FOURTEENERS

Sarah Latchaw

FOURTEENERS

Sarah Latchaw

OMNIFIC PUBLISHING

LOS ANGELES

Omnific Publishing
2355 Westwood Blvd., Suite 506
Los Angeles, CA 90064
www.omnificpublishing.com

First Omnific eBook edition, February 2020
First Omnific trade paperback edition, February 2020

Library of Congress Cataloguing-in-Publication Data

Latchaw, Sarah.
Fourteeners / Sarah Latchaw – 1st ed. ISBN: 978-1-623422-67-7
1. Contemporary Romance — Fiction. 2. Mountain Climbing — Fiction.
3. Bipolar Disorder — Fiction. 4. Authors — Fiction. I. Title

10 9 8 7 6 5 4 3 2 1

Cover Design by Amy Brokaw
Interior Book Design by Amit Dey
Printed in the United States of America

*To foster
Moms and Dads in the trenches
for your kids. You are heroes.*

FOURTEENERS

When a mountain crosses the towering threshold of fourteen thousand feet, it is known as a 'fourteener.' Fourteeners shadow the twisting spine of the Colorado Rockies, and mountaineers, in their desire to be 'above it all,' will face grueling terrain to place these peaks on their mantles.

Chapter 1
ANCHOR

*To offer protection against a potentially fatal fall,
mountaineers will bolt their rope to rock, ice, or
snow at an anchor point.*

Hydraulic Level Five [WORKING TITLE]
Draft 1.100
© Samuel Caulfield Cabral and Aspen Kaye Cabral
EMOTIVUS DROWNICUS NIXIUS

Caulfield sees the half smiles of his wife.

Having her safe in their Bear Creek home, rooted to the ground while he writes and she canoes and hikes, works with her art galleries and cave clubs…she has all of her fingers and all of her toes, but she withers in his hands.

Her mountains are casual acquaintances—warranting a nod, but never an invite. The top-of-the-line hiking pack he gave her for Christmas collects dust in the closet. Next to it rests his own unused pack, bought in a flash of optimism. Every morning she watches the sun hit their mountains in a blaze of gold. Then, at night, they fall into shadow, and another day has passed.

Ever since the avalanche.

Nearly three years ago, they promised themselves to each other again, and when they repeat their vows on this date, every year, they say them with the painful knowledge of what it means to forsake those vows. Their wedding anniversary is a time of celebration. But for Aspen, the days preluding it are a bitter token of ice and panic. She marks them alone, from the safety of her desk chair.

Caulfield's subtle. "Has H contacted you about a climb?" (He has long suspected H is in love with his wife, or was, once upon a time. Now H has his own wife, and he no longer watches Aspen with burning eyes.)

Aspen's not subtle. "How's the new pirate book doing?" She knows this will shut him up. He feels his manhood shrivel at the mention of *that* book—the book with great expectations attached to it. The fledgling fantasy series was supposed to be better than his nixies, and critics couldn't wait to prove those claims wrong. It was lambasted before it hit the shelves. The reviews sit in his brain like his mother's ancient upright piano: dissonant and immoveable.

> "By the standards of his auspicious career, Sea Rovers is a cliché-strangled shipwreck destined for the foreboding depths of dust bins..."

Still, he's a storyteller. He sifts through his brain and seeds of ideas tumble through his fingers where they root on paper. Caulfield writes, not about far-away nixies or water horses, or universally panned pirates. He turns to his beloved Colorado. To the drama of its mountains, where life thrives and dies through sun, and snow, and thin air fourteen thousand feet above the earth.

"And so, Aspen, my wife," Caulfield says, "I propose this: I'll write mountains for you, and we'll conquer them. As much as I want you in my hands, I will not watch you wither there."

Kaye—It has been a long while since we've worked on our book. Are you game?—S

Sam, I'm game for most anything. Not once have I regretted what I did for that Klondike bar. –K

Boulder, Colorado
September, present day

My fingertips skimmed the edge of the glowing laptop screen as I read Samuel's email. The light glinted white against the facets of my wedding diamond and I twisted it, mesmerized. The man who gave it to me breathed soundly into his pillow. Sleeplessness plagued me this time of year, as the mountains trickled from golden autumn to the frozen limbs of winter. Winter brought memories of other frozen limbs, tangled and mangled by the snowy fury of an avalanche on the North Face of Longs Peak, now almost three years past.

Had it really been that long? I counted back the anniversaries to the stretch of time before the Longs Peak climb, when Samuel suffered his last major bout with mania. (Since he'd stormed Fenway Park in Boston with his mother's crematory urn and paid a visit the psych ward, we'd happily had few and far-between slug-fests with his bipolar disorder.)

I'd also eased up on my adrenaline-driven hobbies. Skydiving was a rarity. Kayaking and skiing trips stuck to tried-and-true routes. And my mountains? What Samuel wrote was true. My mountaineering dearth had little to do with Samuel's tenterhook illness and much to do with my fear that the entire mountainside would sweep me away in a wave of snow boulders.

Shivering, I burrowed beneath our comforter and pressed my body against the warmth of Samuel's back. Unconscious, he turned and lifted a bare arm, allowing me a safe haven in his musky embrace.

From the comfort of Samuel's body, I closed my eyes and let my mind carry me back, three years ago ...

Longs Peak, Colorado
November, three years earlier

I'd like to say our Longs climb was as smooth as summer cherries and Samuel worried needlessly. (With a permanent marker, he'd scrawled "I love Samuel Cabral" on my forehead as a Hector deterrent, though the only thing it accomplished was to incur relentless mocking from my pun-happy climb team.) He was a nervous wreck over this winter climb, but he'd still insisted I go. I'd wanted that summit badly and he saw it.

"I can't lock you away in a closet, so I'll have to trust you to take care of yourself up there. It'll be worse for both of us if I hold you back from the things you love."

"Are you and Jaime sure you want to tag along? It'll be a boring couple of days at base camp, just you and Betty the Campervan."

"I'll work on the next movie script for the studio, appease them for a while."

"And from what I hear, Jaime's bringing enough legal journals to argue her way out of Purgatory. Although, she may use them to bludgeon you, so watch your back."

The climb took a turn for the deepest circle of Hell (or at least the circle for politicians and litterbugs) when we met two Canadians at Granite Pass, where the path skimmed along the top of an airy world.

It began with a mysterious red object, wedged in an ice crevasse ten feet below.

I think it's....ah..." Hippie squinted against the sun bouncing off the steep slab of ice.

"Actually, I don't know what that thing is."

Our climb team—Cassady (aka Hippie), Molly, Hector, Luca, and I—crowded around the edge of the slope, wind biting our cheeks as we stared down at the stark blotch of red.

"Do you think it's...*blood?*" Molly, my best friend, would spot a wounded creature on a coke can.

I shook my head. "Some hiker probably just lost a hat."

An unfamiliar voice answered me. "Quite the challenge, eh? C'mon! Let's go after it!"

I screeched and whipped around to find two men already anchoring rappel ropes, their weathered faces creased with glee. We'd glimpsed them some distance down, and they'd already gained us. Longs Peak was a popular destination in the summer, but winter climbs were notoriously demoralizing and weeded out novices.

The sun never graced the north slopes of Longs in colder months, and it felt as though we were scaling the dark side of the moon. We started our climb with six inches of rain, which meant snow and ice, and claw-like crampons fitted on our shoes for the higher reaches of the mountain. I'd done climbs in which the wind howled and, by the time we reached the tundra, we battled a wall of blowing snow. Then, it was turn back or face deadly exhaustion and hypothermia. But this day, weather conditions were mild.

The trek took us through six miles of lush forest, staggering views, and a mountain lake.

A pit stop here and there for solar-powered toilets, water, and nasty but effective Clif Shot Gel. Finally, we broke the tree line and stared in awe at the vast and empty Boulder Field—our high camp for the night. Tomorrow, we would summit the peak via the flat-sided North Face route, which was a grueling, vertical slope that billowed from the edge of the Boulder Field like a cloud pillar.

There were few markers on the Boulder Field and even fewer signs of life. Only a scattering of colorful dome tents nestled in the barren expanse told us we hadn't been drugged and dropped in the middle of Antarctica. At thirteen thousand feet, we'd left anything green behind long ago.

It turned out, the red thing was not blood or a hat, but a Kit Kat bar.

The two climbers who joined us were from northern British Columbia, down for a mountaineering vacation. They also had a sobering adrenaline addiction, and Hector was drawn to them like a marmot to antifreeze.

Canadians have a reputation for being overly polite. They beat us to the field by ten minutes, so by right, the best wind-shielding rock wall was theirs.

"Oh no, we insist your women take the spot." Molly and I smiled at 'your women,' but we appreciated their chivalry, especially as it meant we'd sleep in the snug shelter of a rock wall.

"I love Canadians!" cried Molly. "You are true gentlemen." She kissed their cheeks and I swear their frost-bitten faces reddened like maple leaves.

Evidently, Hector also loved Canadians. He invited them to share the prime rock shelter and they sandwiched their tent between our two tents, making for cramped, but warm, sleeping quarters.

"Fuuu....."

"Again."

"Fuuu...."

"Again."

I scrunched my eyes and shook my head, as if I'd bit a Lemonhead in two. "I can't, Molly."

"Kaye, just say the word."

I scowled at my intimidating linguistics coach, a dirty Henry Higgins popping glass marbles in my mouth.

"Fuuuu...*rick*. Frickety-frick-frick. Mother-frickin' Jacques H. Cousteau."

"Nice, Kaye. The ocean guy?" She rolled off her thick hiking sock and violently rattled a bottle of nail polish.

"At least I have class, you foul-mouthed Amazon."

"Says the woman who wore yoga pants to work."

I tossed my inflated pillow at her head. She deflected and it bounced off the lantern in a flurry of shadows. "One time. *One time*. And they were black."

A deep, lilting Canadian accent rose from the tent next to us, in between wind gusts. I only caught half of what they said given my partial deafness in one ear, but it sounded very Canadian. "You could always say 'fokk.' Like, 'Way to lose yer lumber on de ice, ya fokken bird.'"

Molly's polish brush paused over her foot. (To Molly, third degree frostbite was a fair exchange for perfectly pink toenails.) "I forgot you were over there," she called. "What else do you say in Canada?" We listened with widening eyes as a litany of Canuck-centric curses—from overtly sexual to overtly Catholic—pleasantly filtered through our tent wall. And I thought Samuel and I had been creative with our faux cursing. Molly carefully dotted the edge of her big toenail where the pink had chipped and wiggled her toes in delight.

"I can't believe you packed nail polish for a mountain climb, you overgrown teenager. You do realize temps have been known to drop to forty below at night on the Boulder Field."

"Not tonight." She shifted, her long legs uncomfortable in the cramped tent. "And I can't believe you still say 'frick.' Step off the shiny, it makes me happy."

"So does Cassady. Usually." No one else had noticed the stand-off-ishness between the two of them, but I saw the extra foot of daylight. Molly appreciated frankness. Her eyes dimmed like cooling coals, and I knew I'd unearthed something raw.

"He's leaving, you know. Moving to Breckenridge to work at a ski resort."

I blinked, surprised. "I didn't know. When? Why?"

"When? I'm not sure, but he's restless. It won't be more than a month. Why? Once a nomad, always a nomad, I guess. I didn't expect him to put down permanent roots just because we're dating." She raised a parka-clad shoulder, trying for dispassion but her open heart told a different story.

A year ago I would have said this was complete crap, but life and love had more complications than a Tolstoy epic. "Hippie *has* put down roots. This isn't a casual thing for the two of you, anyone can see it."

"I think I'm going to go with him."

My breath froze in my chest. "Leave Lyons? Really?"

"What, you think you and Samuel are the only ones allowed to nose-dive out of the nest?" Her lips lifted. "I told you years ago I wanted out of Lyons. Just because you two are squawking to get back under mama bird doesn't mean it's the same for me. Besides, Breckenridge isn't far—just a couple of hours. This would be a good opportunity to scout out new accounts for TrilbyJones, and you've already proven that it's possible to telecommute. It boils down to this: I think I might love Cassady and I want to see where this leads."

It was leading my friend away. I had focused so much time on bringing Samuel home, I'd forgotten that life also continued for others. Like when I barged into Angel's hangar and found out in an embarrassing way that he and Danita were trying for a baby. Or when I ran into my old babysitter at the gas station and couldn't believe she had gray streaks and a minivan. In my head, she was still a metal-mouthed teenager hiding in the basement closet while my four-year-old self chucked strawberries at her. (In my defense, I thought she was playing along. I still owed her an apology.)

"I get it, Molly." I tucked limp blonde curls under my stocking cap. "I'll just miss you. Who else is going to ply me with red wine and convince me to send e-mails to my ex?"

"Your not so ex," she amended.

"My *ex* ex."

She gave me a knowing smile. "You're going to marry him again, aren't you?"

"Yeah," I admitted. "I just have to convince him to ask me again. After what happened in Boston, he's waffling between keeping me at arm's length or all in, so at any given moment, it's hard to tell what kind of hint he would welcome."

"Pssh. The Age of Aquarius is dawning, my friend. You should do the proposing."

I was a bit astounded I hadn't thought of it myself. "You think?"

"Mm-hmm. Samuel would take your fine tush right there on Sofia's front porch if you asked him to marry you." She replaced her extreme weather socks and scrambled beneath her bedding, signaling her need for sleep. "Something to think about. Goodnight Kaye."

"'Night, Molly."

"Goodnight, American ladies," echoed a Canadian on the other side of the tent wall. "Best of luck bedding your hosers, eh?"

"Fokking courteous Canucks," Molly grumbled as the men chuckled. I slinked beneath my sleeping bag, as mortified as a sixteen-year-old at a slumber party.

The first time I ever heard 'four-by-four' used as a verb was huddled over the breakfast stove the next morning, between nibbles of freeze-dried food. It was also the first time I'd met someone with a 'gold claim in the bush.' Not a euphemism—I asked.

Dusky pinks of the alpenglow swirled over rocks, though the air was still as cold as the dead of night. There wasn't a cloud in sight, but that could change in a heartbeat. Today would be sunny and warm (relatively speaking for a tundra zone). We watched as early morning climbers trickled onto the field and others stretched stiff cold limbs. A pair of park rangers trudged over boulders, checking ground and weather conditions. I dug through the 'marmot-proof' box and handed out a round of granola bars.

"If you were up in Prince George, you'd just four-by-four those off-roads," crowed one of our new friends, chewing through a bar. "You don't bike the forest during moose-calving season." There was laughter and back-slapping, even though Hector didn't know what the heck they were talking about. My friend was already half in love with his new climbing buddies, and a part of me was relieved he'd made a new adrenaline junkie connection. I had a feeling my cliff-hucking days were over unless they involved a brown mop of hair with a Latin flair.

A heavy boom echoed across the Boulder Field. We stilled, panicked stares flying to the great Diamond slab, then the Keyhole, searching for the beginnings of an avalanche. The loud crackling which followed was too far away to be our snowfield, but the warning was clear. Cassady had been right—warm sunlight after days of snow meant avalanches and, somewhere, a bank of snow had cracked and tumbled down the mountainside.

Minutes later, one of the rangers—I mentally called him Ranger Rick—barreled over to our campsite, a two-way radio clutched in his hand. "Avalanche at Glacier Gorge, just off the west ridge. Don't make plans to take the Keyhole approach today." Cassady raised an 'I told you so' eyebrow. Dang it, that was our return route.

"Was anyone hurt?" I asked.

He smoothed down his grizzled beard. "Not sure yet. Once the sun's high, we'll be seeing lots of slides. Any of you planning to summit today?" We all tentatively raised our hands. The ranger grimaced. "It'll be dangerous. Personally, I'd hold off for the next climb." There was a collective groan.

"Think we could still make the technical on the North Face before the day heats up?" asked Hector. The technical was the most difficult portion of the climb, where all the vertical rock wall training came in handy.

Ranger Rick squinted at the massive face, still a midnight blue hulk in the early morning hours. "It's your risk to take. You're looking at a good five to six hours *minimum*, if you decide to do it. That'd put you up there 'round noon. Then there's the descent."

"We're gonna slide down the Keyhole route for the descent," said one of the Canadians.

"Right on." Hector fist-bumped him. A rabble of butterflies excited in my stomach at the thought of descending after the summit. Sweet Tom, it would be an unbelievable rush. I gazed up the vast snow slope. That summit beckoned me, all craggy ice, thin air and audacity—a siren song to a woman who battled giants. A bushy-tailed fox picked its way over the snowfield and disappeared into what was left of the night. I stared after its path, mind-boggled. This was the sort of thing I loved about mountaineering—something unexpected defying textbooks, nature. Finding life in the middle of nowhere. A Kit Kat bar tucked away like buried treasure. Huffing over rope and axe, higher and higher until there's nothing higher than me—physically and emotionally—in a white, windy place in which humans had no business inhabiting.

I wanted it. Badly.

Could we summit Longs? We'd have to hoof it, push our bodies hard before the sun turned solid snow to fallible slush. No time for pictures or Kit Kat detours; heck, we'd barely have time to slick on sunscreen before we absolutely had to leave.

Hector's bright eyes met mine, making the same calculations. He gave me a nod. "Let's climb it."

Luca jumped in, an eager puppy. "I'm in."

"In," said the Canadians.

"Heck no!" from Molly. Cassady declined, too. All eyes turned to me.

"Trilby? Don't you dare bail on me now." Hector's grin masked the deep disappointments he'd endured since I'd discarded him for Samuel. "You promised me Longs if I was your date for Angel and Danita's wedding."

"I'm here, aren't I? On Longs Peak?"

"All in, Kaye. No time for pussyfooting like these two." He jabbed a thumb at Molly and Cassady.

Cassady held up his hands. "I know when to let sleeping dogs lie, man. Longs Peak obviously doesn't want to be messed with today, and I figure I'd better listen to her growling." He gave me a pointed look that said I'd be smart to do the same. I fretted with the shoestrings of my Tevas.

Hector's face was bright as adrenaline coursed through his veins. I'd basked in his life-loving warmth for so long. *Too* long. Something had shifted in me, slipped away with all the hurt and bitterness I released when I'd embraced Samuel again.

With his shaved head and spiraling kaleidoscope of tattoos, Hector was scary at first glance. He'd scarred his chin in a mountain biking accident when he was nineteen, and women tended to clutch their purses tighter when they passed him outside Paddler's. But his dark, soulful eyes lured them back. Then he further ensnared them with the way his body contorted in godlike stunts off ski slopes, or with a grip so strong, it carried his entire body weight as he dangled from a mountain face.

Hector danced on the wild side of life, and it made people desire to breathe the same exhilarating air he breathed. Women wanted him to risk his heart the same way he risked his life, and each believed she was the one to tame him. But he played those naïve, dreamy females like Morrison played the front row of a Doors concert. Messing with hearts carried a hint of sliminess. Once, I told him as much.

"*Mamacita*, don't be jealous. There's not a girl alive who has guns like yours. I've seen you do things to punching bags that made my balls shrivel." Crudeness and flattery enwrapped laughter so infectious, no wonder his former girlfriends had trouble getting him out of their systems.

Samuel, on the other hand, was Hector's polar opposite. He knew his appeal but was so careful not to give his followers the wrong impression, they couldn't get enough of him.

In my mind I saw Samuel, hunched over his movie script at base camp, thousands of feet down, below the ice and snow, swathed in green. Jaime, Hector's insane sort-of girlfriend, had probably tried to shave his head by now. Yet he was still there, holding me up. Samuel, with a faith in God and in me that was simple and solid, despite the colossal complications of his life.

His love allowed me freedom. He trusted me to come back, and I meant to keep my word.

That summit was not meant for me. Not today.

"I'm out, Hector. Sorry." I wasn't sorry.

Even though we'd ducked out of the summit, the snowfield just beyond the boulders was still a mess of melting ice crevasses. Occasionally we'd hear another tell-tale boom reverberate between cliffs and cleavers, and I hoped no one was buried beneath ten feet of snow. On edge, we passed time with a dice game, though our gloved fingers made things difficult. We chatted up other mountaineers playing it safe at the high camp—one who'd even lived through the horror of an avalanche.

"I was bent over a tree branch like a towel flung over a clothesline, stiff from the cold and ribs cracked from the impact. Snow swept around me, beneath me, over me..." He waved his arms around his torso to illustrate. "It was so cold, I knew I was going to die. But I was lucky the snow wasn't hard-packed around the tree. I wriggled around, like swimming in sand, until I made enough of an air pocket to wait for the Ski Patrol. Then I screamed 'til I heard voices somewhere above my ass..." No thanks.

Around one in the afternoon, Ranger Rick returned with his two-way radio. "Ranger station said to hang tight until things freeze over. You all got headlamps? Night gear?" Most of us nodded. "If not, you got no business being up here, but we'll keep you until we can get you down in the daylight." Man, this guy made me miss my no-nonsense mom. "Is there a Kaye Trilby here?" he asked around a mouthful of orange slice.

"Right here."

"Got your boyfriend at the station harassing the rangers, asking about you. Don't burn up the two-way." He placed the radio in my quaking hand.

"Samuel?"

"Kaye. Thank God!" His voice was warm and melodic, even entrenched in static. When he was emotional, like now, traces of a Spanish accent trickled through. "Tell me you didn't try to summit the mountain."

"Hector and Luca are up there, but the rest of us are safe. Molly just handed me my tail in Yahtzee. We're playing for power bars."

"You have no idea how relieved I am to hear it. I know you promised you'd be careful, but from what we're hearing, the entire mountain is awash with snow today. Just…please stay at high camp until it's safe."

I rubbed my palm against my chest, quelling the ache Samuel's loving concern stirred in me. "I promise. Hey, I need to ask you something. Something really important." Ranger Rick gave me a stern glance and tapped his wrist. I held up my finger for one more minute.

Crackling static. "What was that?"

"I want to ask you something really important and I need to do it now before I lose my nerve."

Another flare of static. "Can you still hear me? I said go ahead."

"Okay. You said you wanted to date awhile and take things slow. Then yesterday, you said you needed me but didn't want to be clingy. And these past few weeks, we've definitely been more…erm…committed than just dating. Are you still with me?"

"Yes."

"Okay," I said again. My palms were sweating beneath my gloves. Ranger Rick gave me the wrap-it-up finger twirl. "I was thinking— well, Molly suggested I should just ask if I didn't want to wait—because I'm kind of a modern girl and all…"

His beautiful laugh. "Firecracker, just spit it out."

"Okay. Ithinkweshouldgetmarriedagain. Whew."

The laughter ended. Then, nothing. Even Ranger Rick looked embarrassed for me as the silence widened, his emaciation of an orange slice grinding to a halt.

"Samuel?"

A shuddery breath. "I'm sorry, I thought you said… Could you repeat that?"

"I think we should get married again. No, wait. That was crappy." I was botching this, big time. I pushed back threatening tears and began again, more slowly. "What I meant to ask was this: Will you marry me?"

Another breath. "Are you serious?"

I tried not to be insulted. "Look, Samuel, I already have 'I love Samuel Cabral' smeared across my forehead. The least you could do is give me a ring to match. Don't you dare second-guess this. Us. Second guess *us*."

And then the beautiful laughter was back. "Oh Kaye, I'm not patronizing you. If you could see my face, you'd know I'm simply shocked and…and beyond elated. I never imagined… I love you, beautiful girl, so damned much."

"I love you too. You still haven't answered my question."

"Yes. I want to be yours again. But then, you know I've never been anything but yours."

"Yours," I echoed, the tightness in my chest unwinding. I glanced at Ranger Rick, whose eyes were suspiciously glassy. "Okay," I said a fifth time. "Well…I'll see you soon. Tonight, hopefully."

"Don't rush. Take your time, watch your footing. I'll still be here with Betty the Campervan and the devil's Latina cousin when you get back."

I laughed. "I'll be safe. Love you."

"Love you, too."

It began with a teeth-rattling *boom*, followed by what could only be the earth cracking and splintering, rending apart.

Molly had just swiped another power bar during our dice game, which we'd moved inside the tent, when it happened. Our faces froze in horror as the entire mountainside crumbled and tumbled around the manmade rock walls of the Boulder Field.

Cassady cursed as we fell to the tent floor and covered our heads with our hands. For long, tenuous seconds we cowered as shadowed blue nylon sagged and rumbled around us. The gear rattled. Power bars and dice bounced around the makeshift table and onto the floor. One, then two sides of the tent popped up, but settled again, thank God. Light no longer poured through canvas—the entire rock shelter dimmed like nightfall. And then, as the snow settled, it was utterly quiet. The idea that the world had ended flitted through my mind.

"What. Was. That?" Molly ground out, her glasses dangling from one ear.

I groaned. "I think it was an avalanche."

"Seriously? We play it safe and seventy-mile-an-hour snow still finds us!"

"I don't think it was a direct hit, or we'd have tumbled down the field," said Cassady.

I pushed myself off the tent floor. "We're lucky the Canadians gave us the prime rock wall." Then, in dreadful unison, we recalled that a dozen or so people were *not* protected by rock walls, but had been boulder-hopping the cobbled field. Leaping to our feet, we jerked on outer garments and gear and zipped open the flap. A wall of snow up to our waists spilled into the tent.

"Cassady, do something!"

He tried to hoist himself onto the snow shelf, only to sink through in a spectacular show of awkwardness. "What do you want me to do, Molly? Build a snow fort?"

After digging and tunneling, eventually we were able to scoot through the opening and up onto a bed of silver.

Straight away, I noticed the snow was not as deep on this side of the field as it was elsewhere. The second thing I noticed was that to the right, just below the Face, the field had been swept clean of equipment, tents, and people. Bright flashes of color peeked through the snow, destroyed by the heavy tidal wave. A handful of climbers pulled themselves out of fresh drifts and tested their limbs. Some already crouched on hands and knees, digging for survivors trapped beneath, frantically shouting for help. Struggling for clarity, I dug out my avalanche beacon and switched it to 'receive.' The sudden pulsing signal from the other buried beacons shot straight into my pounding heart.

"Come on!" Molly grasped my elbow and dragged me toward a tableau of annihilated rock and snow. I fell into step behind her, and we dropped to the snow at the first weak cries for help. "It's been seven minutes," I muttered to Molly. Seven minutes meant the beginning of brain damage. Tears streaming down our cheeks, we burrowed and clawed into the packed snow until we found a knee, then a leg, and finally, the torso and face of a terrified man. Blood trickled from a gash in his head, then grew sluggish and froze as it reached his ice-numbed cheek.

I turned my face from his cracked lips and frost-bitten cheeks, only to spot a blue glove poking through a snow bank several feet away. The glove wiggled and scraped at the surface. With dawning horror, I saw that it wasn't a glove but the bare hand of a woman, her skin freakishly bruised by cold.

"*Help!...Help!*" The feminine voice was weak but unmistakable. I tugged Molly with me and clutched the woman's fingers. She squeezed my hand in return.

"We're going to get you out!" Together we dove back into the snow, fighting time and physics and fatigue to rescue the woman...then another man....and another woman.

Sometime later, overhead, the faint thud-thud-thud of helicopter blades echoed off the craggy walls, coming closer and closer until the sound ripped the air overhead and drowned out the moans of those who had been buried in the snow. We covered our ears.

'*Search and Rescue,*' Molly mouthed. The heli landed on the flat of the field and the rescue team poured from its body, laden with equipment and stretchers. Two black Labradors put their noses to the ground and weaved wildly over the terrain. Jaime's dogs flashed through my head, and I absurdly wondered if Samuel would like one of her puppies someday.

"I've got this one." Two medics knelt next to the woman we'd yanked from the snow. Molly and I stood by helplessly as the team searched long and hard for a pulse, shook their heads and grimly placed a blanket over her face.

Twelve people were buried in the avalanche at Boulder Field. Amazingly, despite severe hypothermia and eventual amputations, all but one of them survived. But that was one life brutally taken by the mountain I loved and, once I saw this young woman with her smothered face and mangled limbs, her last breath snuffed my longing for the wild backcountry.

Two hours later, Hector, Luca, and the Canadians returned, miraculously in one piece. Even the might of Mother Nature hadn't exposed their hubris, the cliffhuckers. They were all smiles and high-fives until they saw the obliteration of the tent city.

"Where's our stuff?" Luca asked, slack-jawed. My stomach turned. Cassady beat me to the head-smack.

We bid adieu to the Canadians. Then we wearily began the six-hour trek down Longs Peak beneath a smattering of emerging constellations. I picked out a proverbial string of stars; Aquarius was bold tonight. If I'd made the summit, my limbs and brain would have been just as leaden. Yet that lost life ate at me. Like a mindless automaton, my body trudged along behind Hector's chuffing shoulders, crouching when I needed to crouch, scooting when I needed to scoot. We broke for water at a marker, and when I realized the ranger station was still a half-mile away, tears of exhaustion rolled down my cheeks and froze onto my scarf.

Then, sometime around one in the morning, I collapsed into Samuel's arms, pressed fervently against his fleece-covered chest. He rested a glove on the crown of my head. "When I heard about the avalanche, I prayed harder than I've ever prayed in my life that you were safe."

"I was. Lots of others weren't." I sighed into his scarf, blocking the image of the woman's blue hand piercing the white of the snow.

"I was afraid for you. *Ay Dios mío,* you're frozen through." His hands grasped my shoulders, waist, cheeks, assuring himself I'd returned in one piece. Satisfied, he tucked me beneath the warmth of his jacket. "Marry me," he rasped into my hair.

"I already asked."

"Then allow me a turn. Please firecracker, marry me?"

Despite pain and fatigue, I smiled. "Mmm-hmm. Yes."

Only Cassady's agonized cry broke through our blissful haze. "What did you two dog ding-a-lings do to Betty?"

Samuel hissed through his teeth. "Oh man, I forgot."

Jaime dashed out of Betty, Cassady hot on her heels. "How were we supposed to know the mountain would vomit all over you?" She ducked as Cassady launched a ball of sweaty socks at her head. "Around mid-afternoon yesterday, Cabral and I got tired of weather reports, so we put my law journals to good use!"

"Who would have thought that Jaime and I would find common ground wreaking havoc in our mutual boredom?" he added ruefully, running a hand through his hair. "Poorly timed, though—we should have cleaned it up. Sorry, Hippie."

I peered into the maligned vehicle...it must have taken hours. Every inch of Betty's interior was papered in pages of Jaime's law journals. Shag carpet wall...steering wheel...brake and accelerator...even the beaded curtains were wrapped like ghetto gifts. I shuddered at the sheer number of neon tape flags it must have taken to play such an intricate, exhaustive prank.

Who carried that many office supplies with them, anyway?

Cassady pointed a bony finger. "After you two juvenile delinquents clean this up, I better not find a single booger of tape residue on that sweet ride, so help me. You better remember, nothing goes over the devil's back that doesn't come under his belly."

"I think he means 'what goes around comes around'," I whispered into Samuel's ear. He kissed my temple and got to work tearing away Jaime's law journals. It wasn't as if she used them, anyway.

An hour before dawn, as the others slept, I flopped around fitfully and woke with a crick in my neck. We had wrapped ourselves in quilts and crashed on the floor behind the pseudo privacy of Betty the Camper-van's beaded curtain. Through the dull blue of morning, Samuel's eyes glittered back, a soft, serious smile on his lips.

"Are you absolutely certain marriage to me is what you want again? That you've had enough time consider the ramifications?" Translation: *this isn't a hallmark "hasty Kaye" move that you'll regret down the road?*

"I'm the one who asked, Sam. Of course I'm certain."

"Our life won't be easy."

My breath lazily lingered over his collarbone, the edge of his tee shirt. I inhaled his heady cardamom scent. "I know." I didn't need to remind him just now what a trip his manic episode in Boston had been.

"We probably won't have children. I mean, we can explore adoption, but…*Kaye*," he breathed when I leaned in and nipped his salty skin.

"Mmm. We can explore it. And if it's a no, we'll hold each other and grieve, and deal with it." I couldn't bring myself to traverse that path of heartbreak, not yet. My lips left his collarbone and found that delicious spot beneath his chin. His scruffy skin set them tingling. "But right now, I don't want to think about that. I just want to be with you." My fingertips deftly trailed down his stomach to the waistband of his flannel pants. "Will you let me be with you?"

He caught my hand and dragged it to the safety of his chest, and nodded to the occupants on the other side of the beaded curtain.

"May I propose something different, yet equally rash?" I liked his playful tone.

"Will you marry me this weekend?"

I gasped. I barely saw the corners of his mouth tug up in the dark.

"I could give you that Elvis ceremony in Vegas you've always dreamed of."

"Why…why so soon?"

He chuckled. "Soon? Oh Kaye, this is seven years too long."

My hand clung to his. I pressed our tangle of fingers to the tears welling in my eyes and nodded. "No Vegas ceremony. But yes, I'll marry you this weekend."

"My wife. I can call you that again," he murmured into our joined hands.

"Yours. Always yours."

Chapter 2
TRAD CLIMBING

When a climber undertakes a mountain face with no pre-bolted slopes, the climb becomes not only a physical challenge, but a mental challenge. Such a climb is ironically termed "traditional climbing" because there is no fixed route.

Boulder, Colorado
November, three years earlier

My head pounded with the need for a deep sleep just beyond my grasp. My muscles were still sore days after our climb, but my mind was restless. I flopped over and patted around for another pillow. In those quiet hours after dark, just two days before to my wedding, I buried my head and prayed for peace.

Until now, my whirlwind workload had kept my doubts and fears waitlisted. Gearing up for Samuel's book-to-movie adaptation had been new and thrilling and, because of his status as a world-famous (and now infamous) writer, he moved in elite circles that were as foreign to me as Tibetan temples. It had also exposed me to a world of backbiting (you couldn't pay me to book that trip again). But once I'd transitioned the last of Samuel's publicity to Patrick and Nat O'Malley—Celeb PR royalty in Los Angeles—I didn't know what to do with myself.

I kicked free from the sweaty sheet and plodded through the pitch-black hallway to the kitchen. I flipped on a light switch and instantly regretted it when my aching brain tried to judo-kick its way out of my skull. Water trickled through my fingers until it was ice-cold. I chugged down a glass, wiped my mouth, and stumbled back to bed.

The Boom Boom Room. Fenway Park. Samuel's arrest and hospitalization. They left a storm of unresolved emotions churning above my head, a storm I'd avoided for the sake of survival. Top that twister off with the Longs Peak climb…the avalanche, the woman I hadn't been able to save…it was too much. For the first time in a long time, I desired to see my thirtieth birthday more than I desired adrenaline rushes.

I hadn't even known her name. But Longs Peak was my next-door neighbor and word of her death spread, even before it headlined the evening news. Daughter. Sister. Girlfriend. Her family's grief-stricken images were captured and captioned, another titillating tragedy that most would shake their heads over and forget.

What if I'd been the one to die in that avalanche? What had I done with my life?

Later that morning, in the quiet of my TrilbyJones office, I stared at my online banking statement. I'd saved millions. Artisan lights blurred into the ceiling, and I laid my head on my arms and cried as grief crashed like a cold front.

Weathering grief is an odd experience. It will drive you under the nearest tree, then lift long enough to let you believe it has finally passed. But the most random thing will bring on a second front of mourning. For me, it was scanning my savings account and realizing that, for years, I'd turned my alimony stockpile into a shrine for an absent love. I'd seen the exorbitant balance of my bank account before. I just never really *saw* it—gilded and obtrusive, collecting dust. What a waste.

I didn't hear my office door creak open. But Samuel crouched next to me, gathered me in his arms. He frowned at my online banking statement, puzzled. Then his face cleared.

"The alimony? Spend it. Let it go."

"How?" I sniffed into the folds of his Henley. He pinched a tissue from the container on my desk and handed it to me.

"That's your choice. Though…can I make a suggestion? If you want to make the mental health benefit concert an annual event, you'll need to establish a fund. I'll have my accountant help you, if you like."

I nodded, names already taking shape in my mind. The Rachel Caulfield Cabral Foundation, after Samuel's deceased mother? Or maybe just the Cabral Foundation?

"I also think you should consider seeing a therapist." Samuel peered at me, eyes soft and cautious. I gave a noncommittal hum. "I'm serious, firecracker. Counseling isn't some New Age thing of your father's. You've collected quite a pile of traumatic experiences and talking to someone might help."

I swallowed. "I'll ask around."

His blue gaze still held mine. *Cripes, here it comes after all. He's going to call off the wedding.* "If you want to wait to get married, if this is too much—"

"No! I want to get married Friday." I shook his hands from my shoulders, closed my online banking profile, and threw myself into a radio ad for the Boulder Bookstore. Samuel opened his laptop on a small worktable across from my desk, but now and then, I felt blue eyes upon me.

Working on the mental health benefit concert filled Samuel with an unadulterated joy I hadn't seen since he'd made his little league team's starting line-up. When Molly and I first tossed around the idea, Samuel had been supportive but cautious. Fundraising for mental health issues was not as widely successful as, say, cancer charities. Sadly, being lumped with "crazies" was a deterrent for sponsors. But in the past weeks, since his spectacularly public 'coming out' during a manic episode, Samuel had whole-heartedly thrown himself into awareness work.

Several national magazines, including *The New Yorker*, were clubbing each other over the heads for rights to a mental illness feature. After checking out of Massachusetts General Hospital, there'd been whispers among media insiders that Samuel had 'gone Garbo.' So Primetime television journalist Belinda Walker made a secret trip to Boulder for an exclusive interview—the first he'd agreed to since his YouTube-worthy arrest in Boston. (That wretched video had gone viral. Last time Angel checked, it had fifteen million hits.) Patrick O'Malley prepped him to discuss his bipolar disorder, but Samuel hadn't needed it. "It's actually easier to respond to questions when my answers are truthful." It was a home run for Ms. Walker, and would hopefully put to rest rampant speculation when it aired tonight.

The flipside was, the heavy media attention would make pulling off our courthouse elopement as complicated as a Vegas magic spectacular.

Samuel grunted in surprise. "The Tripping Marys agreed to play our benefit concert next year."

My head shot up. No. Freaking. Way. "But they're retired."

"I told them we learned to play guitars because of them. Remember? After seeing them in their Planet Bluegrass gig?"

"I remember."

"I told them they're legends."

"Thank you."

"I also told them if they played the benefit, it would get me laid for months to come."

"Really?" My spirit shot up like a sunflower. Frustratingly, the physical aspect of our relationship had been on hold since his release from Mass General.

He fidgeted. "That was a poor joke." Rats. "But," he rose from his worktable and knelt beside me. "I miss you, Kaye. You're it for me. And I wonder if, perhaps…"

"Perhaps?"

"Perhaps we've been overly careful. And we *are* remarrying in three days." *Are we? Yes we are…he won't back out.* "No sex would make for a lousy honeymoon." His sensitive mouth quirked. "And I really, *really* want to have sex with you."

I traced his sharp jawline. "I don't think we're made to handle each other with kid gloves."

"We're too passionate for them." His lips brushed my neck and I shuddered as his eyelashes tickled my skin, the tenderness of it telling me he would be there Friday, and he would marry me.

"*Perhaps* you want to try Friday night? If it doesn't…um…work, that's okay," I added quickly. "I understand, with the meds."

"*Perhaps*," he answered, his voice muffled and gravelly. Samuel's medication change had been a fire extinguisher blast to his sex drive, but my lusty boy was coming around.

"I really wish I could be there, flower."

"It's okay, Dad." I shuffled my phone and my mug, careful not to slosh hot coffee on my hand. Samuel would be here soon, but I'd wanted to call my dad before he and Audrey left for the weekend.

"It's just so last minute. Audrey and I booked this Sacred Sexuality retreat in Black Forest ages ago."

"Dad really, it's fine. We'll have a small reception later, maybe a Christmas party. You and Audrey go on, and…erm…enjoy your weekend." I spilled coffee anyway. With a hiss, I set the cup on the kitchen counter and thrust my hand under a stream of cold water. I grabbed the nearest dishcloth and wrapped it around my hand, hoping the skin around my ring finger wouldn't blister. (Bride priorities.)

"You know, you and Sam could head on down for the retreat after the wedding. Nothing says 'honeymoon' like engaging in tantric acts of self-realization so blissful, you experience a full-body—"

"La-la-la-la! Totally fine, we're all fine there, or will be, where we're going—or not going. Whatever Samuel has planned, which might just be heading up to Estes Park or down to Denver for the night. Anyway, we're covered-up. Er, covered." I tossed the dishcloth and hunted for first aid cream.

Tom Trilby's barking laugh echoed through the receiver. "Oh Aspen Kaye, you never disappoint. Congratulations, flower, and I'll shake my son-in-law's hand when we get back. After I've washed off all the Eros oil, of course."

Like a verbal filter charging in on a white horse, Samuel's entrance through the door saved me. He planned to take me on an afternoon outing under the auspices of relieving pre-wedding jitters, but truthfully, I think he wanted to be sure we were on the same page about remarrying. My eyes flitted over my fiancé, casual in Colorado flannel. With a wave, he yanked his stocking cap from his head and revealed a head of matted brown hair, so different from what I liked to call his polished "executive" coif. I wrapped a bag of frozen peas around my hand and beckoned him over. "Dad, gotta go. Sam's here. You and Audrey have a safe drive, okay?"

"Sure thing, baby girl. Best of luck to you kids."

Samuel hooked a finger in the belt loop of my jeans and tugged me in for a hello kiss. He turned his lips to the blistering inlet of my thumb. "Coffee burn?"

I sighed. "That predictable?"

"Mmm. How is your father?"

"He and Audrey have a sex thing in Black Forest and won't be there tomorrow."

"Are you okay with this?"

"The sex thing? In my opinion, the less info, the better." Samuel fixed me with a withering look. "Hey, we're eloping. By definition, we're supposed to avoid the parents. Seriously, I'm fine. Dad is Dad and, honestly, going to all these retreats with Audrey might be the biggest sign of commitment I've seen from him."

I knew that was unfair and Samuel did, too. But I did wonder how much longer Audrey would stick around. My father and Audrey Wexler had lived together for nearly twelve years, and dated since I was fifteen. In all that time, he'd never call Audrey his wife, though she'd hinted more than once about a common law marriage. If you asked my dad, Audrey's house was "her house." If you asked Audrey, it was "their home."

My father believed formal contracts (such as a marriage contract, hint hint) were trappings of society and 'blackened the prana..' Still, he tried to be a good father. He was there for me when I needed to blow off steam or wanted a bit of levity in my life. I knew he loved me.

I put my hands on my hips in a nerdy gesture similar to a superhero's and scanned the room. "What do I need?"

"Just your fleece and Tevas, maybe a hat. It's warmer this morning."

Samuel took the curves of the blacktop a little too fast as we weaved up into the mountains, before the stray photogs who tailed us found the hidden turn-off into the park. He'd swapped his impractical BMW convertible for a dark blue Subaru—I teased him about purchasing a "backcountry starter kit." All he needed was a full beard and he'd be set. Judging by the boyish gleam in his eyes, the car was a solid purchase. We crossed into the Rocky Mountain National Park at a less trafficked entrance, completely off the grid to the paparazzi who subscribed to Alan Murphy's "Cabral Hometown Haunts" blog.

Home free, the Subaru rumbled over a rutted dirt road into a soaring forest of ponderosas. Hector and I often used this route for backcountry snowshoeing in the winter. Through my window, Longs Peak winked between the trees. Its knobby top was as familiar to me as tracking the pale moon in the sky, but it no longer filled my heart with peace. I closed my eyes and grounded myself in the smell of new upholstery, soft leather under my fingertips instead of the scrape of rock.

Samuel pulled into a nearly empty lot at the Wild Basin Trailhead near the ranger station. He started to leave the car but saw that my hand still white-knuckled the passenger seat cushion.

He eased his fingers over mine and gently unwrapped them. "We're not climbing anything today, firecracker. Just an easy walk up to the waterfalls."

My heart eased its frantic pace. For a moment I'd believed Samuel would try to force me up a mountainside as some sort of therapeutic measure, but we were only hiking along the St. Vrain, the steady creek we'd played in as children, where we'd created our fairytales that inspired Samuel's books. The trail carried us into a haze of gray, the air thick with water and icicles. As we climbed the slick rocks and ice that ran beside the falls, I told him about the chapters I'd written for our 'autobiography' while he was hospitalized in Boston.

"You did what?"

"I wrote for you while you were sick," I yelled above the roar. "Wrote for us."

His eyes widened. His hiking boot froze as he braced himself midhoist on a craggy ridge.

Since our return to Colorado, I hadn't broached our memoir—*Hydraulic Level Five*—or the fact I'd taken us to the collapse of our marriage. Writing the story had been an unhealthy obsession for him during our time in New York and I hadn't wanted to jinx his recovery.

But now, his cheeks were ruddy and healthy. Strong lungs puffed froths of frozen mountain air between us. Flecks of snow clung to his eyelashes and he swiped at them with his glove. Seeing him, robust and clutching at rocks alongside me with the same, lithe athleticism he exhibited when swinging a baseball bat? Oh my, he was breathtaking.

"Incredible," Samuel said when we reached the top of the deafening falls, cascading down the slope like a bridal veil. We took in the wind, the peaks, our home below our hiking shoes.

I reached over and tugged a tuft of coffee-colored hair sticking out beneath his knit cap. "You're backcountry through and through. Don't hide it—you can don flannel and dodge bison with the best of us."

"Mmm, I'm not denying it. But I wasn't just talking about Colorado." His mouth hovered near my good ear so there'd be no mistaking what he said. "I'm amazed by you, all over again. You actually worked on our book while I was in the hospital? My beautiful wife."

Granted, I was all about moving on as adults, but Samuel still made my heart as fluttery as a starry-eyed teenager's. *Wife.* Yes, that's what I'd be again, because he *would* be there. I needed to have a little faith.

When we returned from the falls and swathed ourselves in blankets beside my apartment fireplace, I presented him with the chapters I'd written. He pored over them while I changed clothes. He'd already moved some of his belongings into my—our—bedroom in anticipation of tomorrow's marriage. Among them was an ancient Lyons baseball jersey, well-worn and well-loved. I pulled it over my head, my hair crackling with static. It wasn't lost on me that the back of the jersey read 'Cabral' in big block letters, and I felt that familiar fluttering again. I smoothed static from my hair and pulled an overnight bag from the closet to pack for our weekend.

Sadly, my excavation of the depths of my underwear drawers in search of something sexy for a wedding night yielded few treasures. Seven years ago, in anger, I'd trashed every single piece of negligee I'd worn for Samuel. My handful of one-night-stands hadn't given me cause to replace them, so my stash of lust-inducing lingerie was woefully small. I held up the black lace slip I planned to wear beneath my "wedding dress," and squinted at my reflection in the mirror.

Yes, this would do nicely. It might ignite a few fires.

I zipped up the bag, placed it by the door, and returned to Samuel. Nestled between two pillows, he sat cross-legged, laptop balanced on his knees.

"How's my writing?" I grabbed a couple of waters from the kitchen and handed one to him.

"Not bad at all. Is that one of my old baseball jerseys?" He turned me around so he could see the back, and whistled.

"Yup. What do you think? Still look good on me?"

"My name always looks good on you," he winked. Even his cheesy lines had me twisted up. *Argh. Flutter flutter flutter.* "All packed?"

"Getting there. Don't be disappointed by my lack of silk and lace, I haven't bought anything like that in years."

Samuel chuckled, telltale streaks of red creeping up his neck. "Do I need to resort to two bad pick-up lines in a row? Any lingerie you wear will look nice…on my bedroom floor. Bam."

"Someone's been reading *The Playbook* instead of writing." Still, desire tingled through my body. Setting the notebook aside, he pulled me onto his lap and then his fingers skimmed along my collarbone, resting on either side of my neck. My blood heated as I waited for his kiss. A slow, deep burn filtered through my veins and I hummed against his lips. The corners of his mouth turned up.

"I've enjoyed reading your chapters. I think I like your Aspen better than mine. She's the real deal—not bits and pieces of a memory warped by time."

"I'm glad." He was making me breathless. "I like this Aspen better, too."

With a last peck on my nose, his lips and hands fell away, and he became serious. "The big question is, how are we going to end it? Do we give Caulfield and Aspen a different story?" He gestured to his closed laptop.

"Can you do that in a memoir? Change the ending?"

He shrugged. "It's our story. We can do whatever we want with it. We can make it so Caulfield doesn't leave Aspen. He gets over his hang-ups and confesses everything to her."

"And Aspen finds, at age twenty, she's mature enough to handle their relationship. She loves Caulfield and wants to make their marriage work."

"And they never spend a day apart, happily ever after."

I sighed, bringing his knuckles to my lips. "But that's not how it really happened, is it?"

"How would you end their story?" His eyes darkened and fixed on my mouth as it gently bit his knuckle.

"The truth. Their marriage falls apart. Aspen and Caulfield grow up and move on with their lives. Seven years later, Aspen finds a handsome, successful, sometimes broken man named Samuel, who occasionally reminds her of Caulfield. She loves him with her whole heart and wants to be his wife."

"That's what I want to be sure about." The faint tension in the set of his face eased with my answer. He swallowed, his voice hoarse. "Anyway, it's the same for Caulfield."

"He finds a handsome man named Samuel? Egad, that poison-pen Togsy was right! Curses!"

"Hush, woman. You know I want you, all the time." He wrapped a strong arm around my waist and pulled me against him, easing my mind, reassuring me with unvoiced words that he would be there tomorrow. A toothy grin overtook my face.

"What?" he asked.

"I think we're going to be okay for the honeymoon tomorrow night."

———————————— ••• ————————————

I had just poured a cap-full of jasmine bubble bath into my cherished jet tub, ready to soak muscles still sore from our hike, when I stood up straight, alert. Because of my partial deafness in one ear I could never be sure if someone was knocking, or if it was the old Victorian home's clanking pipes. I shut off the jets and, sure enough, there was another loud rap. Steam billowed from my bath. With pining eyes, I gave the hot bubbles a flick, wrapped my naked body in my bathrobe, and sadly turned away from my bit of heaven.

"Sofia, hello." I opened the door wide and ushered my surrogate mother into my apartment. "If you're looking for Samuel, you just missed him."

"I am here for you, *mija*, though it seems I've caught you at a bad time." Her black hair was looped into an intricate braid that slithered over her shoulder. Even though it was late and I slouched around in my tattered bathrobe, Sofia was pressed and put-together in a blouse and trousers. A tray with two paper cups was in one hand, a cloth bag in the other. Mexican hot chocolate, from the smell of it—Sofia knew me well. "I've had plenty of time with my son this week...and the people with cameras camped on the gravel by our home."

"How are we possibly going to pull this off tomorrow without those vultures present?" Galling photogs. I went to the bedroom and tugged on a pair of jeans and a sweatshirt. Sofia handed me the tray when I returned and followed me into the kitchen.

"You won't. They'll go away after a while, they always do. By the way, you still have two watching your door."

"Ah, Tweedle Dee and Tweedle Dum. We go way back, those boys and me." I resigned myself to the fact that multiple photographers would be snapping pictures at our wedding tomorrow. Well, at least I'd be dressed like a Michelin-star entree instead of thrown together like a leftovers casserole.

Tweedle Dee and Tweedle Dum were the most persistent and ruthless paparazzi I'd had the misfortune to meet. First they'd hounded Samuel because of his books. Next it was his mysterious romance with a Hollywood starlet. Now they panted for an inkling of insanity from their 'fallen' A-lister. At first they were simply an annoyance, but when they'd staked out Boston's Mass General and peppered his family with obscene questions every time we visited Samuel's hospital room, they crossed a line. Now they made life miserable for Sofia and Alonso, just because Samuel was holed up in his childhood bedroom.

I'd expected pushback from Samuel's parents, especially as our elopement came on the coattails of Samuel's manic episode. But it must have been my own fears embedding false ideas in my head, because they were over the moon. Sofia had actually burst into tears. "*Ustedes me traen alegría, mis hijos,*" she'd murmured, kissing our cheeks. "I have prayed for this." I'd even glimpsed a stray tear on Alonso's stoic face. Our relationship was still strained, but perhaps the vows Samuel and I shared tomorrow would ease that strain.

Sofia sat across from me at the kitchen table, to-go cups between our hands. "I want you to have something." Setting her cup aside, she reached into the bag at her ankles and removed a satiny white cloth, perhaps decades old. She smoothed a tender hand over letters fragilely stitched in gold. Then she opened the cover. A book. A Spanish Bible, to be exact.

"This is a Cabral family heirloom, presented to Alonso's great-grandmother by her godparents on her wedding day. She carried it between her hands, along with a bouquet of white roses. It is now yours."

I shook my head. "But Dani—"

"Was also given an heirloom on her wedding day, something of my mother's. Samuel, though…Alonso wishes for you to have this. He admits that he should have given it to you seven years ago, but…"

"But you didn't believe our marriage would last." Well, he had valid reasons for holding onto the heirloom Bible the first time around. Samuel, in his youthful rebellion, hadn't wanted to bring the old Mexican traditions into our wedding. I'd been embarrassingly ambivalent about Alonso and Sofia's wishes, and had rejected the traditions with a 'take it or leave it' shrug. Alonso probably thought we wouldn't have cherished the beautiful Bible, and, at the time, he was right. But now I understood the importance of establishing roots. Having a sense of place.

Knowing where you come from and where you want to go.

Sofia saw my distress and held out her hands. "No guilt, *mi corazón.* It was our fault, too. We didn't have faith in your marriage, so you didn't have faith in it, either. But now, Alonso and I are prepared to give you our full love, openly and honestly." She saw the flicker of doubt as I silently noted that Alonso was not present. She squeezed my hands, solidifying her words. "We are here for you. You are dear to us in your own right, Kaye. In fact, Alonso suggested I come alone. He said you would appreciate the company of another woman the night before your wedding."

"Thank you. That was thoughtful." My lips trembled. Dani and Molly had approached me about an impromptu bachelorette party, but after the devastation of last weekend's Longs Peak climb, I wanted a quiet night to myself. Sofia's presence, though, was as warm and soothing as an eiderdown comforter.

She traced the delicate binding of the Bible. "Samuel has nothing left of his birth father, save for a few photographs given to him by Alonso. Rachel destroyed everything." *She nearly destroyed her son, too.* "There used to be an accompanying rosary, but when Alonso and I left the Catholic Church, his mother demanded it be returned. Alonso travelled all the way back to Ciudad Victoria to deliver the rosary to his mother in person. Facing *Mamá* Marieta after his decision was one of the most difficult things he has ever done."

"I can only imagine." Two enemy lions, Alonso and the Catholic Church, had grappled over Antonio Cabral's suicide. From what I could tell, Alonso now believed his younger brother's tragedy was something he'd never understand in this lifetime. He'd made his peace with God, but not the Catholic Church, to the eternal disgruntlement of the *familia* in Ciudad Victoria.

"Don't think too badly of *Mamá* Marieta. She loved Alonso, but she was heartbroken over the loss of her other son. People act on emotion when they are in pain," Sofia explained.

"You know about Samuel's father, Antonio Cabral Treiño?"

"Yes, but I'd forgotten his and Alonso's second *apellido* was 'Treiño.' Is that a well-known name in Tamaulipas?"

"Marieta was a Treiño, very old family. No relation to those murderous drug lords, mind you—*that* Treiño family is from Nuevo Laredo, and *our* Treiño family is from Ciudad Victoria. The cartels, they are doing horrific things to our home country: kidnappings, ransoms, brutal murders, child trafficking." She tutted, nightmares scrolling behind her eyes.

"Anyway, family names become confusing here in the States, so Alonso and I decided to simply become the 'Cabrals.' Back in

Tamaulipas, they call our family 'Cabral-Llorente.' Both Alonso's and my names, *sí? Familia* is the heart of our culture."

So Samuel's full name was actually 'Samuel Caulfield Cabral Llorente.' What a tongue twister. Growing up, I'd attended the community church with the Cabral family, where they still retained the traditional *apellido* system and I'd found it confusing when Sofia was listed in their membership directory as 'Sofia Maria Llorente Cortez de Cabral.' But the naming system certainly made it easy to figure out how everyone was related.

A thought flitted through my head and caused my heart to pound. Tomorrow, I'd once again be a Cabral. If (when?) Samuel brought me to Ciudad Victoria to meet his family, what would they call me? Would they even want to meet me? I wouldn't beat around the bush. I'd divorced their *familia*, and that was worse than leaving the Catholic faith.

Sofia patted my hand. "Don't fret, *mi corazón*. All will be well."

I rose to start on the dirty dishes. While I washed, Sofia dried and told me more about Samuel's relatives in Mexico.

"Alonso has a host of cousins in Tamaulipas, and several aunts and uncles. Do you remember *Tía* Belinda from Dani's wedding in June?" Boy, did I. She accidentally sent Samuel into a tailspin by comparing him to his abusive birth mother. After he puked out his panic attack, we sat on the bathroom floor and he told me, for the first time, about his parents' suicides.

"Alonso's only sister lives near Ciudad Victoria with her husband. You also met them at Danita's wedding, Mariángel and Tomás? Unfortunately, when you and Samuel married, most of the Cabral family did not attend because *Mamá* Marieta was still incensed over Alonso's conversion." Sofia pursed her lips. "Still at odds to this day, though *Mamá* Marieta is now gone. Hold grudges to the end, those people. Yet it was she who fought Rachel the hardest to see Samuel after Antonio's death, you know."

"I didn't know that."

"She was always a bit aloof with him. She loved him, but distantly, painfully. I'm not sure if it was because he reminded her of Antonio or of Rachel. Maybe both."

"And Samuel isn't either of his parents. That's terrible."

"Yes. My poor son has always battled out of their shadows. Now you understand why we are closer to my side of the family." She gave a wry laugh. "Alonso's family is 'jacked up.' That's what young people say, right?"

I snorted. "Everyone's family is 'jacked up,' to some degree. But where was Alonso's dad in all of this?"

Sofia crossed herself, a remnant of her Catholic past. "Ah, that is a sad story, too. *Papá* Cabral was a law professor at *La Universidad de Tamaulipas*, that's why all three of his children cultivated a passion for scholarship. Not long after Antonio's suicide, his father suffered a massive heart attack in the middle of a lecture. Dropped dead, right there at the podium. Alonso and I planned to move back to Mexico, but *Mamá* Marieta wouldn't hear of it. Despite their falling out, she was extremely proud of what Alonso had accomplished in America.

"She was a...hmm. A difficult woman. She grieved her losses the rest of her life. But even before Antonio killed himself, she was a prickly, distrustful person who made one work hard for a morsel of affection. Many of the Cabral *familia* are such."

"Alonso told me that his grandmother suffered from depression and the family hid it. This would have been Marieta's mother?"

"Yes. It had great influence on her, and thus, her children."

The pieces that formed Samuel's family portrait were coming together. "Long story short, the Cabral-Treiño family has a fantastic mix of mental illness and high-handedness, which actually doesn't mix well at all. And there's a drug lord who is absolutely *not* related to Samuel's dad, whatsoever."

"He's not one of our Treiños."

"He's from Nuevo Laredo."

"Correct. They have nothing to do with us," she repeated with vehemence.

I wondered if there wasn't something to that vehemence. "Neighbors do tend to talk," I prodded.

"They still do." Sofia met my gaze, and I understood a little better why they'd hid Samuel's illness from me. Once Samuel became their son, they'd fought for his rightful place in their family. Battled a matriarch's grief and her own childhood traumas, his father's suicide, his grandfather's subsequent heart attack, and neighborhood gossip. His deck was stacked against him long before he was born, and Sofia and Alonso weren't about to tip his hand…especially to me, his ex-wife. Love and distrust often walked hand-in-hand when it came to shielding one's children.

"Speaking of neighbors, how is Sam handling the Lyons blather?" I asked. "He tells me he's weathering it, but he never wants to burden anyone so sometimes I wonder." I couldn't recall his mentioning any run-ins with the neighbors, other than Murphy's fanboy stalking.

"It's one thing to have unknown people spread gossip about you. It's another when gossip comes from people you say hello to on the sidewalk. But now he has you to help him shoulder this burden. My heart hurts for my son, but I'm not afraid for him." She touched my wind-burned cheek, still raw from the climb. "You will take care of yourself, *mija*? We cannot lose you."

"I think my climbing days might be over."

"Whatever you feel is best. But consider carefully before you do anything drastic, hmmm?"

"Like jump into marriage?"

Sofia's laughter was warm and rich. "Oh no, that is perfectly acceptable. As long as you are marrying my son."

Sometime later, just as Sofia hinted that she couldn't possibly watch another episode of my ghost hunting program, there was a second rap at my door. I glanced at the clock: 9:17p.m. Frowning, I squinted through my recently installed peephole, praying it wasn't a paparazzo. A beady eye peered back and I jumped.

It was my adrenaline junkie friend. "Mother-of-Tom, don't stare into someone's peephole unless you want to give them a coronary."

Hector grinned. "*Ay, mamacita,* but then I couldn't see you flip your gourd every time I did it." He ruffled my head as he passed into my home but stiffened when he saw Sofia. "Oh… I didn't know you had company. I should have, though, it was stupid." He waved to Sofia. "*Hola, Señora* Cabral."

"Hector. I hear that you and my son-in-law plan to skydive Saturday instead of coming to our home to celebrate. You are more than welcome, you know." In honor of our nuptials, Alonso and Sofia were throwing open the doors to their spacious Steamboat Mountain home for a weekend of fiesta-ing. The celebration was very last minute, and Samuel and I wouldn't even be there for the second day, but their Hispanic neighbors loved to celebrate, and our absence would not deter the flow of rum cake and mariachi.

Hector politely ducked his head. "Thank you, *Señora*, but I need some time in the skies with my brothers. It's been a long week."

An observant woman, Sofia often saw into the heart of dramas before the players themselves were aware. Her steady gaze drifted from Hector, to me, and back to Hector. Pity shadowed her smile. "We will miss you. Please come over as soon as you are able. Bring Santiago and my truant son-in-law with you. Oh, and your lady friend."

"Jaime Guzman."

"Her name is familiar." Sofia turned to me. "Isn't...wasn't she your..."

"My divorce attorney, yes."

"I see. So last weekend, Samuel..."

"Spent two days with my divorce attorney in a cramped VW campervan while I climbed a mountain."

Sofia's lips quirked. "We do live in a small fishpond, don't we?"

"We certainly do."

She patted her knees and rose. "Well then. Hector obviously came here tonight to speak with you, not me. Perhaps I will busy myself in the kitchen while you step onto the balcony?"

Had I mentioned how classy Sofia was? Proper and tactful, rolled into one motherly package. Unfortunately, the two classless paparazzi staking out my staircase were neither proper nor tactful. I started to object, but then changed my mind. "You know what? Screw the paparazzi. I'm going to sit on my balcony with my hot chocolate and my friend, enjoy the fresh air, and show them I'm not doing anything wrong. They can publish all the garbage they want about me."

Hector saluted and grabbed my jacket from the back of the chair. Still, I settled far across the deck, a good four feet away so there could be no mistaking the nature of his visit.

We sat in silence for a long time. (Sticking it to the paparazzi wasn't as earth-shattering as I'd thought it would be.) The air carried just enough chill to frost our breath. I burrowed into my pockets and waited for Hector to speak. An occasional light flashed from a camera across the street, but when we didn't embrace or kiss, or toke it up, they lost interest.

Finally, Hector spoke. "Okay, here goes. I'm sorry for leaving you behind to summit Longs. I knew the dangers. But I just couldn't resist bagging that winter climb. It was a crap thing for a friend to do and I should have stayed behind with you and Molly, and Hippie."

I shrugged, not wanting to go there yet. "There was nothing you could have done. Who knows, you might have been one of the people buried alive on the snowfield. You—" I inelegantly wiped my nose on my sleeve "—you might have died, too."

"How are you and Molls doin' after finding that woman? Okay?"

"Well enough. Molly's closed mouth about it. Hector please, I don't want to talk about this, not the night before my wedding." I tried to open the metaphorical door and jump out of this conversation, but he casually leaned back, blocking my escape.

"Are you sure this is what you want, *mamacita*? To marry him again?"

"Of course."

"It's only, this seems kinda...rash."

I gave him an incredulous look. "After all the stunts you and I have pulled? *This* is what crosses the line in your mind?"

"No. But the cliff-hucking and skydiving is all about pushing the limits of the human body, defying physics. We do something crazy and stupid, feel like gods for a bit, then high-five each other when we're done. But this—marrying the man who left you high and dry for seven years?"

"Hey." I straightened my spine. "You know why he left. Heck, by now, every Nixie in China knows why he left. But he came back, and he has broken himself in two trying to make things right between us. You have no idea what he's sacrificed—"

"He convinced you to bail on everything and everyone you love, just so he can have a booty call in L.A.!"

"Shhh!" I pointed in warning to the stalkers across the street. Hector rolled his eyes but lowered his voice.

"It seems like you're the one doing all the sacrificing. Come on, Kaye, don't be a doormat."

I leaned in. "For the record, I left him high and dry, too. I'm the one who filed for divorce, remember? But we've forgiven each other and are ready to move on. I suggest you do the same." I stood, signaling the conversation was over. He only stared up at me, dark eyes wide and glittering. "Look. I know you've never liked Sam, but because you're my friend, I hope you'll be there tomorrow."

"Of course. And as your friend, a *real* friend, I had to speak up. I hope you can appreciate that."

The fight drained from me. "I do. But I disagree with you on this one."

"If it goes south, give me a call and we'll tackle a summit." He caught himself and grimaced. "Or take a quiet tubing trip down the river."

I clenched my teeth to hold back the images of twisted limbs and frozen hands and patted my well-meaning friend on the shoulder. "Have a good evening, Hector. Watch out for the soul-eating parasites at the end of the drive."

"See you tomorrow, Trilby. Or Cabral, I guess." Cameras started to flash again as he jogged down the steps, and I ground my teeth even harder because even though I told myself it was my balcony and I'd done nothing to be ashamed of, I hated that tomorrow, somewhere, hundreds of gullible people would read a blurb about a strange man leaving my home in the middle of the night and believe the real life Neelie Nixie was a cheating tramp.

"I should go home, as well."

Sofia had quietly slipped out of my apartment. Well, perhaps only fifty people would believe I was a cheating tramp.

"Thank you for coming down, *Mamá*. It means a lot."

Sofia pulled me into her warm arms. She always smelled of chocolate and cinnamon.

"Don't fret over the Valdez boy. It is difficult to disappoint someone we care for, but being honest is the best you can do."

"If nothing else, I was honest."

"I have thought of a way to keep unwanted eyes from your wedding tomorrow. Do you trust me?"

"I trust you."

"*Gracias, mi corazón.* Here's what we're going to do…"

Chapter 3
MATCHING HANDS

A climbing hold in which both hands are placed side-by-side to allow a mountaineer to reach the next hold more easily.

Boulder, Colorado
October, present day

Sam—Our Pikes Peak climb last weekend kept swimming in my head, so I had to get it down paper before I forgot the details. Needless to say, I may be working late. Again.

Time for honesty. Next month we'll mark our third anniversary. I know the past couple of years have been rough, with my panic attacks and quirky little phobias. I get that you and Hector think you can fix this by throwing me onto a mountain again…and my therapist might actually agree with you. The Longs Peak avalanche really messed me up.

My fearlessness has been something you've loved in the past and, though you'd never say it, you have to be disappointed. I'm disappointed in me, too.

Perhaps the need to shed this constant disappointment is what made me agree to your and Hector's fourteeners proposal—climb Colorado's tallest mountains. Even writing it makes my heart race with excitement and fright. (Trust me, it's not your combined persuasive skills. But by all means, please continue to 'persuade' me. I kind of like it.) —Love K, who is trying to be brave again.

Hydraulic Level Five [WORKING TITLE]
Draft 1.103
© *Samuel Caulfield Cabral and Aspen Kaye Cabral*
COLORADO THE BEAUTIFUL

"Purple mountains' majesty," Aspen whispers. Katharine Lee Bates had it right, with her 'sea-like expanse.' The mountains circling Pikes Peak are white-capped waves, frozen mid-crash against fourteen-thousand-foot walls.

Aspen's cheeks have numbed and her nose is a solid icicle, but she's glad her first summit in years is in October. The fall foliage is at its peak; the trees that share her name are coffers of quivering gold.

The gift shop behind her certainly lends a surreal element to the summit. It also makes her feel safe, surrounded by price-tagged hoodies emblazoned with 'Colorado the Beautiful' slogans. Now she feels bad for giving H and Caulfield crap about choosing the most commercialized peak in Colorado as the first summit in their fourteener challenge. With the clanking cog railway just feet away and tourists in trendy parkas snapping pictures, potential avalanches are the farthest thing from her mind. Today, their biggest concern is getting down the mountain before a FLASH-BOOM gathers. And that's exactly what it is—thunder and lightning that'll make a gal fear for her soul.

She's still not sure how she landed herself in a race to tackle fifteen of Colorado's fourteeners, but she has difficulty refusing H's dares. Coupled with Caulfield's Sam-I-Am charm, she didn't stand a chance. She shakes her head as she recalls her conversation with H just days ago, his bold black eyes round with innocence...

"I have a proposal for you."

She glances at the office invader over her monitor. "What can I do for you, H?"

"You remember the Canadians?"

"The brothers we met on Longs Peak? Sure."

H gets comfortable in the chair across from her desk and plucks a peppermint from her candy dish. "Well, they have this plan to bag all of Canada's fourteeners this year—that's fifteen peaks."

"I know how many fourteeners Canada has."

"Right, okay. You know how crazy competitive these guys are. They've decided it's not enough to get fifteen peaks in a year. They want me to bag fifteen of Colorado's this year, too, and see who gets their summits first. That's cake, because Colorado has fifty-three alone."

She rubs her eyes, not liking where this conversation is going. "I also know how many fourteeners Colorado has."

"Right, of course. I'll need a good partner. L's in, but they have the baby on the way, so he won't be able to make every climb. Mountaineering isn't really my wife's thing—she's more of a one-sport woman, and that sport's skydiving. Then there's you and Caulfield."

"H, I haven't summited a mountain in three years."

"It's like riding a bike. You just have to get back—"

"Caulfield put you up to this, didn't he?" She shoves his feet off her desk and opens her old-school planner to note of a new client appointment.

"Aspen," he says in a wheedling tone, "it's been three years since the avalanche. When are you going to start living your life again?"

He's beginning to sound like her therapist. "I *am* living my life. I have a wonderful career, a great town, a husband and family who love me..."

"And you also have a daily affirmations calendar on your desk. With mountain views, ironically." She grabs the calendar from him and stuffs it in a drawer. Like a toddler who can't keep still, H next flips open her planner, scans her schedule and jabs a finger at her free weekend. "Look, what you saw on the Longs climb, that woman...I get why going back up there is scary."

Aspen slams her planner shut. "No, you don't. You didn't dig through snow that was packed so hard it was like digging through concrete with your fingertips. Or claw into it with an ice axe and pray to God you didn't kill someone, only to dig them out and find them so..." She buries her face in her hands as the trembling starts. "You didn't see her face, or feel her skin when you had to find a pulse—"

"Aspen, shhh, *tranquila. No te enojes.*" H's arms are around her and she stiffens at their unfamiliarity. He hasn't been affectionate with her in years, not since he walked out of her wedding. "You're right, I haven't been in an avalanche. But I've seen legs snapped in two, heads gashed by ski and skydiving accidents—remember your bounce several summers ago? It's part of the lifestyle." She calms to the point where she sees the truth in H's words.

"So here's the gig: Pikes Peak, super easy. It'll be a late autumn climb, but we'll take it slow. Just you, me, and your ball-and-chain."

Unbelievably, H and Caulfield have reached a friendly understanding in recent weeks. "I haven't been training, not even a rock wall. And Caulfield's never climbed a fourteener in his life."

"You guys run, like, seven miles a day. And the terrain around here isn't exactly flat."

"Yes, but—"

"And you're freakishly strong for a Cabbage Patch Doll."

She shoves his arm, proving his point. She wouldn't say she resembles a Cabbage Patch Doll, though her face does have a baby-ish shape, and she's been plagued by freckles and frizzy ringlets since she was a tot. Ringlets which, when she's active, she'll braid down either side of her head. Fudge it all, she looks like a Cabbage Patch Doll.

Aspen sighs. "You have to admit, we've experienced some incredible things. How many people can say they've climbed above the clouds?"

"That's it, Aspen. We're not like other people. Some would be happy to call it a day after that avalanche, but not you." He leans in with that intense gaze of his. "*You survived.*"

———————— •◆• ————————

Caulfield comes up beside her and together they stare over the rock wall into the fog of a cloud passing through.

"I bought you a bag of cookies." He holds them out to her. She smiles and takes them. The warm chocolate chip cookies have been a favorite of hers since she first rode the cog railway years ago on a school field trip.

The wind bites and whips what little skin is exposed beneath stocking caps and fleece. Temperatures read eight degrees. But Aspen might as well be standing at the golden gates of Heaven, because as much as she's denied it, she's longed for mountain summits. What's more, she's longed for them with Caulfield.

Too bad she chickened out at the trail head and ascended Pikes Peak via the cog railway. H grumbled, but in the end he too boarded the train and slouched next to a toddler with snot bubbling from his nose.

"I'm glad we came up, even if it was just the railway," she tells her husband.

"I was worried I'd made a mistake in pushing you to do this."

"Sometimes we need a little pushing." She peers up at him—another mountain she'd needed a lot of pushing to summit. "Thank you."

Caulfield steals a cookie, though it's not in his strict food plan. "Thank *you* for wanting me along. Though I've got to admit, I'm bushed after climbing those five whole stairs. Any chance I can convince you to take the railway back down?"

Kaye—If you come home on time tonight, I'll personally demonstrate my power of persuasion.

All seriousness now. I am not disappointed in you. I am concerned for my wife. Among everything and everyone under the sun, I love you most. This will never change—I made you that promise on our wedding day, nearly three years ago. This fourteeners challenge is one way of keeping that promise.—Sam

Boulder, Colorado
November, three years earlier

My travel agency clients pushed elopement as the stress-free route to marriage. Ha! Maybe it is in Hawaii, where you can forget the shirt on your back and the sandals on your feet, and still have a beach wedding. A courthouse wedding, however, was complicated.

Five days after the avalanche, I slid into the front seat of Danita Valdez's beautifully restored Coronet muscle car and unbuttoned my red wool coat. I'd creaked down the old servants' staircase of my Victorian home, through my Trilby Jones office, and out the back door without alerting Tweedle Dee and Tweedle Dum. The rest of our tiny wedding party waited across town at the county courthouse—thankfully paparazzi-free. At Sofia's brilliant suggestion, the Valdez boys' parents took Samuel's car for a spin earlier this morning, Tweedle Dee and Tweedle Dum trailing after them, all the way to Denver.

If my string of questionable life choices hadn't clued one in to my impulsive personality, my elopement to a man I'd just as hastily married and divorced seven years ago should've sealed the deal. Fortunately, I had friends who managed to turn our spur-of-the-moment wedding into something cohesive.

My once and future sister-in-law unceremoniously tossed a small bouquet of delicate paper whites into my lap. She and Molly, who fidgeted with her neckline in the backseat, also had bouquets resting in cup holders. "I stopped by a flower shop—assumed it slipped your mind with everything else."

I inhaled shakily. "What else am I forgetting?"

"Forms of identification?" Molly asked.

"Got it." I patted my purse.

Danita drummed the steering wheel with perfect French-tipped nails. "Decree of divorce paperwork?"

I looked to the ceiling. "That'll be fun to explain to the county clerk."

"Hmmm." She gave me her no-nonsense stare. "You're sure about this? Life has been awfully crazy, as of late. Especially after the av—"

"Let's not discuss it today, Dani. Please? Wait until after the honeymoon."

Molly's ginger complexion had gone sickly pale, and I knew the things that flickered behind her eyelids. "I don't want to talk about it, either." Dani relented, for now.

"Anyway, yes, I'm sure about remarrying Samuel. That may be the one thing I'm sure about just now. And before you remind me of what happened in Boston, I know the mistakes I made, I've learned from them, and I know what I'm getting into by marrying your brother. But I also know what I'm getting out of it, and that's a wonderful man who is honest, and kind, and brilliant. A man who loves me and wants to share my life again. We're in this for the long haul. Isn't that what you want for your brother, too?"

A smile played upon Danita's lips. "Something old?"

I exhaled (the defense I'd prepared wasn't needed after all) and touched the satin-covered Bible tucked in my clutch. "I have my something old. Though, I suppose this could also pass." I fluffed the knee-length hem of my dress. No white, just pale gray tulle pulled from the depths of my closet, stored away after a black-tie fundraiser two autumns ago.

I'd forgotten my 'something blue,' though the sky that November afternoon was crisp and clear. I *did* have a brand new gold band to give to Samuel, and that was more important to me than new dresses and manicures.

I nervously twisted my bare ring finger, where Samuel's diamond had once rested and would rest again. Before we exchanged vows, we had to obtain a license from the recorder's office.

Danita steered the car through mid-morning foot traffic near the University of Colorado. Students blearily stumbled through rotting leaf piles toward Pearl Street for coffee and pastries, book bags slung over their shoulders. I bounced my knees and peered down the road.

When we pulled up to the government building that housed the recorder's office, Samuel was already there, pacing the sidewalk, eyes intent on his shiny black oxfords. His hands were crammed in his pants pockets and frenetic energy spiraled around him, so much so that pedestrians gave him an extra foot of space. His head lifted when we shut our car doors. Joy lighted every corner of his face as he strode toward us, a small cluster of paper whites resting in the button hole of his suit coat (Dani had kindly thought of more than my bouquet).

I stood across from him, twisting the paper whites' stems between my palms. His fingers trailed a tamed curl along my temple, down behind my ear to the nape of my neck, where it was tucked into a bun.

"We've been here before," he said.

"It feels different this time."

"Hmm, yes. This is the right time."

I thought of our night spent under the stars after Angel and Danita's wedding, on the Lyons baseball field, finding constellations. *"Timing is crucial,"* Samuel had explained. *"Not only the season, but the hour…"*

I took his hand in mine, touched the tiny white scar between his index finger and his thumb. "Remember Canes Venatici, the hunting dog?"

Warmth filled Sam's eyes. "That constellation isn't up until April. Have I taught you nothing?"

Molly, ever impatient, gave our backs a little shove toward the door. "Hunting dogs my foot. More like a couple of slaphappy Pekingese yapping after a squirrel."

When we'd finished at the recorder's office, Samuel tucked the envelope inside his suit coat and slid into the backseat next to me. "Not so bad, even when the clerk implied we lacked a certain commitment to warrant a license."

"Kaye did just change her name from Cabral to Trilby, back in April," said Danita.

"My favorite part was when he realized who you were and asked you to sign the back of his water bill," said Molly. "Oh! And then he suggested you put all of that income into a big diamond for Kaye."

"I happen to agree. She's earned that sucker." Danita was not known for her frugality.

Samuel played with the blunt edges of my fingernails. "The ring is already taken care of and is in Angel's capable hands." He threaded his fingers with mine. "You are the main show, not the diamond."

My face flushed. Though I'd known him forever, Samuel's admiration still caught me off guard. From the strong Latin angles of his face to the surprisingly delicate turn of his mouth, he continually gave me a moment's pause.

"I can't believe you gave that clerk your autograph. Hopefully it bought us five minutes before he shared it on Instagram," said Molly.

Sam shrugged. "We should be long gone from the courthouse before anyone tracks us down, thanks to Danita's in-laws."

"The Valdezes can only lead them up and down I-25 for so long. *Ave Maria Purísima*, those pests are all over you like *Tía* Lucia on a swap-meet. How are you going to get through Denver International?"

Bingo! We were flying somewhere for our honeymoon. I gave Samuel a sly look.

He narrowed his eyes at his sister. "Fantastic, Danita."

"What? I didn't tell her where you're going."

He turned to me. "We're not flying out of Denver International. We're spending the night in Estes Park and taking a chartered flight to O'Hare tomorrow morning."

"The Stanley Hotel?"

His eyes brightened with desire, and desire also stabbed through me as I too thought of tonight. "You'll see."

A small gathering waited for us in the lobby of the county courthouse, a non-descript office complex with a few interesting windows. Many happy, but hesitant, faces. Well, that was okay...our first marriage had caused so much turmoil.

My mother wore her special occasion dress, a pretty thing she'd bought a decade ago for her annual heirloom tomato growers' banquet and had worn precious few times since. I smoothed a hand down my own little-worn dress and frowned at how scary-similar we were.

Samuel's mother bounced on her heels, ready to fly across lobby and embrace her boy, but Alonso kept her patient. Both Sofia and my mother had matching paper white corsages upon their wrists. Tears pricked my eyes and I turned to Dani.

"Did you...of course you did." I pulled her into my arms. "*Gracias, mi hermana.*"

"It was no trouble. Every wedding needs a touch of elegance."

Cassady was also there, as well as the Valdez brothers—Angel, Hector, and Santiago. Hector had brought Jaime Guzman as a date. She was biting and abrasive, but she'd also made an effort to befriend me. When a person's livelihood dealt out heartbreak on a daily basis, a remarriage was probably a nice change of pace. She gave me an awkward pat.

"Trilby. Don't screw this one up or I'll charge you triple for retainer fees."

"Pretty sure that's unethical. I appreciate the sentiment, though."

Hector tried to meet my eyes, but I couldn't look at him. Nauseating images forced their way into my mind, of him and Luca strolling through the avalanche's devastation like they didn't have a care in the world. I walled them up and out.

Jaime jerked a thumb behind her. "I'm gonna hit the bathroom before the show begins. All that morning coffee."

"Around the corner and to the right," said Molly.

She snorted. "Yeah. I know. Divorce attorney, remember?"

I watched her retreat and avoided Hector's uneasy gaze. He had *that* look, the one that signaled a singular focus, usually directed at the perfect snow or a leggy woman. This time, it was turned toward me. He beckoned me over. I sighed. While Samuel kissed his parents' cheeks and the others exclaimed over Lieutenant Angel Valdez's crisp dress blues, I gave Hector a hurried hug. I tried to pull away, but he gripped my elbow.

"Kaye, please don't go through with this." His words were quiet, rushed. *Oh cliffhuck.*

"Let go of my arm." I twisted in his grip.

"Are you absolutely sure?"

"You bet I am," I said through my teeth.

"He's going to leave again, someday. You know he will. As your friend—"

"As my *friend*, you need to shut up and let me go, right now."

"You're being stupid." He dared me to make a scene.

I saw red. Mustering an old self-defense maneuver, I launched a knee at his tender parts and brought my pointy heel down on his toes. Not hard, but unexpected. He oofed and dropped his hands. Effective. I wasn't subtle, either, because half the wedding party's conversations suddenly stopped.

I lifted my chin. "You're lucky I didn't go for your eyes. How's that for a doormat, *amigo*?"

He coughed. "*Mamacita*—"

"Don't call me that."

By now, Samuel had noticed that Hector and I weren't exchanging best wishes. His questioning gaze met mine.

Angel rushed in to diffuse the situation. "Dude. Is everything…"

"Okay, okay." Hector brushed him away. "I was just telling Kaye I'm happy she's happy."

Liar. My blood still boiled. I closed my eyes and breathed. *Not today. Today is yours and Samuel's.* "Perhaps I'm a bit high strung."

Samuel's face was like a mannequin's—hard angled and impassive. I knew that look, and it meant anger pulsed beneath the polish. "Hector, glad you could be here, man." He held out his hand, but his other hand rested lightly on my hip, claiming me.

"Congrats, Cabral."

"Congratulate me in twenty minutes, when Kaye's my wife."

Good lord, there was nothing to be done for it. Hector and Sam were grown men, but they circled each other like two toddlers after the same Tonka truck. I exhaled. "Hector, are we done here?"

"We're done here."

"So are we."

None of us heard Jaime return (her neon orange moccasins afforded her a stealth the NSA would appreciate). I didn't know how much she'd seen. But Jaime was a lawyer for a reason and, despite her repugnance of the human race, she was a crack shot at reading people. She took one look at Hector, Sam, me…and knew. She rounded on me, finger in my face. "Hands out of my cookie jar, Trilby."

"Hey! Is that necessary?" Samuel said, just as I reached for the sky and said, "No cookies here!"

Spinning on that stealthy heel, she strode right past us and down the hallway. Hector ran after her.

"*Chíngale.* Jaime—"

"I'm not going to wait around while you chase Kaye Trilby *Cabral* for another ten years. You bring me to a wedding then make a play for the bride? *¡Vete a la verga, Valdez!*"

"This has nothing to do with making a play for anyone. This is about keeping my *friend* from making a big mistake. Jaime!"

Then he grabbed *her* elbow, mistake number two. For the second time in as many minutes, a woman jabbed him in the gut.

This time big brother Angel smacked Hector upside the head. "You're the only one who sees it as a big mistake, *manito*. Apologize to Kaye and Sam and then go after your woman."

"Trilby."

"You'd better leave, Hector," I said.

He clenched his jaw, then turned and slammed through the door after Jaime.

Nine faces stared at me, their expressions ranging from baffled to horrified. I buried my head in my hands. Samuel rubbed my neck, but all his reassurance couldn't ease my humiliation. Despite my classed-up hair and heels, I felt too much like a Maury Povich guest for peace of mind.

My mother frowned. "Jaime Guzman's an angry young woman, isn't she? And that Valdez boy's equally rash."

I dropped my hands in resignation. "Rash like me?"

Mom pursed her lips in answer.

Angel shook his head. "Nah. Hector just runs hotter than the rest of us Valdezes, and that's saying a lot for a Latin man. He'll cool off tonight and kiss Kaye's feet tomorrow."

"Except Kaye will be on her honeymoon tomorrow," Alonso pointed out to his son-in-law.

Mom shook her head. "Hector and Jaime will never work, the same reason you and Samuel didn't work. A torch to gunpowder, that's what they are."

I loved my mother. What she'd done for me and Samuel in Boston had been amazing. The way she'd guided us through the fall-out of his manic episode with cool logic…she'd set aside her usual callousness and made her daughter her priority. Perhaps I'd hoped for the same support today. For goodness' sake, I was a twenty-eight year old woman, perfectly capable of knowing my own mind and standing behind my decisions, naysayers be damned. Still, that tiny seed of self-doubt sprouted.

But Samuel, who knew me better than anyone, saw that seedling poke through the ground. He turned to our families. "Well, *Papá*, it looks like we're not bucking *all* of the traditions. A Mexican wedding isn't complete without drama."

"I call dibs on the centerpieces," said Danita.

"Leftover cake is going home with me," added Angel.

Santiago sheepishly pulled a flask from his inside pocket. "I'm covered."

Alonso and Sofia stood there, trying to piece together what had just happened. Then she winked at me. "What did I say? Jacked up."

Alonso tossed up his hands. "*Niños.*"

"And that's how you diffuse a bomb. Come here, firecracker. Let's chat outside." Samuel tucked my hand into the crook of his elbow, and I had never loved him more.

My bare legs turned to gooseflesh, but I removed my heels anyway and let the icy brown grass crackle beneath my toes. The judge agreed to an early lunch while Samuel and I walked toward Boulder Creek. Samuel also removed his shoes and socks, and a shock of cold jolted through his legs. A clicking camera caught our attention… a car across the street.

"Let's wander over to the tree line," I suggested.

"They'll still take pictures."

"We're walking, not stripping naked and going at it in the brush. Let them take pictures."

"I wouldn't mind that." He flipped up the collar of my red wool coat and led me beneath bare aspen branches.

Before we saw the creek, we heard its gurgles and plops. Every crag and snowy slope of Boulder's gendarmes was visible on this crystal clear day…a day for avalanches. I averted my eyes. We gingerly picked our way across the near-frozen ground and into line of evergreens until we reached the creek, swollen with autumn rains. I tested the water and shivered deliciously. Samuel's gaze skimmed down my body and rested on my feet. He fidgeted with the edges of his hair, but it wasn't the manic fidgeting of a month ago.

He cleared his throat. "I need to say something, and I want you to truly listen to me before you rush to conclusions."

I wrapped two protective arms around my waist. "Are you…are you calling it off?"

"Well, that was counterproductive, wasn't it?" He drew me into his arms and soothed my rigid body until it relaxed. I felt the rumble in his chest as he spoke.

"I need to be sure. I can't go into this marriage if divorce is on the table for you. I can't…" A tremble ran through him, leaked into his voice. "Despite his appallingly poor tactic, Hector's concern for you is valid. I know what I'm asking you to do, firecracker. Spending the rest of your life with someone is a huge commitment. Throw a bipolar diagnosis into the mix…"

I pulled back so I could see his face. "This isn't 'ol' Aspen Kaye being rash' again. I know the choice I've made."

"And I know what lies ahead for us. Days, weeks when all I'll want to do is roll over in bed and stay there forever. When simple tasks like eating or showering are as daunting as a mountain climb. Or the next time I run again, you'll be terrified because I've simply vanished. I'm asking you to commit to a lifetime of this."

I slipped out of his arms and meandered along the bank of the creek. "Samuel—"

"But I'm also asking you to commit to a lifetime with a man who would give his right arm so you could have a minute of joy. And for a right-handed writer, that's saying something."

Love tugged at my mouth. "There's voice command software."

He chuckled but didn't relent. "I mean it, Kaye. I will always make sure someone is there for you, even if it can't be me, for the rest of my life. And I swear I will always come back to you as soon as I can." His voice cracked. "Can you promise to stand by me the rest of your life? Even if someday you feel trapped and just want to catch the first flight to Saint Lucia?"

There were precious few times Samuel let me see beneath his carefully-cultivated exterior. Since we'd found our way back to each other, he'd made a herculean effort to show me the *real* him, rather than the fairy tale. Vulnerability was in his eyes. He jiggled his hands in his pockets as he waited for my response. I could say 'yes, I promise,' but that old, old fear of his would still be there. Unless I also laid myself bare, he would always wonder if he'd forced me into a dismal life. So I spoke to him in a language he understood.

"Let me tell you a story." I dipped my toes in frigid creek water. The image of a wild-haired boy, skin browned by endless hours in the sun, splashed through my mind.

"Once upon a time, there was a girl…oh, let's call her Cottonwood Cat."

Samuel snorted. "That's a terrible name."

"Shush, we can't all be writers. CC for short. CC meets this boy when she's, like, five."

"Four."

"Four. He fascinates her, pushes her away and pulls her in. She worships him because he's older, wiser, and makes her feel more treasured than a pile of diamonds. He answers her inane questions, like 'why do dogs go pee-pee on trees instead of toilets?'"

"And he secretly loves her inanity."

"Hold up, this is my story. She lives in a fairytale and this boy is her Prince Charming. But the fairytale gets real."

The smile left my face. "Charming hits a grand slam and, in the thrill of the moment, tells her he's going to marry her someday. Little does this boy suspect, he's just put real money down on her fairytale. Boom, now CC has a life strategy, and that strategy begins with a capital 'S.' Of course the fairytale goes south."

"Kaye, I did love you."

"No interrupting, please, though I appreciate the clarification. It goes south, but CC learns some lessons along the way. The first is that this concept of fated soul mates is bogus." I began to pace again as I explained my theory. "How many people buy into this idea and then end up disappointed when their spouse says or does something very un-soul-mate-ish?"

"Un-soul-ma—?"

"Oh, let's say their soul mate has halitosis. They wonder if maybe they jumped the gun on marriage, that their true 'soul mate' is wandering the streets, strumming a guitar and wailing their name, waiting for fate to throw them together."

He watched my mouth, his own lips pursed to hold back laughter. I put his hand over my heart, feeling its chill through the opening of my coat.

"The truth is, you *choose* your soul mate. Heck, they don't even become your 'soul mate' until you bare your soul to them, and that's really hard. But we're doing it right now, so it is possible. That leads to CC's next life lesson.

"CC thought she didn't have a choice, that this boy was her destiny. And because she saw love as fate rather than a choice, she didn't work at it. Hey, if it's destiny, it'll happen. Right? Wrong. Prince Charming fails her, she's disillusioned, The End. Divorce."

Samuel's eyes shone. "I think Prince Charming suffered from the same questionable fallacies."

"CC *did* make a choice—she chose to love that boy. But she didn't follow through on her commitment, so she was a slave to her washouts for seven years. She failed miserably."

"Kaye—"

"She did. We did." My throat began to close so I swallowed. "The thing is, I'm not wallowing anymore. I'm taking ownership of my choices, and I'm going to love you with everything I have. I promise to stand by you. And if, God forbid, you run again, I *swear* I will exhaust all options. Divorce won't even be on the backburner. It's locked up in a cupboard."

"And I swear I will never underestimate you again." Samuel weaved his hand into my pinned up hair, careful not to ruin my artful construction, and pulled my mouth to his. "I've always chosen you, Aspen Kaye Trilby…tried to, in my warped way. But I can't view us as two separate lives anymore, can I? There's only *us*."

"I really love us."

Sam found my racing pulse. "Your mother was wrong. We're not a torch to gunpowder."

"Unless it's in the bedroom. Because truthfully, once we find our groove again, I think we'll be pretty explosive."

"Seven years' worth of stockpiled gunpowder."

I grew serious. "No matter what Hector, your parents, my parents, or anybody says, don't doubt me. I mean it."

He held my arms with gentleness, so different from the way Hector had grasped at me a short time ago. "I won't. But do something for me?"

"Hmm?"

"Don't doubt yourself, either."

Just as we turned back to the courthouse, someone shouted my name. My father jogged toward us, his old fashioned sports coat thrown over a faded tie-dyed shirt.

"Dad?"

"Tom," Samuel said at the same time.

As I hugged my father, I mouthed a silent thank you to my almost-husband, knowing he'd somehow been instrumental in getting my dad to the wedding.

Dad hugged me back. "Are you already married? Sorry Samuel, I tried to be on time."

I inhaled the weedy and admittedly sentimental smell of my father's coat. "No, you're just in time."

The courtroom was the beigest beige in the history of beiges. The only spots of color in the room were the Colorado and United States flags on either side of the judge's bench, where he reviewed our paperwork. The judge himself was also beige, kind of like a Ken doll in a neck-to-ankle black robe and a suspicious goggle-like tan line that circled his eyes. He probably spent his Fridays on the ski slopes. Only in Boulder.

Sniffles cut through the echo of shuffling papers. My toes felt swollen and pinched in my narrow shoes, and I shifted my weight. Phew, was it hot in here? My head grew fuzzy and my knees began to tremble, so I locked them before they gave out. Another sniffle from our wedding party, this time masculine, had me turning around. It was my father. Sofia too, as well as Molly, Angel, even Danita. The monumental importance of what was happening sank like a stone in my stomach, and nothing good ever resulted from stomach stones. Oh man, I was going to throw up.

Samuel gripped my hand. I glanced up to find his gaze upon me. "I've got you," he mouthed.

He did have me, weak stomach and all. Ah, there *was* color in the room—Samuel's eyes were a vivid blue, so I zeroed in on them until my stomach stopped flipping.

The judge cleared his throat. "Alright, shall we begin?"

Samuel stepped forward and I followed, my hand holding his for dear life.

We repeated our vows and slid rings onto each other's fingers, just as we had before. But now, those words were not a blur in a whirlwind day. "I, Aspen Kaye, take you, Samuel Caulfield, to be my wedded husband to have and to hold from this day forward." All other fancy debris, paper white petals and satin-covered heirloom Bibles, circled that vortex.

I looked Samuel straight in the eye. "In sickness and in health, to love and to cherish until death do us part."

I watched as the blue shone and gathered, until a drop rolled down the crease of his nose, then became lost in the corner of his mouth. But his voice was strong and steady as he placed a ring on my finger, just as it had been all those years ago when he'd barely left boyhood behind. "Kaye, I give you this ring as a symbol of my vow, and with all that I am, and all that I have, I honor you."

"Thank you," I whispered.

I waited for the judge to pronounce us husband and wife, but to my surprise, Sofia stepped forward and handed Samuel a small, ornate box. He emptied the contents in his hands and out spilled thirteen shimmering gold coins. Until now, only by the grace of God had I maintained my composure. But when my husband took my palms and reverently poured the *arras* between them, a sob escaped my lips.

He spoke in lilting Spanish. "I, Samuel, give you, Kaye, these thirteen coins as a symbol of my unquestionable trust and confidence I place in you as my beloved wife..." He put the *arras* box upon the coins.

I accepted the coins and rested my crumpling face against Samuel's shoulder, the gift between us. It wasn't about the *arras* themselves, or even the material comfort they symbolized. In this single act—literally placing his heritage in my hands—he brought me into his *familia*, wholly and lovingly, for better or for worse, a place he'd never granted me until now because he'd never fully accepted it himself...until now.

"Shall we finish?" The judge lifted an eyebrow, signifying he'd performed too many weddings and divorces to be affected by sentimentality. "By the power vested in me by the State of Colorado, I hereby pronounce you husband and wife."

I threaded my fingers behind his neck and pulled him down to me, but instead of meeting his mouth, I whispered in his ear. "If I kiss you, will you kiss me back?" He grinned and sought my lips, his eagerness my answer.

Chapter 4
SEND IT

Slang for doing a challenging maneuver with panache. "You send it, TradMan." The most overused phrase in mountain climbing culture, probably because it's fun to say.

Denver Airport
November, present day

A s I reminisced about our wedding day, I twisted my ring around my finger, a nervous habit.

Today was our third wedding anniversary. I'd hoped to arrive in L.A. early enough to celebrate in his hotel room, but the flight attendant at my gate had just announced another half-hour delay, so the likelihood of getting out of Denver before ten p.m. was slim.

It wasn't flying that made me gnaw my nails to the quick. It was being trapped in a box. I never reserved a window seat now because the feeling of entombment was too much. I'd lose my air. So I'd close my eyes and concentrate on rolling the ball of my foot on the ground as my therapist suggested, feeling its solidness. *Roll...inhale...roll... exhale...roll...*

Any small enclosure or device that constricted my body, like skydiving harnesses and roller coaster bars, caused problems. The 'why' wasn't a mystery. This time of year was always rough since that wretched avalanche, and I found I'd developed a whole host of nervous fidgets. Normally Samuel was next to me, but his trip to L.A. couldn't be avoided and I'd insisted he go ahead of me, that I would be fine flying alone.

I closed my eyes and channeled a different dream, one that brought immeasurable peace.

A tiny head resting on my chest, no bigger than my combined fists. Humid breath against skin.

The slow and steady rhythms of sleep. Breathe in…breathe out… Breathe in…breathe out. The sleep of one who is wholly content, safe, secure…

"Ben Dover and Mike Rotch, please come to the Information Center… Ben Dover and Mike Rotch…"

My eyes popped open. Good lord. Someone would be detained by airport security tonight.

Sighing, I packed away my dream and watched passengers mill about. Two young children ran circles around a pillar until one of them became dizzy and flopped on the stained carpet. I chuckled, though his zonked mother was not in a laughing mood. The couple next to me canoodled, all secret smiles and words. Newlyweds, I'd bet. I decided to be social.

"Are you off to L.A. for your honeymoon?"

"Oh no, we live in L.A.," the woman explained. "We actually spent a week honeymooning in Colorado."

I twisted my ring again. "Wonderful! Did you enjoy your trip?"

The man grinned, and feeling like an idiot, I realized they probably hadn't ventured much out of their hotel room. His wife smacked his arm. "I absolutely adored Estes Park. We stayed at The Stanley. Are you familiar?"

"Oh, absolutely. My husband and I spent our wedding night there. Gorgeous old place. Did you do the ghost tour?"

"Sure did. Though once I heard all of the old stories, my neck kept prickling like someone was watching me." She shivered.

I didn't mention that guests often experienced an eerie feeling, whether they'd done the ghost tour or not. With a last friendly nod, I leaned back in my uncomfortable airport chair and closed my eyes, my own wedding night of three years ago reeling through my mind like a favorite home movie...

Estes Park, Colorado
November, three years earlier

The Stanley Hotel in Estes Park was the very place that sparked my love of a good ghost story, not long after my sixth birthday. Halloween had always captured my imagination, with its spider webs and stockpiles of candy. But hearing about the ghosts that inhabited the stately neo-Georgian hotel scared the crap out of me.

When I was a child, my dad picked me up Saturday mornings for breakfast at a pancake house. As I watched snowy peaks give way to Estes Park through the frosted car window, I spotted a sprawling white building nestled in the base of a mountain, red-roofed, dormers and a portico so grand, it could only be a palace.

"Oh, that? The Stanley Hotel, flower. Hasn't anyone ever told you about it?" Over banana pancakes and orange juice, my father weaved tale after tale of phantom footsteps and tinkling pianos, paranormal partygoers and foul odors, and the infamous Room 217, with its mysteriously unpacked luggage. "Not just spooky stories, either. There was a horror writer who spent the night there, back when they didn't get much winter traffic, and he was so creeped out that he wrote a book about it. I'll let you read it." He frowned across the table at my wide hazel eyes and gapped teeth. "Er, maybe in ten years."

Since then, I'd done the ghost tour countless times and even had The Stanley on my client list. But not once had I spent the night. It was on my bucket list, I'd just never got around to booking a room. So I practically dragged an amused Samuel out of the car and into the main lobby after our wedding, my impatient heels tapping across the glossy wooden floor.

"If I'd known you'd be this anxious to get me naked, Mrs. Cabral, I would have reserved a suite here years ago." His voice carried through the lavish lobby with its high ceilings and dark wood paneling, and curious guests.

"I don't want to miss the next ghost tour. See? They're about to leave."

Samuel's face fell into a weird amalgam of disappointment and restrained graciousness. He scratched the back of his head. "Oh, sure. We can definitely do a ghost tour, if that's what you want. Let me just drop the luggage..."

The laughter I'd repressed burst out, and I couldn't torture him anymore. "Oh Samuel, I'm just screwing with you." I tugged him toward the grand staircase. "C'mon, let's get naked."

A chilly draft ruffled my hair. I pulled my wool coat together while Samuel fiddled with the room key. A feeling of claustrophobia crept over me and suddenly I wanted out of the opulent, empty hallway and into the open sky. Maybe it wasn't claustrophobia. Maybe it was ghosts. Any minute, twin girls might appear at the end of the hall.

Or maybe it was nerves. Because, (drumroll), we were going to, as Samuel used to call it, 'rock the casbah.'

There's something to be said for spontaneity and sex. It certainly helped eradicate performance anxiety, along with time spent questioning whether Samuel would notice my butt wasn't quite as pert as it was when I was twenty. While my body was in decent shape due to my adrenaline junkie lifestyle, that same lifestyle also littered my body with some serious scars. And the wrinkles—the price of a life lived in the sun.

"Your skin is so soft." Samuel's nose traced the line of my neck and warm air tip-toed over my flesh, raising goosebumps. He didn't seem to be aware of the scars. Or if he was, he didn't care.

I brushed his stomach, felt the muscles clench beneath his shirt. "Aren't you nervous?" My voice quaked like an over-tight guitar string. He fumbled with our room key, swiping it twice and jiggling the knob before it clicked. He ushered me through the door, let it swing shut and didn't even turn on a lamp before he had me against the foyer wall, the light switch digging between my shoulder blades.

"A little," he admitted between kisses. "Why, are you?"

"A little."

He paused and explored my mood, and saw I was more than 'a little' nervous. He eased me down. "Kaye. We don't have to have sex just because it's our honeymoon. After the last time, in New York ..."

"Don't be ridiculous, I want to."

When we'd slept together at the New York apartment, in the throes of his manic episode, the sex hadn't been an expression of love. It was a desperate attempt to ground his mind, to tie him to me somehow before he slipped away. Fear and desolation had driven me to Samuel's body, and neither should have a place in our bed.

He groped behind me and found the light switch. A string of lamps lit the room like hundreds of candles and I squinted. *Argh! Bright!* Samuel muttered an apology and turned off all the lights but one. But I'd seen the doubt creeping across his face. He was mentally talking himself out of sex (oh Samuel). Seven years of doing just that had become an ingrained habit.

Open him carefully, Kaye. Quit being such a bumbling amateur.

As my eyes adjusted to the low light, numerous gestures leapt out like a hidden picture puzzle. Flower bouquets (as in plural) were placed on tables and a bureau, from brilliant roses to delicate mountain columbine. I rolled a sprig of green between my fingers. Aspen leaves. A tin of pricey hot chocolate rested next to the percolator, along with my favorite red mug from the apartment (I'd wondered at its absence). My droid docking station was on the desk. A lingerie box rested next to it and I peeked under the lid.

"Open it," Sam encouraged.

Something silky and indigo slithered through my fingers...he'd really gone all out.

Red crept up his neck. "It's cliché, I know. But I wanted this to be special. It's not our first time or even our first honeymoon..."

"I know you'll treat me like a queen, Sam. You already have." I hadn't been romanced like this in years, and I felt like the Algebra student who'd been handed a Calculus book with instructions to solve for 'x.'

He nodded to the box. "We'll save that for later."

As he eased the coat from my shoulders, I screwed up my courage. This was Samuel. Heck, in college we'd gone after it like champions despite a three-day exam cram. A memory flitted through my head, one that involved a black beehive wig and the best night of sex ever. I smirked.

Yes, that would do to lighten up this party.

I pointed to the edge of the mattress. "Sit here, please."

Samuel slowly sat and watched my movements with wary eyes. Embarrassment settled into my stomach like a brick, but I pushed it aside because now was the time to remind him what he'd been missing in his sex life for the better part of his twenties. Casting a sultry look over my shoulder, I leaned over and docked my phone.

"Kaye?" Husky voice, good sign.

"Just a sec.'"

I scrolled to the E artists. When Samuel was a teenaged music snob, he used to say Elvis' charm was all exploit-expertise, but then I'd busted him curling his lip in the mirror. I knew his secret kink. Now, piano chords pounded from the dock speakers and EP's rich voice warbled a 'Lord Almighty.' Samuel threw back his head and laughed. I placed my hands on his knees and leaned into him, trying to keep a straight face.

"Girl, girl, girl, girl, you gonna set me on fire…" he sang quietly, resting his forehead against mine.

"Samuel Caulfield Cabral, you know this song?" I brushed my fingers through his thick hair, gently tugging at his roots.

"Yes. You're feisty tonight." His hands slithered around my waist and drew me closer. Our mouths met in slow, playful kisses that quickly became more as we realized, holy cliff-hucker, we were going to get— Oh yes. Elvis is the King.

He gripped the hem of my black slip and lifted it, carefully working it over my head and hair, and threw it behind me. Huh. I'd agonized over that lingerie dearth, but Sam had been right.

It hadn't made much difference.

He dragged me to him until his face rested against my sternum. "It's a pleasure to see you again," he crooned to my cleavage. I smacked his shoulder and he laughed. *This.* This was what I'd missed in those few sexual encounters, those tragic blurbs on my sex life timeline. Warmth.

Laughter. Love. Simple delight in each other…not just our bodies, but the hearts that beat within these flesh-and-blood frames.

My conscience was still tinged with shame over our fear-driven sex at Samuel's New York apartment, but he tenderly wiped it from my mind with every caress, every smile, every whispered '*mi vida.*' My life. I *did* live for him, and that choice didn't overwhelm or trap me. I felt liberated. Adoration welled in my chest, and I was pleased to see it reflected.

"If you can remember the last time Elvis serenaded us," I whispered into his ear, "I'll break someone out of the jailhouse." Terrible line, I knew. But Samuel loved that kind of stuff.

"Halloween, the year after we married. You made me dress like a lounge singer, complete with white blazer and blue suede shoes, and that horrible black hair gel. The stuff got all over you and our sheets after Danita's party…Oh Kaye, *right there.*"

He still remembered how my Priscilla beehive wig caught in the links of his watch— though he struggled with other memories. His kisses never forgot the crook of my elbow, the skin beneath my knee, the white-ink trilby hat tattooed over the delicate bones of my foot.

A single song, annoying with its lord almighties and burnin' love, looped for the fourth time.

Samuel froze, his arms shaking. Wait, where was he going? He stalked across the room and, if looks could fry electrical devices, my smartphone would have been a pile of ashes. The room fell silent and he lunged back into bed.

I lifted an eyebrow. "Happy?"

"Elvis has left the building. I'd much rather be the only man rocking your world."

"That may be the worst line on the books." But it worked. He tangled his hands in my hair and he showed me why he was the only man who had ever and would ever "rock my world."

"I belong to you," he whispered some time later. He pressed his lips to my earlobe. "Do you know that?"

"Mmm, I do." *That's why I'm holding you, silly man.*

We lay there on the white duvet, limbs tangled. Breeze from the air vents in the ceiling wafted over our skin and cooled it. I was too relaxed to move. And honestly, I didn't think Samuel could twitch a pinky if he'd wanted to. I lifted his jelly arm and let it drop across the bed, confirming my theory. Finally, he rolled to his side and cocooned us in the duvet.

"Wow," I said after ten minutes. "We needed that."

"We didn't last very long, did we?"

"We have all weekend."

"Oh firecracker, we have much more than that." His mouth curled. "Next time we should see how long we can hold out."

"I'm not waiting another seven years for a repeat performance."

He laughed—heartily, fully *laughed*—and nothing was more exquisite than the sound Samuel made when he was happy.

"This is Guzman. Don't bother with a message unless it's business-related. Just try again in an hour..."

I frowned and tossed my phone on the hotel bed, where Samuel scraped the last bit of frosting from a room service plate. We'd foregone a wedding cake, but the Stanley Hotel was nothing if not accommodating, and they'd sent up complimentary plates of petit gâteau, thus making my fantasy of wedding cake, a bed, and Samuel a big whopping reality.

"Kaye, let it go. I know you want to believe that underneath Jaime Guzman's Rottweiler exterior is a cuddly puppy, but she isn't a nice person. Jaime overflows with bitterness and hatred. Today she turned it onto you, and I won't be silent while you beat yourself up trying to justify her actions at our wedding. Hers *and* Hector's."

I tightened my new robe and leaned against the window frame, watching the mountains fade into the deep blues of dusk. "Hector's just...he doesn't understand. And he's hurt."

"No, Kaye. He's dangerous. Please don't think I'm being patronizing when I tell you I've known people like him, befriended them only to find they're the type of person who keeps his buddies in addictions to justify his own destructive behavior."

"You're referring to Lyle Togsender." Togsy, who'd only just begun to rake in the profits of his tell-all book lambasting Samuel and other New York artists. Last I checked, it had cracked the Amazon Top Five Hundred and was rapidly climbing the hill toward a bestseller's slot.

Caroline Ortega, who'd also sold out Samuel, had timed the book release perfectly. When the *Water Sirens* movie hit theatres in two weeks, Togsender's book would be battling for a number one ranking.

He continued. "I'm sorry for the things you saw in that avalanche. That woman…" He shook his head. "But I'm relieved it wasn't you. And I'm certainly not sorry you had a wake-up call. If that makes me seem calloused, so be it."

The sun dropped behind the mountains. As a moonless night crept in, only the absence of electric lights marked where the Rockies towered over the city. I shuddered. "Well, you don't need to worry about Hector dragging me down. There's no way I'm going up a mountain again, on foot or skis."

"That's not what I want for you, either." Samuel watched the mountains with me. His words were quiet, but they packed a mean punch. "I don't want to bury my wife before her fortieth birthday."

"You won't." A few bricks toppled. The anguish he'd experienced before he found out our climb team survived had been intense.

Samuel rubbed the back of his neck. "No skis, huh? Our honeymoon destination suddenly seems entirely inappropriate. We're supposed to fly to Zermatt tomorrow."

"Oh."

"I know that look. Is Zermatt that bad of a place for a honeymoon? We don't have to spend the day on the ski slopes—just roll around in a feather bed. Maybe I should have listened to Dani and chosen someplace warm."

"It's not that. It's only…it's Zermatt. I know what that town means to you, and I know why." The Swiss Alps were like Camelot to Samuel. His birth mother had taken him on a ski trip to Zermatt when he was five. It was the one and only 'family vacation' she'd ever spent with him.

"Honestly, I thought that spreading my mother's ashes would be a fitting way to begin this new chapter, make new memories. But when I say it out loud, it does sound like a horrible idea for a honeymoon trip; completely self-centered. Let's go someplace warm instead."

I traced swirls in the fogged glass. Light snow flurried, stuck to the windowpane and melted to glittering droplets. In truth, Zermatt wouldn't have been my first choice, or even my fiftieth. But Samuel wasn't just trying to please me. He'd promised to guide me down the most private avenues of his life. "Since when have we ever done anything by the book?" I pointed out. "I want to see Zermatt. Take me to Camelot, King Arthur, as long as we're back in time for the *Water Sirens* premiere. Can you imagine what would happen if *the* Samuel Caulfield Cabral didn't put in an appearance on the red carpet?"

Now he studied the Oriental rug beneath our feet. "Ahhh…That's the other thing I wanted to discuss."

Holy fish buckets. *He wasn't going.* "No. Are you serious? Sam, you can't miss your movie premiere! That's…that's like skipping prom, or worse, missing your wedding reception."

"You've actually made my point." He held up a finger. "One, we both hated prom because there's only so long you can bop around to Top Forty hits in tuxes and heels. Two, as we speak, our wedding reception is happening…without us."

"At least we made an appearance," I weakly countered, but he had me.

"*Water Sirens* has become a creature of its own. It's grown up, moved out, and shacked up with Hollywood. The publicity hype? The red carpets and screaming fans? I'd rather have a quiet book signing with twenty readers."

"I know." I rested my head against his shoulder and relaxed into the familiar scent of cardamom and juniper. "How did Patrick and Nat take it?"

"They advised against missing the premiere and then told me they'd back me one hundred percent. I promised them, if the movie was a hit, I'd walk the red carpet into the sequel…Are you…are you smelling me?"

"Yep. And you're absolutely sure this is what *you* want?"

"Absolutely." He chuckled as I sniffed and sighed.

"Okay. We'll go to the hometown showing like normal people, and that I insist upon. We have to celebrate somehow."

He raised a single brow, leaving no doubt how he'd like to celebrate.

Los Angeles, California
November, present day

Half an hour to midnight on my third wedding anniversary.

Three years later, Samuel was finally making good on his promise to Nat and Patrick.

The movie was a hit. Then the sequel was a hit (though he didn't attend the premiere to that one, either.) Now, his third blockbuster was set to hit screens, and Samuel could no longer avoid the inevitable. We were attending his movie's red carpet premiere in L.A. tomorrow night.

My taxi pulled into the circle drive of the Hollywood Roosevelt. A bellboy rushed out to take my luggage, but I only had a garment bag. I trudged across the lobby to the front desk, weary. The attendant politely smiled at my travel-rumpled tee shirt and jeans, dismissal flickering in her eyes.

"What can I do for you?"

"My husband left a room key for me. Samuel Cabral?" She lifted an eyebrow and I mentally kicked myself. "Sorry, that's Mr. Calvino." We rarely had problems with the photogs now, and only the occasional uber-fan found their way to our home. But social media was a little stirred up by the private author's re-entry into the limelight, so better safe than sorry.

She slid a key envelope across the granite counter. "Please enjoy your stay with us, Mrs. Calvino."

I thanked her and crossed the empty lobby for the elevator bank, half-collapsing against the rail as the doors closed. I'd worked nearly seventy hours this week at TrilbyJones to cover the time I was taking off. The holiday gear-up was an insanely busy time in the world of nonprofits and tourism, but Samuel needed me here. He was as nervous as a high school freshman about this very public appearance, especially since it came on the heels of his derided *Sea Rovers* book.

I swiped the key and cracked open the door. Darkness.

He'd wanted to pick me up from the airport, but I'd insisted he get some sleep. Honestly, he'd looked rather wan this week. His stress levels were elevated and though the fresh air of the Pikes Peak trip helped, we had to be careful and watch for shifts in his mood.

I patted my way through the dark until I hit the edge of the bed. As my eyes adjusted, I peeled off my travel-weary clothing, sticky with airport grime and L.A.'s acrid air and slipped beneath covers already warmed by my sleeping husband. He rolled over and pulled me against him.

"What time is it?"

"After midnight."

"Mmm. How was your date with *el changuito*?"

The little monkey was my boisterous two-year-old nephew, the spitting image of Dani. "We played Candyland for all of ten minutes, read a few books, and then I let him run laps around your folks' back-yard until bedtime. Go back to sleep."

He buried his face in my hair, puffs of air tickling my scalp. "Mmm. Happy anniversary."

"Happy anniversary." Content in Samuel's embrace, I gave in to exhaustion.

That night, I dreamed of a baby boy.

Chapter 5
CAMS

When fitted into a crevice, the spring-loaded camming device will expand or contract until it is secure. Climbers may then fasten their rope to the cam and continue on, trusting the cam to catch them should they fall.

Warm Los Angeles sun spilled through the open curtains of our hotel room. Samuel was already gone for the morning, so I stretched, groaned, and enjoyed a leisurely sprawl in the middle of the bed. Then I recalled my dream.

In the two-and-a-half years I'd wiped clean my baby nephew's leaky orifices, scrubbed spit-up out of my shag area rug (very difficult), and looped trippy Baby Einstein episodes on my tablet (who needs 'shrooms?), I'd never handed him back to his mother with a strong "gosh, I want one of these" urge in my uterus.

Not even when I held Gabriel Angel Valdez, aka "*changuito*", for the first time, his red, wrinkled hand curling around my gigantic index finger, did I pine for the fjords of "Mommydom." Dani had been half-blitzed on gas in her hospital bed, telling me, "It's way more fun going in than coming out." (Angel informed me that, during her delivery, she bellowed at the O.B. team to keep "those giant salad tongs" away and then wheedled Sofia into fetching a grilled cheese from the cafeteria. Danita and Entonox don't mix).

It had been difficult for her, being pregnant while Angel flew back and forth to the Middle East. Active duty Air Force pilots were called up at any time for one-off missions, and Angel frequently was, especially since he'd switched planes. Dani did what military wives do— took care of the home front. They relocated to a low-maintenance townhouse. Sofia and I went to doctor's appointments with her when Angel couldn't. We spent a weekend putting together the nursery, Samuel and Santiago hunched over crib assembly instructions while Dani and I sanded an old chifforobe.

When I first saw the sweet, crumpled face of our *changuito*, love surged for this tiny being. No desire to have one of my own, though.

That is, until the Baby Dream.

I'd had dreams that knocked around my brain, remnants of stress that surfaced in the midnight hours. Dreams of the long-ago New York brownstone and Samuel's cocaine-fueled affair. The monster-like "Other" of Samuel's books. More recently, mangled limbs packed in avalanche snow. But this dream wasn't horrific. It was gentle. Pure bliss, as if I'd zipped into a feather-down parka I'd never known I'd wanted, and it fit me to a T.

The first time I dreamed of the fragile infant was several months ago, and he lingered in my thoughts until breakfast.

The second time I dreamed of him, he hung around past my morning meetings.

The third and fourth times, I couldn't let him go until afternoon. I pushed him from my head, but during our sunset run, as we heaved and panted up a mountainside, I mused that the infant's dark locks and long lashes were a lot like my husband's.

The sweet smell of baby powder clung to my pillow. Sighs and coos echoed in my ears. Baby fingers clutched my sleep-tangled hair and retreated into hazy memories as I pushed through real life. Every time I dreamed of him, my heart pulsed in my chest and I felt the heaviness of a feather-light head resting there, downy hair tickling my neck, breath warm and humid on my sternum. I realized, with life-altering clarity, that Samuel had been right.

One day, I'd want this.

"One day" was now.

That evening, I ran a flat iron through my blonde kinks with the gentleness of a chainsaw. Guilt crept, painted my mood purple. Wasn't Samuel enough? Lord, how I loved him, almost to the point of ridiculousness. We could be perfectly happy, just the two of us. Telling him now that I wanted a baby, changing the game, would be unfair. He'd be devastated he couldn't (*wouldn't?*) give this to me. (No, *couldn't.*)

Heck, it had been hard enough for him to approach me about something as simple as his aversion to my carb-loaded meals, for fear of disappointing me. He had sat me down at our kitchen table, all sober-eyed and serious.

"I have a confession." His eyes had darted down, across the room, anywhere but my steady gaze.

"Oh?" Ghastly scenarios spun through my head like a roulette wheel, before landing between 'I'm using again' and 'I hate this shirt you bought for me.'

He took a deep breath. "I don't eat bread anymore. Or dairy. Or caffeine." My eyes widened. The bread and the dairy, I could deal with. But coffee? *Hot chocolate?* "I should have told you sooner, but you're such a foodie, I wanted to enjoy it with you." He gestured to my mountain biking gear, piled at the door where I'd left it before I'd hit the shower. "You're so active, you burn off anything you put into your body. But it's not so simple for me. Healthy food keeps my mind healthy. You know? I need to get back on track."

"Oh. Well, what do you eat?"

"Mainly green and sprouted things." He laughed and nudged my stiff shoulder. "Relax, firecracker. You can keep your sugary breakfast cereal."

"No no, I can do this with you. We can eat the same things."

Cinnamon rolls. Cream cheese. Bacon. I bit my lip to stifle a sob as I realized I'd have to learn how to cook all over again. I'd known my lifestyle would drastically change when I'd married Samuel because he needed structure like a tree needed roots. But no ciabatta? No tortellini? *No, no, Kaye, you unsupportive glut. Your husband's health is more important than a cheeseburger.*

"Fudge, that means I'll have to ask Dad for his hippie recipe book."

"Hmmm. I've tried his brownies. Best consult your mom's organic farmers collaborative instead."

It had been good for us. I lost a few pounds and he gained a few. His routine kept me organized and, as long as he didn't try to sell me on his noxious bulgur wheat bowls and I didn't shove my tuna melts in his face, we were solid.

If only our honesty extended as easily to heavier things. I was still afraid he'd go manic and leave, and he was still afraid I'd serve him with a second set of divorce papers if the waters roughened. Hopefully, as time passed, trust would outplay our fears.

I glanced at the clock above the hotel room door—fifteen minutes until the car arrived. I tugged my flat iron through another strong-willed curl. It sprang back the instant I released it and I waved a white flag. My hair was not meant to be straightened. Ever. It wasn't in my genes. Not part of my life plan. Straight hair was *not* a possibility for me.

Crud. I would *not* think of that baby again.

"Problems?" Samuel was already buffed and polished in a classic black tuxedo. His gaze darted to my discarded flat iron, then my hair. "Huh. I wondered what that thing was for."

I flung a defeated hand over my mess. "I should have made an appointment with a stylist like Nat suggested."

"You look amazing."

I began the tedious task of pinning up my hair. "You have to say that."

"Fishing for another compliment?" He caught a stray blonde curl and twisted it around his index finger, humming a familiar tune.

"'Sister Golden Hair'? Really?"

"You like the song."

"I do," I admitted. "But you hum it so much, people will think you're a serial killer."

Samuel snorted. "Hey. It's hard to find good lines you haven't already fallen for."

As we hammered out a life together, I saw the wisdom in Samuel's choice not to attend his first movie premiere, three years ago. His very public manic episode lent his fame those few extra letters in 'infamy', and it reached frenetic heights just before the movie hit theatres. Every 'Cabral siting' only fed the insatiable beast.

Wild headlines about our elopement (*Shocker:* Water Sirens *author weds real life Neelie! Indigo Kingsley in tears!!!*).

Death threats from the zombie faction of Indigo's fan-base (*UR a #manstealer #homewreckingbitch i hope you die die dieee!!!*), all of which the O'Malleys documented 'just in case' (in case of what, my grisly murder!?) Hermetic life looked pretty good.

But as hullabaloos do, it died down. Now it was time to step out for an honest-to-goodness Hollywood premiere.

A bobby pin fell out, and another, then my up-do collapsed.

"What are you doing to your hair?"

"Not helping, Sam."

"You don't usually fix it that way."

"That's because it's a red carpet event." For a man who'd once lived in the limelight, you would think he'd know this.

"You should leave it down." I fixed him with a glare that could wither a still-life painting. "Okay, not my area of expertise."

I sighed. "Yet you still manage to be correct." Yanking out all the pins, I twisted back a few strands and called it good.

I'd probably be the most inelegant attendee walking the red carpet at Samuel's movie premiere and that was fine. Been there, done that, had the ridiculously expensive, out-of-style Thakoon dress in the back of my closet to show for it. Tonight, a simple, desert-hued cocktail dress hung on the shower curtain rod. Samuel said it played up my freckles, and he really, *really* liked my freckles. (For years, I'd loathed my freckles because they kept me in perpetual tomboy status.)

In small-town Colorado, heels and dresses that skirted the edge of fashion were not a necessity. Still, there was one woman who oozed into my mind and, even three years later, filled my belly with jealousy. I stared myself down in the mirror.

"Do you think *she'll* be there?"

"Who is this '*she*' that warrants such foreboding emphasis?"

"*She.* Caroline."

"I can't think of anyone who demands less worry, Kaye." He winked in such a superfluous way, I realized I should be worried.

"Mother cliffhucker, she *is* going to be there. How on earth did *she* get an invite?"

"Caroline knows people. Nat says she attended last year's premiere as well." He shrugged, but anger burned in his blue eyes as he adjusted the cuff of his sleeve. "She doesn't matter. Togsy doesn't matter, and when we're back home in Colorado, none of this will matter. Ten minutes?"

As I grabbed my make-up bag, I wondered how much this *did* matter to Samuel.

The Chinese Theater was across the street from the Roosevelt Hotel, but for appearance's sake, we'd toured around in a limo with Patrick and Nat before 'arriving.' I hadn't been to the Roosevelt since Samuel's manic episode three years ago, and bad memories beat the door like cranky neighbors.

Journalists lined the red carpet leading into the Theater, followed by a *klöosterföocken* of fans in Nixie gear (yes, they warranted a '*klöosterföocken*'), leaning into the metal barricade with a barely-contained madness. White label cards were placed at the feet of each media outlet and camera team. We'd known the premiere would be a big deal. Instead of shrinking in popularity, Samuel Cabral's *Water Sirens* series had gained a legion of new readers with each movie blockbuster that broke box office records, clamoring for more, more, *more*.

"Ready Mrs. Cabral? Or does that remind you too much of my mother?"

"Pssh. Sofia's got nothing on these guns." I flexed my toned arms and steeled my spine.

As the car door opened and Patrick handed me out, I took a moment to enjoy the balmy air on my skin. The mild November sun was a welcome relief from the biting cold winds of the Front Range. Then the shrieks of super-fans hit our eardrums with the violence of agitated howler monkeys because "OMG Samuel CABRAL is here!!!", and poof went my moment.

I scanned the cards along the red carpet. *New York Times. USA Today. Huffpost. The Hollywood Reporter.* Samuel bantered with the outlets who'd been tactful in their coverage of his spectacular fall from grace three years prior, but politely side-stepped those who were dogged little cockroaches. Why make it easy?

There was a host of celebs in attendance. Most looked younger/older, taller/shorter, thicker/thinner, paler/tanner than they did on the big screen. All were accompanied by their entourages and were relatively off-limits. Samuel spent the majority of his red carpet walk greeting his fans, signing books and smiling for pictures. I stood quietly at his side, flanked by Patrick and Nat.

"Admiring your stilettos?" Nat asked.

"Is that what these spiky things are?" I grinned at her confounded expression. "Relax, I'm not that backwards, though at star-studded events like this, sometimes I feel it. Good grief, is that Johnny Madrid?"

"You're fine. Just keep your eyes off your shoes and a smile on your face."

I realized any photographs taken of us had a lovely shot of the sunburnt crown of my head and I kicked myself, because I'd warned my own clients about this very thing. Doing my best June Allyson, I turned to Sam and the fan with whom he currently spoke. A blow-up doll gaped back at me, blonde wig obscuring her face. I leapt back.

"Oh. Wow!"

"Whaddya think?" asked a keen young man in fedora and tee shirt that depicted the Stay Puft Marshmallow Man sandwiched between graham crackers. The doll was suspiciously familiar.

"Is she your…date?"

"I was just telling Mr. Cabral here, I've already sold a dozen Neelie Nixies—well, 'Nellie Nymphos,' don't need a lawsuit—on the NixieNet.net forums." NixieNet.net (members pronounced it "nixie-net-net") was Alan Murphy's fan site, which he'd expanded to include the wildly popular *Cabral's Hometown Haunts*, his "*Baedeker Guide*" for stalkers. I wouldn't put it past that monkey rump to have a Nellie Nympho stuffed in a suitcase under his bed.

Samuel grimaced. "Very entrepreneurial of you, though I don't think Kaye likes it, nor do I. Not exactly respectful."

"Not at all!" I agreed, but I'd become background noise to the perv once his idol author acknowledged him.

The guy blatantly leered at my chest. "I'd try to sell you one, but you've got the real thing. A bit smaller in person."

"Oh no you didn't! That's it." My oh-so-cool husband grabbed my elbow and steered me away, just as I prepared to launch myself at my sex-toy doppelganger and stab out her beady eyes with my stiletto.

"Not here, firecracker. Let the lawyers crack down on him." I opened my mouth to demand he march back there and deflate that affront to Fiction Me, but remembered his hazardous position. If Samuel so much as lifted a hostile pinky, the tabloids would question his sanity. Talk about grinning and bearing it.

He turned to Patrick. "Contact the fan sites. Pressure them to shut him down internally before we're forced to take legal action."

"Why give him more attention? You know he just showed up here to plug his blow-up doll." I nearly choked on my breath mint.

"Just a minute." Samuel couldn't lift a pinky, but I could. In a spur-of-the-moment decision, I removed one of my chandelier earrings and made a beeline for the perv. I pointed to the guy and crooked my finger.

"Excuse me, can I please see your lady friend?" Palming the earring, I gave the confused man a dazzling smile as he handed over the doll. Then, like a lion cub pouncing on its prey, I drove the lethal post of my earring between Neelie/Nellie's ample bosoms and ripped, and the piece of plastic grievously deflated in my murderous hands.

"One-star rating for durability." I tossed the wilted thing back to the guy, ignored his string of stunned obscenities, and acknowledged the scattered applause from Samuel's more decent fans. The earring glittered like a gilded dagger as I refastened it into my earlobe.

Samuel shook his head as I returned. "Was that necessary?"

"I think so, yes."

Patrick ran a hand through his salt-and-pepper hair. "You certainly know how to make friends with Mr. Cabral's fan base, don't you?"

"*Hollywood Days* and goodness knows who else got the entire exchange on camera," Nat chimed in as she jogged to our sides.

"So did a dozen fans," I admitted, the high of the kill wearing off. "Ah well, at least Samuel didn't slug anyone."

"This time," he muttered.

"His fans probably would have eaten it up if he had," said Nat. "Defending his woman, going all caveman. Ladies love it."

"So do personal injury lawyers," Samuel deadpanned.

"You always were the chivalrous sort...usually," said a voice, still as sultry as North Carolina in July.

The hairs on the back of my neck pricked.

"Kaye, on the other hand, is a PR disaster." She squeezed out a tight smile. "Look on the bright side, Samuel. If the pervert sues, that kind of seedy story will keep your movie in the news for weeks."

She looked much the same: lithe and stylish, one of few women who could make a pants suit cutting edge. Her black bob was so glossy, I saw my reflection. This time, though, she had a different man on her arm.

Samuel's face was a blank page. "Caroline. Always ready to find the gold in garbage."

An awkward silence settled as Nat steered us through the theater entrance. "Perhaps we should move this conversation off the red carpet? Don't want *Page Six* drumming up a feud."

Which was exactly what Caroline would have liked. Disappointment flitted over her features before she slipped into her usual bored air.

I studied her date, tried to place him. Bullish frame, heavy eyebrows, waves of dishwater hair and beard. He could have emerged from the alley if not for the pressed tux and an aloofness that was more Tribeca than Skid Row. I gasped. Sam's old "college buddy" from the brownstone. *Togsy.* He was older, of course, still well-heeled. But there were the same telltale nuances I once saw in Samuel: hollowed cheeks, dark circles, mottled and sallow skin. The hand that didn't rest on Caroline's shoulder drummed a discordant, restless rhythm on his hip. So he hadn't kicked the drug habit after all. Poor Ms. Ortega. Her brittle eyes caught mine and I glanced away, too late.

Sam saw it, too. "Lyle."

"Samuel."

Caroline cleared her throat. "I apologize, where are my manners? Lyle, this is Samuel's wife, Kaye Cabral. Lyle is my..." She looked lost.

"She's my publicist," Lyle finished. *Hmmm, I thought she was a lot more than that, Mr. Togsender.* Caroline's cheeks reddened. *Well, she did make her bed when she screwed over Samuel for this walking wedgie.* Still, I pitied her.

"Considering Ms. Ortega quit a lucrative book series to risk her career with your mediocre tell-all, I'd think she at least deserves a 'Caroline makes the sun rise.'" I sweetly smiled at the ego-on-legs.

Samuel's hand pressed into my back, warning me. Caroline gaped, a bit like the blow-up doll I'd just stood down. Lyle's eyes darkened. A nasty memory nearly bowled me over, one of a sneering frat-boy who'd taken pleasure in exhibiting Samuel's demons to his nineteen-year-old wife and then laughed at her heartbreak.

"Still a sniveling little drama queen, I see." He turned to my husband. "How are the mental wards in the Rockies?"

Oh, he did not. Harsh words bristled on my tongue, but Sam gripped my waist. "Kaye, he's a bitter and unhappy man. And we've had enough drama tonight."

I wanted to rail at Samuel to flipping stand up for himself. But then I saw his lips were thinned in repressed rage and his fist was so tightly clinched, his knuckles were white. He was trying to take the high road, not cause a scene…which was what Togsy and Caroline wanted.

My fingers weaved between his. "You're right. My apologies." I nodded to Samuel's former friend. "Sorry for your disappointment, Caroline."

Later, at the after-party, Caroline sought me out. Samuel was deep in conversation with a *Water Sirens* producer, and as I made my way to the restroom, she pounced.

"I truly am happy for you and Sam, you know. He needs someone in his corner. I tried to be that for him, especially after the scandal in Tamaulipas with that woman. He was devastated. But in the end, I couldn't give him what he needed."

"What woman?" I racked my brain for some past conversation about a woman in Tamaulipas but came up empty.

Caroline looked down her perfect nose. "Ah, I see he still doesn't tell you everything. Sorry to disappoint you with the truth, Kaye."

After that, we only saw Caroline and Togsy from afar, and I assumed they'd moved on to greener pastures.

The movie itself was fantastically over-the-top and Samuel's script was perfection. No surprise. We put in a brief appearance at the after-party, long enough to witness A-lister Indigo Kingsley and her hunky Latin lover, Marco Caldo, demonstrate their dental-polishing techniques.

We promised the O'Malleys we'd see them after Christmas, shook a few spa-softened hands, and beat feet for the Roosevelt.

Sometime around one a.m., after we shed our costumes and "got reacquainted," Samuel pulled my feet into his lap.

"Mmmm. That is amazing. I love writers." Every last ounce of stress seeped from my muscles and into a cloud of comforter and pillows.

"Thank you for not attacking Caroline and Togsy with your earring. I've seen the damage you render to over-inflated poseurs and their 'heroine' addicts."

"Ha ha. That's me, The Blinged Perforator: ridding the world of perverts, one blowup doll at a time." I grew serious as I remembered Togsy's drooping eyes and skin. He looked like he'd aged thirty years since I saw him in that New York brownstone. "Is that what he's on? Heroin?"

"Some sort of opiate. Maybe cocaine, too."

"I feel bad for Caroline." I reached behind me and bunched up a pillow. I may have imagined it was Togsy's face. "Why do you think she hasn't left him yet?"

"She did leave him, last April. They only have a working relationship now."

I paused. "How do you…have you talked to her?"

He kneaded my foot a little harder. "I called her last summer after I saw a photo of Togsy on social media. It was pretty obvious he was using again…if he ever stopped. I told her, as an old friend, I was concerned. She told me, very matter-of-factly, not to worry and that they no longer shared personal space." Samuel watched me closely. This was the part where we trusted each other, and that included our dealings with our exes.

"I'm sure it was more heartbreaking than that."

His grip on my foot relaxed. "You know Caroline."

"Not really, but I don't think anyone does. She said something odd tonight."

"Hmm?"

"Something about a scandal in Tamaulipas involving you and a woman?"

His fingers froze. "It's nothing to worry about," he said rigidly. "Our interactions were completely blown out of proportion by my Cabral *familia*. I...I haven't spoken to the woman in five years."

"Oh." I scooted into bed, irritated that I'd once again been suckered by Caroline's drama. *But if it was only mindless drama, why was Samuel squirming?*

The television flickered light and shadow over our posh hideaway. An infomercial played, some sort of food processor that baby food-ized vegetables. I shivered. Samuel tucked the blanket around my legs, but I hadn't shivered from the cold. This room at the Roosevelt was much too similar to the one I'd stayed in when I first became aware of Samuel's bipolar disorder. "Samuel?"

"Hmm?"

"Do you ever...After seeing Togsy again...do you ever think about ..."

"Do I ever want to take a hit of coke? Sure, especially if I've had a rough day." Clear blue eyes met mine. "But then I remind myself how it nearly cost me my life and everything in it. For me, it's all or nothing. No flirting with boundaries." Yes, this was Sam.

He didn't flirt with commitments, either. Commitment to his mental health. Rehab. Writing. Charities. Marriage. If he made a commitment, you could be darned certain he'd follow through because the last thing he wanted was to be a burden. Sometimes I worried he didn't allow himself the grace of humanity.

"That's why you don't drink, too."

"The main reason I don't drink is because it's a trigger, and if I have several shots I start to think 'man, I remember this feeling, and I remember something even better.' It's healthier if I just abstain from the whole line-up, you know? Booze, cigarettes, weed, porn. Carbs," he teased.

"No *Debbie Does Sourdough*? Pity."

I remembered something Caroline once said: '*He's never actually been an alcoholic. Just cocaine. But he would have become one if I hadn't intervened.*' At the time, it seemed as though she'd known him better than anybody. But she'd never acknowledged how hard Samuel had fought. It had only ever been about *her* and what *she'd* done.

"Samuel," I hedged, "why didn't you tell me you kept in touch with Caroline? It wouldn't have upset me."

"I didn't want to trouble you. You have enough on your plate." There was that nervous kneading again. I swapped feet.

"Really?" *Keep it calm, Kaye.* "Are there other things you've kept from me because you don't want to 'burden' me?"

"Sure, but nothing of importance. Every person needs to retain some shred of privacy, don't you agree?"

I nodded. That was fair.

"And what about you? Do you keep anything of importance from me because you're afraid you'll send me into a downward spiral?"

Faint baby powder perfumed the air, and I felt a tickle of downy hair across my cheek.

"No. Nothing of importance." I brushed my toes along his ribs. He flinched and grasped my foot. Samuel was ticklish.

"You're really good about going to meetings, too," I said, taking the focus off of me.

"If I stop going, I'm setting myself up for a relapse. Too easy to convince myself I can control it, next time."

"Hey." I pulled my foot from his lap and sat across from him, hands on his thighs. "There is no next time."

Determination hardened in the creases around his eyes, his mouth. He gently cupped my face. "There is no next time." And then he pressed his mouth to mine, my skin to his, love tempering the harsh edge of lust, and showed me precisely why he would never take a hit again.

He made love to me, and I'd lied to him.

I told myself it hadn't been a selfish lie, that I'd hidden my desire to be a mother because I didn't want to stress him out. But wasn't it selfish to cut him out of decisions we were supposed to make together? Isn't this what he'd done to me a decade ago?

The kicker was, I expected him to trust me with the sensitive details of his drug addiction, yet I hadn't trusted him with one of my deepest secrets. So deep, I wouldn't acknowledge it, even when it left me with aching, empty arms. Not *it*. *Him*. Because the truth was, I did want to have a baby. Wanted it so badly, I dreamed about an infant boy whose father was obviously Samuel.

'A soul mate isn't fate…it's a choice. And they don't become your soul mate until you bare your soul to them.' These were the words I'd spoken to Samuel three years ago, on our wedding day. What happened to that wise woman? Who was this little coward who'd taken her place?

As he trembled over me, and as my body reacted to the skilled attention of the man I adored (but lied to), my head mourned the biological fact that this child whom I loved—yes, *loved*—could never be.

But I didn't tell Samuel.

The orchids and roses of *Tía* Lucia's autumn garden emitted such a heady fragrance, her in-ground pool could have been filled with Chanel No. 5. We sat on the patio of her Mission Viejo home with sweating glasses of lemonade and watched the California sun call it a day. *Tío* Carlos swam lazy laps in their pool, his wake rippling golden as the last rays clung to the horizon.

Samuel stifled a yawn. It had been a grueling day of press interviews. Mainly fluff about the new movie, though a journalist went rogue and asked him about his arrest three years ago. Old news. But if a gossip columnist could dredge up a new revelation, old news became new news, and that meant web hits. He'd handled himself well, but he wasn't used to the back-to-back interviews anymore. I grabbed his empty glass before it slipped from his sleep-limp hand.

"Sofia mentioned you and Carlos were in Ciudad Victoria last month. How is your mother-in-law?" I asked Lucia.

"Still refuses to move to L.A., even after Carlos offered to build a suite onto our home. We visit often enough to keep an eye on her health, but I'm afraid Carlos will have to put his foot down." Uncle Carlos was an investigator with a firm that helped families locate their missing immigrant relatives, and frequently traveled to the Mexican border. I often wondered if "visiting his mother" was code for something else.

She pulled her black braid over her shoulder and toyed with the ends. Lucia's features lacked the soft roundness of Sofia Llorente de Cabral's, and whenever I saw a Frida Kahlo's self-portrait, I was struck by the likeness between them (minus Frida's daring uni-brow). When I was young, I'd thought Sofia's sharp-faced sister was the epitome of California cool, with her bright, breezy skirts and even brighter smile. She'd always tell us stories about celebrities who walked into her custom furniture gallery, which were polite as peas and which had sticks up their wazoos. One had to be cautious when chatting with Lucia; she had a knack for drawing the juiciest stories from people. Still, she lured me into her web of gossip.

"Do you ever see any of the Cabral *familia* when you're back home?"

She flipped her braid over her shoulder. "Not if I can help it."

I glanced at Samuel, now wheezing in sweet oblivion. "That's surprising. I thought you got along?"

"Sofia's in-laws think they are haute society of Ciudad Victoria because *their* family used to be in maize and cattle. Ha. All of our grandfathers were cheap laborers at the *maquiladoras* when the hacienda system ended."

I'd heard Alonso mention the old Cabral hacienda, just south of the city. In its heyday, it had been a thriving plantation in the Spanish style, lush with citrus trees and agave plants. "What happened to their hacienda?"

"The estate was broken up not long after the revolution—1920 or so. Whatever remained declined until the sixties, when the Cabrals simply didn't have the money to continue farming. If it hadn't been for Professor Cabral's job at the university, the hacienda would be in ruins like the others. The family used to live there in the summer because the city was too hot. In the summer, when we were children, we used to hang sheets between the concrete blocks for shade. I was glad when cooler months returned, because it meant the Cabral boys also returned to Ciudad Victoria."

She gathered our empty glasses and rose. I grabbed the pitcher and followed her into the kitchen. "That's what I don't understand. Your families were friends when you were young."

"No no, only Alonso and Antonio played with us. Mariángel, their older sister, was too much like her mother. She oversees the hacienda now, but no one lives there." She rinsed the glasses. Through the kitchen window, I saw that the patio was completely dark and flipped on the switch. Yellow light flooded Samuel. He twitched and turned onto his side. Beyond him, Uncle Carlos climbed out of the pool, his carefully groomed handlebar mustache now a sodden dishrag. I averted my gaze before I got an eyeful of his very European swim attire.

Beside me, Lucia took in her twilight garden, her eyes somewhere in Mexico. "Marieta Treiño, their mother, was an old witch. Antonio was such a sensitive, serious little thing. Samuel is much like him. My poor boys." Ghosts were in her voice. "I never see them now, and I couldn't give two pennies for the Tamaulipas Cabrals, especially after they told Samuel to stay away."

"Wait, what?" The pitcher nearly slipped from my fingers, but I caught it before it clattered to the counter. That wasn't typical in Mexico, where their entire culture was built around *familia*. "Why did they tell Samuel to stay away? When?"

"Oh, I suppose it's been five or six years now."

Caroline's words from the other night echoed: '*a scandal with a woman from Tamaulipas*'…

Lucia continued. "Once he became a famous writer, he used to visit us every year during the L.A. leg of his book tour. Next he'd travel down to Ciudad Victoria and stay with the family for a week, a little R-and-R. One year, he told me he wasn't travelling on to Ciudad Victoria, like before. When I asked him why, he only said he wasn't welcome there. You know how Samuel is, never one to bad-mouth. So I asked Sofia, 'your son tells me the Cabrals don't want him to come home. What's going on?'"

"What did she say?"

She leaned in. "Supposedly, there was a huge fight between Samuel and his aunt Mariángel. Sofia was extremely angry that Mariángel made some unfounded accusations, something she'd read on those ridiculous gossip sites. I guess she's never heard the saying 'don't believe everything you read.'"

"A relationship with a woman that was completely blown out of proportion by his Cabral relations," I murmured.

"That's it. She said he was a drug addict and philanderer like his father, and he wasn't to set foot in the old family hacienda again."

"Whoa, whoa, whoa, which father was supposedly a philanderer: Alonso or Antonio?"

"Antonio, of course. Samuel's birth father."

"Wow. Is that true?"

She shrugged. "There were rumors he'd had an affair with a rural woman while Rachel was back in Boston and pregnant with Samuel. He'd had trouble with his law firm, so he traveled home to Tamaulipas to escape those hoity-toity Caulfields for a time. No one knew if it was true because he died not long after that. Rachel denied it, said the Cabrals were spreading vicious lies and they'd never meet her baby because of it."

"I've never heard *any* of this."

"Like I said, there may not be an ounce of truth to the rumors about Antonio."

So that was why Samuel had ducked my suggestions we visit his family in Ciudad Victoria. They didn't want him there and he was too hurt, too ticked, too embarrassed to tell me. I had half-a-mind to march across the border, over the plains and mountains of Tamaulipas, and tell them they were horrible people for rejecting one of the greatest men I'd ever known. Samuel had struck pay dirt for cagey, haughty families whose values were so skewed, they framed their social diary clippings instead of their children's artwork. Thank goodness for Sofia and Alonso.

"Oh Kaye, you look like you're ready to take names." Lucia patted my hand. "I'm glad my nephew found his way back to you, even if you did pop a child's Neelie Nixie balloon with a penknife at his movie premiere, then told her to 'get a real friend.' That was a tad extreme, *mi cielo*."

I looked heavenward. The click-bait bloggers had hit this one out of the park. Unfortunately, now I needed to explain to Lucia why she, too, shouldn't believe everything she read, and that explanation would include the phrases 'knock-off Nellie' and 'illegal sex toy.'" Not exactly the conversation you want to have with your in-laws.

***

After a delay, we debarked from our plane in Denver and cruised across windswept flatlands toward our mountain home. He hummed the harmony line to "Wednesday Morning, 3AM," and I dialed the radio down so I could hear him. He had a pleasant voice, quiet and unassuming, with a lilt to his phrasing that told the listener he loved language, loved words. I'd informed him, once, that if he ever decided to stop publishing, he could have a successful career narrating deep sleep apps. (Then I had to backtrack and assure him his voice was soothing, not boring. Samuel didn't see the compliment).

"What are you thinking about?" he asked as the song ended.

"I don't believe Simon and Garfunkel really robbed a hard liquor store for twenty-five dollars."

"Probably not. Although, they could have gotten some great material out of it, maybe stayed together for another album or two before they broke up."

"Such a sad song, though. Watching the one you love sleep away the last few hours of morning, knowing you might not ever be with them again."

"It's so maudlin, it's ridiculous."

I punched his shoulder with the strength of a teddy bear. "Allow me my sentimentality, you stone-hearted statue."

"Kaye, Kaye, Kaye. Haven't you been listening? Rocks don't feel pain."

I mumbled something about a lack of crying islands, because I had nothing else.

As Samuel's Subaru eased around the curving highway south of Boulder, I recollected on a visit from Alonso's eccentric *Tia* Belinda years ago, when I was about twelve. They'd invited me over for *tres leches* and I'd stayed until my father's shift ended at The Garden Market. It was growing dark, so we'd retired to the Cabrals' family room in the basement and I listened, fascinated and confused by the mix of Spanish and English flying back and forth. But the summer heat soon caught up with me and I leaned my sweaty head against Samuel's knee, their folktales blurring with my half-asleep dreams.

"...Antonio and I climbed the Sierra Madre Oriental in Tamaulipas, high up, into the oak forests," said Alonso. "The mountains of home aren't like Colorado. Smaller, isolated, thick with desert thorns and tall grass. We would travel through the villages...once, they gave my brother *toloache* for a sprained ankle and he hallucinated he was trapped inside its thorny fruit...It is what the Aztecs used to subdue their human sacrifices, *sí*...

"...The village is where we first heard about the *leoncillo*...Yes, Samuel, there is such an animal. Most call it a jaguarundi. Smaller than a puma, solitary, secretive. They almost look like otters."

"You never see them, which is why spotting one is the stuff of legend," added Great Aunt Belinda. "They are harbingers. It's true, young man, don't shake your head at me. If you see one, it's because he wants to be seen. He's warning you."

"Antonio spotted it first, so perhaps the *leoncillo* was meant for him..." There was a long stretch of quiet. I wasn't sure if I'd drifted or if no one had spoken. "Not long after that, we received our acceptance letters to Boston University."

"If only Antonio had listened..."

As I fell off completely, with Samuel's touch gentle against my hair, one thought lingered: *if Antonio had listened to the leoncillo's warning, Samuel wouldn't be here...*

I lifted my head from the car window and rubbed tired eyes. There had been a wildcat on the rocks, I was sure. Too small for a mountain lion—a bobcat, or a lynx?—but he'd darted behind a boulder before I could identify him. The warmth of the sun had lulled me to a cozy place and who knew how long I'd snoozed, so perhaps there hadn't been a wildcat at all.

Beyond the road were the Rockies, streaked in November snow. It wouldn't be long before winter found us in the Front Range. I groaned and stretched.

"Can I ask you something delicate about your birth father?"

"Ah…Sure."

"Lucia mentioned it and I'm wondering if it was true," I hedged. "She said he had an affair with a woman in Mexico, when your mom was pregnant with you."

Samuel frowned. "How on earth did that come up?"

"Well…she said you had a falling out with your family there over that woman in Tamaulipas, something about your father being a philanderer and the garbage in the gossip mags."

"Lucia needs to rein in that wagging tongue. I suppose she also mentioned I'm barred from visiting?"

I nodded. "Why didn't you tell me before, when I asked to visit the hacienda?"

"I guess it falls under that 'nothing of importance' category." We both knew it wasn't 'nothing of importance..' He sighed. "No one can prove he had an affair, but I'm ninety-nine percent certain it happened. My dad—Alonso—has a letter from Antonio that hinted at it. As for my argument with *Tia* Mariángel, it was more complicated than a misunderstanding about a woman."

"You weren't buying drugs, were you?"

Samuel opened his mouth but bit back whatever he'd planned to say. He narrowed his eyes thoughtfully. "That would make sense, wouldn't it? Tamaulipas's cartels are notorious. But no, I didn't visit for drugs."

"Your bipolar disorder? No, no one knew about it five years ago. Or maybe Mariángel did?"

"No, she didn't."

"A romantic entanglement?" Silence. Bingo. "That's it, isn't it? This woman—"

"Firecracker, please let it go. It's in the past, and my relationship with the Tamaulipas Cabrals won't change in the foreseeable future. It's a non-issue."

"Then why—"

Samuel smacked the steering wheel in exasperation. "Look, Kaye. I know that asking you to drop this is incredibly unfair. I recognize that as my wife, you should be privy to my secrets." *And as my husband, he should be privy to my secrets,* I silently added. Apparently this was a lesson we both still needed to learn. "The last time I was there, some… shady things went down. This is one secret you don't need to know about. Please, just trust me."

Shady? Chilling ideas flooded my head. What the heck happened in Mexico? Did someone die? Was Samuel caught up in something illegal? Given the organized crime problem Tamaulipas suffered, it was possible. I didn't believe he'd lie to me about buying drugs. So what was the deal with this woman?

I turned back to the window. We were in the homestretch; the foothills and cliffs on the outskirts of Boulder flew by.

Perhaps he'd had a lover in Ciudad Victoria, like his father had—a lover to whom Mariángel had objected. I could understand him not wanting me to know. Was that why Samuel didn't want to take me to Tamaulipas? Because he'd cared for someone there, someone special he never told me about, and it ended badly?

But why would he have revealed his other romantic entanglements and not this?

Maybe you just answered your own question…she was special. Or maybe I was just being a paranoid wife/ex-wife/wife.

Whether there was any truth to my speculation, I knew one thing: I didn't like the idea of another woman being so special to Samuel, he couldn't tell me about her.

Not at all.

Chapter 6
BELAY MONKEY

A mountain climbing addict's significant other,
who desires to share in the climber's passion but gets
suckered into long hours of belay duty.

Hydraulic Level Five [WORKING TITLE]
Draft 2.106
© *Samuel Caulfield Cabral and Aspen Kaye Cabral*
MOUNTAIN HOLLIDAY

The air of Leadville is so thin, the winter so chilling, it's little wonder it killed Doc Holliday. Consumption, not a gunslinger, got him in the end, and Caulfield thinks this Old West town must have been booming in silver and law and order to keep Holliday alive when he'd made so many enemies along his flamboyant lifespan. Why would a man whose lungs were emaciated by tuberculosis live his last years in a mining town at an elevation of ten thousand feet? Maybe it was a leisurely suicide. Maybe he had friends here. Or maybe the silver song of profit was too alluring to turn a deaf ear.

Their climb team didn't plan to stop in Leadville, but Caulfield's swollen ankle set them back several hours and now they need to eat before they hit the treacherous mountain roads to Bear Creek. His foot throbs with every heartbeat. His head and stomach ache from altitude sickness courtesy of Mount Elbert, but he would rather secretly vomit in a grimy old saloon bathroom than appear an anemic Gumby to Aspen and the man who used to pursue her.

Aspen sees anyway—his face is clammy and pale. She grasps his hand under the table, not a pity move but one born of genuine gratitude. Mountain climbing is her passion and not Caulfield's, and he's suffering all the indignities of a novice to restore some of that passion to her soul. His hand was steady as they trudged over routes packed in ice and snow, his whispers encouraging when panic set in and she lost her breath, her brain. He was there, always there, pulling her back to earth with his mantra of "slooow breaths, slooow breaths. You want to feel okay. Say it now, Aspen."

She wants to feel okay.

She felt okay when they reached the summit, astoundingly okay. Caulfield saw the brightness of her eyes, the invincibility as she pumped her fists and laughed, collapsed into the snow and closed her eyes in pure joy, pulled him down next to her.

He's so damned proud. It's a high he remembers well, this adrenaline coursing through his veins, though there's nothing synthetic or false about it. The high of conquest. Of eminence.

Remnants of that high still glow in Aspen's freckled face and he can't stop watching. They're ensconced in a red pleather booth at the Silver Dollar Saloon, straight out of an Old West movie with swinging doors and wood so dark, Caulfield squints to see the menu. But he sees Aspen, loud and clear, and she validates his gamble. A sprained ankle is his summit trophy. Pushing her up that fourteener was the right call.

H and L sit across from them. Banter flies over a plate of fries, beers, and they fist bump as if a director has instructed them to "show me bromance and really play it up for the camera." L has replaced Aspen as H's daredevil go-to, and Caulfield wonders if this hurts her feelings, because she watches them with plain envy and recalls those post-climb plates of fries, beers, and fist bumps *she* used to share with H. But then Caulfield asks her, "Do you want to split an order of fries, too?" and he is now her hero. In his current state of nausea, combined with the turmoil of a stomach that hasn't digested anything fried and greasy in over a year, that plate of fries is so far off his food pyramid it's in the Gulf of Suez.

H nods at Caulfield with newfound respect.

The second platter arrives. They douse their fries in ketchup and laugh as L tells them all the funny nicknames he's given his pregnant wife.

H shares how *his* wife locked his favorite skis in a utility closet at the hospital, so he'd have to spend tomorrow with her instead of Copper Mountain.

Then Aspen tells how she had a heart-to-heart with her intern about the importance of commas in design copy, after a poster advertising a family fun day/ASPCA bake sale nearly went to print reading:

Join us if you love
Baking
Your Family and Your Pets!

She jots it down on a napkin and their laughter roars.

Caulfield recognizes his cue—the ritualistic 'sharing of inside jokes' that informs him he's now inner circle. Frankly, he would rather scrub gas station bathrooms than spend another Saturday immersed in machismo conversation with H and his sidekick. But he loves Aspen, so he launches into his story. "Ever hear what happens when someone puts powdered milk under your bed sheets? Lemme tell you about this one time my wife…"

Sam—Out of curiosity, do guys really swap inside jokes as some male sign of respect?— K

Kaye—Don't question the bro code. Trust me, there are three ways into the inner circle.
1. Buy them a beer.
2. Tell them a story about your woman (sorry), kids, family.
3. Laugh at their jokes.

Sam—This "bro code" sounds suspiciously like something from a Judd Apatow movie.

Thank you, by the way, for bagging Elbert with me. It speaks volumes.

I'll always bag Elbert with you—that's how much I love you. Let's not put it on a bumper sticker, though.

Mount Elbert
November

Perhaps the wildcat I saw on our return from the Denver airport was Colorado's version of a harbinger of doom, warning us to turn the Subaru around and head back to the airport or face certain death. Drama worthy of Dr. Phil hit us from all directions the minute our tires found foothill blacktop.

The media circus surrounding Samuel's blockbuster premiere left him social-weary as we sat down to a Thanksgiving turkey with my mother, father, and Audrey. It left *me* with a string of high-profile gossip stories to account for, namely to parents who wondered How in the Name of Jack they'd raised a daughter whose fictional alter-ego inspired fanboys to worship her in effigy...er, blow-up doll. Poor Dad. He couldn't even meet my eyes. I was amazed he hadn't run Samuel out of town with a baseball bat.

Mom, on the other hand, hadn't been this tickled since Dad accidentally left his car in neutral after weekend drop-off, and it rolled down the hill and into Mom's koi pond.

"Tom, can you please pass the quinoa corn bake you made? It's absolutely delicious." *Wait. Did Mom just smirk at my dad?*

"Not as delicious as your tomato pie. Cherokee Purples, are they?" *Flipping hamster balls, did Dad wink at my mother?*

Something was not right. Audrey prattled about how my hair had gleamed against the red carpet in the premiere photos. I widened my eyes at Samuel. He widened his back and gave a quick shake of his head. I narrowed my eyes at him. Of course I wasn't stupid enough to call them out at our Thanksgiving table, but I swear to the Almighty, my mother and father were flirting. Which wasn't unusual for most people's parents, but I couldn't remember a time when my parents hadn't been frosty toward each other.

"So flower, you and Hector are heading up Mount Elbert Saturday? He was in The Market stocking up on fruit leather."

"Ah, yeah," I stuttered. "Samuel and Luca Guzman, too."

"Good for you, baby girl," said my mother as she held out a Corning Ware dish. "More carrots?"

Just like that, it was as if the exchange had never happened.

"I'm not imagining things, right? You saw it too? My folks' flirting?" I asked the next day, as Sam and I huffed along the East Ridge approach of Mount Elbert, the next fourteener on Hector's to-do list. Somewhere ahead of us, Hector and Luca's laughter bounced over ice and snow and I looked around, hunting for prognostic signs of an avalanche.

At fourteen thousand, four hundred and thirty-three feet, Mount Elbert was the highest peak in Colorado, but also one of the easiest climbs. It was a good route to tackle in winter because the snow was packed from high traffic and summiting was entirely possible, as long as the wind was minimal. The cusp of winter brought with it a biting breeze. Sweat on my neck and back prickled like drops of ice. I zipped my fleece to my chin and yanked down my stocking hat.

"Once upon a time, they were in love," Samuel theorized. "I don't know if that ever, one hundred percent goes away. Most people just don't act on that sliver of love."

"And they have a child—me. They can never be rid of each other entirely."

"If you want to put a negative spin on it. I think it's more likely they appreciate the life they've created together. While their relationship didn't pan out, the evidence of the love they shared still exists in you. Sadly, that evidence is currently the butt of late night television jokes."

I groaned. *The Tonight Show* even hash tagged "#MyNightmareDoll" in Nellie Nympho's honor. It was a trending topic within fifteen minutes.

Conversation died as we ascended into higher elevations. The climb had challenged my long-distance stamina, but in terms of difficulty, it was a Class 1. We stuck to the ridge proper, navigated rocks and tundra, and only needed snowshoes to traverse slick ice slabs above the timberline. But I tensed at each crackle or far-away boom, which may have been, but most likely wasn't, an avalanche. Samuel watched me closely, gripped my hand whenever I'd start to panic.

There were no avalanches on our climb, and the wind died down to a gasp once we reached fourteen thousand feet. By the time we summited, that familiar high raced through my body like a shot of pure oxygen, lost to me for three years. How could I have forgotten this feeling?

Compared to Himalayan peaks, our Colorado fourteeners were babies. But as I discovered this unearthly corner of the earth, washed in indigo and ice, over the clouds and into the sun, I was struck with the thought: *this is what it's like to stand on a different planet.*

"She's baaack," Hector smirked. I rolled my eyes—yes, I enjoyed the climb. I turned my grin to Samuel, but it fell from my face as I assessed his health. He pressed his fingers to his temples and swayed. I caught his arm and guided him down to a rock.

"Whoa there. Have you been drinking enough water?"

"Nearly a liter."

That should have been plenty. Worry pounded in my chest. "Headache? Nausea?"

"Yes to both."

Crud, not good. Hector slung his pack from his shoulders and rummaged through it.

"Altitude sickness, man. Here's a couple of Tylenols. Take those and if you start feeling really bad, like you're going to pass out, let us know.

I agreed and helped Samuel to his feet. "Sounds mild, but we better start the descent before it gets worse."

It did get worse, but not the sickness. Samuel had ankles as strong as sequoias from all of his running and strength training. Seriously, even a chainsaw couldn't bring down those things. But toss in the dizziness of altitude sickness and uneven ground, and his ankle rolled like a rock star. He splinted it and we helped him limp the rest of the way down Mount Elbert.

Altitude sickness and sprained ankles aside, we had our first fourteener in the bag (Hector said we couldn't count Pikes Peak because we took the tram). It was ugly, but it counted.

I thought of my mother as I steered the Subaru around black, mountain curves, while Samuel rested in the back with his foot propped on the counsel. She'd been on my mind since Thanksgiving. I'd never believed that every woman's destiny was to be a mommy. Take my mom, for example. She could nurture the blight off of a tomato, but she'd been lost when it came to hugging her own daughter. I was eternally grateful my mother decided to have me, and she taught me how to be strong in the face of adversity. She was a pillar when we'd hunted for Samuel in Boston during his manic episode—practical in the face of panic. "Wipe your eyes and walk it off, Aspen Kaye." I told myself this was how she said, "I love you." But in the deepest recesses of her heart, I wondered if she regretted becoming a mom.

For so long, I'd assumed I was like her. Spectacular auntie material, but a mother? Not so much. But now there were moments...

When I saw a mom clasp her daughter's hand as they sauntered down Pearl Street, arms swinging.

Or the mother in the grocery store line ahead of me, leaning over her cart so her sticky-fingered son could wrap small arms around her neck and kiss her cheek.

When my nephew instinctively grabbed my index finger as we inched closer to a group of twitchy-eared mule deer browsing the forest line.

Each time, I was swamped with love. I didn't know what to do with this love. Tears burned behind my eyes and this...unanswered *yearning* to be some little person's protector welled inside of me.

I left Samuel and his injured ankle at home Sunday morning to drive to Lyons and attend church with the Cabrals. He had said nothing more about this mysterious woman he'd known in Tamaulipas. Perhaps there was nothing to know. But if there was nothing to know, why didn't Samuel simply tell me about her? (And for that matter, why did I have such a hard time trusting my own husband? No one could deny we'd messed up royally a decade ago, but since we'd remarried, Samuel hadn't once given me reason to question him.)

Over lunch at the Lyons Café, I subtly fished for information about the Cabral hacienda in Mexico but came up with little more than what Lucia had offered. Still, what Alonso shared was fascinating.

"We spent many a summer climbing in the hacienda's fruit trees, eating mangos and oranges. '*Lita* would chase us because we'd knock the fruit down before it had ripened. She made the best mango pie."

"The same pie I make," Sofia smiled. "I'll have to give you the recipe. Samuel loves it."

I returned her smile, acknowledging the momentous gesture. The Cabral mango pie recipe had more security detail than the POTUS; Sofia didn't hand it out to just anyone.

Afterward, I drove out to my mom's farmhouse. When I pulled into the driveway, I saw that my dad's Prius was parked on the far side of the shed, peeping around the corner as if it was in the middle of a vehicular game of hide-and-seek. Odd. Mom had asked me to swing by and grab extra pumpkins that hadn't sold. Maybe she'd asked Dad over, also. I jogged up the stairs, empty crates in hand, but froze before I pushed open the screen door. Giggling. Schoolgirl giggling, but not a school girl. My mother.

Then my father's laugh joined hers, and in retrospect I should have known better than to enter that kitchen because I might learn things I shouldn't learn, but dammit she'd asked me over, so it was her own fault. At the time, I assumed they were playing a hilarious game of Parcheesi. I entered.

Dad had Mom pressed against the counter, his body (still partially clothed, thank heavens) covering hers. Her farmer tanned arms were wrapped around his back and his hands were doing something in between them that I couldn't see, and never did see because they jumped apart when the screen door slammed shut behind me. Oops.

I dropped my crates and covered my eyes. "Arrrgh! No *no*, I did not see that. Did. Not. See. That."

Mom cleared her throat. "Sorry 'bout that, Aspen Kaye. I forgot you were coming over."

There were the rustles and zips of clothing being put back into place, but I refused to open my eyes until I received a verbal "all clear." I'd have to tell Samuel he was wrong. My parents were definitely acting on that "sliver of love" left between them.

"You want to explain what's going on?" I asked my mother later, after Dad took the lily-livered route and hauled tail.

"Honestly Aspen? You really need to ask?" I arched an eyebrow. She gave me a flustered "hmph" as we filled another crate with small pie pumpkins. "We haven't been doing…that…for long. We started talking again, oh, a few months after your wedding. Going for walks, gardening. We found we missed each other's company, the stories we used to tell, interests we shared. You know that much."

Yes, I'd caught them elbow deep in potting soil on more than one occasion, but gardening was a far cry from what they'd been doing against that counter. Ugh, Audrey would be heartbroken. I wondered if she knew what (who) her "common law husband" was doing when she worked shifts at her organic grocery store. She was either a very good actress, or she trusted Dad so much, she hadn't a clue. Gah, I wanted to tie them up and force them to watch *Unfaithful* a dozen times.

"Friendship is one thing," I spat. "Boinking behind Audrey's back is another."

"Aspen Kaye, watch your tongue. My sex life is none of your business."

We heaved up the pumpkin crates and tottered toward my jeep. "Really, Mom? Have you thought about Audrey in all of this, or are you too self-interested to care about her feelings?"

"Audrey Wexler has done quite well for herself and will continue to do so. She loves that grocery store of hers more than anything or anyone."

"Whether or not that's true, it doesn't give you and Dad the right to treat her like trash. That poor woman! She has tried for over a decade to be a part of our dysfunctional family, and here you are, having an affair right under her nose while we all sit around the dinner table."

"That's a bit of the pot calling the kettle black, isn't it?" She shoved the crate into the back of my jeep and slammed down the back door, then tried to storm to the house. I grabbed her sleeve and forced her to meet my eyes.

"Are you talking about Samuel and Caroline? Because Sam was upfront with her from the beginning. And you two need to be honest with Audrey before she catches you in the act, like I did."

Mom sighed. "Baby, I know. Believe me, I know we're in the wrong, here." Her eyes looked old and tired. Even her hair kerchief drooped. I remembered when Dad and Audrey first started seeing each other when I was a teenager, and how it broke Mom. She loved him after all these years and had hoped one day they'd find their way back to each other. It wasn't in me to stomp out her hope.

I softened. "May I ask why Dad hasn't ended his relationship with Audrey?"

"We haven't talked about it yet. This is too new."

"Mom…what if he's not planning to end it with Audrey? What then?"

Her kerchief drooped even further. "Then I'll have played a fool a second time."

I called my father twice, but he sent me to voicemail. I calmed down after my initial shock and decided it was best if I distanced myself from this ticking time bomb, but not until Dad received a clear "if you hurt my mother again, I'll caponize you" warning. Words a woman should never have to say to her father.

Samuel was holed up in our apartment when I returned from the Love Shack, hopping around our kitchen and tossing kale and blueberries into a blender. Bleh. His ankle had puffed up to the size of a butternut squash and I gave him a death glare as I hauled one of the pumpkin crates onto the counter.

"Okay, okay, I'm on my way to the couch." Smoothie held high, he hobbled to the living room, crashed atop the sofa and swung his leg onto the ottoman.

I handed him a bag of ice wrapped in a towel. Just as I finished scrubbing the first batch of pumpkins and prepping them on my cutting board, there was a knock on our door. Nothing good ever comes from late-night knocks on your door. I checked the peephole—Molly.

Her face was blotchy and makeup-less, and her eyes were red and puffy behind her glasses. I ushered her out of the cold night air. Samuel's smoothie cup froze halfway to his mouth. She gave him a small wave, barely composed.

"Molly?" I steered her into the big leather chair. "What's going on? Why aren't you in Breckenridge?"

"I need to talk to you. I need to do it now, in person, before I lose the nerve." And then she burst into tears.

"He wants to live in a cabin. It doesn't even have indoor plumbing!" she wailed. "What is a composting toilet, anyway?"

"It won't smell as bad if you add peat moss after..." Samuel's words died as he caught my stink-eye.

"What cabin? Where?" I asked, baffled.

"Alaska!" she wailed, and my heart sank.

What was happening to the strong women in my life? (To be fair, I also had my hang-ups, and to claim otherwise would smack of self-righteousness. Words straight out of a therapist's mouth: my own insecurities caused me to hold others to unrealistic expectations.) Still, my structure of female solidarity was shaken, and not in a "shattering glass ceilings" kind of way. My no-nonsense mother was my dad's secret on-the-side honey. Dani was so exhausted by her strong-willed toddler, she hadn't picked up a blow torch in ages. If I could count Caroline as "in my life," her career was shellacked for a man who had no intention of kicking his drug habit. And now Molly. *Oh Molly.* Moving to Clam Gulch, Alaska to harvest razor clams was *not* her dream. It was Cassady's dream (until three years from now, when his dream would probably be to herd cattle in Montana or wrestle gators in Florida).

Later that week, I tried not to glare at Cassady as he hugged friends he hadn't seen in months, swapped trail condition reports with Luca and Hector. Instead, I watched two tourists comb the aisles of Paddler's Outdoors Adventures and stop between the snow shoes and ski poles. (In a small town, everybody knows everybody, so if I didn't know them, they were tourists.) Judging by their flimsy shorts (in December) and sparkly pink phones, which they strategically positioned over their shoulders for 'candid shots,' I didn't think they were in Lyons for the mountains. Maybe I was a prejudiced old hag and they were visiting family for winter break. Or maybe they were the new stars of the next Warren Miller ski film. But my gut (or their Nixie tee shirts) told me they were here for Samuel.

"Luca! Get your baby face over here with those 'biners." Hector yanked the harness of his hiking pack and rocked on his heels as he tested the weight balance. Luca emerged from the equipment closet and chucked a pack of carabiners at his stomach, making him 'oof.' Earlier this year, Luca had picked up a part-time job at Paddler's when he and his wife of barely three months found out she was pregnant. When they'd shared their news with our stunned circle, he simply said, 'one helluva honeymoon.'

"Why is your husband in the closet?" Luca asked me.

Angel grinned and opened his mouth, but I pointed at him. "Don't even say it. For the love of my sanity, no more innuendos."

It was our traditional Friday Lunch at the Valdez family's store, and Hector and Luca geared up for another mountain climb. I'd declined. We'd barely made it down Mount Elbert with Samuel's sprained ankle, and I wasn't ready to tackle another winter route.

We circled a shiny new tailgating grill, containers of carry-out spread across its plastic-wrapped rack. Molly was perched on a ladder, draping red and green tinsel across antlers. If anyone noticed her anxiety, they didn't bring it up.

Behind us, Santiago manned the register, miserably munching on a veggie lettuce wrap (his bluegrass chick had eliminated meat, dairy, gluten, flour, caffeine, and sugar from their diet. I wondered if this might be the death of their relationship).

The Longmont premiere of Samuel's movie was tonight (Samuel would be sporting a new pair of crutches). Though small scale compared to Hollywood's red carpet shindig, it was a crucial appearance for us. I loved my town on the edge of the Rockies, but gossip was its bread and butter. Sometimes, your biggest fans can also be your harshest critics, and it was no different for Samuel Cabral, acclaimed Colorado author and social misfit. Even though his return to the Front Range brought him back to the people who loved him, it also dropped him in the center of an aquarium. He was the sole exotic fish among a school of guppies. Their eyes followed him through grocery store aisles and waited for him to up-end a holiday poinsettia display. If he spent an afternoon in the library, heads peeked around shelf corners to make sure he wasn't defacing books. The last straw was when Molly let it slip that Alan Murphy had added a "Cabral-Watch" app to NixieNet.net and was making a killing on advertising. (Alan's parents were now demanding he move out of their basement since he had a steady income.)

Curiosity waned as time passed. But it returned like a charging bull every time a *Water Sirens* movie hit theatres, like now. That's why Samuel currently hid in a literal closet.

Santiago fixed his meticulously-styled hair and approached the two sparkly phones staking out Samuel. He flashed a row of white teeth. "Lemme guess, you found the 'Cabral's Hometown Haunts' map on NixieNet.net."

The girls exchanged a secretive look. "Yeah, the map said he's sometimes here on Fridays." She shrugged. "We saw *her* here and thought we'd take a chance." Judging by the way the word 'her' dripped like poison from her lips, I didn't think she liked me. A small yet vocal faction of the *WS* fandom believed I'd caused Samuel's bipolar disorder.

"That's great you're into his books." Santiago the Salesman. "Here's the thing. You've loitered here for an hour and haven't bought anything. So I'm going to have to ask you to leave." He lifted an eyebrow. "Unless you plan to make a purchase."

The girls grabbed tubes of Burt's Bees lip balm from the display and plunked them on the counter. "Have a nice afternoon," said Santiago, then politely but firmly hustled them from the store, observing the youthful cheeks spilling out of their shorties. "Still can't believe Samuel never took advantage of that," he mumbled. Yep, his bluegrass chick was definitely on the way out and I wouldn't blame her one bit. Santiago could be a bit of a dillweed.

Angel still beamed at me, lips scrunched together.

"Don't say it."

He held up his hands. "All I'm gonna say is, that Togsender guy did raise some interesting points. Samuel always was a little too touchy-feely after baseball games."

"Cripes, Angel! Togsy wrote that he was gay, not a flipping molester. Besides, gay humor sailed years ago, on the same ship as blonde jokes and Your Mom."

"Then there was the whole team showering thing during baseball season."

Ugh, Latin machismo was the worst. "From what I hear, you did your fair share of towel-snapping. Aren't you supposed to pick up your son by two?"

Dani shot her husband a withering look and turned to me. "Seriously, why's he in the closet?"

"He's writing."

"And he finds inspiration amid Paddler's rafting equipment?"

"Samuel just needs to chill before the crowds tonight, Dani."

"Okay, sure."

At first, our friends tiptoed around what happened in Boston. Words like "bipolar" and "episode" were mouthed, the way people mouthed "sex" in polite conversation. Then Dani, blunt as a butter knife, asked Samuel how the new meds were working. The floodgates opened and no question was taboo.

Molly snickered as she arranged a Santa in skis. "Maybe you should help Samuel with those 'metaphors.' Relive glory days in the equipment closet."

I froze, water bottle halfway to my mouth. "What do you mean?"

"Oh please," Santiago mumbled through alfalfa sprouts, "everyone knows you and Cabral used to get it on like bunnies in that closet behind the life vests. Our long-time customers still joke about you guys 'breaking in' our new gear."

"We did not!"

"Alan Murphy should add that closet to his Cabral tour map, right after the ball diamond," Danita teased. "Well, *beneath the bleachers* at the ball diamond."

I spewed water down my shirt. "Does everyone really know about that?"

The circle erupted. But really, what did I expect? The town had known much more about its teenage population's shenanigans than we ever gave them credit for but, in my defense, hormones had wreaked havoc on my judgment. I cringed at what our parents had been aware of and never mentioned, save for Sofia's occasional threats to take Sam and me to a Boulder workshop called *What's NORMAL Anyway?: Facts and Fallacies of Teen Sexuality*. I wiped dirt from my rear and joined Luca as he inventoried fishing lures.

"Hey. Did you ask your sister about tonight?" Down the aisle, Hector's back stiffened at the mention of his ex.

"Yeah. Jaime said, 'If your 'Care Bear'—she means you—'calls me again, I'll give her a reason to file a restraining order.' So I don't think she's coming."

Disappointment clenched my gut. Ever since the blow-out at our wedding and Hector's elopement with Dr. Tricia not three weeks later, I'd seen Jaime precious few times. "Quite the hubbub happened while you were in Zermatt," Sofia had tactfully put it.

"Attention everyone." Molly hopped down from the ladder and frowned at the back room. "Cabral! Time to come out of the closet, your presence is required!" At last, Samuel appeared from his hideaway of musty life vests and kayak paddles, laptop under his arm and blue eyes squinting like a cat's in a suddenly bright room.

"As you know, Cassady and me...the thing is..." I winced, because I knew what Molly was about to announce. Her lower lip trembled as she looked at me. I gave her an encouraging nod. "Well, there's not an easy way to say this. We're leaving Colorado."

A chorus of "oh no" and "aw man" rose and died. She continued. "We won't be a world away. Well, kind of. Cassady wants to go to Alaska and I've never been."

I was glad to see Cassady reach for her hand. I hoped he wouldn't abandon her and drive Betty the Campervan somewhere into the wild, ala Chris McCandless.

"Anyway, Kaye and I think we could make this work in TrilbyJones' favor, since Alaska and Colorado have similar clientele. There are the mountains, the national forest, lots of outdoor tourism. We'll hire a couple more employees, expand our base." She nodded, as if convincing herself.

Cassady pulled his long, shaggy hair into a tail. "We'll come back to visit."

"And we'll definitely be back for the benefit concert in June."

It's just time to move on, ya know?" He held out his fist for a bump from Samuel, which was reluctantly returned. "Sorry man. It's tough leaving behind friends."

"I'm sure we'll still cross paths," said Samuel.

Angel cleared his throat. "While we're making announcements, we also have news to share."

The air in the room was thick with tension, at odds with the sparkling decorations and holiday tunes tinkling from the speakers.

Danita turned to her brother. "We didn't want to announce this until after Thanksgiving. *Mamá* and *Papá* already know."

"I'm being deployed," said Angel.

Oh no. No, no, no. We'd all known this was coming again, but so soon, and just after Christmas? I tallied the months...two...three... four years since his last deployment. Son-of-a-Nutcracker, not soon, after all. Where to now? Iraq again? Afghanistan? How would little Gabe handle the separation?

Then Danita said something I was *not* expecting to hear, though I should have.

"Angel's being deployed for eight months," she said with a quake, "and I'm going to have another baby."

Chapter 7
ROCK!

When rocks fall, a climber shouts a warning
'Rock!' to those ascending below them. A heads up
is always polite.

Winter wind bit our cheeks and gray slush clung to our boots as we huddled together at Buckley Air Force Base to wish Lieutenant Angel Valdez and the 460th Wing farewell. Christmas had been a quiet affair. We made it special for *el changuito*, but our joy was marred by the bitter taste of Angel's deployment. When he returned next year, he would find a two-month-old infant and a son who'd grown a foot.

No one dared consider that bleak conjunction: *If.*

Angel frowned at my long face. "Oh Kaye-bear, none of that. After all, 'It's the mooost, wonderful tiiiime, for a beeeer!'" he sang with all the boisterousness of a North Pole bartender. I hugged his neck and smiled through watery eyes.

"Take Dani out every now and then, will you? Get your nails done or something," he asked. "Don't let her sink into herself."

"Dani's usually the one who calls me out on the sad state of my nails. I don't think that will change anytime soon."

"Still."

"We'll take good care of her and the kids, Angel." I flicked a fuzz ball from the shoulder of his fatigues. He was so dashing and heroic.

Angel gazed behind me at his wife, who conversed with another military wife as their toddlers darting around their legs. "They tell us that spouses withdrawing from us is normal, in the days before we're deployed. That…that they do it to cope. Sometimes they even wish we'd just go ahead and leave already, so we can get the deployment over with. It's damned awkward, though."

I didn't know what to say, so I reassured him again we'd take care of his family.

He choked back the tears he was loathed to showcase and grabbed the duffel bag at his feet. "Don't you sell my kayak seat on the Glenwood Canyon trip. I'm reclaiming it next May."

"Never. I am so proud of you, Angel. Danita is, too. Be safe."

That night, like the children we once were, Samuel and I slept on either side of Danita in her old bedroom while she wept into her pillow.

Two weeks later, Molly and Cassady left for Alaska. Why someone would move to Alaska in the middle of their dark and endless winter was a mystery. I couldn't understand Cassady's peripatetic lifestyle… staying somewhere long enough to establish roots, only to yank them out of the ground on a whim.

After a hurried goodbye, Samuel and I zipped up our coats and turned toward St. Vrain. His ankle sprain had all but healed, but long runs were dicey so instead we strolled through the stripped winter trees along our creek.

"Talk to me. Every inch of your body is tense."

I sighed. "Life is changing too fast. It's like being in the middle of a paintball fight without a paintball gun. There's my folks and this ridiculous affair that's going to blow up in their faces. I need to step up my game for Danita and *el changuito*. Now there's this uncertainty at TrilbyJones. Our employees are worried about Molly's move to Alaska. They depend on their jobs to pay rent and feed their families, so of course they're concerned. I'm concerned, too."

Samuel lifted a branch weighed down by ice and snow. "Do you believe expanding into Alaska is a foolish business risk?"

"Risk-taking is how businesses put a pin on the map. Alaska's a good move, but…" How to voice my feelings? "The thing is, I don't feel comfortable with the reason behind the expansion. If Molly hadn't decided to follow Cassady to the clam capital of the Alaska—and I have no idea how we're going to position *that* on our website—we would never have considered this. Watch the ice."

He jumped over the slab. "Most new opportunities come from unexpected avenues."

"I suppose so. But expansions are usually chosen through careful market research."

"Molly brought in new clients when she moved to Breckenridge *and* managed the payroll, correct?"

"Breckenridge is still Colorado. We have connections in Breckenridge."

"Knowing Molly, you'll have connections in Clam Gulch in no time."

I waved my hands, frustrated. "It's Clam Gulch, Alaska! How many connections can she possibly make?"

Samuel's smile was wry. "Alright, city girl."

We breathed in air that made our nostrils tingle. The creek split here: one branch traveled north and the other, south. "Left toward Old St. Vrain Road, or right toward Planet Bluegrass?" Sam asked.

"Let's try Old St. Vrain today. I want to see if there are any acreages for sale." We wandered through the woods until we hit blacktop.

"Has Molly ever dropped the ball with TrilbyJones?"

"No. She's a rock."

Ah, there it was. She was my rock. She wasn't supposed to up and move across the country for a guy. Shame at my selfishness burned in my cheeks.

Samuel continued, gently. "Don't forget how supportive she was when you shouldered my promotional tour several years ago."

"And I followed a guy halfway across the country, too. Man, I'm a ho-bag."

"No. You love your friend and your employees, and you want to see them happy. You're asking the questions you should ask and I'm merely helping you find perspective."

I squeezed his hand in mute thanks. "What do you worry about?"

Samuel grew quiet as we walked along the deserted road. A home-owner had recently placed a herd of papier mâché sculptures in their yard. Dragons? Iguanas? With snow in the forecast, they wouldn't make it through the week, but perhaps that was the intent behind the art. In Lyons, who knew?

"What do I worry about? No matter how much of myself I put into my novels, no matter how I push to be a better writer, I'll never again have a book as well received as the *Water Sirens* series. I worry that my career has peaked in my first decade of publishing. Sometimes I obsess about this, play those negative reviews over and over in my head, and I don't know if it's because of my bipolar brain or if it's a hit to my ego, but I have trouble letting go. Is that a gecko?"

He studied one of the sculpted lizards— painted red, white, and blue—as puzzled as I. Patriotic or satirical? We shook our heads and he continued.

"I worry that I've disappointed you."

"Samuel, no. I've told you a million times how amazingly talented you are. It's just *en vogue* for critics to tear down writers who've gone mainstream."

"Most of the reviewers were fair in their crit. *Sea Rovers* did lean too heavily on cliché. You can't win 'em all." Samuel kicked a stray rock into the ditch. "I worry you might have enough of my moods and leave. I worry about *you*, too. That I'm stifling you, keeping you from doing the things you love. And those panic attacks."

"Sam—"

"I make issues out of nothing. I *know* I do this, it's okay. That's why I'm constantly moderating my head. Catastrophes happen when I act on instinct and don't evaluate whether my thoughts are normal or extreme."

"Sounds exhausting."

"You have no idea."

What thoughts did I moderate? Nearly two months after our L.A. trip for Samuel's movie premiere, I still hadn't told him about my desire to have a baby. I should. But I also knew what his response would be, and I was absolutely certain my telling him would drive a wedge between us.

Isn't your silence also driving a wedge between you?

He reached for my hand again. "I don't think my worry here is extreme. You're unhappy. You've been unhappy for a good six months now, and that goes beyond your parents' affair, Angel's deployment, Molly's move. I don't believe it has anything to do with mountain climbing and panic attacks, either. What's going on?"

The trunk of an old cottonwood encroached upon the road. Someone had carved the face of a wood spirit into its bark, as angled and creviced as the bark itself. I patted its cheek. "You know how you asked me to trust you on the matter of your visit to Tamaulipas, how it was better if you didn't tell me? Well, this is the same situation. It's best if I not say anything."

He gave a brusque nod, but he was as satisfied as a squirrel with an empty nutshell. He'd broach this again. We often had talks like this along our creek. It was our place of candidness.

Some people imagine Colorado as arid. It's dry, to be sure, but in our corner of the state, streams weaved through red rock foothills, lined by evergreen shrubs and trees that dappled sun-beaten waters with shadow. Creeks froze over in the winter months, and Samuel and I crunched our way through ice in our winter boots. In the spring, melted snow and rain from the Rockies flooded these narrow creek beds and rushed down the mountains, gurgling full to their banks.

Summer heat tamed them into trickles of lifeblood that sustained all things green and breathing on the Front Range.

My hometown of Lyons was triangled in a watershed, where two of these mountain streams converged: North St. Vrain and South St. Vrain. The creek slithered east into ranch country where it eventually spilled into the South Platte River.

What would Lyons be without the St. Vrain? Our farms pulled from its waters. Planet Bluegrass was nestled into its curve. All roads in and out of Lyons crossed the St. Vrain—there was no other way. The St. Vrain was my lifeblood, too, this creek of childhood fairytales, and now, my marriage. This creek was in me. The season didn't matter, because one can overcome any type of weather with good shoes and waterproof layers.

Early spring, I was kicking off my heels and struggling to unzip my shift after long hours at the office, when I spotted my hiking boots and fleece laid across my bed. Samuel came up behind me, removed my struggling hands and dragged my zipper the rest of the way down. His arms circled my bare waist. His breath was warm and inviting on my neck.

"I have a surprise for you." He kissed my skin once, twice, making me shiver. Then he groaned and removed his hands, to my great reluctance. "But we'll need the last bit of daylight. "Change and we'll go?"

Cliff-hucking tease. I conceded and pulled on my active wear. Lately, Samuel's mood had teetered on the edge of mania. He was aware of it and tried to check his exuberance, but it was still hard to keep up with someone who had the speed and panache of Chester Cheetah.

The office had been a road race today. Bathroom breaks were nearly impossible, and lunch was out of the question. A rival firm in Breckenridge poached our ski resort campaign, I presented to a potential client in Alaska whose signing was as likely as Clam Gulch becoming a spring break hot-spot, we were in the middle of tax season and, to top it off, one of my IT guys quit and the other was ready to murder me if I didn't hire a replacement soon. I normally wouldn't handle some of these details, but our office manager was on maternity leave and her temporary replacement's résumé proved to be vastly overstated. Frankly, all I wanted was to curl up in my comfy chair with my comfy blanket and a comfy bowl of popcorn.

I threw together cold tacos for an "on-the-road" dinner and followed my husband out the door.

We didn't travel far. Samuel drove us out of Boulder but before we reached Lyons, he turned west onto a two-lane blacktop called Left Hand Canyon Drive. The area was familiar. Left Hand Creek had a wild, class five mini-gorge rapid that was only reachable by squeezing a kayak through a small culvert (river rats called it the 'Fighting Miner' because it resembled a mine's log entrance and beat the piss out of you). Next, you passed under the road, then zigzagged into a boulder garden and hit a cascade. Hector and I occasionally took our kayaks through the obscure whitewater. Well, we used to. If I closed my eyes, I could feel low-hanging willows comb my arms as we sped into the canyon.

A few miles farther, Sam pulled onto a driveway that was little more than two muddy tire tracks. We meandered up a hill, around rock walls and groves of shimmering aspens, cottonwood and pine. Samuel parked. I followed him up a gentle slope and wondered why the heck we'd stopped in the middle of nowhere. The sun skipped along the tops of the mountains and soon it would be dark, so there was no time to hike. Below us, Left Hand Creek sputtered and gasped with the first of the snowmelt. In another month, ice water would roar over its bedrock.

"What do you think of this place?"

"It's beautiful. I think I've noticed this spot before, where the creek curves. It has a nice vista, good for biking when it warms—"

"It's ours."

"Say what?"

Samuel jammed his hands in his pockets, pleased. "I bought it. Thirty-five acres of prime mountain-view real estate. I thought we could build a house over here…"

My brain struggled to catch up with Samuel's boisterous plans, but it was still stuck at 'thirty-five acres..' "How much did you spend?"

"Seven-fifty." Given his royalties intake, not bad for a land investment. But still.

"Why didn't we discuss this first?"

"I told you, I wanted it to be a surprise. Although…judging by your expression, you're not happy."

I tightened my ponytail and walked the line between gratitude and exasperation, a well-worn path. "I couldn't have chosen a better place myself, but we never even talked about it. Buying a house, yes. Building, no."

His smile fell. "Sometimes you make me feel as though I can't do anything right."

Argh, argh, argh. So frustrating when he was like this.

"Listen. It's an extravagant gift, incredible. And this is possibly the best view in Boulder County. I just…"

I looked over the land again. We were far enough into the mountains where bare rock face gave way to lush green, even in winter's last gasp. Purple haze, gleaming aspens. The valley below teemed with color and wildlife along the creek. But the really amazing thing about this place? There was a grocery store ten minutes away. Now I felt like an ungrateful chit.

I tried again. "Tell me why you chose this place."

"See the tree line on the edge of the field, where the hill crests? That's the property line. Thirty-five acres gives us an amazing amount of privacy. Snoopy paparazzi and fans couldn't get close to our home without trespassing."

"Fair point."

"It's between Boulder and Lyons, not a long commute."

I loosened to the idea. "Again, fair point."

"And we can build a home together, just the way we want it, down to the last sink fixture."

Ah, I got it. "It'll be *our* place, while the apartment above Trilby-Jones is still kind of *my* place."

"It's time to move this marriage out of a holding pattern, firecracker. Let's build something permanent."

"Fair point, times three."

We hiked up and over rock ledges, through thick canopies of pines that had blanketed the ground in needles. A dirt path snaked into the forest, darkening as twilight loomed. This was no deer trail. Someone had lived here before. We climbed further and I nearly stumbled on a wooden staircase, crumbling and rotted. Behind the overgrown brush on either side of the stairs ran an old rock wall.

"Good lord, it's the Secret Garden."

"Not quite. Look at the top of the stairs."

I took the stairs two at a time lest they disintegrate beneath my shoes and a solid stone building, no bigger than a shed, came into view. A fragile-looking wood door clung to rusted hinges. I looked back at Samuel, confused.

"An old mine entrance, probably gold and silver. See how it's built into the hill?"

I could just imagine a grisly miner laboring on this very hill and then stumbling back to a shack that surely must have been here, once upon a time. The actual mine shaft had been filled in and bricked away, perhaps a hundred years ago. Ancient, musty air filled my nostrils as I stepped inside. I pressed my hand to the wall, the ceiling, stomped the floor—sturdy as the mountain it inhabited. What a spectacular playhouse for a child.

"No danger of the ground caving into collapsed shafts?"

"It's already been inspected. Any remnants of the mine shafts collapsed decades ago and settled nicely."

"Water?"

"Also inspected and tested for lead, arsenic and thallium. All clear."

I lifted an eyebrow. "This wasn't a spur-of-the-moment buy, was it? You've been at this for a while."

"It was in the works before this latest manic episode, if that's what you're getting at. Give me a little credit."

I winced at his harsh tone, but let it go. His mind was on the mend, no need to pick a fight.

As we explored the property, it burrowed its way into my soul. Samuel was right. We could grow roots here, build a home. Log cabin? Spanish style? It would need thick walls and a deep foundation, here on the mountainside, with the wind. I closed my eyes and the breath of the mountain fluttered across my cheeks, my hair. *Home.*

Samuel took my hand with apology in his eyes. I smiled and we explored our property, pointed out locations to build. Years could pass here. I saw our family sitting on a deck in relaxed conversation as the sun sank. We'd take *el changuito* and his little sibling down to the creek to splash and fish. There'd be other children, perhaps. Birthday parties on the mountain, piñatas and baseball cakes, knowing Sofia. I saw the baby boy of whom I dreamed growing and toddling over rocks as our hands hovered near his little belly, guarding him. The field to the right was open enough to be a good sledding hill. We'd huff up the hill with our boy under one arm and a sled rope looped around the other, because his snow gear would make movement as impossible as pushing through a vat of honey. At night we'd read one last book and he'd glide into dreams against my chest, his starlight lamp swirling gray, blue, green colors upon his nursery ceiling.

Samuel gripped my hand. I hurriedly swiped away the tears running down my cheeks, but it was too late.

"Kaye. *Talk to me.*"

I covered my face with my hands, but he pried them away. Blue eyes met mine. Earnest and familiar and pained, promising they'd be in my mind until I made my last memory.

"Tell me why I'm making you sad. Tell me how to fix this."

I shook my head. "It's not you."

"Then what is it?"

"I don't want to stress you out."

Exasperation flooded his face. "Aspen Kaye Cabral, this has gone on long enough. You talk to me now, or we're going to marriage counseling."

That pushed me over the edge, and my barely dammed emotions bawled over. "It's this dream, this idea I can't seem to get out of my head and it's driving me—" I caught my breath and slowed, slowed, to coherency. Samuel watched, patient and alarmed. When I was in control of my emotions, I tried again.

"What sort of rooms should we have in our home?"

Samuel's confusion deepened, but he answered. "The obvious: kitchen, bedrooms, bathroom, living room. I'd like an office or library for my writing, and you'd need one for business. We could share an office, I suppose. We'll want a rec room and a place to store all of your outdoor equipment...Actually, we may need to buy the neighboring acreage for that."

"What about a nursery?"

Samuel stared at me, then dropped my hands like a hot pan. "What? How? Are you—?"

"No! Not pregnant." I flushed. "That isn't possible for us, is it? But..." I bit my lip. "Have you thought anymore about it?"

His eyes widened. "About getting you pregnant? Kaye, I can't—"

I shook my head. "Have you thought about our having a child?"

Samuel exhaled, as if he'd been slammed by a Greco-Roman wrestler. "I should have seen this coming. Here and there, I suppose. Nothing serious. Why? Have you?"

"Some. A lot."

"What have you thought about? How long have you been thinking about this?"

"Months now. I've had dreams. I'm sorry I didn't tell you."

Samuel plopped down on the ground of what would one day be our backyard, the lingering spring muck soaking through his jeans. I sat next to him. "I knew something was bothering you. I just assumed you were disappointed in our marriage. But you know what they say about assuming."

"You wouldn't have had to assume anything if I'd told you in the first place."

"That's true." His eyes were as unfathomable as a thick fog. "But my track record for being open and honest isn't exactly stellar, so I'll not hold it over your head. Don't beat yourself up about it."

"Thank you." I mentally kicked myself in the shin. Why did I always underestimate Samuel?

His restless fingers tugged brown grass and twisted them into spikes. "Do you want to tell me about these dreams?"

So I told him. The dark-haired infant with his dark eyes, sleep-slowed breath and baby powder, everything. All the while, as eagerness and longing bubbled over and spilled into the space between us, Samuel watched me as one watches a tragic news story unfold. Sad and removed. When I finished and saw the way he looked at me, I knew what he would say before he even said it.

"Kaye. Oh Kaye. You would be a wonderful mother. I can see it too, you know? A baby we made, sleeping in your arms. Sometimes I imagine you nine months pregnant, all rounded and glowing with excitement, and I feel excited too. But..."

"But?"

Samuel's face darkened, and in that darkness was a self-recrimination I knew all too well. He rose and turned away from me, hands on his hips. He stood there, silent and tense, before his head fell back and he uttered several expletives. "I'm so damned sorry, firecracker. I can't tell you how much I want to give this dream to you. But I can't."

Fear rose in my chest. "Well, of course we can't have biological children together. But there are other options. A donor, maybe—"

"That's not what I meant—"

I rushed on. "Or adoption. Samuel, there are so many possibilities. It would take research to find out what we can and can't do, with your mental health history—"

"And my arrest record."

"People with drug arrests in their past are still able to adopt."

"How about my very public meltdown? Have you forgotten about that?"

"No. But...there are ways around it. We have resources."

"Unethical ways that involve money under the table. Absolutely not."

"Not necessarily." I stood up. "I'm not talking about child trafficking, for Pete's sake. What if the biological parents choose us? If we make use of the media, tell our story."

"No. Absolutely not," he repeated. "Can you imagine the backlash if we used my connections to adopt a baby? My health struggles and indiscretions are under a microscope as it is. It would be a bloodbath in the petri dish. Imagine putting a child through that kind of lifelong scrutiny, always having people speculate if daddy's neglecting him to break into major league ballparks with cremation urns."

"Samuel," I chided.

"And what about my reasons for not wanting children? Have you forgotten them, or are you simply discounting my wishes in the matter, thinking I'll 'come around' eventually? Because let me tell you, Kaye, this is deadly serious to me."

"It is to me, too!"

"No, it's not! It can never be, because you don't have bipolar disorder!"

I pointed a finger at him. "That's not fair."

"Have you thought of the ramifications of bringing a baby into our lives, completely dependent upon us for everything? I have nightmares about slipping into a depression or a manic episode and somehow mistreating you and the people I love, let alone a little child."

"You are *not* your mother, Sam. Besides, I would be there."

He dragged his hands through his hair. "What about TrilbyJones? You work insane hours as it is, and it will only get more insane with this Alaska expansion. Are you going to sell your share of the business and be the primary caregiver?"

I paused. I loved TrilbyJones. I'd worked hard to build it when I had nothing, not even Samuel. Selling…no. No. *Could I? For our baby?* "Maybe, I don't know. It's not like we're hurting for money. We'd have to figure it out."

"Exactly." He jabbed a finger toward the ground. "You haven't thought this through."

"Isn't this what we're doing? Thinking this through, now, *together?*"

"I've already thought this through, a thousand times!" His voice cracked. "The sad, messed-up fact is, I would love to be a dad. In a perfect world, I'd have one kid on my shoulders and two hanging on my ankles. But this isn't a perfect world, and I'll not risk the precious trust and vulnerability of a child simply to satisfy a selfish desire to be a father. That's what parents do—love their kids so much, they put their children's needs before their own. And I'm doing that by choosing not to be a parent in the first place."

"Samuel, you don't have to be perfect to be a good father. And you *would* be." I tried to grip his hand but he shook me loose. "We have an incredible support system here in Colorado— "

"You're not hearing me, Aspen Kaye. *I'm screwed up.* You knew this when you married me."

Anger flared. "When I married you, you promised me we'd explore our options. You did *not* give me a definite 'no.'"

"Would you have chosen not to marry me if I'd given you a definitive 'no'?"

I paused, biting back hurtful words I couldn't take back. "I still would have married you. But three years ago, I also didn't think I'd want to be a mom."

"And now you do."

I nodded. "That's why I didn't say anything about it—to be fair. But I also think it's fair to acknowledge that people grow and change. That's what living *is*. We aren't etched in stone, Sam."

"Our genes are."

And that was the kicker, wasn't it? There was no magic cure for bipolar disorder. You coped as best as you could, you made sacrifices, you accepted you could never quite be 'normal.' What did that mean, anyway? 'Normal.' I snorted. Didn't everyone have their burdens?

People who had no business having children had one, *had ten*, then hurt them and resented them for taking away their freedom, for getting in the way, for putting a cramp in their miserable, selfish lifestyles. Then there were people like Samuel, who was so far from selfish he was Mother Theresa compared to these child-abusing louses. But he'd been born with a curse on his brain. It sucked. It wasn't fair. Then again, God never promised us life would be fair, did he?

I wiped my eyes with my hands, knowing we were at an impasse. Samuel half-heartedly gestured to the sky. "It's almost dark. We should head home."

Chapter 8
MANK

When climbing gear is rusted or otherwise unsafe
(due to age, carelessness, or inexperience) it becomes
a danger and is said to be 'mank.'

In the days that followed our fight, I tried to bargain with God. If he would just cause Samuel to have a change of heart, I would be the very best mother I could be. I would take our child to Sunday school, teach him or her about Jesus, all of it.

I railed at God. What had I done to piss him off? Had I proven myself to be sub-par parent material? If he was God, why didn't he show a little mercy and fix this?

Late at night, as Samuel soundly slept off his latest episode, I pleaded with God to take this hurt away, to ease this bitter disappointment and anger I felt toward Samuel, toward my friends, toward the world in general.

Nothing.

Samuel and I reached an unspoken, uneasy truce to shelve the issue. On the tail-end of an episode had been a craptastic time to have the baby discussion. But I couldn't blame his bipolar disorder for the lingering cold. Gruff goodbyes and hellos, three feet of personal space on the couch, in the bed. We'd never made good on what we'd started before our trip to Left Hand Canyon. In fact, we hadn't had sex in three weeks and I was twitchy.

One evening, as I hacked away at a pile of zucchini and onions *he* insisted on eating (you know, for *his* healthy eating plan) I felt particularly combative, even to the point of sautéing the whole thing in delicious slabs of butter. Oh, he could keep his secrets about a woman in Tamaulipas, but I had to tell him mine? And then he had the gall to be angry? How was this fair?

Maybe he's not angry, Kaye. Isn't it possible he feels really bad about the argument, and even worse that he can't give you what you want?

But I wasn't ready to let go of my anger. Samuel was in the living room, feet propped on my coffee table, tapping away on his laptop while two loads of unfolded laundry sat in the hallway. Was it too much for him to fold a rat-friggin' basket of towels? Pungent onion fumes burned my eyes and tears streamed down my cheeks, blinding me. I pressed a towel to my face for relief and my kitchen knife clattered against the counter. His head shot up from his computer screen.

"You hurt?" he asked. When he saw there was no blood, he turned back to his writing. *Yep, he's angry.* Well, someone had to step up first, and I was just as capable as Samuel. I marched into the living room, wiping my hands with a dishcloth.

"It's your turn to talk."

His gaze flitted over my pursed lips, tear-streaked face. "Okay. About what?"

"Despite my reservations, I told you my secret. Now will you tell me why you went to Tamaulipas the last time?"

He clenched his jaw, refusing to take the bait. "No, Kaye. This isn't quid-pro-quo. It's about your safety and I won't compromise that."

I slung the dishcloth over my shoulder with a huff. Five minutes later, when the irrational haze of anger and onion vapors cleared from my brain, I realized what he'd said.

My safety? What did an ex-girlfriend in Tamaulipas have to do with my safety?

The next morning I travelled through Lyons, making the rounds to our benefit concert donors. June would be here before we could say "gee-tar pickin'" and we'd need to advertise soon. But I was ahead of schedule and, on a whim, turned north toward Steamboat Rock. Dani had cut her hours at Jeff's Welding and Machine to ten-a-week, to the despair of her admiring welders. I was pretty sure this was her morning off, and I wanted time with *el changuito*.

The doorbell went unanswered. Sofia's car was gone, though Dani's car was in the driveway. I heard a high-pitched shriek in the house and I barreled through the door. Gabe streaked past my legs, tee shirt riding above his belly button and not a stitch of clothing from the waist down. He pivoted mid-run and skidded toward me. I caught up my little monkey in a hug, and he wrapped his arms and legs around me. For the sake of my pencil skirt, I hoped he was pants-free for reasons unrelated to the potty.

"Aun' Kaye, I go poopoo. Hurray!"

Dang it. "Oh splendid, *changuito*! Such a big boy. What have you got here?" I tapped one of the fists he'd looped around my neck. He pushed the cloth into my face.

"Underwear!"

"Wow, are those trains? Your mama must be so proud of you."

Dani appeared, pull-ups and wet wipes tucked under her arms. Her black hair was piled and lopsided on her head, and flannel pajama bottoms sat low on her waist, underneath her growing mid-section. What appeared to be either pure heroin or baby powder was splattered against one leg. Of course it was the latter, though her desperate and pleading eyes gave me a split-second pause.

"We've been working on the potty today. I want this boy out of diapers before this one goes into them." She pointed to her stomach. Then she noticed the baby powder across her pants, chuffed, and shook them out. "You should see the daybed in the guest bedroom, looks like an ATF sting gone south. You turn your back for two minutes…"

Last Saturday, as I babysat Gabe while Danita went into the shop, he'd emptied three boxes of elbow macaroni onto the kitchen floor in the time it took me to drop trou' and empty my bladder, and was about to top it off with an economy-sized box of goldfish crackers when I caught him in the act. Knowing that Gabe also punked Dani made me feel better.

My nephew slithered to the ground and held out his underwear. "On, Mommy, now!"

"Saying 'please' will get you farther in life, *changuito*." She helped him step into his underwear and he yanked it so high, I winced. He ran up the stairs, hopefully to vacuum the baby powder and shake out the quilts on Sofia's daybed.

Dani slowly circled the main room, her expression vapid and defeated as she took in the disaster of toys and random objects strewn across the room. Her gaze turned to me and she blinked, as if she'd forgotten I was there. "What brings you out to Lyons on a Wednesday afternoon?"

I gestured to my skirt and heels. "I've come to watch my nephew while my sister-in-law takes a long, relaxing shower. Isn't it obvious?"

Dani's eyes lit. "Kick off those heels, Kaye. I'll be back in twenty minutes. Vacuum's in the hall closet."

An hour later, Danita dropped onto the couch across from me, ten years younger and damp hair streaming down her back. *El changuito* sat on my lap. Two fingers were in his mouth and he absently rubbed his stuffed monkey's tail across his cheek while he watched cartoons.

I swiped hair out of Gabe's sleepy eyes, sooty like his dad's. "Have you heard from Angel?"

Dani rubbed her rounded belly. "We talked a few nights ago. He's okay, though he wouldn't tell me otherwise, you know? Gabe has finally stopped asking about him. It breaks my heart." She closed her eyes. "Three months down, six to go."

"It'll go fast, with the baby on the way."

She smiled gently as I rested my head against Gabe's fine hair. "Sure you don't want one of those?" The expression on my face wiped away her smile. "*Ave Maria Purisíma*, I'm sorry. Sometimes I can be so thoughtless."

"Don't worry, I wrote the book on speaking before thinking. It wouldn't bother me, but Samuel and I got into it a few days ago."

"He still doesn't want kids and now you do. Is that it?" I nodded. "*Ay.* That's rough. But to be fair, he warned you."

"Believe me, I know."

She patted my knee. "This was bound to happen, but you two will work through it. Samuel's not going to give up on your marriage again. And you're not, either, or I'll kick your birth-marked butt all the way to Clam Gulch, where Molly will kick it back." There was my pushy Danita.

I tucked straggling curls into my hair bun. "In retrospect, we probably should have waited to have that talk until he's getting at least four hours of sleep a night."

"Is Samuel through this episode yet? We miss him around here, especially Gabe."

"He's getting better."

She went to the kitchen, grabbed two bottles of water and handed me one. "Just because he's a little wilder doesn't mean he can't be around his nephew."

"He doesn't like being unpredictable."

"At least it's not as bad as it was during those episodes in L.A. and Boston. His meds are still working, right?"

I nodded as I uncapped my water and took a swig. Gabe pushed my hands down so he could see the television. "Speaking of L.A., *Tía* Lucia mentioned something curious awhile back, when we were there."

"Did it have to do with *Mamá* buying her that horrible vintage tunic off Etsy for her birthday? She swears it looked better online."

"Funny, but no." I glanced at Gabe, who only had ears for his train show. "Ever hear of the Ciudad Victoria family asking Samuel not to visit again?"

Dani puffed her cheeks and blew. "Yes, but not much. You know how my family is. *Mamá* said Sam and *Tía* Mariángel had an all-out smack-down over some *loca* in one of the mountain villages. Something about the gossip magazines ruining his reputation, and how she was bad news and he should stay away from her." She widened her eyes. "I can see what you're assuming, Kaye, but it was strictly platonic with this woman."

"Then why would *Tía* Mariángel ban him from the family hacienda?"

"You'll have to ask him." Great. We'd been down this road before. She bit her lip. "You already have, huh? *Pendejo.*" She grumbled some unflattering things about her brother. "Walk with me to the kitchen?"

I settled Gabe into the corner of the couch, tucked his stuffed monkey in his arms, and followed. She tossed snack bowls in the sink as she collected her thoughts.

"Okay. I don't know why this woman was so special he'd choose her over his family. But *Papá* talked to Tomás not long after this happened, and he insinuated she had ties to the Zacatón Cartel. Tomás said if Samuel associated with her, he wasn't to visit anymore."

"Wait, aren't the Zacatóns those ex-police and military deserters who turned mercenary? The ones who are always on the news?"

She rolled her eyes. "No Kaye, they're a frat house."

Holy Tom. No wonder Samuel didn't want me involved. The Zacatóns were butchers. Drugs actually made up only half of their revenue. The other half came from kidnappings, extortions, assassinations, and protection rackets. They didn't use money to get what they wanted. They used brutality. Beheadings, wholesale slaughter, torture...the stuff of nightmares. The crime organization was headquartered just over the border from Texas in Nuevo Laredo, but they had operations throughout Tamaulipas, not to mention Mexico, Guatemala, and the good ol' USA. Samuel might be of interest to them if he ever came to their attention. Wealthy, high profile, family in Tamaulipas...

The idea of those murderers coming after Sam filled my gullet with ice. I'd once read a news article about how a man was kidnapped and kept in a standing-room-only box more than a year, until his family raised enough money to pay his ransom. Then the Zacatón Cartel killed him anyway.

"Honestly, I kind of agree with *Tía* Mariángel," Danita murmured. "Mexico is an amazing place to live—beautiful, friendly—as long as you don't go looking for trouble. And no one wants their family on the Zacatón Cartel's radar." I didn't argue.

At the end of my workday, I drove past The Garden Market and saw my father's car. I pulled into a parking space, grabbed my grocery bags from the trunk and pushed through the jingling door.

"Is Audrey here?"

Dad chuckled. "Hey flower! Nice to see you, too."

I looked around the store for the woman who loved my dad but would fire his cheating butt if she knew what he was up to.

"Audrey's at her brother's place for the weekend, helping her niece shop for a prom dress. Remember when I took you prom dress shopping? First time I realized you were all grown up, so beautiful."

Man, Dad was smooth. But he tended to sentimentalize my childhood, because I definitely did not remember prom dress shopping going down like that. Tom Trilby may have been the 'accepting parent,' but then I dragged him to a dozen formal wear stores across the Front Range because I couldn't find the perfect anti-prom dress: no bling, beading, ruffles, princess skirts, or anything girly. (What did he expect? He'd raised me to be a proper little bohemian.) Dad blew his Zen. Explaining why I didn't need underwire was the superlative memory of that day.

Snarky words withered on the tip of my tongue. I gave my father a hug. "I was in town so I thought I'd stop in, pick up a few groceries. You have big Saturday plans?"

"Just work, maybe head out to Ol' Man Elias' place in Jamestown and restock on incense." I gave him a charry eye. Ol' Man Elias had a state-of-the-art hydroponics system that was the envy of the Front Range. "But I don't have a date with your mom, if that's what you're getting at."

"Dad. Listen. It's supposed to be none of my business, but it *is* my business. If this sours, you tear apart the fragile mends to this family. Not to mention Audrey will avoid us like anthrax, and I love her. I've known her half my life."

"Which is why she'll never, ever bail on you, baby girl. My scumbag butt, maybe, but not you."

That was my dad, the dreamer. Maybe he was right. Audrey might want to see me when—and I meant *when*—their dying relationship 'ran down the curtain and joined the choir invisible.' But I knew

about shelving the *Sea Rovers* series and picking up the new book idea I pitched to them."

"But Holy Week begins this weekend. Your mom is going to flip."

Samuel chuckled humorlessly. "Understatement of the century. I plan to return Saturday night, though, so I'll be back for Palm Sunday."

"I didn't even know you were working on a new series."

"We haven't exactly talked much, have we?" He grabbed a handful of boxers and undershirts from a dresser drawer.

I ignored his arctic tone, determined to thaw the coldness between us. "What's it about?"

"It's a surprise," he said, a touch too sarcastically.

Nope, still frigid. "I think I've had enough surprises for today, thanks."

He paused in his packing and frowned. "What's that supposed to mean?"

I crossed my arms. Here we go. "This woman in Tamaulipas, the one who wasn't a lover and was obviously important to you, but you won't tell me a thing about?"

"Kaye, for the love of—"

"Does she have ties to the Zacatón Cartel?"

His expression was a study, which told me my sister-in-law was correct. "How did you…?"

"Dani told me, and she heard it from your father, who heard it from Tomás!"

His brow furrowed. "They know a lot more than I thought they did. That's troublesome."

"I swear, your family needs to rent space in Area 51, for all the secrets they have."

He braced his arms on the dresser, head down. "Listen to me. We weren't lovers, but she was important to me. Yes, she had ties to the Zacatóns. I haven't heard from her in years and, as far as I'm concerned, the matter is finished."

"One more question."

Samuel sighed, resigned. "Fine."

"If the matter is finished, why are you still barred from visiting your Ciudad Victoria family?"

"It's not that I *can't* go back to Ciudad Victoria. It's that I *won't* go back. I pissed off a few people, and it's best if you not know the details. Now *please* let this knowledge be enough for you."

My hands flew to my mouth. "Oh my God, Samuel." People only said this kind of stuff on *Dateline.* "Did you do something illegal?"

His voice was rough. "Something that was necessary but morally gray, not to mention illegal, dangerous, and probably stupid."

"And because it was illegal, you can't tell me about it." Did I believe him? I wasn't sure, and that was a giant problem.

He continued, either ignoring or not seeing the distrust in my face. "It's in the past. All I want is for our marriage to thrive, to keep rebuilding our lives in Colorado, and be an uninteresting yet meaningful part of our community."

"One last question, I promise."

He sighed. "Fine."

I bit my lip. "This woman. Is she alright?"

Samuel's eyes softened. "I believe so."

We spent a half hour playing catch-up with each other's skin before Samuel had to catch his flight out of Denver. The air between us was strained, but I was able to forget the truths he had (and hadn't) revealed, at least for a time. I couldn't bear to let him fly off to New York without telling him I was still in this marriage, and I believed he felt the same. Wasn't that a form of trust?

His suitcase was packed and ready at the door, yet we were still in bed. He straddled my back and ran fingers along my spine, dug thumbs into my shoulder blades. He cupped my bottom.

"Come here, let me put my arms around you before I have to go." I crawled into his warmth.

"Tell me about your book."

"I promised you mountains, remember? For our anniversary?"

"But we're already writing about mountains together."

"And we'll continue to work on *Hydraulic Level Five.* This is another fantasy series. A wife and her husband—the heroes—buy property in the foothills of the Rockies. On this property is an entrance to an old mine shaft."

"Hmmm. Familiar."

He kissed my forehead. "'Write about what you know.' But this is where the story skews from reality. One day, the wife goes into the mine shaft and vanishes. See, it isn't only a mine shaft. It's an ancient portal that can carry a person to different mountain ranges, all over the world. The conundrum is, how do you control where the portal carries you? She tries to return, but the portals shift. The woman has nothing on her, no identification, no money, only the clothes on her back. She tries to work her way home. Meanwhile, her husband hunts for her, travels from mountain to mountain to find her."

"Does he find his wife in the mountains?"

"They find each other, eventually. It just takes time." He gently poked my ribs. I laughed and squirmed. He held me tighter and trailed his lips along my neck, breathing in our scent. "I love you, Aspen Kaye Cabral. Too much for reason."

"I love you, Sam." I kissed his chest, brown hair tickling my nose. "I'm glad you're writing a new series. I think it's brave of you to admit when something isn't working and start from scratch. It can't be easy to shelve three years of work."

"Honestly, it's freeing. I feel excited again, passionate about what I'm putting onto paper."

"What's the rest of the series about?"

Blue eyes danced. "The husband and wife travel mountains together, solve mysteries and hunt down bad guys, of course. The Sherlock Holmes of modern mountaineering."

"Ooh, you could send them to the Himalayas, maybe Bhutan or Nepal. Did you know Everest is exactly twice as high as our Mount Elbert? Doesn't that blow your mind? They'd need oxygen masks, though, and a Sherpa guide. They are the most amazing climbers, it's unreal how fast they are. Can you write in a Sherpa?"

Samuel chuckled. "I'll write a dozen Sherpa. An army of Sherpa ninja warriors who fight an epic battle over the Khumbu Icefall."

"That would be hazardous. The Khumbu Icefall has terrible avalanches." My eyes blurred on a random object across the room, seeing that blue and battered hand, trapped in a landscape of pure white.

"Kaye? Kaye." Samuel jostled my body, bringing me back. "Don't return to that place, *mi vida*. Just forward."

I rubbed my cheek against his bicep. "Hector asked us to climb Torreys Peak this weekend. You'll be out of town and Luca's wife is having the baby any day now, so it would just be the two of us. Are you okay with it?" I searched his face for any sign of discomfort. His mouth lifted in a telling, overly easy smile.

"Yes. Just let Hector know if you start to panic, okay? Last I heard, no one's giving out medals for bravery on Torreys Peak."

Apart from the occasional business trip, Samuel and I never traveled without the other. I could count on one hand the number of times we'd slept apart since remarrying. Even when we circled each other like hyenas in the sun, come nightfall we shared a bed.

I couldn't sleep. The possibility that Samuel had been involved with the Zacatóns, even in a minor capacity, blared through my head like an emergency siren. No matter how much Samuel downplayed it, "pissed off a few people" did not sound minor.

Earlier, I'd been gleeful with the prospect of sprawling across the entire mattress, all to myself. I'd stolen Samuel's pillow and propped myself up with a book and a slice of French silk pie from the deli. But once the lights went out, our sheets were too cold without the warmth of Samuel's body. The room was too quiet without his soft snores.

The French silk pie had been a bad idea. Sugar trembled through my veins and I flipped and flopped, kicked off the covers, and finally rose. When one isn't sleepy enough for sleep, one cleans. I dug out an arsenal of spray bottles and sponges from the laundry closet and tackled the kitchen floor, the counters and floorboards, then the bathrooms until exhaustion crept into my muscles and fogged my brain. Not long after one a.m., I collapsed into bed. Sleep should have come quickly and peacefully in the satisfaction of a spotless home, but my mind was as relentless as a summer drought.

Won't go back to Tamaulipas…

Should our new home have a first floor laundry or second floor laundry?

Pissed off a few people…

What about a mud room? Definitely a mud room, especially for *el changuito* and his sibling.

Did something illegal...

A toy room would be a nice addition, or even a few well-placed baskets filled with toys.

Of course, if Samuel changed his mind someday about children, we'd want a toy room.

A darker idea—would we need some sort of safe room? It would be too easy for a Zacatón mercenary to slip into the immigrant communities of Colorado. If we had a family in the future, we'd need extra security measures.

It's in the past...

My mind needed a safe room. Soon, my thoughts drifted into tangible imaginings of a small, warm body curled into my lap, of whispered nursery rhymes and hugs from tiny arms, and before I could chide myself for indulging in dreams that could never happen, my mind gave way to weariness and I slept.

Chapter 9
WHIPPER

When a climber takes a significantly long and hard fall, enough to lift the belayer into the air and past the first point of protection.

Hydraulic Level Five [WORKING TITLE]
Draft 1.109
© Samuel Caulfield Cabral and Aspen Kaye Cabral
COLORADO IS FOR BOTANISTS

Aspen knows she's in for a wild ride when H calls at two a.m. and tells her to pack her ski gear, they're not just climbing Torreys Peak. They're skiing Dead Dog. So here she is, lugging not only her hiking pack, but skis and poles up the trail ridge toward the "saddle" between Torreys and Kelso Mountain. When she was a child, she'd peer at the mountains through the car window as her mom drove down I-70 and she'd imagine a giant Pecos Bill who rode the "saddle" between the peaks. Now she squints up at the saddle and, through the sun of early spring, sees a cowboy's outline in the clouds. Her eyes water. Though the sun is low, it blazes against her black fleece, which haywires her nerves all the way down to her frigid toes as she mucks and sucks through snowmelt.

The ascent is not bad, but whoever set the boot pack must've had a stride the size of her imaginary cowboy giant. By the time they reach the top of the snowy apron, Aspen will be walking like him, too.

Torreys Peak is named for a botanist, of all professions. She's met plenty of rough-and-tumble botanists in her Colorado adventures, but she can't shake the image of John Torrey as a bespectacled, lily-faced researcher, bending over seedlings in a Columbia University greenhouse.

Once, she joked about this to Caulfield. He didn't find it funny.

"Scientists have an undeserved "nerd rep," simply because they're curious about the natural world. If not for the 'nerd scientists,' the backcountry would not have been explored and catalogued."

"True."

"How can you possibly consider explorers like Lewis and Clark 'fragile'? Or Linnaeus, Carver, Mendel, even Beatrix Potter?"

"Well, the last one wrote bunny books."

Caulfield eyes Aspen the way a vegan eyes a hot dog. As a child, he was the owner of a plethora of botany books, not to mention a rock collection that claimed a whole bookcase.

She kicks it in gear to catch up with H. Torreys Peak ducks above the trail ridge…just a couple more hours to the technical. She thrusts her hand in her pocket. Even through gloved fingertips, she feels the familiar edges of the Rose of Sharon rock, smooth and cold. A few years ago, she plucked it from Bear Creek in the middle of an epic fight with Caulfield at Maria's wedding rehearsal cookout, of all places. She gave it to him as a memento (of what, she's not sure. Their lost childhood? A relationship gone sour?) Caulfield must have read it with a dose of optimism, because he returned it to her—a good luck charm—to carry in her pocket when she climbed.

Her mind sees him waking in a New York hotel bed, bleary-eyed and rumpled, the staleness of a good sleep clinging to his skin. Is it ten o'clock there? He's already showered and shaved, buttoned into an immaculate suit, and off to his publisher in the Bertelsmann building.

She rubs the Rose of Sharon rock and picks up her pace.

H is bounds ahead, a blue push-pin in a map of white.

Her friend always treats her as an equal and though he's slowed his gait to allow her to catch up, H hasn't taken any of her gear. It's fine. She doesn't expect special treatment because she's a woman. Still, Caulfield would have at least offered. She would refuse, of course, but the gesture alone would have burned in her heart.

It's unfair to compare what H does to what she *thinks* Caulfield would do, so she concludes she's spoiled rotten, hitches up the skis strapped to her back, and boots through eight inches of snow.

"Thought I'd lost you to the mountain goats!" H calls above the roar of the wind and points across the snowfield to several goats on slope crags, hooves tucked beneath their bellies.

He says something else she can't catch so she taps her bad ear and shrugs. He points to a solo skier at the base of Mount Kelso. They wave him over.

"How's the snow?" Aspen asks.

The skier wipes his face. "Blowing powder over rocks, fine as flour. I'd take a different set of tracks." He gestures to footprints leading up the northeast face of Grays, sparkling white and washed in morning sunlight.

Turns out, the tracks belong to one of the mountain goats. The goat has a smaller stride than the giant cowboy, and now she has no trouble keeping up with H. Soon they trudge into the saddle between Grays and Torreys, and it's just a quick jaunt up the summit. Well, as quickly as a mountaineer can jaunt through five feet of snow, when said mountaineer is five-foot-two.

At last, she and H stomp onto the summit overlooking Denver, smug and on top of the world.

"Hey H, did you know this massive piece of rock is named after a *botanist* from New York City? Isn't that funny?"

He gasps in faux horror. "*New York City?* Hilarious!"

Sam—how's your trip? Are you coming home tonight?—K

Kaye—I'm not even sure how you want me to react. Is this chapter some sort of passive aggressive vent? Are you upset because I believe your botanist joke isn't funny, or is it something else?

Samuel—I just want to share my climb with you and tell you, in my own way, how I miss you despite your 'awesome' attitude about the botanist joke. Are we really wasting page space on something so silly?

Kaye—I'm positive I don't need to bring this to your attention: you intentionally drew a stark contrast between your husband and the man you spend time with when your husband is away. Take my name off this chapter—I want nothing to do with it.

Sam—Can we take this from email to phone?

I reread the chapter I'd sent to Samuel. Admittedly, I'd taunted an already snarling tiger. I knew I'd made a mistake in writing about my Torreys Peak climb while I was still upset, but that little friend called "rationalization" got in the game:

He needs to know what you're thinking, doesn't he? How he hurts your feelings. How you are trying to be the bigger person. Besides, he hid things from you, too. He ticked off a drug cartel!

True. But he hid it to protect you. Just like you hid your desire for a baby to protect him. You both made crap calls.

Sadly, this seemed to be our MO.

It doesn't have to be.

An hour after our heated email exchange, my phone rang, cutting short this flash of hopefulness.

"Hey Samuel." I was outside, viciously scrubbing my hiking boots clean of caked mud.

"What just happened?"

"I think we had our first e-fight. Not bad for three-and-a-half years of marriage."

I heard the buzz of what sounded like a cocktail party in the background, but it grew fainter and then ceased altogether. "Kaye, listen. I know when I left for New York, the air between us wasn't great. Well, it was amazing right before I left. Really, really amazing…"

I shook my head, smiling in spite of myself. "One track mind, I swear. Are you at a party?"

"Dinner and drinks, celebrating the new book deal. Honestly, it's turned into more of a party. I stepped out, but I think I'll call it an early night. There are only so many mocktails I can swill. Bottom line: I overreacted to the story about Hector in your writing and I apologize. But firecracker…I think you wanted to make me jealous."

"That's ridi—"

"You're kidding, right?" His tone sharpened. "I'm trying to talk to you and you're going to discount me?"

"No! Why on earth would I want to make you jealous?"

"Because you're angry with me."

"About the woman with Zacatón ties? Scared out of my mind, maybe, but not angry. I understand—"

"You're angry because I don't want to have children. You want to hurt me the way I've hurt you, and the quickest and easiest way to do that is to throw Hector in my face—that tried-and-true fallback. Then you cushion those barbs with passages about how you love me, how you appreciate my kindness, so you can label your bitchiness as honesty."

"Excuse me?"

"You know I'm right." I heard a muffled question from what sounded like a female. Samuel told her "no" and "goodnight."

"Was that a woman from your publicity team?"

"Who else would it be?" Sam paused. "Are you jealous, Kaye Cabral?"

My cheeks heated. I didn't know whether to be pissed or turned on. I jumped to my feet and paced the small balcony like a caged ferret. *Rein it in, Kaye. He's still coming down from his last episode.*

"What I know is I've married a man who refuses to share himself with me. You take, take, take, keep taking until I'm stripped bare, yet you're buttoned and zipped so tight, I have to move mountains to get anything from your mind." *And that was reining it in? Well done, Kaye.*

Samuel's voice rose to match mine. "What more do you want? I *have* given you everything. My writing. My broken mind. Every damned fear."

"Then why didn't you tell me you were involved with the Zacatón Cartel?" I all but hissed into the phone.

"Because I want to protect you from—"

"Drug thugs? Or maybe you wanted to protect yourself." My neighbor halted halfway to his mailbox and peered at me, and it hit me how quickly our fight had escalated. But we'd always fed off of the other's emotions, even when we were children. I lowered my voice. "It's like you have this deep need to make people believe you're a saint. Sam—I know you're not perfect. I love you anyway."

"I love you, too. And yes, perhaps I have hidden my interactions with this woman because she reminds me of a time I was ruled by drugs and illness, and I never want to be that man again. God knows it's selfish and unfair, but some days I'm dangling over the edge of a cliff with only a few fingers gripping sanity, and it's all I can do to keep myself from tumbling over." He sighed. "But my failures aside, we can't make the animosity between us go away by saying 'I love you.' This fighting…it's too much."

"What do you suggest?" I said quietly.

"I don't know. Counseling?"

I dropped into a chair, the metal cold on my back. "Together or separate?"

"Together, of course. Marriage counseling."

"Fine. But the only way this will work is if we do it right. No more hiding things."

"That goes both ways, Kaye."

I rubbed my eyes, exhausted. "Do you want to call, or do you want me to?"

"I suggested it. I'll call."

"Alright. Back to my original question—you'll be home tonight?"

"I'm planning on it, as soon as I check out of this hotel. I'll catch a redeye."

Despite Samuel's plans, he did not return from New York Saturday night. Berkshire House's marketing team asked (begged) him to attend a launch party for an author whose sales needed a boost. I grumbled but saw the necessity. His professional image needed polishing, so it was the perfect opportunity to drop bread crumbs about his freshly inked deal to write the mountaineering series. "Keep the bloggers buzzing," he told me early Sunday morning.

"That's two parties in a handful of days. How's your health?"

"I'm okay. I'll definitely be home Tuesday night. We'll repair this, together."

Which meant I had to explain to an already concerned Sofia why her son skipped out on one of their most treasured family holidays. His head on a platter, not mine.

After lunch on Palm Sunday, she pulled me into their quiet library.

"He's not in trouble again, is he? Is the bipolar making him out of control?"

"No, nothing like what happened in Boston. He's kind of volatile right now, but life's also been volatile, and I haven't been the easiest of people. It's a perfect storm."

Sofia wrapped her warm, pillowy arms around me. "I know, *mi corazón*. I see more than you think I see."

Of course she did. She was a mother.

<hr>

Monday night passed, and no word from Samuel. I assumed he planned to return tomorrow, though doubt and dread stomped through my head.

Wrapped in a throw blanket, I toyed with its tassels as I watched the sun sink below the mountains. The spring breeze still carried a hint of snow and a shiver ran up my back. My phone rested on the patio table beside me, silent.

I should call him.

No, I should give him space.

I picked it up, scrolled through my recent calls, then cursed and dropped it on the table. A pick-up truck bellyached and lurched into the parking lot across the street. Hector. Seeing my blanket-burritoed form, he saluted.

"Hey *mamacita*. How're the calf muscles?"

I groaned. "As stiff as a corpse's. I'm way too out of shape to ski Dead Dog like we did."

"Nonsense, you owned that little bitch." He peered behind me, into the apartment. "The ol' ball and chain back yet?"

"Nah, not 'til tomorrow. Change of plans." He plopped next to me, at the base of the stairs. "What brings you to this neck of the woods?"

"I was at the hospital to see the Guzmans' new baby. Looks a whole lot like Luca."

"Which means she'll have a baby face forever, sweet girl." Luca was known for (and plagued by) his angelic, baby-like face. I tucked my knees into my chest. "Do you ever think about it, Hector? Having kids?"

"With you? Sweetheart, I'm flattered!"

I shoved his shoulder. "Be serious."

Humor drained from Hector's face, and he suddenly seemed worn down, weathered. "I dunno, Kaye. With our risky lifestyles, kids would suffer."

"You wouldn't give up the dangerous stuff for them?"

"Sure I would. But I'd hate it, you know? Miss it, too. I mean, you gave it up for Samuel. Don't you miss it?"

"Half the time I'm scared out of my mind to try it again, and the other half I miss the rush so much, I physically tremble like a junkie. Isn't that insane?"

"Nope, it's an addiction. I know I'm addicted and I'm fine with it. If I go down in flames someday, I won't regret that last hit. It makes me feel…like I'm a god, and I've seen the world from places regular folks never tread. I've been awakened."

A cold finger of fear poked me. Hector was strong, invincible. Nothing would ever bring him down. "And if you went down in flames, where would this leave Tricia?"

"Sometimes I wonder if I was meant to marry Tricia." He looked at me. "I wonder if I was meant to marry someone else. My soul mate."

I looked at the ground. "There is no 'meant to,' Hector. Your soul mate is the person you choose to give your soul to. If you made the choice that she's it for you—which you did when you married her, may I remind you—then she will be. But you've got to be in it together. It sounds like Tricia's in it for the long haul."

"You're right. Absolutely." His tone lightened. "And listen, I love you. You know I do, and I always will. I think you could have been a person I'd give my soul to."

"Hector—"

"But it takes two, right? You've never been into me like that. I get it. You gave yourself to him before I was even in the picture."

"Think of how happy you and Tricia could be. Let *her* be your adrenaline rush, not the stupid stuff like skydiving in the rain and cliff-hucking."

He nodded at my advice, but I might as well have given it to a polar bear. "Do you ever see Jaime?" he asked.

"No. I think she wishes that avalanche had carried me off three years ago."

"Don't say that. Her pride was hurt, but she cared about you, as much as Jaime can actually care about someone."

"I think her feelings run a lot deeper than anyone gives her credit for."

"Yeah, *mamacita*, you're probably right. *Todo está bien.*" He slapped his palms on his knees and hopped up. "Let's grab dinner. I need to reclaim my man badge after all this talk about feelings."

I tossed my blanket inside the door and yanked on my shoes. "Perfect. I could kill for a burger and fries."

***

My jeep rumbled along the rutted dirt road Tuesday after work, the faded Spanish signs and Madonna statues of the Mexican-American neighborhood in my rear view mirror. I hadn't been down this private drive in ages, not since Jaime Guzman told me to "go fuck a duck" (her words, not mine), and slammed the door in my face. But Dani suggested I swing by.

"I saw her at the diner the other day, alone. She looked sad," Danita had said as I left the Cabral home on Palm Sunday.

Of course Jaime was sad and alone. That's what happened when one alienated their friends and family. But I'd always grieved the premature end to our friendship, twisted though it was, and with great leeriness I sought her out.

Her car still ticked as it cooled in her driveway. Just as I reached her back steps, she pushed through the door, already changed into chore clothes, kibble bucket in one hand and an unidentifiable tub in the other.

Her eyebrows shot up and she froze. Then she strode past me with a casual nod, as if we'd only spoken three days ago. "Hey, Kewpie doll. What can I do ya for?"

"Just thought I'd swing by."

She snorted. "You're the crappiest liar this side of anywhere. Let me guess—your sister-in-law told you I was hoarding pain pills and razor blades after she saw me eating at the diner all by myself."

"Something like that."

"Ridiculous. I was waiting for a client. Woman and her ex spent four hours arguing over the meat in their deep freeze. Cost them three hundred an hour on both sides. While you're here, you might as well entertain me as I clean out the kennels." Jaime raised purebred Labradors. She swore they were better company than humans.

I racked my brain for something that would entertain a semi-sadist. "What do you want to know?"

"I see you and your nutcase husband are doing that benefit concert again. Fourth Annual such-and-such, blah blah."

Indignation fizzed. "Watch it, Guzman. No one likes a playground bully."

She scoffed but dropped the name-calling. "I assume volunteers get into this thing for free, right? With food vouchers?"

"Are you volunteering?"

"I wouldn't mind a day at Planet Bluegrass. Hold this."

She handed me a plastic tub of what looked like ground up raw meat and smelled like it, too. I wrinkled my nose. "Please don't tell me you've murdered someone and are feeding them to your dogs."

"Relax. He was a Denverite."

We talked for the next hour as she dished up something I wouldn't feed my worst enemy, but swore up and down liver was the Godiva chocolate of doggy world.

"How's that caveman ex of mine? Still wrapped around your wrist like a slap bracelet?"

"Let's not talk about Hector, okay?"

"Does he ever ask about me?"

I squirmed, uncomfortable with this line of questioning. "Jaime. He's married."

"Doesn't stop *you* from spending time together."

"But we've only ever been friends."

"Have you?" She scratched the neck of one of her dogs. Its tongue lolled happily, and a string of drool dropped from its mouth onto her knee. She wiped it off with her sleeve. "He would have stayed with me forever if I hadn't broken it off when I did. Man was in for a world of hurt. As my ex-husband is so fond of telling people, I'm the type of crazy that makes men sleep with one eye open." She gave a strange, brittle kind of laugh. I'd long ago learned her hackles hid a soft underbelly. "I give it another two years."

"Can we not put an expiration date on their marriage?" I snapped. "Allow them a fighting chance."

"Be honest, Kaye-bear. We know Hector's type and we know Tricia's type. She'll want him to stop with the dangerous stunts and have babies. He'll complain she's trying to cage him like a damned bird and 'babe, don' you know that birds gotta fly free?'" I smothered a chuckle. Jaime's 'Hector' impression was spot on. "That's how it'll go down, I bet a million bucks. Isn' dat right, puppy? Such a good boy." The dog nuzzled her face.

She didn't know how spot on she was, though I'd never divulge it. I had been just like Hector for seven years, romanced by the adrenaline rush before Samuel came back into my life.

"A man typically chooses his family over a woman," she continued. "In this case, Hector's 'family' isn't Tricia. It's the guys at Paddlers." For a misanthrope, Jaime often had keen insight into humanity. Being a divorce lawyer will give that to you. But being a divorce lawyer will also make you a misanthrope.

"Is there any situation in which a man will choose a woman over his family?" I asked.

"Sure. If she's family, too."

My eyes widened and my feet rooted in place.

Holy mother.

My mind raced back to Samuel's mystery woman, and the questions I'd struggled to answer aligned with Jaime's bit of wisdom, now perfectly clear.

Samuel's mystery woman in Tamaulipas wasn't a girlfriend. *She was family.*

Perhaps I was overreacting. Maybe this woman was simply a distant relative or friend that Samuel felt obligated to support. But an entanglement with the Zacatóns? Not even his inflated sense of chivalry would drive him to risk his family's safety.

Unless she was also family.

A close cousin? No, Mariángel wouldn't have banned him from the home.

A relative on Sofia's Llorente side of the family, then. But wouldn't *Tía* Lucia have known...what was it she'd said? Mariángel had accused Samuel of being a drug addict and philanderer, just like Antonio... *because Antonio had an affair with a local girl...* Like that, out of the bluest of blue, it hit me.

A sister.

It was so ridiculous I wouldn't know Sam had a biological sister, but entirely possible. Occam's Razor: the simplest solution. My mind fitted together the puzzle pieces. He had a half-sister somewhere in Tamaulipas, someone the Cabrals wouldn't have claimed because of Antonio's affair. *Especially* if the cartels were mixed up in this. But the minute he discovered it, Samuel would have searched for her regardless of the family's warnings, because that's what you did when you were an adopted kid and you found out you had a biological sister. There was no other explanation that made as much sense, no other reason he'd risk a falling out with the Cabral *familia* and an entanglement with criminals. Only love would have driven him to do it.

And if he had a sibling with ties to the Zacatón Cartel...

My hands were clammy. I tried to shake them out, but they were welded to the steering wheel so tightly, my arms trembled. Oh crud, a panic attack was coming on. Somehow, I got myself to the side of the road before it hit. My chest ached. I gasped and gasped, never able to inhale enough air. Tears leaked from the corner of my eyes. I opened my mouth and sucked in air again, a gaping fish struggling to find water.

Breathe.

Breathe.

I rolled down my car window and rested my head on the frame, incanting:

I want to feel good. I want to feel good. Feel the upholstery under your hands. See how soft it is, against each tiny groove on the pads of your fingers? Feel your feet resting solidly on the floor mat? Ground yourself, Kaye.

Minutes later, I wiped my sweaty face with my discarded sweater and breathed cold, fresh, spring air, deeply and fully. I had to be rational about this. Letting my emotions control me would not get the answers I desired from my husband.

My husband. *Oh no.*

My head thudded against the seat rest.

Samuel was home by the time I slipped through our apartment door. His suitcase was already unpacked and I heard the washer and dryer tumbling in the laundry closet, so he'd been back for a good while. I should have called to tell him I'd be late.

I fell onto our bed, drained. He emerged from our closet with a dress shirt and hanger in hand.

"Hey. I was worried."

Sam looked at me more closely, my splotchy face, streaked mascara, and crossed the room to take me into his arms. The hanger in his hand dug into my back.

"You had another panic attack. I know you don't want to, but we need to bring this up when we start therapy. Or perhaps we should try a specialist this time—"

I shifted out of his arms and he dropped them to his sides, confused.

"Samuel, I have to ask you something really important. I don't need details, but I do need the truth."

"Alright." He slipped the shirt over the hanger and hung it on a dresser knob.

"Do you have a half-sister?"

He halted, and then his restless fingers burrowed into his dark hair. I absently noted that he needed a haircut. Finally, he nodded.

"Is she affiliated with the Zacatón Cartel?"

"Not anymore."

"Do you still keep in touch?"

"No. Five years ago, the last time I was there, I paid money—a great deal of money—to help her disappear into the States. We haven't been in contact since, for safety reasons." His eyes narrowed. "How do you know this? No one knows I have a sister, not even my parents."

"Are you sure?"

He thought. "My Aunt Mariángel might have suspected, but she never pursued it. The Zacatóns…they're evil, Kaye, and that's putting it lightly. Please understand why I don't want to involve you anymore than necessary. The less you know, the better."

"I understand." My voice shook. "Just one more question, though. Have you ever, in any way, aligned yourself to the Zacatóns?" His silence spoke volumes. I groaned and bent over, resting my head between my knees.

"If anything, I've made myself an enemy by helping her run. Her maternal uncle was in deep with the Zacatón Cartel."

"Do they know it was you who helped her escape?"

"Not really. It's complicated."

"Oh dear lord," I groaned again. "I don't want to know."

He gingerly touched me between my shoulder blades. "Now do you see why I won't go back to Tamaulipas, ever? I made enemies when I helped her escape, but they didn't know my identity. I'd like to keep it that way."

I closed my eyes. The fear I'd pushed down only an hour ago reared its ugly head, but I held it at bay. "Who did you pay to help her escape?"

"There's bad blood between the cartel and a radical group of hackers on the Dark Web who call themselves 'Unknown.' I used them to get the documentation she would need to start a new life in the U.S."

"I've heard of them before." Vague clips from nightly news stories about the hacktivist group attacking corporations and government sites ran through my mind, their Guy Fawkes masks always prominently featured in flashy graphics. They were everything that was right and wrong about the internet: so loosely centralized, they had no agenda and no common morals and members did everything from protect freedom of information, to cyber-bully preteen gamers.

Apparently, they also sold fake passports.

"So the cartel could potentially trace you. Oh my God, Samuel."

"If it makes you feel better, all interactions were done via a third party. No one could connect my name and face."

"That you know of."

"And most of the Zacatóns with whom my sister was involved are now dead or in jail."

"Jail doesn't seem to deter criminal activity."

"They were henchmen of Treiño-Herrera. When he was extradited to the U.S. and incarcerated in a federal prison, his followers scattered. The bottom line is, I believe I'm in the clear after five years, but better safe than sorry."

"Treiño…that's your father's second *apellido*. Sofia said the Cabrals' Treiños weren't any relation to the Nuevo Laredo Treiños."

"They aren't. But back in the day, his last name sure caught the eye of a girl whose older brother was a smuggler for the Nuevo Laredo Treiños." Samuel stretched across our bed, but his bunched muscles revealed he was anything but relaxed. "She was barely an adult," he muttered, "but she became my father's mistress. She thought he was someone powerful, not a washed-up, crooked lawyer from Boston."

"You mean, this all began when a teenager propositioned Antonio Cabral Treiño because she thought he was part of the Treiño crime family in Nuevo Laredo? And he totally *went* with it?" I sank onto the bed beside him.

"Yep. My birth dad was a real winner."

"Let me see if I've got this. This affair produced a daughter whom nobody, save you, knows about. The daughter gets caught up with this dangerous drug cartel, but she wants out. So you paid mucho dollars to a hacktivist group on the Dark Web to illegally smuggle your sister into the U.S., thus ticking off said dangerous drug cartel. Now you steer clear of Mexico to stay off their radar. Sam…" I shook my head, stunned. "And you call skydiving dangerous?"

Samuel ran a hand through his hair, sheepish. "There's a bit more, but that's the crux of it."

Stuff like this didn't happen to people from Lyons, Colorado. "You can't ever go back," I rushed on. "I don't want us to end up on a *Forensic Crimes* episode."

He reached for my limp hand. I let him take it. "I promise, Aspen Kaye. Believe me, no one wants me to live more than myself. Now let's never speak of this again. I don't want you entangled in this."

I bobbed my head, speechless.

"Kaye? I hate that you know. But…I'm glad that you know."

Once again, it hit me that I would never fully know Samuel Caulfield Cabral: husband, childhood friend, baseball golden boy, brilliant and mentally complicated artist, former drug user and, seemingly, duper of deadly drug cartels.

At least he'd come clean with the truth, crazy though it was. And because he'd told the truth, a bit of trust chiseled through that wall.

Chapter 10
GOING TO CHURCH

*When climbers skip Sunday church services
to tackle a mountain.*

I needed a change, so I grasped the most immediate, most attainable form of change that wouldn't leave me jobless, homeless, or limbless.

The day before Easter, I went to HeadCase Hair Salon.

Cynthia, the owner, was one of TrilbyJones' first clients. In fact, the salon's name was mine and Molly's brainchild (which might have been projection). But it lent itself well to quirky ad campaigns and became a favorite among the CU students who bothered with haircuts.

I watched Cynthia in the mirror from her styling chair as she fluffed my long curls.

"Chin-length? Are you sure?"

"Absolutely."

"That's what I like to hear—confidence. I'm going to bob it, glam it up silent film style, like Anita Page." Ooh, old Hollywood. Cynthia knew my kinks. "I'm thinking coifed curls."

"I'm thinking you're a genius."

"I'll show you how to fix it…"

A half hour later, six-inch clumps of wet hair were scattered under the chair and I turned my head, eyeing the new cut. My giddiness soured because I did not see Anita Page glam. Just Kaye, but with an old lady haircut (lacking the strange blue rinse that had permeated the church potlucks of my childhood). "Wow. I look older."

"Not older. Professional." She studied me, her red penciled eyebrows shrewdly slanted. "Hmm, I know that look. Not happy?"

"I like it. It's just…" I sighed and tugged at a short blonde curl, let it spring.

"You can relax your curls."

"Not enough."

"You want me to take off more?"

"Definitely not, it'll be a ball of frizz." I tapped my chin. Well, if I was going to embrace my inner granny, I might as well do it thoroughly. "Let's go blue. Bright blue."

"You serious?"

"Absolutely."

Later, when I returned home, Samuel mumbled a "hello" from behind the screen of his laptop.

I shook my cerulean-hued waves and dumped my purse and jacket on the table next to the door. My dress felt confining in the comfort of my home, so I unzipped it and shrugged it off on my way to the bedroom. Oops! A resounding "*¡Pollas en vinagre!*" hit the walls behind me.

As I hung my dress in our closet, Samuel's arm snaked around my bare waist. I stiffened automatically. Crap. Before he could retreat, I turned around and wrapped my arms around his waist.

"Do you think I look like your *abuela* with a blue rinse?"

Wary eyes searched my face. Hands skimmed my hipbone, all the way up to the ridges of my neck, now missing its heavy curtain.

"If *Mamá* Marieta had paraded around like a blue-haired Betty Page, *Tia* Mariángel would have had her committed." He lowered his lips and I sighed, having missed his touch for too long. "Let's leave my grandmother out of this conversation."

I traced the contours of his chest over his tee shirt. He flinched in that good way, the one that told me he desired my touch. "Let's leave the conversation out of this conversation…"

Reactions to my experiment in geriatric fashion varied.

"Only pop stars and teenagers have blue hair," Dani said, pointing at my locks. I noted that her fingernails sparkled with purple glitter.

"Nonsense. The Queen Mother wore it very well."

Thanks Alonso.

"How festive. Like an Easter egg," Sofia added, her dark eyes round with forced sincerity.

My cheeks flushed. "It's only temporary." I peeled an Easter egg and flicked pastel-dyed shell bits from my fingers. "I'm going to grow it out again, change it back to blonde in a couple of months."

Dani sagely nodded. "It's not exactly appropriate for a thirty-year-old professional."

Samuel rose to my defense. "Why live and die by the code of some fashion editor? I think Kaye looks sexy."

I winked at my husband, grateful. "It *is* growing on me."

"Then you should keep it." His eyes burned with candor. Despite our issues, he always captured me with the depth if his devotion.

Alonso shrugged and grabbed a bright pink boiled egg. "*Niños.*"

One night several weeks later, Samuel went to bed early so I mellowed on the balcony of the old TrilbyJones Victorian. Hidden in the cluster of trees across the street was a pair of Great Horned Owls. Their gravelly hoots had reached through the window and called me outside (Molly said the Audubon Society named the Great Horned Owl the "Barry White of birds"). I cradled my guitar in my lap and strummed soft chords until I matched their pitches. Not content to leave the crazy on the strings, I added lyrics. The owls hooted and again, I strummed.

"Baby your screech and hoot and howl, makes me one Great Horny Owl, oh, oh, oh..."

No answer. Perhaps they'd heard it one too many times.

My ears attuned to the owls, I didn't miss a conspicuous rustle in the brush. I leaned forward, listened. Another rustle, then all was quiet.

My bad ear was acting up. I ditched my attempt at owl R&B and texted Molly:

Singing Barry White and thought of you.

Molly and I spoke every day about client projects, administrative issues, financials and investments. But we hadn't had a long, personal chat in over a month. She didn't text back, but moments later, my phone rang.

"I'm so glad you texted, but Barry White?"

"Owls."

"Oh, that makes sense." That, right there, was why Molly was my friend.

"I can't wait until our rafting trip at the end of May," she continued, "but it won't be the same without Angel. How is he? Have you heard anything?"

And so it went, as I caught her up on local news and she filled me in on life with Cassady in Alaska. "I hardly ever see him, our schedules are both so opposite. When we *are* together, sometimes I get the feeling he'd rather be alone, you know? It's still so cold here, but the light is coming back so I'm hoping we can get out into nature more, see Denali even."

I stared into the black backyard and froze when something moved. Yes, definitely a shadow shape against the silvery trees. Too tall to be a coyote. Deer? *No, it's human-sized.*

Freaked out, I abandoned my balcony and returned to the bright safety of my apartment.

I refocused on Molly, answering with "oh" and "hmm" and "goodness," wishing I could reach through my phone and pull her onto my balcony. We both needed an outlet, a friend. But she never asked about Samuel and I lost my nerve to blurt out "my marriage is rocky" without invitation. It was probably for the best. What was it my grandmother used to say? "Don't go to your girlfriends before you go to your man. If you blab about your marriage, it'll just make things worse when your gals give him the stink-eye."

Our marriage counseling began the first week of May. It was, to put it bluntly, a big, fat, blue-faced turkey.

SARAH LATCHAW

The therapist came highly recommended by one of my TrilbyJones colleagues, who had undergone sessions before his marriage ended in an all-out-brawl-of-a-divorce (that should have been a red flag about our new therapist).

"Mother of pearl, you're the one who insisted I climb mountains again with Hector, and now you turn around and accuse me of having an emotional affair?"

"I didn't say you're having an emotional affair. I said you might be in danger of one."

"So you don't trust me."

The therapist stroked his goatee as he leaned forward, barely disguising his glee in our fireworks. "Remember, Aspen, what we're doing is learning how to resolve conflict in a healthy way. You need to hear what Samuel is saying, not what you think he *meant* to say."

"It's Kaye," I growled for the tenth time.

"Mm-hmm." Joe jotted in a notebook. I hoped it was my correct name.

"I trust you," Samuel pressed, a bubbling pot on the verge of boiling. "But you have a big heart and sometimes you give too much of it away."

"We've beaten this dead horse for years, but has anything more ever come of my friendship—I stress *friendship*—with Hector? No! Because there is nothing there, Sam."

Embarrassment burned the back of my eyes and produced hot tears. "And I have to ask, is this paranoia truly *you*, or is it a side effect of your disorder?"

Samuel's face darkened considerably. "Even if it is my bipolar disorder talking, does that give you a green light to race right over my concerns?"

"Okay," Joe said brightly as he made another mark in his notebook. "Let's step away from this issue and go back to buying a black-market baby."

I threw my hands in the air. "I never said I wanted to buy a black-market baby! Only that we should consider nontraditional options." Now I had to face off with both my husband and my therapist?

"We've been blessed financially, and I'll not use it for questionable purposes." Samuel's voice was calm and patronizing; I was a shrieking banshee in comparison.

"So you were willing to pay off ….people with very bad morals to help your half-sister, but won't consider using our substantial resources to help us have children? Do you not see the hypocrisy here?"

"Careful, Kaye." Sam's eyes darted in warning to our therapist.

"Don't worry, Samuel. Therapy is confidential." Joe popped the collar of his yellow polo shirt. I wanted to pop him one in his face.

"How is it any different?" I argued.

"Saving this woman wasn't a choice. It had to be done."

"But both are doing a little evil for a greater good."

Samuel's voice rose. "Perhaps if I believed being a father was a 'greater good,' which I don't. Even if I did, I wouldn't do it."

"Why not?"

"Yes, why not, Samuel?" Joe Cool of the Popped Collar chimed in. I shot him my iciest glare.

"Because I've bargained with evil people to make evil go away, and all it did was perpetrate more evil."

I couldn't argue with this, but man, I wanted to. I felt like a bad person and in front of a complete stranger, to boot. Samuel may have won the argument, but it would be a bittersweet win.

Joe Cool wasn't letting us leave without one more piece of the action. He patted our backs as we filed out of his office. "The fighting? You may not believe it, but it's good." (I was fighting to keep in that eye roll—*this* was good.) "It shows me you still care about each other. Now, if all I'd witnessed was silent indifference, then we'd really have our work cut out for us." Okay. I could hang my hat on this bit of wisdom.

Turned out, Joe Cool was a prophet. Over the next week, silence hung between us like a soundproof drape, though our muffled words were louder than our shouts had been.

Sunday morning, I stretched and contorted my arms until I zipped myself into a chambray dress (Samuel didn't offer to help). Surely I could still dress myself. Cooking, cleaning, paying bills, taxes, servicing my car. I'd done it all alone for years but didn't relish the prospect. I also didn't relish that wretched absence of Samuel's company. Even as Samuel dressed beside me, knotted a tie at his near-perfect throat, he was here, but not here.

The shoes I'd selected had mud splatters, so I dashed to the closet for a last-minute switch.

Perhaps this wretchedness had nothing to do with Samuel and was simply inside of me.

Let's explore this a little, Kaye.

I dropped to my knees and dug through my pile of shoes until I found one of the flats I wanted.

Was it fair to ask Samuel to fill an emptiness he couldn't possibly fill?

No, that's on you and God.

But he could at least be a present partner. Where was my other shoe? I shoved a row of dresses aside.

I bet he thinks the exact same thing, Miss High-and-Mighty. Your shoe is behind the designer heels you never wear.

Sometimes, my internal voice of reason needed to buzz off. I unearthed the missing mate, slipped them both onto my feet, and jogged to the front door where Samuel waited.

We sat side by side in our church pew, the Cabral family on either side of us. To my left, Danita squirmed in discomfort, her ever-growing middle causing her lower back to ache. I bunched up my red wool coat and passed it to her. She tucked it behind her tailbone and squeezed my forearm in mute thanks.

I heard very little of the minister's sermon because my brain over-flowed. Did his family notice the ice between us? How would we ever get through a Sunday dinner? Heck, last month, Sofia had asked what was wrong before I'd even picked up my fork, and our relationship hadn't been nearly as strained, then.

As I stressed over Samuel, his fingers graze the top of my knuckles, soft, like tallgrass tassels. I glanced up to find his eyes already on me, dark and pleading. He offered me his hand again, and this time I took it.

My ears opened as I really heard what the minister spoke about—forgiveness.

Forgiveness from above. Forgiving others. Forgiving ourselves.

Easier said than done. No babies. No trust. No honesty. But there were two babies to my left. And my hand was in Samuel's…this was honest, wasn't it? Trusting?

Tension leaked away and I relaxed into the pew, content to sit in this moment of peace.

It would end soon enough, but for now, I embraced it.

Our truce extended into the afternoon, and we made it through our family dinner better than I'd anticipated (only one eyebrow raise from Sofia). I'd tensed when *el changuito* asked me if I was having a baby like his mommy. I played it off with a chuckle, asking him if he thought I'd eaten too many donuts like his mommy. Danita kicked me under the table.

She still seemed weary, slouching as if two invisible sandbags rested on her shoulders.

Beside her, Angel's empty chair wasn't empty at all—his absence was ever-present. But she'd video-chatted with him yesterday and today, so she managed to smile at her father's jokes.

After lunch, Samuel complimented his mother on the meal and rose from the table. He reached for my hand.

"Kaye and I are going to walk out to St. Vrain."

Sofia tsked. "She'll ruin her lovely shoes."

I flicked my wrist. "Oh, don't worry about it. I always keep a pair of sneakers in the car, just in case."

Alonso licked the last bit of pie from his fork. "Sofia does the same. Sensible, our women."

"That they are." Samuel winked at me, but there was no light in it. This wasn't a simple stroll along our creek, and soon his fear was mine. Was this it? Was he calling it quits on our marriage, cutting me loose again? Perhaps the hand-holding, the peace and kindness, the forgiveness I'd felt during the worship service had simply been *his* peace. His goodbye. By the time I'd laced on my sneaks and the creek's gurgles reached our ears, I'd worked myself into a frenzy. I wiped clammy palms against my coat.

Samuel turned to me, emotion flowing as cold as creek water. "Do you want a child enough to leave me?"

"What?" I asked, startled.

"A baby. Will you leave me if we don't have children?"

I exhaled and laced my fingers over my head. He wasn't ending our marriage. But then I really, truly listened. In a way, he was. Rather, he placed the choice at my feet.

Water lapped against the bank of the creek bed. Sunlight dappled the surface and I looked up, seeing for the first time that fragile leaves peppered the branches. Green had returned. My heart ached as I pondered his question. The persistent lump in my throat whenever an acquaintance announced they were expecting. Hearing clients chat about the quirky things their kids did, how they never knew how much love they had inside of them until they held their children for the first time.

But then I remembered the deep sorrow of living without Samuel.

"No. Our marriage comes first. I made a vow."

"I made a vow, too." He drew me into his arms and I went, reluctantly. Despite today's ceasefire, anger and bitter disappointment still twisted my insides. "And I told you we'd explore our options, didn't I?" His warm lips grazed my scalp as he breathed, coming to some sort of decision. "Very well. We'll research our options."

My head shot up. "Really?"

"Just research."

Hope burgeoned through the muck of disappointment. "I have piles of research already. Parenting with bipolar disorder, articles by doctors and therapists. International adoption guides, domestic adoption guides, foster care." I ticked them on my fingers. "There's even a support group in Denver for parents with mental illnesses who've been where we've been. There is so much information out there."

"Please don't get your hopes up, Kaye," Sam said quickly. "I don't think this is a wise idea, at *all*. Honestly, I believe any legitimate answers we're given will only lead to heartbreak. But I'm willing to listen to what people have to say."

My arms came around his middle, now completely willing. "Thank you so much. I love you, Samuel Caulfield Cabral. You are the most selfless man I've ever known."

Samuel sighed. "I love you, Aspen Kaye. Too much for reason."

Later, as the intense glow of happiness gave way to reflection, I realized this wasn't the first time he'd declared he loved me 'too much for reason.'

Chapter 11
FREE CLIMB

*When a climber chooses to summit a mountain without
the aid of manmade devices.*

The evening Tom Trilby showed up on our doorstep, duffel bag in
one hand and hookah in the other, was the night I knew my marriage was being put through some sort of trial by fire.

"Audrey found out about Gail and kicked me out."

"Wow Dad, that's rough." Now was not the time to say, 'I told
you so.'

"She also fired me."

"Understandable. So you don't have a job or a place to live?"

"Sounds about right."

"Come on in." I pushed the door open for him to enter and cringed
as a week's worth of body odor filled my foyer. He dropped his duffel
bag and stretched out on my couch. His Prius was absent from the
parking lot. Had he hitchhiked from Lyons? Mom's farm would have
been closer.

"Dad, can I ask why you didn't go to Mom?"

He flung a tanned arm over his face. "Aspen baby, that is one can
of worms I don't ever want to open."

"Are you going to tell Mom what happened, though?"

"She'll hear about it soon enough."

"She'd let you stay at the farm, you know. Maybe even give you work until you found something more permanent. There's loads to do right now, getting ready to plant."

"Flower, believe me, I know there's loads to do. Which is precisely why I'm staying out from under Gail's handkerchiefs. Her tomatoes were the death of us before and they'd kill us again."

I delved through the hall closet for travel-sized shampoos, soaps, toothpaste. "You don't know that. It's been twenty-five years."

"Oh, I know. Besides, things are rocky between us just now."

He wrapped up his filthy body in my favorite chenille throw blanket and I stiffened with repressed fury. "Because cheating's not as fun, now that Audrey knows?" Not so repressed after all.

"Watch your tongue. I may be a good-for-nothing, but I'm still your father."

"I'll get the guest room ready." I stormed down the hall before I said anything regretful, such as 'DNA doesn't merit respect.'

As dad rummaged through our refrigerator, Samuel helped me stretch a fitted sheet over the guest bed.

"How long is he staying?"

"I don't know. I don't think he knows. Do you mind?"

Samuel rubbed his neck. "The timing isn't ideal."

"What did you want me to do? Turn him out?"

"No, but I wish you would have discussed it with me first."

I started to argue but squelched the fiery words. "You're right. I should have run it by you before I let his drama through our door. Goodness knows we have enough of our own. But he's my dad."

Samuel grabbed a spare pillow from the closet and tossed it on the bed. "I know. I also know you've spent a lot of your life chasing his affection. How about we set some boundaries here?"

"What do you suggest?"

He leaned in and whispered. "Two weeks, then he needs to find a place of his own."

"A month," I countered, "and we help him financially if he still hasn't gotten a job."

"Three weeks, and if he hasn't found work, we talk about a loan."

That night, I sat on my sofa, tucked between the two most influential men in my life. A bowl of popcorn rested on my lap and three sets of eyes were glued to the inane comedy airing on our TV.

My dad, showered and as fresh-smelling as a summer garden thanks to a stockpile of rose-scented hotel shampoo, rubbed my neck like he used to when I was single digits and couldn't sleep. Just like that, tension melted away, leaving only resigned exasperation.

"How do you do it, Dad? Ensure no woman will ever stay mad at you?"

"I shouldn't really be telling my daughter this, but—"

"Never mind." I placed his hand back on my neck.

"I was only going to say that I'm not above admitting I'm a huge screw-up and I need the women in my life to make me a better man. I need you, too, flower. You're the only family I can count on."

Next to me, Samuel's fuming was so palpable I felt the heat. But I was too overwhelmed by the blissful hope my dad's words had cracked open.

That night, as I listened to the choking snores of my father in the room next to ours, I couldn't stifle my giddiness. My father needed me. When he was in trouble, he turned to *me* before he turned to anyone else. This meant something, didn't it? After all these years, was it possible this was the beginning of my dad's journey into adulthood? I could swing by over my lunch hour and take him to Fischer's Deli. He'd tell me about his job leads, we could hunt apartments together, or maybe a little bungalow out by Jamestown. We'd have meaningful talks about what he wanted from life or if he still loved my mom. He'd tell me he regretted missing out on stuff when I was young. I'd tell him I forgave him, because I had, long ago.

I fell asleep anticipating morning, when I would place a steaming cup of coffee in front of my dad and a bowl of our favorite generic cereal. I'd hug his shoulders and he'd pat my hand, and I'd tell him how glad I was to have him with me.

But when I stumbled into the kitchen just after dawn, bleary-eyed and wrapping a tattered bathrobe around my body, my father was not there. I peeked into the guest room, the balcony. Nothing. Samuel was out on his early morning run, and I briefly wondered if Dad had joined him, but dismissed the idea. When I returned to the kitchen, I spotted it—a small, square paper from my sticky pad, fluttering on the countertop with each pass of the rotating fan:

> Flower—my guy who sells incense (wink) knows a guy who might have a job as a property manager up near Cheyenne. Can't beat working outside with your hands. My buddy's putting me up, so no need to restock the fridge. –Dad

I crumpled the note in my fist, changed my mind and smoothed it across the cold granite. Then I grabbed a dispenser of clear packing tape and flattened several pieces over the top, sealing it to counter. It would remain there in case I got big, ridiculous ideas about my dad. I was a grown woman. Yet, now and again, those girlish wishes wouldn't stop humming in my ear.

Samuel came into the kitchen, scrubbing his wet hair with a towel. I hadn't even noticed he'd returned from his run. He read the note over my shoulder and chuffed.

"Let's hope the job pans out."

Pure anger streaked through me and I slammed my palm on the counter, over the note.

"Since when is being kind to my father an imposition?"

Samuel's face immediately tightened. "Did I so much as suggest he was imposing?"

"You did, last night."

"I simply want to see him get back on his feet and for once, keep the promises he's made to the women in his life."

"He worked at the Garden Market for fifteen years. He was with Audrey for fifteen years! How is that not commitment?"

"Again I ask, did I so much as suggest he's flaking out by going to Cheyenne?"

"It was implied."

He wrenched open the dishwasher, grabbed a cup from the rack, and set about making one of his disgusting kale smoothies. "Look Kaye, whatever wrongdoings you have floating around in your head, don't pin them on me. There was nothing subversive in my tone, no reason to read into sentiments that simply aren't there."

I promptly burst into tears. Samuel cursed and leaned against the counter, arms crossed as he waited for me to scoop up my spilled emotions. "I know. I'm sorry I tried to pick a fight. It's just..." I searched for words to express my deep disappointment. "I got my hopes up, you know? Despite the spectacularly unfair way he treated Audrey. Despite his messing around with my mother. I thought maybe I was different."

"You *are* different. You're his daughter and he loves you."

"But not enough to have anything beyond a superficial relationship."

Samuel crammed kale and blueberries into a blender. "I'm not defending his past actions or the haphazard way he has darted in and out of your life. The thing about Tom Trilby is, he's like Cassady. He gets restless because there's this emptiness inside of him and he thinks it can only be filled by the next job, the next new age practice, the next woman. But what he wants can't be filled up by any person, any profession, anything external he finds on this earth."

"Are you talking about God?"

"I think so. Yeah, I am." Samuel reflected. "He's the only thing I've found that tempers the restlessness. Everyone hungers for peace, but not everyone knows where to find it."

"I don't have much experience with that kind of peace, long-term, anyway. I mean, I've sat in a pew, I've felt peace, but it goes away when the next crisis hits."

"I suppose it comes down to believing this kind of peace is uninterrupted by crisis. That it persists, in spite of the next crisis."

I remembered peering into Samuel's hospital room after the terrible episode in Boston to find him praying with the priest. At the time, I'd been resentful that he'd allowed God into that hospital room before he'd allowed me. But I now knew I couldn't give the kind of peace that calmed a haunted mind. In fact, wasn't it terribly unfair to expect another person to be responsible for providing inner peace?

So was it fair for me, a thirty-year-old woman, to blame my father for not sticking around my apartment to make me happy?

I put away the empty bowl and cereal box I'd laid out for my dad. "Your comparison to Hippie hit the nail on the head. The way he squirms when his life becomes too settled, or the way he keeps Molly at a distance when she just wants him to lean on her." I put a glass under the faucet, not blinking as it flooded and water spilled over the rim. "We can wish they would change, we can try to make them change, but in the end, it's like asking the Rockies to pack up and move to Iowa. The only way it'll happen is if the mountains sprout legs."

"Or if someone gives them a push."

At some point, I'd closed the gap between us and rested my cheek on his chest. He rubbed my back. "It's time for my dad to move on," I whispered. "He stuck around Lyons for me. Not for Audrey or Mom, or the Garden Market. He waited until he knew I'd be okay, and then he moved on. This has to be enough."

"Whatever faults Tom has, he loves you, very much. I know it's hard to understand, especially as a child—leaving someone because you love them. But for those of us who have been toxic to the people we love, we thought we could give the people we love a better life if we weren't *in* their lives..."

"Sam, goodness knows I don't say this enough, but the way you've changed, the things you've overcome? It's a miracle."

He shook his head. "You didn't see the struggle. I tried, over and over, to change for you, for my family..."

"But in the end, you changed for yourself."

He nodded. "I couldn't bear to lose my soul."

———————— •◆• ————————

Later that week, we sat side-by-side on a couch as comfortable as granite, grim faced as we listened to the resource worker at Bright Hope Adoption Services.

"After you complete your evaluations, the next step in the application process is an extensive background check. Anyone with a felony offense on record is going to face a long, hard road. We can't even allow convicted felons to adopt internationally, per U.S. regulation." I internally cringed. Samuel wasn't a felon, but he'd come pretty darned close and only escaped jail because of Caroline Ortega's connections. Court-mandated drug rehab and AA meetings, community service, involuntary hospitalization...The way the worker eyed Samuel, I think she knew it, too. One couldn't live in Boulder without having heard, seen, or read about his infamy.

"If your background check's clear, then we'll conduct in-depth interviews where we focus on the stability of your relationships, conflict management, how you were raised. Please understand it's necessary to scrutinize everything about you in order to protect our kids. They deserve stable homes." We'd both have to lay ourselves bare as strangers combed through the most painful, intimate facets of our lives.

"Lastly, you must be absolutely certain this is what you *both* want. If one of you is on the fence, then my recommendation is not to pursue adoption. Trust me, if you're not all in, it will rip your marriage apart and only lead to heartbreak for your adopted children. I've seen it happen one too many times."

I closed my eyes, not wanting to hear the truth in her words. But I knew. Deep in my heart, I heard. Samuel didn't want kids. Out of his love for me and commitment to our marriage, he had tried to set his trepidations aside. What was it he'd said? *I love you, too much for reason...*

Now, because I loved him, I couldn't force this upon him.

I threaded my fingers through his, squeezed, and let go. Stony-faced, I gathered up my coat, purse, and reached across the table to shake the worker's hand.

"I appreciate your candor and willingness to meet with us. But I don't think adoption is an avenue we'll pursue, after all."

That night, I dreamed Samuel left. It was an old ghost from our college days, when I'd walked into our apartment to find him sprawled across our bed, despair exuding from weary limbs punished in a morning run. I jerked awake. He was still beside me. I wrapped myself around his warm body.

"Trouble sleeping?" he asked groggily.

"Nightmare. Sorry I woke you."

'S'okay, it's been a rough day." He cupped my cheek and, only then, I realized tears streamed down my face. "Lemme help." He fumbled around in the dark room until he found his Spanish guitar. Mellow chords twanged and he sang quiet lyrics about beds of lemon balm and fragrant jasmine. The lullaby echoed through my head and I remembered, just before sleep reclaimed me, that I'd heard Sofia sing it when we were children.

———————◆◆◆———————

Friday lunch at Paddlers, Luca brought a tiny guest. "Whoa Kaye, what did you do to your hair?"

I waggled 'gimme' hands for his new little one. "I joined the Blue Rinse Brigade. My knitting bag is in the car. Come here, sweet baby, Auntie Kaye wants to kiss you."

"You look like that crazy pop star, but without…" Luca clammed up and his face went red. I chuckled.

"Without the rack? That sounds about right." I peered down at the tiny tot rooting around for lunch and the even tinier chest beneath her. "Nothing to eat there, babe. But we've got plenty of pizza, nom nom nom." I cradled the infant and sighed as painful knots eased and loosened.

"What does Samuel think about the hair? Hey, where is he, anyway?"

"Conference call. And surprisingly, he loves it."

The door jingled and a young woman entered. She was Latina–strong jaw, high cheekbones, wide mouth. Her wavy black hair was pulled back in a mess of a ponytail, her clothing was rumpled and worn, cheap but sturdy, like something one would wear to hike through mountains. I nearly wrote her off as a tourist, but something about her…

She was striking, or would have been, if not for an air of uncertainty displayed in the hunch of her shoulders, her downcast gaze, crossed arms. *Shatterable*…that's how she seemed, as if she were desperate for a smile, and at the same time, fearful. It was clear she hadn't been in Paddlers before, but she was familiar. Had I met her in the Mexican neighborhood out by Steamboat? No, I'd definitely know her, the entire community turned out for backyard fiestas at the Cabrals.'

Her eyes swept the aisles, the displays, as if searching for someone. She called out to Santiago in Spanish with a lilt so recognizable, I knew at once she was from Tamaulipas.

Santiago pointed to me. I stepped forward, curious.

The woman stared at me with wide eyes as she took me in, from my blue hair to the infant gumming my sternum.

"You are Aspen Cabral?" she asked in broken English.

"Yes, but most people call me 'Kaye.' What can I do for you?" I replied in Spanish, and her shoulders eased.

"I am sorry to disturb you. I'm looking for your husband—Samuel Cabral?" I narrowed my eyes. Certainly she wasn't a Nixie? But she was from Tamaulipas…

"How do you know him?" I asked, suspicious.

"I…I don't mean any harm," she said quickly, her eyes darting between me and the baby in my arms. I snuggled the child closer. "And I promise not to bother you. Only…would you mind terribly if you carried a message for me?"

Surely passing along a message was harmless. I relented and held out my hand (the one that wasn't holding a baby). The woman's face flushed, embarrassed. She slid her frayed backpack from her shoulders and crouched to rifle through it, her skin reddening by the second as she came up empty.

I took pity on her. "Santiago, toss me those sticky notes and a pen, will you?" Santiago, deep in conversation with Luca about The Colorado Rockies' minor league prospects (this shy young woman had lost his interest), chucked the requested items at my feet. I rolled my eyes and scooped them up.

The woman laughed nervously as I handed her the paper and pen. "Men are not much different here than they are back home, *ay?*"

Another wave of familiarity struck me, and I couldn't help but smile. "Doesn't matter whether you live in Colorado or Cameroon. If a dude's talking sports, a raging wild fire wouldn't get their attention."

"Maybe one of these." She patted her rear, then seemed to remember she was swimming in baggy cargo pants. "Well, maybe not today." A wave of self-consciousness claimed her as she took in her disheveled appearance. "I'm so sorry, I'm not usually crude, or so…" She swiped away the tangled wisps that had escaped her ponytail.

Lord, I just wanted to scoop up this woman and hug her. "Hey! You look like you've been outside, doing what people do in Colorado. But you're not from here, are you?" I dug a little. "Tamaulipas, is it?"

Just like that, the woman's face shuttered. She quickly scribbled her note, folded it in half, and passed it to me. "I apologize, I have to run. Thank you very much!" She heaved her bag onto her shoulder and was halfway out the door before I realized she was leaving.

"Wait! I don't know your name."

She paused, and then, barely above a whisper, said, "Marieta. Just Marieta."

"Just Marieta," I repeated.

The tiny girl in my arms gave an angry mewl, demanding my attention. Marieta watched her, a deep sorrow behind her eyes. "Congratulations," she murmured. "I didn't know…"

"Oh, this little sweetheart isn't mine, although I'm still working on a deal with Luca." I gestured behind me. "He's the proud papa."

The melancholy lifted as she comprehended my words. With a rushed "goodbye" she was gone, and only the fragrance of citrus lingered.

It took a cistern-full of self-control not to unfold that neon yellow slip of paper and read Marieta's words. I was Samuel's wife, after all. But because I was his wife, I needed to trust that he himself would inform me of the note's contents.

He paced our living room, tugged his hair, barely containing the freak-out. "You honestly couldn't tell that she was my sister?"

"Well, of course I can see the resemblance, *now*. It's all about context. Your long-lost sister was the last person I'd expect to waltz into Paddlers on a Friday afternoon."

Samuel placated. "I know, I'm sorry."

I gestured to the note. "What does she want?"

"She wants to meet tomorrow afternoon, says she needs my help with something. She left a phone number." *Pace pace, tug tug.* "God knows it's risky for her to be in town, especially when there are so many migrant workers up for the summer—people who might recognize her." *Pace pace, tug tug.* "But I can't help it. I'm so damned glad to see her again. She wants to meet at the Mount Sanitas trailhead, on the edge of town."

"Isn't that rather secluded?" I raised an eyebrow.

Samuel met my eyebrow and raised his chin. "Santiago will go with me."

"If you think it's safe…"

In the end, it hadn't mattered whether it was safe or not. Samuel waited three hours (Santiago bailed after two), called her prepaid phone countless times.

She never showed.

If Samuel had made a pact with his sister to sever contact, one wouldn't know it by the way he threw himself into tracking her down. He began with discrete inquiries in the Chicano communities along the Front Range. *Nada.* Then he moved on to migrant services, but her false identification said she'd been born in the U.S., so of course she didn't register in their database.

Her last known address—in Texas—proved to be a dead end…she hadn't lived there in three years.

I scoured the internet and social media, but any half-brain knows you don't post about hiding from a drug cartel and expect to live, so that was fruitless. When I mentioned that maybe she'd changed her mind about meeting him, he reasoned that a person doesn't travel all the way from Texas to Colorado, only to 'change their mind.'

"North Texas or South Texas?" I asked. He replied with an ice-blue stink-eye.

We were chasing a ghost. She'd manifested for five minutes, this girl with no name and no home, and vanished into the blinding sun. "Am I going crazy?" I asked Samuel. "I swear she was there."

He shrugged, defeated. "I never told you her name was Marieta. Your description is accurate. Who else could it be?"

He didn't even own a picture of her.

The weekend of our fourth annual mental health benefit was nearly upon us, and I'd drafted my Cabral family to help with the gory details, from hanging Chinese lanterns to placing neon signs along the roadside. Morning drizzle swathed Lyons in a fine sheet of clamminess and taunted draught-plagued ground with rain, but it dried up as the sun baked the mountainside. Sofia and I unzipped our raincoats as we bounced between restaurants and art galleries, restocking flyers.

"We're good to go," said the frazzled waitress at the Lyons Diner as I filled out a donation receipt. "Thirty pre-sliced fruit pies for the benefit concert, delivery scheduled for eight a.m. to Planet Bluegrass. I've heard it'll be a heck of a concert."

"We've got a great line-up."

She leaned in, conspiratorially. "I've also heard that Indigo Kingsley's putting in an appearance."

"Er…that I can confirm is not true. She's filming the next Nixie movie."

"Pity. Loved her in the last one. Your hair's different." She eyed my blue curls and not in an admiring way.

"Oh wow, the morning has flown by so fast!" I glanced at my watch, then to Sofia. "We really need to hit the other businesses."

"Sure thing," the waitress said.

I loved Sofia, but I missed having Molly by my side. She would have convinced me that I totally rocked this color. Sofia simply said my untamed blue mop was 'classic.' Victory rolls were classic and Sofia was a fibber.

Molly and Cassady were flying back from Alaska, and I bounced on my heels like a kid hopped-up on Red Bull. Yet another reason I needed to get out of town and into the mountains— to burn off this nervous energy.

Sam and I had planned to spend the afternoon hiking the mountain of my nightmares…Longs Peak. My therapist insisted the climb was a necessary evil. But we'd had a row this morning, before the coffee had even filled my mug, and now I'd be climbing Longs Peak solo.

It all began when I'd hinted that he needed to tell Alonso and Sofia they had a niece… "Kaye, I can handle my family," he'd said, still rubbing sleep from his eyes.

"They're my family, too." I stirred creamer into my coffee a little too vigorously and sloshed it down the side. "Sooner or later someone at church, or the magazine, or the grocery store is going to ask them why their son is looking for this strange girl. What will you tell them?"

Sam slammed a cupboard shut. "I'll figure it out myself."

"You've always been this way, it's like pulling teeth to understand you."

"This is who I am. You knew this the first time you married me, and you knew this the *second* time you married me. If it's a facet of my personality you can't live with, then perhaps you should ask yourself why you married me at all. Where are you going?"

"To hand out flyers with your mom, and then on to Longs Peak." He scrambled to clean up his breakfast things and gather up his gear. "I'm not ready yet. Let me change."

I shoved several power bars and a new pair of gloves into my hiking bag. "I'm going by myself."

"No. I'm coming with you; that was the plan. Don't leave like this." He placed his hands on my biceps, beseeching me to wait. I stepped out of his grip.

"I need some time alone, Samuel. I'm not storming away angry, I just...I want space."

"What if you have another panic attack? What if you're injured and climbing by yourself? That's too risky."

I grabbed my day-pack and stalked toward the door. "You knew this about me when we married. Perhaps you should ask yourself why you married me at all." With this parting shot, I realized I had stormed away in anger, after all.

The bell tinkled above the door of a Main Street boutique as we distributed the last of our flyers. Sofia walked me to my car door and casually leaned against it, preventing me from leaving.

"What troubles you, *mija*?"

I bit my lip and glanced down the street, at the blue sky overhead, anywhere but into her loving eyes.

"A mother knows things."

Shame reddened my cheeks as I remembered the terrible things Samuel and I had shouted at each other this morning, and I feared we'd said one hurtful word too many. "Did you ever ask God to change Samuel, when he was deep in addiction? Or even to heal his mind?"

"Oh, many times. Have you?"

"Yes."

She patted my hand. "But I should have asked God to change *me*. I needed strength to forgive my broken son and love him, just as he was."

She tucked my hand in her elbow and we sauntered down the sidewalk, toward the greenspace with the park benches. "For so long, we hid our son's bipolar disorder because we were too concerned with keeping our family affairs private. Can't let others see we aren't perfect, oh no. But God has a way of tumbling pride. I had to pull back the curtain and let people see us—*me*—for what I am."

"What are you?"

"Real. If I'd learned this lesson sooner, I might have spared so much heartache." She slid her sunglasses up and scrutinized me. "I assume this has to do with the woman Samuel is searching for?" She smiled at my bug eyes. "My son thinks he is so clever, with his New York ways, but in Lyons you can't keep your parents in the dark. Is this the same woman who caused such a fuss in Tamaulipas?"

I warred with telling her the truth about her niece. It's not an easy thing, to do what's right at the expense of one's marriage. Didn't she deserve to know? Now I realized the dilemma Sofia, Alonso, and Dani had faced when they'd hid Samuel's bipolar disorder. If the tables had been turned, I might have done the same.

As it turns out, I did do the same. I didn't tell her, not because I lost the nerve, but because an unexpected visitor plopped onto the park bench beside us. Her hair was bunched into a top knot and giant sunglasses half-covered her face, but I'd recognize that A-list, Aussie incarnation of tenacity anywhere, on and off the big screen.

"Kaye Cabral, you freckled, sexy beast. What have you done to your hair?"

I leapt to my feet. "Indigo!"

She laughed and threw her arms around me. "Surprise!"

"Rumors were flying that you planned to crash our concert, but I've been telling everyone they're false."

"Nothing like a well-placed rumor to drag people out of the woodwork. Hallo Mrs. Cabral."

"My dear, a pleasure to see you again."

Indigo Kingsley was Hollywood royalty and was best known for portraying Neelie Nixie in *Water Sirens*. She also used to date Samuel and, once upon a time, stole the tootsie roll center right out of my candy-coated day whenever their steamy photos were splashed across magazine racks. (Grocery shopping had been awesome.) They split because Samuel was still in love with his ex-wife (me), and Indigo was in love with gourmet cheeseburgers (and Marco Caldo).

"Where's your dreamy chef?"

Indigo waved her hand. "Off chasing moose and other Colorado-y things. He wants a picture of a bighorn sheep, but Samuel said unless he goes up early morning, spotting one is akin to spotting modesty at an awards show."

"You've talked to Samuel today?"

"I did." She peered at me over her glasses and I shifted. For as chatty as she was, Indigo was surprisingly observant. Back when they'd dated, she'd noticed Samuel's manic moods, right away. Now, concern was written all over her face. "He didn't sound right on the phone. Is there anything I can do?"

Sofia and I exchanged a worried glance. I squinted up at Longs Peak and regret and relief warred in my bones. It would still be there to climb another day. "Thanks Indigo, but I was just on my way back to Boulder. I'm sure there's nothing to worry about."

When I was in middle school, I ran hurdles my one and only track season. To hit the three strides needed to find a rhythm and clear a hurdle, you have to be tall or really fast. I'm neither. Watching me run hurdles was probably like watching *el changuito* try to scale his baby gate. My coach said I needed to shave seconds off my time, and I tried, I really did, but speed was not my thing. I was stubborn, though. It took pathetically hobbling over hurdles after a bad tumble in the middle of a track meet for me to call it quits.

Long story short, no matter how much you desire something, certain dreams just aren't possible (despite what motivational posters will tell you).

I texted Samuel to let him know the Longs Peak climb was off and I'd be home soon. He replied with a brief: *Writing all day, do what you like.* Ugh. I chucked my phone into the counsel.

Dread roiled my stomach because I knew what the next few weeks would be like as he slipped into another episode.

I rounded the curves toward Boulder and Left Hand Canyon Road came into view. In a split-second decision, I cranked the wheel.

Cars, billboards, civilization fell away the deeper I drove into the canyon. I rolled down the jeep windows, opened the skylight. Fresh mountain wind blasted my skin and cleared away emotional debris that had collected in hard-to-reach crannies.

The creek was no longer swollen with spring rain and now trickled along the base of the canyon, nearly obscured by thick ribbons of cattails. I slowed until I spotted the tire-track drive that ascended up the mountainside to the property Samuel had purchased. Wildlife went silent at the slam of my car door. I crawled onto the hood, statue-still.

I listened. Waited.

I slid to the ground, felt dirt and gravel beneath my hands. I waited for words, struggled with what to say. Finally I gave up and listened to a quiet that wasn't really quiet at all. Insects resumed their cricks and buzzing, and birds warbled from the crowns of giant ponderosas. Up the hill, a woodpecker hammered at a skeletal tree with bones bleached white by many summer suns.

The breeze whistled the tall grass; conifers and their leaves rustled in answer.

Quiet.

Was this the peace Samuel spoke of? To meld into the cadence and grandeur of the natural world, to be a part of something greater than you and know, deep down inside, you were made to be loved?

Maybe finding the right answer wasn't the key.

Maybe it was finding the right question.

I didn't know the words to say, so I thought…

You know what's in my heart. I can't ask you to change him anymore, so will you change me? If I'm not meant to be a mom, please, please take away this longing inside of me. All I'm asking for is a little peace.

Peace is what I was given, beneath the ponderosas and warblers and blue sky, where our home would one day sit.

Chapter 12
DRAG

When a rope runs through several unaligned
points of protection, friction is created and can
throw a climber off-balance.

The rising sun painted the sky in early morning hues as I turned onto the drive of Planet Bluegrass. It was the day of our long-planned mental health benefit and my jeep was laden with heavy duty plastic tubs, boxes of performance schedules and electronic equipment. A world news anchor's somber tone sanded the rough edges from my jagged mood. But then I listened to the next story...

"The internet activist collective referred to as "Unknown" released a statement yesterday, indicating its refusal to cease its campaign against the Mexican criminal cartel, Zacatón, and their government supporters. Animosity between the amorphous collective and the cartel peaked last Thursday, when Unknown demanded the release of Daniel Rodriguez, a hacker allegedly kidnapped by the Zacatón Cartel in April of this year. Unknown has threatened to make public information damaging to the cartel's smuggling operations. In national news..."

I turned off the radio and killed the engine. Sitting in the deep blue of early morning, I forced my mind away from Samuel's mysterious involvement with the Zacatóns and Unknown. Today was about giving the local mental health clinic a show of support, the likes of which they'd never seen.

A bleary eyed Molly stifled a yawn and waved into the beam of my headlights. She and Cassady had caught the red eye from Anchorage, and I questioned whether she'd even been to bed. Before I'd unbuckled by seatbelt, she ripped open my door and flung herself on top of me.

"Kaye Bear, you naughty girl." She backed out of my car and allowed me to exit. "What's this I hear about Indigo Kingsley dragging her L.A. entourage to our concert? How amazing is that?"

"Believe me, I'm as shocked as you are. But you know Indigo's a big ol' softie when it comes to Samuel."

"Does that worry you?"

"Not like it used to." Warmth burned through my chest like a good whiskey. The sun had yet to peak over the mountains, but Molly's light encompassed me. I pulled her around to the trunk. "Wait until you see how the merchandise came out. The temp tats you designed are trill." I dug out the plastic tub.

"I don't think you can use 'trill' unless you're a millennial or you've been in prison." She held up a fake tattoo, the phrase 'Embrace Your Crazy' tangled in a lick of wicked black flames.

"I think I'll put it here, just above my cleavage. See how many hugs I get."

Molly and I dragged crates over to where the rental company had assembled vendor tents. We spent the next thirty minutes applying tattoos and unpacking gear while we waited for the first wave of volunteers to arrive.

"What's Hippie up to this morning? I thought he might be here."

Molly inspected her sandal strap. "Cassady's trying out a new trail bike with the Paddlers boys. Supposedly it has Bluetooth capability, logs your trek. He can't stop talking about it. He and Santiago said they'd swing by before crowds really pick up."

"Assuming crowds pick up."

"That's my Debbie Downer." She hugged me again. "Attendance has trended up each year, no reason for that to change. Besides, the doors haven't even opened yet, the weather rocks, and we've got local bands with big followings."

"And temporary tattoos for the kids." I flashed my thigh, which now read 'Broken Crayons Still Color.'

She whistled. "Not sure what kids you're hanging out with."

Just as Molly predicted, as the early June sun warmed the towering, red rock mountain faces above Planet Bluegrass, people arrived. They came because the Tripping Marys hauled themselves away from their rounds of retirement golf and played three encores. The came because we'd saturated social media with quirky tag lines and invites. Many came because Indigo Kingsley haunted the food tents. I spotted Indigo just before noon next to a grateful meatball sub vendor, surrounded by security detail and a hundred jostling camera phones.

"Kaye!" She waved a lily arm over the heads of her admirers. One of her guards maneuvered me through the crowd.

"What's up?"

She pointed to the menu. "Do you want Marinara Parm or Spinach Alfredo? We're all in for the Marinara, so if you try the Spinach Alfredo, we could go halvesies."

How Indigo maintained her thigh gap, I'd never know. I grimaced at the rich, greasy alfredo-smothered meatball and my stomach turned. The vendor handed me a soggy sub sandwich and once we rounded the tent corner, I passed it to the starlet. "Sorry Indigo, but this thing looks as appetizing as the scum my mom dredges from her runoff pond. Anyway, I have a date with Samuel for chicken curry."

"The River Styx flows with curry." She shivered, somehow elegant even with marinara squishing between her fingers. "That's why Samuel and I never worked out, you know. He eats too much Indian food. That, and he was still in love with his ex-wife."

"Minor obstacles."

Indigo snorted. "Oh! There's your heavenly husband now."

I followed her finger and saw him weaving around blankets and umbrella chairs, one eye on the stage. A backpack was slung over his shoulder, probably containing his laptop.

"Crikey, is he wearing cut-off khakis? I never thought I'd see the day."

"Ah, yes. What you are witnessing is the result of what happens when one buys their entire summer wardrobe at REI."

"Crikey," she said again, such an Aussie. "It looks like he's on his way to a Dave Matthews concert. The Sam I knew would rather cover his bits with fig leaves than shop off the rack."

"Was that Samuel's preference or Caroline's?"

"Ooh, good call. Caroline might have dissed buying off the rack and Samuel never corrected her. That happened, you know. He didn't care enough to speak up for himself, as if they'd skipped over all the romance and went straight to lukewarm. Anyway." Samuel sauntered up, clasped her hand and kissed her cheek with the elegance of a flamenco king, despite the cargos.

"Indigo. Kaye." He brushed his lips against mine, a perfunctory motion he greeted me with every morning. I stood by silently as Samuel smiled at Indigo and gave her his undivided attention. He wasn't laser focused on his computer screen while she spoke to him. He didn't offer one-word, half-hearted answers when she asked about the next book. Familiar resentment rumbled inside, but I stifled it.

Big picture, Kaye. Your husband kissed her cheek, not her lips. He's respectful. He's here, supporting you.

Still, dissatisfaction spread like a slow-growing cancer.

We reclined on a blanket and enjoyed the twang of banjos and guitars, the whine of fiddles. Dani was beside us, her swollen ankles stretched in front of her. She still had a couple of months to go, but the heatwave was merciless. Sofia took pity on her and offered to babysit Gabe so she could get out, hear the music. I wondered if a lazy boy recliner and air conditioning unit would have been more up her alley.

To my relief Samuel had not brought his laptop, but he wanted it. His fingers twitched nervously, picked at blades of grass. *Relax*, I mouthed, and patted my thighs. He lay down and placed his head in my lap, closed his eyes. I watched the breeze play with his soft brown hair and ran my fingers through it, toyed with the ends until his body went slack.

After a while, Indigo and her detail left to explore the vendors. But not twenty minutes later, she returned, her arm looped around Santiago's.

"Look who I found!" Santiago called.

Samuel scooted over on the blanket, and they plopped down. My eyes widened when I witnessed Santiago's fingers slowly drift from Indigo's hip to her back, subtly playing with the strap of her sundress. Marco Caldo would not be happy that the biggest flirt in Lyons was working his game on Indigo. But she didn't seem uncomfortable, so it was none of my business.

Samuel was not amused. "Marco find his bighorn sheep, yet?"

"No. He's visiting a farm-to-table restaurant, talking to the chef, getting menu ideas." She took the hint and put an inch of space between her and Santiago. The youngest Valdez boy, though, didn't notice how Samuel's icy eyes tracked his every pinky twitch.

"So then this guy asks when we'll get the next shipment in, even though I told him we don't carry Bald Mountain brands because we want our gear to make it through a hike. *Ay ay ay*, Dani, you look exhausted. Need a foot rub?" She shrugged noncommittally, but he took that as a yes and placed her right foot in his lap, dug his thumbs into her arch. That was enough for Samuel.

"Fuck, Valdez, if you don't quit being such a douche, someday some woman is going to hit you with a lawsuit."

Fire lit Santiago's brown eyes. "And what's that supposed to mean, bro?"

"You know exactly what it means, *bro*. Indigo, and now Danita? You'll hit on any female within walking distance."

"Excuse me?" Indigo and Dani said in stereo. Both men jumped to their feet and stared each other down, posturing like a couple of alpha dogs. Dani smacked her brother's leg.

"*Cállate la boca, pendejo*, you just insulted every single person in this circle except Ms. Kingsley's security detail."

Said security detail was ready to pounce. "Let it go, Sam," I pleaded. "Santiago's just a stupid flirt."

"Lay off, Kaye. Someone has to stand up for my sister, with Angel gone." *Crap, here we go again.* I'd seen this quick anger before (New York, in his fight with Mr. Avant Garde), but Santiago didn't know the warning signs.

"Don't you dare bring Angel into your crazy, Cabral. You mention my brother again and I'll beat in your teeth." Oh wonderful.

Dani grabbed Santiago's elbow just as I grabbed Sam's. "Whoa, whoa, whoa, you two," she said, "cool it down before you get thrown out of here." But both hot-headed men were too far gone to listen. Samuel shot off his mouth in rapid Spanish, something about Santiago being a self-centered jackass who went through women like cat food (my translation may have been incorrect), and it was game on. With a quick burst of fury, Santiago thrust both hands against Samuel's chest and shoved, hard. Sam stumbled back into Indigo, Indigo's security detail swarmed like drone bees around their queen, and both men were bodily dragged to the ground and pinned by a combined six-hundred pounds of muscle. Meanwhile, Indigo's growing circle of fans cheerily held their phones aloft. This thing would be on Twitter in twenty seconds.

Dani sighed and rubbed her belly. "With uncles like that, this little one will be incarcerated by the time he's fifteen."

Indigo chuckled. "At least he's got Kaye to bail him or her out of jail." I didn't laugh. "Oh darling, look on the bright side. Once this fight hits YouTube, Samuel's books will be golden again. That's what celebs do when they want to take a month off, you know? Do something risqué and then 'lay low to avoid bad press.' The gossip sites squawk and speculate, the celeb finds a quiet resort in Kauai, bang. Autopilot."

Dani snorted. "Better pack your bags for the beach."

Indigo had a way of making the stress of bad press sound appealing. "As lovely as Kauai sounds, I have to make sure Samuel isn't thrown into the clinker by my event security. Indigo, Dani, enjoy the rest of the benefit."

Unfortunately, I did not get to my boys in time to save them from an evening in the Boulder County jail. Just as well, they needed to cool their heads. But that meant Santiago couldn't return to work at

Paddlers. I needed a breather myself, so before my next shift at the concert, I walked down the street to one of my favorite haunts.

Paddlers bustled with their typical Saturday afternoon crowd. Cassady manned the register, stuck until Santiago returned. Customers browsed through aisles of fishing tackle and life vests. Perhaps this wasn't the best idea. I turned to leave but wasn't paying attention and crashed into another customer.

"Oh geez, I'm so…" The words died on my tongue as I gripped the arms of the woman I'd plowed into, steadying her.

"Marieta," I breathed.

She wore the same baggy cargos, which couldn't have been pleasant in this heat, but had stripped down to a tank top. She was painfully thin, lithe like Samuel, but not strong. I searched for tell-tale injection bruising on her arms but saw nothing. She backed away from my scrutiny.

"Tell Samuel I am sorry I didn't meet him. I wanted to, but…" She glanced over her shoulder, worried, and I realized she was going to run away.

"Wait! You've been like a ghost to find."

"Sometimes I feel like a ghost," she said flatly. Before I could question her further about her vanishing act, she ducked past me and out the door. As she retreated up the hill toward the music festival, I thought it strange I'd bumped into her not once, but twice, at Paddlers.

But I didn't ponder too long, because Hector was already making his way over, just as I prepared to run after Samuel's sister.

"Hey *mamacita*." He pulled me into his warm embrace and steered me toward the backroom. I craned my neck and peered out the window, but she was long gone. "I wasn't expecting to see you today, with the benefit. What's up?"

"I just came by to let you know the sheriff has Santiago cooling his heels in lock-up, so he probably won't be back until this evening." Dammit, I'd never find her now.

Hector's eyes widened. "What kind of shindig are you throwing over there at Planet Bluegrass? Maybe I need to close up shop and head over."

I sighed. "Just a couple of testosterone-driven egos settling a score in the middle of a crowded music festival. He and Sam now have the opportunity to make nice behind bars. Unfortunately, Hippie's probably stuck behind that register for the rest of the day."

"Do you need help over at the benefit, with Sam gone? Seriously, I could just close up early for the evening. You look frazzled."

"Thanks, but you can't give up revenue on a busy weekend. We're covered."

"Let me call Pops out of retirement for a night. Just a sec.'"

"Hector—"

"I'm doing this, *chica*."

Fifteen minutes later, once *Señor* Valdez had jerked an old Paddlers polo over his gray head, we strode up the hill toward Planet Bluegrass. I scanned the crowds, desperate for another glimpse of Samuel's missing sister, but finding her would be as likely as reclaiming an oar carried away by a swift-moving current. Damn. One more thing to upset Samuel.

"Time to come clean, Kaye. You could have called to tell me Santiago had gotten himself arrested."

I refocused on Hector. "I needed a break. Sam's..." I paused. Was I willing to go down this road? Talk to another man about my husband? But I needed someone to listen, someone on the outside of this marriage who cared and could speak with bluntness. So I talked. I told Hector how difficult it was to watch Samuel slip into yet another episode and to have my concern thrown back in my face. It wasn't about the lack of sex, though Samuel had to be just as frustrated as I was. I told my friend that sometimes all I longed for was to have Samuel put his arms around me and tell me he heard my fears and saw my struggles. I told Hector I felt like the 'bad guy' if I so much as mentioned my desire for children.

When we'd nearly reached the gate of Planet Bluegrass, I realized that I'd spent the entire walk yapping like the very female stereotype I despised, while my friend had listened, helpless. I groaned and rested my head on Hector's shoulder.

"I feel like an idiot."

My head gently bounced as he chuckled. "If I thought you were an idiot, I would have ditched you twenty years ago, when you took that stinky Nutty Buddy I had for youth baseball and used it as a boat for your Barbie doll."

I laughed. "Oh man. It sank right to the bottom when water leaked through the air vents."

"The boys have to breathe."

"Give me a break, I didn't know what it was. No brothers."

"Me, Angel, and Santiago—we were your brothers. Samuel, too."

"Yeah."

The benefit was still bustling with people of all ages, from babies to geriatrics. A fiddle whined from the stage as the next act tuned up. Another success, and I knew Samuel was mainly to thank. He'd thrown his clout behind our TrilbyJones brain child, even after our first concert garnered mediocre attendance. But the music was good and the day was cloudless. Samuel's hard work should be recognized, and I would.

As soon as he was out of the slammer.

Hector folded his tattooed arms. "Listen, I know sometimes we need to get the crud out. But the stuff you said? Tell it to Samuel, not me, and be loving and respectful about it. You chose to marry him and if he's a decent guy, he'll treat you right."

"Even when he's a land mine, like today?"

"Even then. He might be angry and hurt, but he'll sort it out when he's back to himself. If he doesn't, give this hunk of meat a call. *Ay, Dios mío*, is that Jaime Guzman?"

I followed his riveted gaze and saw Jaime staring down a cluster of children who circled her for a free pinwheel. She showed a boy who couldn't have been more than four how to blow air through the blades and it whirled, much to his delight. Then he tried, with very little success, and showered Jaime in a spray of spittle. I braced myself for a hallmark Guzman hissy fit. But she simply tugged up the collar of her tee shirt and wiped germ droplets from her face. An unguarded Jaime was as rare as a dodo bird.

Now I saw why Hector had been so hung up on her. He saw too and, for a moment, he forgot he had a wife, whom he loved very much. Slack-jawed, black-eyed...

I gave his spine a smack. His black Paddlers polo was clammy with sweat under the punishing midday heat. He shook himself out of his stupor.

"Make sure Tricia knows how much you care, okay? The minute you get home."

"Point taken." His eyes grew distant and his mouth tightened. "I give great advice, don't I? If only I listened to half of it."

The drive home was fraught with unspoken words. Headlights hit the double yellow lines as we curved along the foothills highway that lulled me into a weary stupor. Samuel drummed his knees, messed with the radio until he found a station he liked, then changed it during a commercial break. I searched for that optimism Hector had injected into my spirit during our afternoon walk, but Samuel was crestfallen when I told him about my encounter with his sister. A full five minutes passed. "Are you going to say anything?" I finally asked.

"The only new thing we know is that she was in town this afternoon, and she's probably gone again because I landed in jail."

"Why did you go after Santiago?"

"Technically, he went after me."

"You threw the verbal stone, Samuel."

He clenched the steering wheel and braced for what was rapidly degenerating into another argument. "You know the cause as well as I do. I'm teetering on the edge of an episode again. I can tell it's coming, but I'm not sure which way it's going to tip."

"You mean manic or depressive?"

"Hmm."

"Do you think the latest meds adjustment was correct, or do we need to try something else?"

"*You* don't need to try anything, Kaye. It's my brain that can't seem to keep my mouth and my body out of a damned jail cell."

I gripped the steering wheel. "Okay okay. Doctor this week?"

Samuel scoffed. "Which one? Mental health? Therapist? Marriage counselor?"

I half-smiled in spite of myself. "Maybe we should have all of them over for coffee."

Samuel's mouth quirked. "We could just sit back and let them talk about us to each other."

I longed for his hand to snake across the counsel until it found mine, a bit of loving contact for an affection-starved woman. He didn't. Such a little thing, but as little disappointments go, they add up and you're left with a big fat pile of unhappiness.

"Why don't you hold my hand anymore?"

Samuel looked puzzled. "I do."

"Here and there, and usually only after we have sex. Which has been practically nonexistent as of late."

Just like that, those walls of ice went up. "Well, my dear, if you weren't so prickly, I'd probably want to hold your hand. It's difficult to hold a hand covered in thorns."

"And it's even harder to have sex with someone who doesn't give affection." Ouch. So much for a loving discussion. "I'm just..." I pressed the heels of my hands over my eyes. "I'm so tired of this. I need a break."

"From our marriage?"

"From our animosity." My sniffles filled the silence in the car, along with that relentless drumming of his fingers. A memory hit me, one not in the too distant past, of a late-night car ride on this very road, in Cassady's campervan. I'd just told Samuel I was unhappy, that I hadn't fared well after he left me for New York. "I need you to talk to me. I want you to look into my eyes when I tell you about a stressful client or the next climb. I don't want to see the back of your laptop screen when I ask what's troubling you."

"That's fair."

"That's it?"

"I'm not sure what else you want me to say. I agree with you. Do you want me to argue?"

My head ached. "No. Fine. That's...that's it."

Very early, around three, I awoke to a dip in the bed as Samuel quietly climbed in, finally putting aside his writing for much needed sleep. Even though we fought, his presence was more comforting than our warm blanket.

"Kaye."

"Hmmm?"

"I hate to see you cry. I think I hate it more than anything."

"I cry when I'm upset. I cry when I'm happy. I cry at flippin' rock concerts. It just leaks out."

He searched through the blankets until he found my hand, and tucked it, safe and secure, between his two palms. "Do you ever wonder if our marriage was a mistake?"

I frowned. He'd asked me this more than once. Did *he* believe we'd made a mistake? "Occasionally," I hedged. "But I always come to the same conclusion—it was a choice. I chose to marry you, and I don't regret it. So no, it's not a mistake."

"Okay." He exhaled and closed his eyes. "Okay."

A week after the benefit concert, Molly and I had a lunch date with a potential college intern. She and Cassady would return to Alaska in early July. Molly was strangely tight-lipped on the status of their relationship, but there was little closeness between my friend and her beau. I hoped for the best for my friend. After all, she'd uprooted her entire life to chase adventure with Cassady in Clam Gulch. But if she returned to Colorado before the year was out, I wouldn't be shocked.

Molly checked her watch for the third time as we stood outside the Fighting Mango, a lunch spot neither of us had ever visited but was popular with the Communication Arts department at the University of Colorado. TrilbyJones had been asked to consider their PR majors for internships, but the interviewee was late.

"Five more minutes, and we go inside and try those mango cocktails."

"We have to go back to work, Mol.'"

"We can split it."

Just then, a harried young woman who couldn't have been more than twenty rounded the corner, loaded with a book bag that looked heavier than my hiking gear. She swiped her blue-streaked hair into a bun but came to a dead stop when she spotted us.

"Neelie!" Tears gathered in her eyes and something inside me withered. "I love you, so much. And Oh. My. Gosh. I love your hair!" An uninvited hand touched my bobbed blue locks. "I've never seen someone your age pull it off!"

"That's it. I'm going back to blonde first thing tomorrow."

"Don't you dare," said Molly.

The student shook her head, as if every piece of knowledge in her world had been turned on its head. "A blue-haired Neelie Nixie. I can't...wow. This will change everything when I read the books again." She remembered herself and thrust out a hand. "I'm so, so sorry, I'm Ashley. I know, me and every other twenty-something. Just call me Ash, it avoids confusion. Let's eat mangos!"

We settled into a table and perused the menu. Mango chicken, mango sandwich, mango salad...

"I sense a theme," said Molly as she cleaned her glasses with her shirt hem.

A distinctive chuckle caught my ear and I followed it to a booth across the dining area.

There was Samuel, seated across from a man I'd never seen. He was in his mid-fifties, though his sunbaked skin belied his age. Steely locks tufted around his ears and beefy hands paged through the menu. His clothing was work-worn and stained with the same clay that was impossible to wash from the knees of my jeans after weeding my mother's gardens. Though I couldn't understand their words, I saw, without a doubt, the lilts and trills of the Spanish language.

Agricultural worker? A new employee with Alonso's magazine?

Ash clutched my forearm. "Shut. Up. That's Samuel Caulfield Cabral! I love his books, though the pirate one kinda threw me. Wow, he's even hotter in person..." She covered her mouth. "Aaaand he's also your husband. I'm sooo sorry, it's just that I'm a huge Nixie fan. Neelie Nixie got me through a really rough time in the fourth grade." I choked on my ice water. Ash blinked rapidly.

"Oh, I know SCC is *never* happy to hear elementary kids have read his books, but my parents are very modern. It's all good." She gasped. "Do you think you could introduce me?"

My eyes darted over to Samuel's table. After the jail incident his mood tipped neither toward mania or depression, but stabilized, a small miracle. He wasn't better…just not worse.

By now, he too had spotted us. He gave a quick shake of his head. I narrowed my eyes in confusion. He widened his, silently telling me in no uncertain terms was I to bring my student over to his table. Odd.

I turned back to the girl, who was touching up her orange lipstick. Me and my blue hair didn't judge. She showed me her teeth.

"Any mango stuck in there?" Yeah, she didn't stand a chance.

"Sorry Ash, but I don't think this internship going to work."

Her face fell, as if I'd told her Indigo Kingsley had been recast. Then she squared in her shoulders in a way that reminded me of (and I hesitate to say this) me. "Look, I know I'm a ditzy, crazy Nixie fan, but here's the deal. I'm also creator of YourNextBook, an app that connects readers with authors and their work."

My eyebrows shot up. "Samuel told me about this, it's really popular. That's yours?"

She shrugged. "A good book can change a life, and that's what Samuel Cabral's did for me. Authors have more control on the app and so do readers. It's the way of the future. Now, take my track record with app development and translate it into consumer relations. With the right algorithms, you could shine through the thousand other PR campaigns and place yours directly in front of your target audience."

Molly was speechless. Me too, and I loved it when people surprised me. "If you'll do our social media too, you've got the job."

Ash squealed. "Thank you, thank you! I wanted this so badly."

"Now it's truth time. You could have an internship with Google. Why us? Is it because of Sam's books?" Ash's face reddened and I softened toward her. "Tell you what. If you let Samuel and his guest enjoy their lunch while you tell us about your awesome tech skills, I'll invite him to our next luncheon and he can sign your books. Deal?"

Joy blossomed and she shook my hand. Somehow, I thought our next luncheon at the Fighting Mango would be attended by five bouncing Nixie fans. "Deal. Oh, and I'm doing the Google thing next year."

I slid into the passenger side of Samuel's Subaru after a quick change into my trusty Tevas. We were heading up to the construction site of what would be our new home to check the freshly-lain foundation. Admittedly, I'd had very little involvement until now. The idea had been Samuel's. He'd purchased the land. He'd chosen the builder and selected the floor plan. It dawned on me how much my disinterest in the project hurt him. It all clicked when our marriage counselor asked, "how would you feel?" Joe Cool could bring the guilt in five seconds flat. Since that session, I'd thrown myself into creating this home together. Building materials, architectural features, bathroom placement, all in.

The foothills slid by. As the canyon grew taller and narrower, it left one with the claustrophobic feeling of being trapped in that Death Star garbage compactor in *Star Wars*. But soon the canyon widened and I exhaled. For June, the sun was absolutely scorching, the air dry and dusty. Left Hand Creek barely trickled as it played peek-a-boo with the road. One final bend and there was our new home up the hill, the concrete foundation now visible. I broke into a smile. Samuel grinned, also. We got out of the car and strode up the hill to where the foreman packed up for the day.

"Everything go okay?" Samuel asked.

The man flicked a speck of dried cement from his forearm. "Cement's poured and we'll give it a month to cure, then build the frame mid-July."

We explored the construction site. Typically, house foundations looked smaller than their true square footage. But even without the walls, the footprint was massive. This would be a big home for just the two of us. My heart saddened at the thought of never filling this great home with children, but I pushed through it.

"Do you like the house?" I hadn't even heard Samuel approach, but I now saw the foreman had departed and it was just the two of us.

"It's missing a few walls, but open floor plans are all the rage."

"Cheeky."

"I like the house. No, I love it. And I love you."

He kissed the top of my head, proof that he was trying. Satisfaction bounced through me at this small, yet huge, gesture. I wrapped my arms around his middle and squeezed. "Walk with me?"

We wound our way up the maze of trees, now vibrant and quivering in the flush of summer. The ground was pocked with shady soft spots where spring mud had yet to harden and crack, and soon my Tevas were caked. I scraped off the soles on a nearby rock. To my left, the old mine entrance peeked through the undergrowth.

"Are you going to ask me about lunch today?" Samuel asked.

"I was getting around to it."

His smile was a bit sad. "The man's name is Javier. I met him when I was locked up after my run-in with Santiago Saturday. He was in on a misdemeanor charge, driving without a license and slapped with a three-hundred dollar fine. He belongs to a group of seasonal laborers on guest visas who journey up from Mexico City in the spring to work the farms around Greeley, then head back after harvest."

I nodded along, wondering what this person had to do with Samuel.

"Javier says he knows my sister."

"Danita?" His look told me otherwise.

"Supposedly, they're neighbors."

Concern filled me. "Do you believe him?"

"What else do I have to go on? The thing is…she doesn't live in the States anymore. Her address is in Mexico City."

"She returned to Mexico!? But you went through so much trouble to get her out!"

"That's why something is wrong. Javier doesn't know why she wants to see me, but believes she returned through the cartel tunnels and one of their thugs followed her—that's why she didn't show. He thinks she's probably skipped town, and if I want to find her, I should start with her home address in Mexico City."

"That's insane. What did he say when you said you wouldn't go?" His gaze was riveted on the gravel he ground beneath his boot. My gut turned to ice. "Of course you told him no."

A long pause. "Kaye, she's my sister."

"Oh my God! You have no idea who this Javier guy really is, if he even *knows* your sister!"

"Don't you think that has crossed my mind?" Samuel was a genius in many ways, but he had a history of putting his faith in the wrong people. "Firecracker..." His tone was too patronizing for my liking. "I can't abandon her. Besides, Mexico City is fairly safe. Most of the Zacatón activity is concentrated in north Tamauli—"

"Then get the Mexican law enforcement to help."

"Been there, done that, they're 'still investigating' the first time I went to them. For all I know, she simply needs to get back on her feet."

I grew desperate. "Why are you doing this? You hardly *know* this woman."

"If I don't help my sister, no one will." He placed his hands on my shoulders. "*Mi vida*, I need you. I won't travel alone—I'll ask Santiago, Uncle Carlos to go with me—he's a pro at finding missing people."

"It's also time to tell your parents about Marieta."

Samuel dropped his head in concession. "I never wanted to tell you about any of this."

That hurt. "Well, you married me. Complete honesty comes with the territory, bub."

"I know. And I'm trying. But sometimes, complete transparency is more complicated than strutting down Pearl Street buck naked."

My lips twitched. "The hippie performance artist on the old capitol lawn would disagree."

His eyes softened. "I love you, Kaye Cabral. Forgive me for dragging you into this mess."

"That sounded a lot like 'forgive me for what I'm about to do.'"

"That too."

I straightened my spine. "I'm going with you."

"Like hell you are."

Samuel's tone was as hard-set as concrete and arguing would be a waste of breath.

Instead, I planned. What would I need for an emergency trip to Mexico? My passport. International data plan for my phone. Snacks... lots of snacks. What would Samuel's sister need?

With a start, I realized I knew very little about her.

Chapter 13
DOWN CLIMB

*Moving down a rock face rather than up. Usually done
when climbing without a rope, in emergencies,
or when a climber has ventured off-route.*

Hydraulic Level Five [WORKING TITLE]
Draft 1.113
© *Samuel Caulfield Cabral and Aspen Kaye Cabral*
VOLCANO SLUM

It's dusk in Mexico City. Aspen has her mountains back home: Mount
Holycross. He glances at his watch. She must have summited by now.
This is my mountain, thinks Caulfield as he, Uncle C and S edge along
a backstreet piled with a dull rainbow of garbage and work their way
up rough-carved roads, higher and higher toward the summit of this
dormant volcano, now only an anthill for the dense lines of humanity
that march its slopes. He wouldn't have involved them, but traveling
alone to a place like Tizilicho is akin to taping a sign to one's back that
reads 'KIDNAP ME.' Tizilicho isn't in the part of Mexico City where
families drive nice cars to restaurants when dad works late and mom
doesn't feel like cooking.

"That girl from my store—she lives in a place like this?" says S.

"I'm not sure."

"This doesn't feel right, man."

"What choice do I have?"

Uncle C doesn't question, never does. He's just visited his mother in Ciudad Victoria and what's a nine-hour detour south to Mexico City? The man is as easy-going as the broken-in cowboy boots he's worn since the eighties. He adjusts his giant belt buckle, smooths his mustache. He just wants to get out of the slum before the sun dips below the hills and plummets them into darkness.

But S halts under a flickering streetlight, the only one on the hill. Deep lines are made deeper in its amber glow. "What are you hiding? Who is this girl to you?"

No suspicion or accusation—just questions. S seems to have forgotten that Caulfield called him a 'womanizing douche.' He strongly suspects Aspen ran a below-level operation to talk S onto the plane with him.

Forgetting isn't always a bad thing. Because of his broken head he forgets quiet often, mainly small, useless memories. Millions of trees grow because squirrels forget where they bury nuts. That's all he wants for his sister, to help her grow roots, to thrive far away from this place. "She's my sister."

"Maria—"

"Not Maria. Another sister."

Uncle C's handlebar mustache twitches but he says nothing. More unraveling...only a matter of time before his parents learn of what he's done, but it's too late, the mesh is a tangle of threads between his fingers. "She's my half-sister. My real dad and a woman from Tamaulipas had a *thing*."

Isn't that a hang-up: his 'real' dad, as if the man who raised him isn't 'real..' It's a pungent leftover he should have tossed fifteen years ago when he became a man and realized who stood beside him and who didn't.

Caulfield was the product of a broken man who found a broken woman and together they made a broken child. The same for his sister, and that's what binds them together—not blood or family. Mental illness. Both fought demons and lost, and won, fighting, always fighting. She claimed Caulfield was her light and maybe that's why he now stands under a dirty streetlight in Tizilicho. Who else is left to be her single beaming lampstand, cutting through the smothering, overwhelming fog of drug use? That fog uses up person after person like sulfur mustard, steals their light, absorbs their light. Had she grasped and clawed for his light, only to find he wasn't a true light at all but a weak imitation?

Caulfield remembers when he dragged her to the rehab center in Ciudad Victoria nearly six years ago, ratted hair and clammy skin, her body trembling as poison leaked from her pores...

"Why did you bring me to *this* place?" she snarled.

"You need help. They'll never find you here."

"They'll *always* find me, Caulfield. They'll find me because I'll always find them first. That's how messed up I am."

"You can overcome this. I did."

"I don't have *familia*, like you."

"You do now."

She did overcome. She completed rehab, found cheap housing in Ciudad Victoria. But the cartel was always three steps behind with another 'job' and promises of more drugs. She needed to leave the country and he helped.

"You can never contact me again," she said as they left the cross-border tunnel behind in Texas. "It is safer this way..."

What if he hadn't listened? Would she still live in this slum? Tizilicho, built on top of a World Heritage site where ancient Aztecs eked out a living forging canals and artificial islands.

What little grass grows between grimy cinderblock apartments is crowded out by volcanic rock.

No electricity, no running water. People siphon it from the neighborhood down the hill.

Caulfield inquires at the grocery store at the bottom of the hill (little more than a shed with basic food staples on teetering shelves), the clerk says he saw her a few days ago. "She looks like you. Tall, skinny, wide mouth. Sweet girl, comes in every other Friday from the slum with money. Brings children —neighbors pay her to watch them."

Caulfield pulls out the yellow post-it note, flimsy as fabric from carrying it in his wallet:

Hermano, I need you. There is no one else. Meet me at the Mount Sanitas trailhead tomorrow at six in the evening.

"Why didn't you come?" he murmured when he called the number she'd scribbled, but only a dial tone answered.

Now, Uncle C waits for them at the top of the stairs, thumbs hitched over his belt buckle like a true vaquero. The outline of a gun holster is visible beneath his embroidered shirt. It's illegal to carry a firearm in Mexico, but as often as Uncle C drives the dangerous northern Tamaulipas highways, he doesn't blame him for packing heat.

He and S climb open-air stairs, wobbly and uneven. His breath catches. His sister lives here. He's only seen her three times in his life, but he loves her. Or maybe he loves the idea of her. He'll bring her to Bear Creek, where he and Aspen can lease their apartment to her once the new house is finished. It all begins with a knock on a flimsy plywood door.

No answer. He knocks again, runs a hand through his hair while S takes a turn, as if Caulfield's knocks aren't sufficient. Then he bangs his fist against the door and curses.

"Does she have a night job?" Uncle C asks.

"I don't know."

"What next?"

"I don't know." He doesn't know anything about her, does he? Nothing, except the fairytales he's woven in his head.

A door down the hall creaks open and a woman peers at the three strange men. "Who are you?"

"I'm her brother."

Faded flowers paint her apron, washed and rewashed. Her posture leaves little room for luxury. She isn't one to soften words. The woman takes in the look of him, S, Uncle C. Her eyes rest on the gun bulge beneath Uncle C's shirt. "How do I know you aren't one of them? A Zacatón?"

"I guess you don't."

She nods. "Either way, she's gone."

"When will she return?"

"She's gone, as in moved. Don't know where."

Just like that, hope morphs to alarm, hard and porous as the volcanic rock below. "Please. I need to find her."

"If she wants you, she'll find you."

"But what if she's in trouble?"

The woman's eyes glisten, just slightly, and Caulfield suspects she may be the migrant's wife. "I believe I spoke to your husband. Is he a farmhand in Colorado?"

Her shoulders ease. "Do you want to see inside the place?"

She slides by him and the smell of herbs tickles his nose, causes him to sneeze. She jiggles a key into doorknob. The plywood creaks.

The room is indeed empty of life. A bit of furniture, a mattress thinner than the ones in the various jail cells he's inhabited. A table with two chairs. An empty hamper, pink plastic hangers dangling from a clothesline running the length of the tiny room. No clothes, no toiletries, nothing that indicates she was abducted or in a flight for her life, which is comforting. A trace of orange and lye lingers in the air.

A massive thud echoes behind him and a small object flies across the floor. He jumps, turns around. S is flat on his back, groaning. "Tripped," he mutters as Caulfield gives him a hand up. He finds the small object in the corner of the kitchenette, cocooned in dust bunnies, and smiles—how unexpected.

"What is it?" asks S.

"A matchbox car. See?" He plops the yellow corvette in S's palm.

"I had a thousand of these things when I was a kid."

"Me too, though most of them ended up buried in the creek clay behind our house. Aspen flushed one down the toilet, once. Mom had to call a plumber."

S holds the toy out to the woman. "Your son's?"

Her face is a blank slate. She takes the car and tucks it into the pocket of her apron.

Caulfield puffs his cheeks, exhales. "Not much for us to do."

Uncle C grunts. "At least she's safe."

"Yeah," he says, though he honestly has no idea. Some dark thing clouds inside of him, call it sibling intuition or a gut feeling. But what else can he do, aside from wait for her to reach out?

Once they are in the hallway, the woman closes the door behind them and locks it, *click*.

Locks away all traces of his sister.

Locks away the clues to where she's gone.

They stand outside the apartment and watch the sun release one last encore of gold before it bows and a curtain of darkness falls.

Now what? He turns to S and Uncle C. "Let me be the one to tell my parents."

S frowns. "Do it quick, man."

He would, as soon as he figures out what to say. Right now, he just needs to sink into a mattress and sleep for a thousand years.

Later, in a hotel room flooded with city lights, as S snores in the bed across the room, and as Caulfield "wavers" in that place between awareness and nothingness, he quietly laughs at the neighbor woman's parting words...

"I like your Nixies."

Whatever

S—I'm sorry you didn't find her, but you tried. I know you're drained and discouraged.—

K

Mount of the Holy Cross
July

"Any panicky feelings?" Molly asked.

"Not yet. You?"

"No. Give it another thousand feet and we'll see." This was Molly's first climb since the avalanche, and she was as rigid as the stick her Black Lab, Tito, chomped between drooly jaws.

We took the North Ridge approach up the Mount of the Holy Cross because it was only a Class Two and she was out-of-practice. Hector and Luca, showboats that they were, ditched us for the Cross Couloir ascent and would 'wait for us' at the summit. Ha. Not if we got there first.

"Kaye, you're killing me. If you don't ease up, any time advantage we gain will be lost when I pass out in the tundra zone."

I slowed my short, zippy strides to match Molly. Tito darted between us, vibrating with unspent energy. It was hard to imagine an avalanche tumbling through this thick forest, hoisting and heaving our bodies over a trail that was more of a giant rock pile. Once we broke the tree line and met nothing but rock, moss, and thin air, how would she fare?

"When does Samuel get back from his book signing?" she puffed.

"Wednesday." Molly had assumed he was in Mexico City for a book signing, and I hadn't corrected her. Lying by omission didn't sit well with me. Neither did worrying whether my husband had been kidnapped and crammed in a box.

"And you're dropping us off at the airport tomorrow, don't forget. Argh, I'm going to die. My calves are cramping!"

Break time. I scooted my rear onto a flat rock and unhooked my water bottle. Molly patted the ground for Tito to settle at her feet.

The trees on this side of the mountain were old, more than a hundred years, untouched by disease or fire. "Samuel said something interesting last week. Our lives aren't remembered beyond two or three generations." I breathed in cool, crisp air. "Think about it. Do you know much about your great-grandparents? How they spent their afternoons, their hobbies, their beliefs? Do you know what they worried about?"

"Mine worried about whether grasshoppers would get their corn crop. For the first eight years of my life, I actually believed grasshoppers were called 'Long-Legged Beelzebubs.'"

"Gran said her dad griped about how the Irish were stealing all the jobs because they worked for pennies. Then Gran would remind him that *he* was Irish, and he'd laugh and say, 'You just proved my point.'

"But it's a speck in time, swept away when our parents die. Once we're gone, most people won't even know they existed. One day, our descendants won't know anything about *us*, other than public records and a small branch in their family tree."

"When we get back to Boulder, we're going to see about Prozac for you, sweetums. That's the most godawfully depressing thing you've said in months. Cripes, I think I'll just lay down right here on this mountain and call it quits." She sprawled across the rock.

"Well, he also said it's one reason he has faith in God. Who else is going to remember us forever? Why would we be so complex, love so deeply, if in the end, no one is left to acknowledge our existence?"

"I guess that's comforting if you believe in God."

"And naively optimistic if you don't."

Molly dug through her hiking bag and tossed a dog treat to Tito. "Look on the bright side. Samuel will be remembered for a couple of centuries, at least. Do you think his books will be considered classics a hundred years from now?"

"Hated by high school students far and wide: the dreaded mandatory reading list." I sighed and unwrapped a bar. "Sometimes I wonder if anyone will remember me beyond this generation. Danita's children, I suppose. A dead-end branch on a great grand-nephew's tree."

Molly frowned. "Oh Kaye, don't think like that. Is it really certain that you and Samuel won't have children?"

"He doesn't want them, and I can't force fatherhood on him. It would be unfair." I scratched the top of Tito's head and he panted happily as I swallowed back tears.

"But what about you? I can't believe you'd have such a strong desire to be a mom if you weren't meant to have kids."

"I've turned it over a thousand times in my head, believe me. I've tried to make sense of it. I've begged God to show me the big plan. I mean, does he think it's hilarious to place this love in my heart for Samuel and then to make me want children so badly, I can feel them in my arms?"

Tears gathered behind Molly's glasses. "I can't answer that. All I know is there's a lot of cruddy things in life that can't be explained. Remember what happened to my sister Holly several years ago? How horrible her post-partum depression was? But now she's come through to the other side and has a lot more gratitude because of it. It shifted her entire worldview."

"Sofia told me that a person's suffering is a horrible, temporary window. But once we've stared into that window, we're able to see sunlight shining through, feel it on our skin, allow it to illuminate dark corners of our lives and expose the bad things that lurk there."

"Sofia is, like, the wisest person I know."

"Sometimes. I don't agree with everything she says and does, but she knows how to love people."

"So do you. And so does Samuel, because of her and Alonso." She snapped her fingers. "You know, our descendants won't remember a thing about us one day, but I bet they'll know how to love. They may not realize that, four generations back, a special aunt loved their Great-Great Grandpa Gabriel, but the love itself will be ingrained in them. That's what you pass down. Not worries or hobbies, or what you ate for lunch."

We sat in silence, tossed a stick into a creek much too cold for our feet, but perfect for Molly's slobbering dog.

"I miss you, Molly."

She nudged my shoulder. "You have a standing invite to dig up clams with me on the beach."

As we heaved ourselves onto the summit of Holy Cross, we found our friends collapsed across the ground in pure exhaustion.

"Really guys? You're that competitive?" Molly tapped Hector with her boot and he simply flopped over.

"How long have you been up here?" I asked.

"At least an hour," Luca groaned. It was possible we'd have to roll them down the mountain.

We rested and pointed out a herd of mountain goats, mere dots on the purple slope of the neighboring mountain.

I thought about what Molly had said. Whatever choices Samuel made—both good and bad—were driven by love. It was his guide through a field of sinkholes that could have swallowed him up if not for the rope he clung to. When he didn't know which direction to go, he pulled out his compass and asked: which is the most compassionate path to take?

This was why he'd gone to Mexico City to search for his sister, despite my strong objections. He'd been driven by love and, in the end, that's why I gave him my blessing.

———————◆•◆———————

I'd wondered which way this latest episode would go before he left for Mexico City. Given his spiraling mood swing, not to mention his brawl with Santiago at the mental health benefit concert (oh, the irony), I'd have placed money on mania. But when I collected the boys from the airport, depression rang loud and clear. Dejection. Mexico hadn't gone well but he was sealed up tighter than one of Sofia's Tupperware bowls.

"Did you find her?" I glanced at Samuel in the rearview mirror, feeling very much his chauffer.

"We were too late. She was gone."

"Gone where?"

He closed his eyes and I felt the sting of his dismissal. He probably just needed sleep. In five hours' time, after he rested and ate, he'd open up.

But five hours turned into fifteen and an uneaten plate of food.

Early the next morning, my fingers fumbled with the zipper of my pencil skirt as I quietly got ready for work, trying not to wake him. Startling me, he brushed my fingers away and finished the job.

"Feel better?" He didn't look better. Purple circles rimmed his eyes, skin was paler than normal, and I suspected he'd return to bed after I left.

He rested his chin on my head. "I found her apartment, spoke to whom I assume was Javier's wife. She's a spindly thing. No Marieta. Nothing." His tone grew angry. "I don't understand. I gave her more than enough money not only to live comfortably in the U.S., but to have a place in Paris if she so chose. Why did she return to Mexico, only to scrape by in that decrepit place? Where did the money go?"

"Drugs?"

"How else could she blow so much money so fast?" He thumped a fist on the wall. "I'd hoped she would stay clean. I should have brought her home to Colorado."

I ran my fingers through his hair, eased his mood. "Perhaps she sent some of it to her family in Tamaulipas."

"I'm the only family she has."

"What about her friends in Mexico City? It sounds as though Javier and his wife could use a bit of help."

"He never mentioned it."

"Maybe she had a lot of debt that needed to be repaid. Or someone she paid off under the table?"

"Possibly."

We lapsed into uncomfortable silence as I struggled to tame my mane and he brushed his teeth. He followed me into the living room and dropped onto the couch with his laptop. I grabbed my briefcase and gestured to the coffee table.

"Can you please pay the water bill online today? Otherwise I'll have to drop it over at the waterworks."

"Mmhm." His eyes didn't deviate from his laptop.

I nearly walked out the door, but I remembered a mistake I'd made, so long ago. I turned back and sat next to him on the couch.

"Hey. I love you, Samuel."

He glanced up, a soft smile on his mouth. "I love you too, Aspen Kaye."

As I jogged down the flight of stairs and into my business, beautiful hope unfurled in my chest, the kind of blindness that made everything in the world shine. As long as I had his soft smiles and an 'I love you' every morning, this marriage would work. He'd be okay, I'd be okay, *we'd* be okay, nothing would rip us apart, whether it was the most fundamental of disagreements like money and kids, or the havoc wreaked by mental illness.

But as I unlocked the door and slipped out of my heels just after six p.m., that roller coaster high bottomed out. Samuel was still on the couch, asleep. Still unshowered. The unopened bill still rested on the coffee table. His laptop word processor had only several paragraphs of writing about his visit to Mexico, which ended in a single word: "Whatever."

The cycle began. 'Whatever.' Really? Was he a teenager? Of course, before long, *I just knew* he'd be holed up like a hermit playing the Xbox. (Never mind that he'd never owned an Xbox.) Oh, I was irritated. Dirty bowls on the counter, mostly filled with uneaten cereal. *My* cereal, because he didn't eat that 'toxic stuff' anymore, right? Unwashed clothes tossed on the floor next to the hamper. Was this some passive-aggressive message he wanted to send? 'I am perfectly capable of putting this stinky tee shirt in the hamper, but I'm going to leave it on the floor right *beside* the hamper.' I snagged his clothes off the floor and stuffed them in the hamper, then the clothes he'd draped across the footboard of our bed, *then* tackled the clean clothes in the laundry basket that hadn't been folded for a week and, because I was really in a tizzy, his deodorant, toothbrush, mouthwash, and shaving gel that cluttered our counter. He had three empty drawers next to his sink! 'Normal' Samuel was fastidious, organized. 'Normal' Samuel would never leave clothes on the floor, hygiene things all over the counter, dirty dishes in the kitchen. If he was typically messy, it wouldn't have bothered me one whit. (Okay, it would have bothered me, but for completely different reasons.) Why was I so worked up about it now?

"Damned bipolar disorder," I gritted through clenched teeth. "Why can't you leave him alone for just one month?" I grabbed a half-empty bottle of fabric softener and slammed it onto the top of the dryer. The metallic thud rang through the hallway. "Give him one!" *Slam.*

"Single!" *Slam.* "Month!" *Slam.*

Like an idiot, I stood in the hallway, waiting for 'bipolar disorder' to answer.

It didn't. Neither did Samuel.

For two weeks I secretly monitored his meds. He took them.

I monitored his moods. Apathetic. Anxious. Angry, all the 'A's.

I monitored his physical symptoms. Back aches, no appetite, and definitely no sex.

I dragged him out, hoping to draw a genuine smile. The Twiggies played a rip-roaring gig at the Boulder Theater. Samuel leaned against the wall next to his stool, false smile plastered on his lips, standing with the rest of the crowd in a show of appreciation. But it was just that—a show.

We saw his doctor, which came to nothing. "I don't think a meds adjustment is what's needed. I can give you a dose of Depakote and additional psychotherapy."

But the thing that pushed me from concern to panic was the evening I returned from work to find an open bottle of port wine on the counter. The thing had been a thank you gift from a client and I'd stuffed it high above the cabinets, intending to send it home with our IT guy. I'd forgotten and, being inches shy of elf status, I couldn't see it. But Samuel could, and had, and decided to break out the brandy-heavy beverage today after how many years of sobriety?

Oh my God, his meds. I burst into our room, spilling light behind me. Samuel jerked a hand up to his eyes.

"How much of it did you drink?"

He groaned and fell back into his pillow. "Just a little. It turned my stomach and I wretched it up."

"Are you telling me the truth? Because if you drank more and it's mixed with your meds, we could have a serious problem."

"I suppose there's no way to prove it, is there? You'll have to trust me." I returned to the kitchen, speechless.

Was it possible to feel such relief and, at the same time, such heartbreak? I held the bottle up to the ceiling light. The iris of the wine glowed dark red, nearly three-fourths full. I watched the burgundy liquid gush out of the bottle like blood from a vein and splash down the drain, its deeply painful color blurring through the mess in my eyes. He hadn't even tried to hide it. Did he care so little? So much? Was he so defeated? Or maybe he was asking for help?

Another thought crawled in: What if we'd had an infant in our home? A toddler? An eight-year-old? Would I have sent him to Sofia and Alonso while I cared for my husband? Or perhaps I would have sent Samuel to his parents' home. I'd have been in way over my head.

Perhaps it's for the best, this thought whispered. I shrugged it off, a sweater that was too warm.

By the time the port bottle was emptied of every last drop, I'd made a decision.

In the morning, I would go to his parents for help.

———————————— •••• ————————————

As I held the receiver, I played out different conversations in my mind:

Alonso, Samuel's depressed again.

How long? How bad?

It's really bad this time. He drank again, kind of.

Ay Dios mío, his medication. He needs to be in the hospital...

No. Take two...

Alonso, Samuel's had a rough time, ever since he came back from Mexico—

Why on earth was he in Mexico? Nobody mentioned to us he'd be out of the country...

No. Take three...

Alonso, Samuel is depressed because his secret illegitimate half-sister needs help and even Interpol can't track her down. So he's lying on the couch in four days' worth of stale sweat and filth, contemplating whether he's going to renew his acquaintance with alcohol.

Silence...

It had potential.

As it turned out, I didn't get a chance to make that phone call.

Early the next morning, a rapid pounding sent us tumbling from our bed in a heap of blankets. I glanced at the alarm clock: five-fifty a.m. I hadn't slept much, instead holding vigil while Samuel tossed and turned, watching for any breathing difficulties or convulsions.

Sam jerked on his pants and peered through the peephole, as if he didn't already know who it was by the trills and tildes fired at our door. Perhaps he was taking stock of Alonso's fury before he admitted the Spanish cyclone. I couldn't make out his words until Samuel opened the door, and it all became clear. My mind rushed to translate.

"A sister!? Why in God's name did you not tell us this woman in Tamaulipas you befriended is our niece?"

"I had my reasons." Samuel shot me a look, but I wasn't the droid he was looking for.

"They had better be good reasons."

"My reasons are my own. Perhaps you could afford me a modicum of trust?"

Alonso clutched Samuel's bare arm and steered him into our living room, as if he were a naughty five-year-old who'd just kicked the cat. Kudos to Samuel for not shaking him off, though he was entirely capable.

"I'll trust you when you can prove to me you aren't ruled by your moods and whims!"

I almost went to bat for Samuel, but Sofia beat me to the swing. "Alonso, that is entirely unfair. You know he has put forth great—"

"He hid our niece from us!"

"He said he had his reasons."

"What if she needed us? The Valdez boy says she's in trouble." Oh, Santiago was a dead man.

Samuel's neck reddened and his eyes flared. Now it was game on. He stepped right up to his father, emphasizing the full six inches he had on Alonso. "Don't you have any faith in me, *Papá*?" he said in Spanish. "Do you believe I am a fool? Your own mother kept the girl a secret, took it to her death. Your own family turned her away."

Alonso grasped the back of his son's neck and pressed their foreheads together. "*Mijo*, do you honestly believe I would have done the same? You of all people should know better."

"Because you adopted me?"

"Because you are my child! Because I have given you my life, fully and freely!"

Samuel bit his lip and stepped down. Tears shone in his eyes. One sob, two. Alonso yanked him into a hug. Everything in me wanted to go to my husband, but in this moment, he was a son, first. I quietly stepped onto the patio and allowed Samuel time with his parents.

The sun was now a brilliant orange in the eastern horizon. I trailed my finger through the dew on the railing, the patio chairs, and waited with a strange detachment for the drama to unfold, relieved, for once, not to be in the middle. My phone buzzed in my sweater pocket. I glanced at the caller and grimaced. Santiago.

"Samuel's going to murder you. Couldn't you have waited until daylight?"

"I'm guiding a group of German tourists into the National Park this morning, and I wanted to call before my signal got spotty. Listen, Kaye. I know this has caused an all-out-smack-down in your family, but it had to be done. I asked myself, 'what would Angel do?' He'd do the right thing. And it wasn't right, the Cabrals not knowing they have a niece."

My thoughts exactly. "I should have said something sooner. I'm sorry, Santiago."

"Nah, you're in a rough place. Consider this a late Christmas present."

I flinched as the raised voices of Samuel and his father thundered inside our apartment.

Sofia slipped through the screen door. I ended the call.

"Walk with me?" she said.

I nodded and yanked on my ecosneaks. We clomped down the outside stairs and turned north, toward Pearl Street. Summer air hung heavy this morning, unusual for Colorado's arid climate, but the sun would soon dry up any lingering humidity. It promised to be a hot one. Pearl Street was quiet, save for a handful of bakeries and coffee shops open to early-birds. Sofia twisted her long, heavy hair over her shoulder. They had left home in such a rush, she hadn't taken the time to braid it.

"How long has Samuel been this bad?"

I sighed. "A couple of weeks, though it's crept up for a while. Ever since..." I bit my tongue, but Sofia knew.

"Ever since you argued about children."

I rushed to explain. "I love your son, Sofia. I'm in this with him. And I knew when we married that children might not happen."

"Oh *mija*, your mouth says one thing but the pain in your eyes says another. You can be honest with me."

The dam broke one time more than I cared to count. "I brought this episode on with the way I harped at him about kids. I *knew*. I knew it would distress him, but I did it anyway."

"You are my whirlwind child," Sofia smiled. "It would have been wrong for you to lock up all of this feeling, to hide it away from your

husband. You must be *real* with each other. As for causing him stress..."
Her face filled with a world of worry. "I believe this horrific web in
which he's ensnared has placed a lifetime's worth of stress on his shoulders. The Zacatón Cartel." She shook her head. "My poor, confused,
heroic boy. Always charging in on his white horse to right wrongs,
always shielding those he loves. A sister! I wish he had told us."

"He was scared, Sofia. He didn't want to bring it to your doorstep."

"Oh, I know. Only three weeks ago, another fifteen bodies were
dumped on the highway north of Ciudad Victoria, their heads, hands
and feet removed so they couldn't be identified. Four were children."
She crossed herself. "I tell *mi familia*, every time I speak with them, to
be vigilant. The people are sick of it. Lucia told me about the hacker
group...Incognito?"

"Unknown."

"Yes, that's it. There is a branch in Ciudad Victoria that publishes
addresses and photos of homes and businesses belonging to the cartel,
to drive them out of our city. Just last week, they released information
that caused near riots around these Zacatón places, the people hate
them so much. Lucia tried to google it, but you have to know how to
access the Dark Web."

"Listen to you, you techie."

Sofia shrugged. "Now tell me more about last night."

So I did, starting with the open bottle of wine and then the
depression.

"What do I do now? I've watched his meds, got him to the doctor,
even took him out for his birthday."

Sofia stopped beside a bed of day lilies and stooped over to finger
one of the delicate petals. She always sought out flowers. "He needs
work away from his laptop. Something to get him outside, into the
air. Manual labor. Not a cure, I know...but it may help him to 'switch
frequencies,' so to speak." Her eyes shown with an idea. "What is your
mother typically doing this time of year?"

Oh, Sofia was a genius. "Her early root vegetables—beets, rad-
ishes, carrots—might be ready for harvest. English peas and snap
peas will need to be picked soon. Otherwise, lots of watering and
weeding the other plants." I pictured my mother in her tattered straw

hat and gardening gloves browned by the dirt. Last time I saw her, she was up a ladder replacing glass panes on the roof of her greenhouse. "Greens like kale, spinach, and arugula will be in the greenhouse. Planting squash maybe. I think she'll have a couple of lambs by now, and chickens every day."

"Could she use a farmhand?"

"Oh, I think she could definitely use the help."

Sofia winked. "I wonder what sort of fastidious, detail-oriented, hardworking person we could find to assist her?"

Chapter 14
GASTON

*Named after a French mountain guide, this is
a climbing hold that looks as if one is using their
hands to pry open elevator doors.*

I yelped as some wild animal streaked from my mom's living room and through the kitchen, leaving a trail of bleats behind. An old cloth was wrapped and safety pinned around its rump. Its stump tail wagged through a round hole cut in the cloth. I stumbled into a rack filled with blue, green, and orange glass bottles and they rattled, scattering rainbows throughout the kitchen.

"Cheese and crackers, Mom! Why is there a diaper on that lamb?"

Mom looked at me as if I were crazy. "You think I'm going to let a lamb take a big ol' dump on my carpet?"

"Why is there a lamb in the house to begin with?"

"Her name is Loppy." The lamb butted her head against Mom's leg, and she scratched it as if it were a cat. "Her momma rejected her, so I've been bottle feeding."

"Can't she stay outside?"

"Nah, still too cold at night. She sleeps in a laundry basket by my bed. She's a sweet, playful thing, but she chewed the heck out of the furniture I got from your Gran."

Not a big loss. If not for its sentimental value, that old plaid couch would have been retired with 8-tracks. (Although, I'm not sure Mom had retired those, either.)

Loppy bleated again and nudged my mother, then moved on to my shoes. She sniffed the Tevas, sucked one of the shoestrings into her mouth and chewed.

I dodged Loppy's chompers. She followed me across the kitchen, into the living room. I tried to hide my feet behind the table, but she pushed past the table legs and lapped happily at my favorite climbing shoes.

"Aspen! Don't let her eat it, it'll make her sick."

"Kinda don't have a choice here." I jerked the shoes off my feet and shoved them in the cabinet under the sink. Loppy dived for the shoes and ran smack into the cabinet with a surprised "maaa!" I chuckled. "That'll teach you, you cute little garbage disposal."

"Might have to go to the pet store and buy a few toys."

I smiled knowingly. There was a distinct possibility Loppy might not ever be put in the sheep pen. "Hey, is Samuel out back?"

"He's in one of the west gardens with the migrants digging weeds out of the beet rows. Man's a hard worker, does good, too."

"Is he okay?"

Mom nodded, understanding what I meant. "We spent most of the day in the back field thinning out those damned prairie dog colonies with my twenty-two. Does wonders for dark moods."

"Murderers."

She snorted. "Wreak havoc on the land. They signed their own death warrant when they collapsed my fence line with their burrowing."

"Hey." I touched my mother's hand, rough and cracked as I always remembered it to be. "Thanks, Mom. I know I don't say it often enough, but I'm grateful."

She looked away, embarrassed. "I know I'm not a normal kind of mother, but I do try, Aspen Kaye, in my way. Now get some fresh air with my new farm hand."

I grabbed my Tevas from beneath the sink and high-tailed it out the door before Loppy nipped my ankles.

"Don't let that lamb out!" Mom called, just as I closed the screen door to Loppy's bleats.

The mosquitoes were visible clouds of annoyance, this close to the St. Vrain. The combo of water and my mother's delicious gardens made her farm a blood-sucker breeding ground. I grabbed the insect repellent from her work shed and sprayed myself down, slipped into one of her old flannels, and hopped onto her four-wheeler.

Gravel spit behind the tires when I accidentally peeled out (I hadn't driven the old thing in ages), but I found my bearings and floored it once I reached open field. Wind beat against my face and water streamed from my eyes. I swerved around a low-hanging tree branch, just in time. Gravel gave way to two tire tracks, and soon I bumped and thumped through waist high pasture until I reached her back gardens. I use the term 'garden' loosely. These things weren't your neighbor's five rows of beans and tomato plants. This two-acre stretch of baby green tops was her livelihood. Nurturing fragile plants from seedlings, watering and weeding round the clock as they unfurled their leaves and stretched their stalks, picking their fruits—these were her babies. As a child, I'd hated weeding and bitterly complained about how sunburned my neck was, how my back hurt. She'd get a good hour's work out of me and send me off to play under the auspices of chasing rabbits from her vegetables.

I heard the laughter of the seasonal workers. They were at the far end of a row of young turnips whose tops were barely distinguishable from weeds. A trail of uprooted thistles and tall grass marked their paths. I grabbed garden gloves from the ATV compartment and knelt in the dirt on the other side of Sam's row.

"Hey, firecracker. Your mom put you to work, too?" He smiled softly and reached up, untangling something from my curls. He held up a grass tassel for me to see.

I returned his smile. "She sent me to make sure you weren't yanking up the root vegetables with the interlopers. I can't believe how quickly they took over, it looks like she just weeded a week ago."

"She hired a couple of high school students to work weekends. I heard all about how kids these days can't tell a radish from a carrot, because any vegetable they eat comes canned and smothered in cheese."

"The smothered in cheese bit doesn't sound so bad," I laughed. "Mom used to go to Denver and talk to classes about responsible agriculture. One of the kids actually told her that farms would be obsolete in five years, because most people shopped at grocery stores. That Mom didn't chuck a big fat textbook at the kid's head is pure luck."

"Given the way she lit into me for offering to buy a bottle of Round-up, I'd say it's a miracle of God."

"I'd say it's a miracle of God that you didn't end up in a pile with those dead prairie dogs. Don't you know that Round-Up is to organic farmers what cliff notes are to Lit professors?"

Joy leapt in my heart as I saw laughter in his eyes, his mouth, his body. Sunlight beat down upon his face and red streaked his skin, revealing the places he skimped on sunscreen. The burns would hurt if he didn't put on lotion soon. I brushed dirt from his forehead. He caught my hand. Gently pushing the glove up, he lowered his head and kissed my wrist, ever so softly.

"Thank you, Kaye. Somehow, you always know just what I need."

"I'd love to take credit, but it was your mother's idea. Look, I know the sadness and the anxiety is still in there…"

"A healthy outlet is never a bad thing. But you didn't have to drive all the way out to Lyons every day after work, just to keep me company."

"I like keeping you company."

"Come here." He helped me step over the garden row, led me away from the field and the other workers. Then he pulled me into his arms. Fresh earth, grass, and sweat filled my nostrils as I breathed. His muscles bunched and tensed under my embrace. He'd pushed them hard today. "This week out in the air, just me, the ground, and the things that grow? It lends honesty. Do you understand?"

"Yeah. It cuts through all the world's crap."

Samuel chuckled. "Exactly. Why do I hide so many things? Why do I let myself be swept up in wickedness?"

"'Wicked' is a strong word."

"Oh *mi vida*, there are wicked people in this world. Here's a lesson in root words from a writer: 'wicked' comes from 'wick.' In other words, 'twisted.' Wicker furniture, a candle wick. All twisted. And when a person twists something out of its natural state—the truth, for example— then they are wicked. I'm afraid I'm as wicked as the next person."

"If that's the case, anyone who's ever lied is wicked."

"Hmmm, I think it's more a state of being. A habitual liar, if you will."

"Are you a habitual liar?"

"I didn't think so. But Gail reminded me that a lack of transparency is just another form of lying."

"My mother is the most brutally honest person I know. Awesome when you want the truth. Disillusioning when you're a four-year-old who wants to believe in Santa Claus."

"In this instance, I asked to hear the brutal truth and I got it. Tricking people into believing you are something you're not is lying. Keeping secrets from the people you love... Oh, I may tell myself I'm protecting my family. And I am. But there's a layer of self-preservation at the bedrock of secrecy." Samuel rested his chin on my head. "I don't want to be a wicked person, Kaye. It's time to come clean."

"What are you saying?"

"Tomorrow evening, after *el changuito* goes to bed, I'm laying my cards on the table."

Samuel was perfectly composed in the Cabrals' formidable library, the last traces of his depressive episode having dissipated like a spent thunderstorm. He sat beside me on the stiff company couch. Across from us, Alonso and Sofia each claimed an armchair, and Dani propped her very swollen feet up in the recliner, the room's only comfortable piece of furniture. I wasn't sure why Alonso hadn't led us to the cozy family room of our happiest memories. Perhaps for that very reason: Alonso was not happy. He was furious, despite Sofia's persistent intervention.

A tiny, snide voice whispered that he now reaped what he'd sown (after all, hadn't they hidden Samuel's bipolar disorder for years?), but 'I told you so' had no place in this conversation.

"I couldn't forget the letter my father wrote to you," Samuel said to Alonso. "How he found the country girl in the mountains where you used to hike, how he lusted after her. In the exaggerated imagination of my childhood, he had been a hero. I didn't want to believe that he could cheat on my mother and me, so I decided to unearth the truth.

"I combed every street, tavern, business within a five mile radius of La Vereda, Tamaulipas. The village is only a scattering of homes on two mountain slopes and a valley, more burros and cows than residents. My sister—Marieta Sanchez is her name—told me that many of the residents are *campesinos*, making them attractive recruits to the cartels. The homes are cinder block, small, brightly colored like you find in most of the mountain towns on the outskirts of Ciudad Victoria. Kitchens are outside on the patio and everyone cooks with wood...the smells in the evening were incredible. Mexican orange blossoms everywhere; they all plant them, crush them into fragrances."

"Not much has changed in fifty years." Alonso's expression was wistful.

"La Vereda is no different than any small town, in that everyone knows everyone's business. But the cartels have made them tight-lipped and it was impossible to convince anyone to help me with what little information I had: Young man from Ciudad Victoria, Harvard educated, used to visit thirty years ago? But an old woman *did* remember a well-dressed city-slicker named Antonio Cabral Treiño, and warned Marieta I was asking questions. So, in the end, *she* found *me*.

"I was eating lunch at the only store in town, a white-washed grocery with tamales that reminded me of home. She pulls up a chair and says, 'I hear from the *señora* that you're looking for my mother. This is her.' She shows me an old photo and there's my dad with his arm around a young village woman. She wore one of those brightly colored flower headdresses women make on festival days, and she looked at my father as if he were a king."

"The Cabral men have always been too dashing for their own good," Sofia tutted.

Samuel shifted uncomfortably but pressed on. "See, this woman thought he was a golden boy because his second *apellido* was Treiño, like the wealthy family from Nuevo Laredo. This also pleased her older brother and he encouraged the relationship. When the brother found out the Cabral-Treiños were has-been hacienda owners, he told her to break it off, but it was too late. She was in love with the '*pocho*.'

"My father trysted with her whenever he visited his family in Ciudad Victoria. Then he stopped."

"Because he shut himself up in his garage with a running Chrysler," Alonso grimaced. Samuel nodded. "Once the girl discovered she was pregnant, she tracked down *Mamá* Marieta in the city, searching for Antonio. There, she learned of his death. She had no money of her own and she feared once her pregnancy became apparent to the older brother she lived with, he'd turn her out. She explained her plight to *Mamá* Marieta. For all her hardness, I believe *Abuela* grasped at this connection with her dead son and helped this scared, pregnant girl."

Alonso shook his head. "*Mamá* never said a word to us."

"From what I understand, the last thing *Mamá* Marieta wanted was another scandal darkening their door. She kept them secret from the entire family, even you and Mariángel. But *Mamá* Marieta visited La Vereda every March until the year she died, to mark Antonio's birthday. And, given my sister is also named 'Marieta,' I don't doubt *Mamá* Marieta was a godsend to a cast-off, scandal-plagued single mother and her illegitimate child."

"What happened to the woman Antonio had an affair with?" Dani asked.

"She passed away a decade ago. Cancer. Even then, Marieta still felt the sting of her origins with every whispered word, every bit of gossip. She told me the neighborhood was disappointed to learn I was her brother instead of a secret lover."

"Why didn't she just leave?" Dani asked.

"It's more complicated than simply hopping on the first bus out of town, sweetheart," said Sofia. "It sounds as if she had no money and no acquaintances outside of La Vereda. Because you've never struggled to survive, you've had the opportunity to plan a future, make big dreams. When every day is a fight for food and safety, there is no future plan. You cling to what you know. That was me until my child-hood friend opened my mind to a bigger world." She held Alonso's gaze, the air thick with unspoken memories.

"That's how she got involved with the cartels," Samuel said. "Her uncle had a foot in the door with drug smugglers. It was a lot of money, and the small bit *Mamá* Marieta squirreled away for her had been burned through by the time she finished school. For a poor teenager plagued by debt and depression, the 'easy money' was difficult to resist. She was a drug mule up and down the Tamaulipas highways, Texas, New Mexico, posing as a college student, a waitress, the daughter of such-and-such. Then she graduated to running valuable drug ship-ments through the cross-border tunnels. And, as we all know, when someone struggles with depression, ready access to drugs is like flicking a Bic next to a powder keg.

"The second time I saw her, six years ago, she was forty pounds lighter, gaunt, messed up. But she wanted to get better. She wanted out. So I took her to rehab and, while she detoxed, I researched ways to help her escape this cartel. The problem is, the U.S.-Mexican border is so pocked with drug tunnels, it resembles Swiss cheese, and Marieta knows where half the tunnels are located. The Zacatóns don't allow those who know the tunnels to escape and live." Samuel focused on the laces of his shoes. "That's where my involvement gets dicey."

"What did you do?" Alonso pressed.

"I obtained false documentation for Marieta—new name, identifi-cation—and accompanied her on one last drug run under the border near Nuevo Laredo. The tunnel was six football fields long, began in a Mexican cemetery and ended beneath a pool table in the backroom of a Texas bar. You would not believe how sophisticated this thing was... electricity, ventilation, automated carts. The plan was to dump the drugs and settle her into a new life, far away. But there was a hitch. When her 'cargo' arrived, it wasn't just two kilos of cocaine. It was ten kilos of 'pure cocaine,' packed in coffee crates from Colombia. We wore ski masks so the distributor wouldn't recognize us, but he might have known Marieta."

Sofia's face was a study. "And the drugs?"

"We never delivered it. Marieta tased the receiver, then we dumped the crates in a farm pond and ran."

Dani snorted. "Bet you OD-ed an entire school of carp. Way to kill the ecosystem."

Sofia pressed a palm on her chest. "I'm glad you got rid of that poison."

"But don't you see the dangerous position in which he's put the whole family?" Dani said. "Ten kilos! Over a million dollars' worth of cocaine is literally swimming with the fishes. They just don't forgive something like that, and everyone knows the drug mules are considered expendable. They either get arrested or murdered." She shot daggers at Sam. "You're going to end up on *Forensic Crimes.*" *My fear exactly.* "Furthermore, any road that leads to this 'sister' leads to Samuel, to Kaye, to us, and my *kids*. I should just kill you with my bare hands and get it over with!"

"That's why Sam kept it a secret." I touched Dani's arm. Her blood pressure was already precariously high. "And it's been so long. If something were going to happen, wouldn't it have, already?"

Dani's look could have melted rock. "Nice, Kaye. Let's just tempt the hell out of fate, shall we?"

"Is my niece safe, wherever she is?" asked Sofia.

"I don't know. I'm trying to find out."

"Is she trustworthy?" Dani glared at her mother.

"I believe so."

Samuel may have had faith that this woman he'd only met a handful of times wouldn't give him up, but I sure as heck didn't.

Why would she return to Mexico after Samuel went through so much trouble to get her out?

Why would she ask for his help once more, only to vanish?

Well, I had my summer project list: Run a business, build a house, climb mountains, and find out everything there was to know about this woman, down to how she took her coffee.

Empty soda cans stood yards away on Jaime Guzman's gravel driveway, lined up like condemned men on the top of an old wire kennel.

"Tell me again why I need to learn to shoot? I carry pepper spray in my purse."

"An anonymous little birdie thought it in your best interest."

"Have your brains and those of your little birdie—whom I assume is Samuel—gone to absolute mush? On what planet is putting a gun in my butter fingers a good idea?"

"Normally I don't agree with your fancy-pants playboy, but in this case, I think he's right. He didn't say much, but it sounds as though a shady character is skulking around. Better safe than sorry."

Samuel was in L.A. for a script meeting he'd put off for as long as possible until the *Water Sirens* producers all but threatened legal action. His dynamic PR duo also booked several signings, a talk-show or two, a comic-con, and any other promo events he could do to cultivate interest in his upcoming mountain climbing series. He hadn't wanted to leave, as this Javier fellow still frequented our Boulder County haunts. Despite the man's claim of friendship with his sister, Sam didn't trust him. Thus, the firearms training.

"I don't know what good this will do, because I'm not about to start packing heat."

"I do."

"You do?"

"I've heard about one too many divorce attorneys gunned down by their clients' raging ex-spouses. Received a few death threats myself."

"I had no idea. Can I see your gun?"

"What are you, five? It's in your hand, Kewpie."

"Ah." I inspected the gun, turned it over, careful to keep the muzzle away from my person.

"Argh! Don't *ever* point a gun at someone else, even accidentally, unless you're ready to stare down manslaughter charges. Rule number one in gun protection."

"The safety is on, right?"

"Yes, but it doesn't matter. Always, *always* point it toward the ground." I saluted, gun prudently pointed toward the ground. Jaime glared. "You're going to shoot off your toe."

We practiced hitting targets on the back of Jaime's property for a couple of hours, until my ears rang and my finger joints ached from the kickback. As the sun set, we packed it up and waded through waist-high prairie grass toward Jaime's home. Her kenneled Labs barked with hyperactive glee and, one by one, she set them free. Two tried to take me out. I shoved them back and wiped streaks of slobber on my jeans.

She grabbed two beers from her fridge, and we settled onto her deck to watch her dogs run laps in her yard.

"You gonna tell me why your husband is worried about this person?"

I fished prickly burrs out of my shoelaces.

She took a swig of her beer. "What would you say if I told you I already had an inkling?"

"How could you possibly?"

"I have connections."

"I don't think your gossip magazine contacts are going to be much help in this situation."

"Yeah, probably not. Heard an interesting news story a few weeks back."

"Oh?"

"Things are heating up in Tamaulipas, what with the cartels stomping all over the highways like bulls wagging their balls. I have family there, you know. I'm concerned." I bit the inside of my cheek.

"That's where the Cabral family comes from, isn't it? Ciudad Victoria?"

"What are you getting at, Jaime?"

"I'm not finished with the news story. A man named Daniel Rodriguez released a slew of information on the Dark Web linking various people to the Zacatón Cartel. Addresses, photos, pseudonyms, cross-border tunnel routes. I bet Samuel's worried."

I met her stare for stare. "Why would he worry?"

Jaime smirked. "You can't lie to save your life. He's worried because somewhere, sometime, he got tangled up with the Zacatón Cartel. He's worried because the information released on the Dark Web might lead back to him."

I rubbed my forehead. "I remember hearing this story on the nightly news a couple of days ago. The man that released the info is a member of the hacktivist group 'Unknown.' He's missing, possibly dead…" My brain made the link.

"Those 'connections' you always brag about. Are they able to access the Dark Web? We might be able to see if there's anything of concern. Hypothetically, *of course*," I added. "Samuel's never had any dealings with the Zacatóns."

Jaime held up her hands. "No judgment here. He's too pretty and rich for them to ignore."

"The connections?"

"You're kind of relentless."

"Jaime, dammit! Can you or can't you access Daniel Rodriguez's information dump on the Dark Web?"

"I can."

I sat up straight. "Flaming hamsters, I knew it. You're an Unknown! Oh man, it makes so much sense. You hate lying, cheating scumbags. In fact, you hate most people but especially people who prey on others. You're a loner, but you must have some social interaction."

"What a lovely picture you paint."

I ticked my fingers, one by one. "You're sneaky. *Snarky* sneaky, constantly have these 'operations' up your sleeve. And you can always, always find the dirt you need. Your 'connections' are other Unknowns— even the gossip magazine connection. You're a member of Unknown!"

Her face reddened, and I knew I'd cracked her M.O. "Why would I play war games with a bunch of entitled college brats who think hacking is some sort of service to society?"

"Because sometimes it is. Freedom of information, right? And I'm betting while Unknown has its fair share of hanger-on goobs, at its core they're serious business. You said yourself you're concerned about your family in Tamaulipas, and isn't Unknown trying to pick off the cartels? You're one of the good guys. You're a secret superhero, Jaime, and I just 'Lois-Laned' you!"

Her face had soured so much, I swear fermentation oozed from her pores. "You are batshit crazy!"

"Says Batman. Where do you keep your Guy Fawkes mask?"

"Honestly, do I look like a disaffected protester to you?"

"Honestly, yes. Is it in the top of your closet? Under your bed?"

"Shut up." She shoved my shoulder, not hard enough to bruise, but enough to mean business. "Even if I were an Unknown—which I'm *not*—I wouldn't tell you. The whole point of Unknown is to remain *unknown*."

She leapt to her feet and grabbed an empty water pail. While she sloshed out to the dog kennels, I scanned her property. Beautiful house all alone in a wide-open meadow, just on the fringe of the foothills. Accessible only by a dirt road off a blacktop, off a two-lane highway, on the fringe of the grid. Her address bordered the Mexican neighborhood in Lyons but was not a part of it. Jaime herself, always watching, never a part of society. Always on the fringe... Everything about her cried 'fringe activist.' How did I not realize this before? Now that I'd found this missing puzzle piece, the picture of Jaime finally became clear.

"Did Hector know about your alter ego?" I called.

"That's it! Give me back my beer." She yanked the sweating bottle from my hands and stomped up the stairs. I followed, catching the door before she slammed it in my face.

"Marieta Sanchez, age thirty-three or thirty-four. Grew up in La Vereda. Last known residence was Tizilicho, a slum in Mexico City. That's all I ask."

She sighed. "What about Samuel? Want me to see what's out there on him, too?"

"Just...be careful not to tip off anyone. But I definitely want to know anything you can find on Marieta."

"Marieta...Sanchez." She jotted the details on the back of a napkin.

"Does she have anything to do with this mystery woman Samuel visited in Tamaulipas? The one you were twisted up about earlier?" I pursed my lips.

"Kaye Cabral, with nothing to say. I bet this whole 'practicing discretion' thing is killing you." She tossed the napkin in a desk drawer, among a dozen other notes scribbled on napkins. "It might take a while, but I'll see what I can do."

"I can pay you."

"And now you go and insult me. Just let me be a nice person for once."

"Okay." I went in for a hug, but she dodged me.

"Quit blowing sparkles out of your ass. This is hush money, not a favor. No one finds out about my alter-ego, got it?"

We sat on her deck for another hour, her dogs panting contentedly at our feet. The sun dipped below the mountains and soon the sky was brilliant with stars. It was a moonless night.

"Do you know the Unknown hacker responsible for the data dump? Daniel Rodriguez?"

"We may have interacted online once or twice, but no. My people are from Tampico. He's from a little mountain town outside of Ciudad Victoria."

"La Vereda," I murmured, without thinking.

"Yeah, that's it." Her tone shifted from incredulity to concern. "Same time tomorrow, Kewpie. You need to be proficient on that firearm."

***

I had a theory about how this Javier seemed to be in the same places as me and Samuel. Because of all our trouble with paparazzi several years ago, we were extremely careful with social media, cell phone locations, and other tracking devices. But the occasional thorns in our sides were well-meaning fans desiring personal access to their favorite writer and shared his comings-and-goings on Alan Murphy's NixieNet.net, aka NNN.

Friday morning, I ducked into Ash's cubicle: our resident app genius-slash-Nixie fan.

"Can you try something for me? Just after one p.m., share on NNN's Cabral Sighting app that Samuel is pushing a grocery cart at The Garden Market in Lyons, Colorado."

"Isn't he doing a comic-con in L.A.? None of the users will buy it."

"I don't need them to buy it. Just a stalker."

"This'll ruin my Nixie cred," she grumbled, but agreed.

During lunch at Paddlers, I checked my watch: one o'clock.

While Hector rang up customers, Tricia and I leaned against the counter and shared a contraband cream cheese and bacon pizza she'd picked up from the Lyons Diner. I'd inhaled a slice in four bites.

She raised an eyebrow. "You and Samuel still gluten free at home?"

I groaned as I licked sauce from my fingers. "We're delicious-free. But he's in California for the week, so…"

She shrugged in that awkward, surface-friends manner that defined our relationship.

"Everything in moderation. It's a slippery slope, carb addictions and sugar intake."

Tricia could never quite turn off the physician switch. To her, my marriage to Samuel was more of a case study and our conversations often evolved into unsolicited medical advice. How she stayed married to an adrenaline junkie with a death wish was beyond me.

I glanced at my watch again. "I need to pop over to The Garden Market before I head back to work. Thanks for the company, Tricia."

"I've always wanted to do more of your Friday lunches."

Oh honey, these lunches ain't what they used to be. Molly, Hippie, and Angel were all far away. Dani was feeding *el changuito* mac 'n cheese at home. Samuel was traveling. Santiago was usually good company, but he had his eye on a disillusioned musician at the boutique next door who'd recently dropped out of college to 'find herself,' moved to Lyons with her North Face gear in tow, and was on the hunt for a kayaking instructor. Santiago could sniff out those types a mile away.

That left me, Hector and Tricia, and the ice between them could inflict frostbite over a twelve-mile radius. I was glad to scoot out of the Valdez seat of power.

The hairs on the back of my neck prickled as I walked next door to Audrey's store. I glanced over my shoulder. No one was there. Now wary, I instead crossed the street and passed the diner, the rows of boutiques and law offices. Yes, someone was definitely watching. Had this been a good idea, baiting Sam's stalker?

Finally, I doubled back, pushed through the glass door and into The Garden Market, the little bell tinkling my arrival. No one followed.

Audrey peered out from the bread aisle. Her expression was calm, but her left eye twitched in a dead giveaway.

I gave a little wave. "Hey lady. Long time no see."

Audrey brought me in for a weak hug. "Still kind of uncomfortable, I suppose. Miss ya, though."

She was rounder, sadder. Like me, Audrey tended to eat her emotions. I'd always known when Dad had rejected her marriage advances because she'd break open a tin of turtle chocolates.

She placed a tin on the counter between us. I grabbed three.

She lifted an eyebrow. "You and Samuel still sugar free?"

Apparently my eating habits were atrocious today. "What he doesn't know won't hurt him." A string of caramel stretched from the turtle to my mouth. I flicked it with my tongue.

"Not the best philosophy to employ in a marriage. But what do I know about marriage?"

I placed the turtle down and met her gloomy eyes. "Listen, Audrey. I have to stay out of this because, well, Tom's my dad. But I'm going to say this: You deserved better. I love you, and no matter how ugly things ended with you and Dad, you will always be my family."

She touched my cheek. "Back at you, kiddo. So what brings you by?"

"Dad asked me to return something to you. This is really bad, since I just told you I prefer to stay out of his mess."

She shrugged a pale shoulder and I caught a glimpse of her floral tattoo. "Tom Trilby is persuasive. It's the dimples…makes him seem sweet and boyish. You have it, too—your dad's smile."

"Unfortunately for me, it just makes me look like a Cabbage Patch doll."

"Nonsense. Men always swoon for the girl next door. Or in Tom's case, the girl on the farm."

Yeah, this was going south. I dug through my purse and set a bottle of expensive-looking lotion on the counter. Audrey snapped open the lid and a light fragrance hit my nose. Mint and water lilies? It was Audrey's 'signature' scent, a perfume I'd always associate with her.

Her eyes welled. "It's so stupid. I stuck the bottle in the glove compartment of his Prius on purpose. I imagined him smelling it, remembering and regretting all he'd given up. I bet he didn't even open it."

I was ninety-nine percent certain he hadn't either.

The bell over the door jingled. Sure enough, it was the man, Javier, who had been ten steps behind Samuel half the summer. Flippin' NixieNet.net. Tall, skin browned and leathery from years of sun exposure, late-fifties, Aloha shirt draped over a beer gut, sunglasses pushed up in thick gray waves. Now, my mother often hired seasonal laborers and I knew they typically didn't ditch the fields in the middle of a work day (they also didn't wear floral shirts to work). But a lack of rain threatened to dry up even heavily-irrigated crops, which dried up jobs. Perhaps employment hadn't panned out. I flicked my gaze back to Audrey so he wouldn't catch me staring.

"He's watching you," she said softly. "Not one of those photographers who used to chase Samuel around, is he?" She smoothed a hand over her hair. Audrey had always taken a not-so-secret glee in Samuel's celebrity-level attention. (Or perhaps she was simply interested in handsome strangers, now that she was free of my father.) "He and Sam had lunch one time. Excuse me, Audrey."

"Good to see you, Kaye," she said, suddenly concerned.

I grabbed a basket and browsed the shelves, one eye on the man. He also browsed groceries, never more than an aisle away. By the time I checked out, I was positive I was on my way to the inside of somebody's trunk. This had been a stupid, stupid idea. He stepped around me and headed for the door. Finally, he left.

Audrey's wide eyes darted toward the alarm button under the counter. I shook my head.

"He's gone now."

"That was freaky."

"Give me a call if you need me," I said as she finished my order.

"You too, kiddo." She passed me my groceries.

I exited the store and hustled down the sidewalk, only to find the man followed several paces behind. Now my heart pounded in my ears, my chest, and the familiar gasps for air began.

My free hand slid into my purse and fisted my pepper spray. I pivoted.

"Is there something I can do for you?" I fought to keep the tremble from my voice. I said the same thing in Spanish and his eyes lighted.

"My apologies, *Señora*. Trust me, I'm harmless."

"What can I do for you?" I repeated.

"I thought I recognized you, but I'm not sure. Are you Samuel Cabral's wife?"

I was two steps from bolting. "*Señor*, why are you following Sam?"

"I don't mean to alarm you. I recognized your blue hair." His smile was guarded. "I'm a friend of his sister's, you see."

"Dani?" I tested.

"Marieta Cabral Sanchez. I apologize for bothering you, but could I have a moment?"

I took in my whereabouts. The street bustled with shoppers, tourists and townies alike. Surely he wouldn't be so brazen as to attack me in broad daylight. I glanced at my watch. My meeting with the Front Range Historical Society wasn't until three. "I can give you twenty minutes, right here."

"*Gracias, Señora*. Please, call me Javier." He gestured to the very public bench in the greenspace.

"How do you know Marieta?" I asked as we sat.

He reached into his shirt pocket and pulled out a creased Polaroid. Three people stood in front of what looked like a historic fountain. Marieta, Javier, and a second woman. The sun was bright, and their faces were partly shadowed, but the woman on the left...now I could see the resemblance to my husband was uncanny. I traced her sharp cheekbones, soft eyes.

"A gift for your husband. I know very little about him, but he and Marieta seem very similar." Javier smiled, a bid to put me at ease. "A while ago, my wife—the woman on the right—broke her foot. Marieta came every day to help with our son and keep house, what little we have. When she was done, she'd sit beside my wife and read to her Samuel Cabral's books. She'd brag about how the author was her friend and how proud she was of him. She never told us he was her brother, but we weren't blind."

"I hope your son didn't find the books too scary. Samuel's always saying he doesn't approve of children reading them."

Something flickered in his black eyes. "My son doesn't have the understanding for the books. He's just turned three. I missed his birthday."

In spite of my wariness, my heart went out to this father, so far from his family. "If you don't mind the observation, it seems you waited awhile to have children."

He laughed a warm, delightful laugh, and I had to remind myself I knew nothing about him.

"I waited awhile to settle down. I was much wilder in my youth, and very handsome. Then, one day at the open air market, I saw this colorful woman selling dried *toloache* and I thought 'who is this brazen thing peddling devil plants to tourists?' I had to have her and convinced her to marry an old man."

The alarm on my phone buzzed, yanking me out of hazy, far-away places. "Rats, I should have been on the road by now."

"Oh! I've completely forgotten my original purpose in approaching you." He took a piece of paper from his wallet and handed it to me. "Please have Mr. Cabral call me when he returns from Los Angeles. I have an idea of where Marieta might be and would like to accompany him when he goes south."

My guard snapped up, and I remembered the 'trap' I'd set. "And you know he's in L.A. because…"

Javier looked embarrassed. "His fan page. They post his upcoming appearances, usual haunts. I thought he'd be at the grocery store…."

I pocketed the paper and crossed my arms. "You're really good at this. If you hadn't stalked my husband all summer, I'd trust you. But the probability of Samuel going with you to Mexico is zero. He's contacted Mexican law enforcement, Border Patrol, the International Commission on Missing Persons, *Grupos Beta*, and Uncle Carlos. The fact is, unless there is proof she's in trouble, we can't do much. Do you have proof?" Silence. "I didn't think so."

It was eerie how the jovial man grew detached, ice-cold in the beat of a bird's wing. He looked down his sharp nose. "You're quite a rude little girl, aren't you? Nevertheless, my number is there, so do with it what you like. I won't keep you, *Señora*." Javier placed his ball cap over his matted hair, then paused. "A word of warning. The Zacatóns frown upon their drug mules dropping precious cargo into lakes. If I were your husband, I wouldn't call such great attention to myself by strutting around with Border Patrol. *Ya me despido. Cuídese.*"

When I returned to my office after my meeting, the first thing I did was put in a call to Samuel's lawyer about nixing Alan Murphy's 'Cabral Sightings' feature on NixieNet.net.

I told Jaime about the odd encounter as, once again, we fired bullets at soda cans.

"Now we know how he tracked Samuel. It sure isn't via the Dark Web."

My ears perked up like one of her Labs. "What did you find?"

"Not much of consequence on Marieta Sanchez—I'll have to dig more." *Pop pop.* I jerked in reflex with every loud discharge. "I found absolutely nothing on Samuel Cabral, which is balls. With his level of notoriety, you'd think there'd be info about him all over the place. But he's squeaky clean, as if someone intentionally wiped his info. A few inquiries about him have popped up since April, but nothing before."

"Why would someone do that?" *Pop pop.*

"To protect him, or someone close to him."

I froze mid-aim. "Marieta…"

Jaime plucked empty shells from the ground, deep in thought. "I think I know how to find more on Marieta Sanchez. Give me a few weeks."

Chapter 15
SANDBAG

A route is called a sandbag when it's more difficult
to navigate than its designated grade.

In the early morning hours of the first Wednesday in July (as in, *three-twenty-two a.m.*), I received a desperate call.

"Aspen Kaye Cabral, get your gringo lily-ass to the hospital right this instant. And I mean, *now*. I love my mother, but so help me I'm ready to have the nurses throw her and her helicopter parenting license out the door. You promised Angel you'd be here for me, so you better make good on that promise or I'll have his squadron break sound barriers ala Maverick and Goose over your home every day for a year!"

Ah. Dani was in labor.

Already having leaped out of bed the minute she called me a "gringo lily-ass," I slipped into an ugly pair of spangled leggings and a thermal. Angel had given me fair warning about what to expect: "She could scare the piss out of a marine, the way she talks. Just remember, talking is all she can do to you, once the epidural kicks in. That, and throw things..."

Samuel flopped over and squinted at me, his brown hair a bedraggled mess. Lord, he was sexy when cruelly and abruptly yanked out of a good REM sleep. His mouth was all pouty, his skin flushed...Argh!

It had been awhile since we'd had sex, and if my dear friend and sister weren't about to give birth, I might have pounced on him.

"The baby?" he muttered.

"Yep. You coming with?" He buried his face in his pillow and, for a moment, I thought he'd actually go back to sleep. But then he kicked the covers away and stretched his long, lanky frame, all glorious six-foot-three-inches of brown skin laid bare for my eyes to roam. He sat up, and I watched his abs contract with starving eyes. *The baby, Kaye.* I scrubbed my teeth a little too hurriedly, twisted my insane hair into a clip and struggled to get a grip. "Mother-frickin' chicken peckers."

"That's a new one. I'm not sure, but I think you just insulted me," he said around a toothbrush. Then he jerked a black tee shirt over his head and I bid farewell to his abs.

"Not you, my libido. Shall we go?"

Sam popped a mint into his mouth and offered one to me. "Lead the way, birthing coach."

We sprinted down the hallway and into Dani's hospital room. But the instant Samuel got a peek of his sister up on all fours, huffing and puffing and sweating like she was in (oh, I don't know) *labor*, he pivoted faster than a Radio City Rockette and fled the room.

A flood of Spanglish gushed forth from Dani's mouth, but that was the only "gushing forth" that had happened since I spoke with her twenty minutes earlier.

"Ave María Purísima, hermana, what did you do? Swing by Starbucks first?"

I dropped my purse in the closet and mumbled something about a gripe-fest.

Dani shot me one of her most contemptuous glares, a special reserve only taken off the shelf when someone did something really, really bad.

"It's Womb Eviction Day. This child has been notified and pink-slipped, and I'll be damned if he comes into this world disobedient and defiant."

"You know what they say about karma."

"Damn, Kaye! I didn't ask you to the hospital for your pithiness. Now get over here so we can talk without staring over my giant birthing hips."

I slid a sturdy-looking chair to the head of Dani's bed. Beside her, a heart monitor beeped. The little one's beat fast and steady, but every time Dani lowered herself to the bed, its heart rate would slow, a lot. I wasn't a medical professional, but even I understood this was concerning.

"How long have you been at this?"

"A few hours. Seems like days."

"What have they told you?"

"Not much," she huffed. "The baby's not dropping. They're going to give this method a little more time and if there's no progress, a C-section. Mom's down the hall trying to get answers from my doctor. He's delivering another baby, so it might be awhile." She tried to blow a piece of hair out of her face. I tucked it behind her ear. "I told them to do whatever they had to do to get him out safely."

"*Him*? You're having another boy?"

She growled at me. "I have no idea, but he's not a piglet! It's just annoying to say 'it' all the time!"

"Okay, okay. Tell me what to do."

"Entertain me. I can't watch TV like this and I need a distraction."

I racked my brain for stories that would utterly engross my high maintenance friend. "Got it. I'm going to reveal to you all the dirt I have on Samuel's Hollywood acquaintances if you promise not to breathe a word."

"I'm as high as a kite. The likelihood of my remembering any of this is zilch. But spill away."

I assumed the position of a good gossiper and leaned in. "You remember how some tabloids said those two celebrity judges on *Cooking with the Stars* were having an affair, and the rest of the media, handlers, fans jumped all over the mags for peddling filthy, home-wrecking lies? Turns out, the mags were true."

"Whoa, I thought he left for a better show, not because he slept with his co-star."

"Nope! The series dumped him before he could dump drama on their set. It didn't help that the woman's now ex-husband is a producer..."

I told her seedy insider stories until my voice grew hoarse and she could no longer crouch on her hands and knees. A nurse eased her to her side. Tears spilled down Dani's cheeks. "I'm so, so tired, Kaye. I wish to God that Angel was here."

I gripped her hand. "Your child will be born very soon, and he's going to be okay. You're going to be okay, too. We won't let anything happen to you."

She sobbed harder, and I glimpsed a Dani I'd rarely seen. "I want Angel so bad. I need him *here*, with me, not half a world away!"

I looked straight into her eyes. "Dani, listen to me. You've got this. We've got this." I closed my eyes. *Please protect her. Protect this baby.*

"What are you doing? Don't you dare punk out on me with a panic attack!"

I jerked my hand away as her fingernails embedded themselves in the flesh of my palm.

"Watch the talons! I'm just praying, you hormone-riddled hag."

Her own panicked eyes softened. "Oh *manita*, thank you so much." Determination flashed through her face as she shored herself up for battle. "Right. It's all going to be okay."

At ten-forty-two a.m., twelve hours of labor and one C-section later, Christina Sofia Valdez made her yowling, shrieking-mad entrance into our bright and airy world. As her doctors suspected, her umbilical cord was wrapped around her neck, effectively bungee-ing her up every time she tried to bust out of the womb. I stood beside Danita in Angel's place, phone aloft, stroking her hair and laughing with her when we heard the first high-pitched power wail that was all female. She became my special little princess the moment the nurse placed her in my arms and I realized: *I'm the first familia to hold this tiny, squirming body.* Love wrenched through me.

I crouched next to a weeping Dani, my own eyes overflowing. "*Mi hermana,* meet your daughter."

I hung back as my nearly incoherent sister-in-law introduced Christina to her four grandparents. Gabriel bounced in Samuel's arms, his young eyes glued to his baby sister, and I hadn't realized a toddler was capable of so much love and adoration. Yet again, he taught me not to underestimate a two-year-old.

Next to me, the nurse watched. Then she leaned forward conspiratorially. "Your turn will come someday."

Mild irritation mingled with sadness. "No it won't. You shouldn't say that to people you don't know."

"Oh, you'll be a mom someday. Trust me."

I scowled, ready to go report the woman when I saw Sofia catch my eye and give a shake of her head. Later, she found me as I filled my thermos at the water fountain.

"The nurse was right. Someday, somehow, you'll be a mom."

Anger clouded my brain. "Not you, too! Do you know how painful it is?"

"Kaye. Keep your heart and mind open."

I screwed the lid on my thermos, tightening it until it broke past the thread. *Bite your tongue.* I breathed deeply, counted to ten.

"Look, I appreciate your optimism. And I get that when someone in the family has a baby, all eyes then turn to the woman who doesn't yet have kids. But it hurts my marriage, my husband, and me. The best way you can encourage me is to help me fill this void."

Sadness touched her expression. "I can do that, *mi corazón.*"

Later, I rocked my sweet niece as Dani slept in her hospital bed. Sofia and Alonso had taken *el changuito* home. Samuel was down in the cafeteria, buying food for dinner. I grazed her paper-thin eyelids, watched as her mouth moved and sucked, listened to her mewls and sighs.

With each touch, each sight, each sound, I said goodbye to my imaginary child.

The weight of the bundle in my arms... *Goodbye, warm little body.*

Wisps of air on my neck... *Goodbye, tiny lungs.*

Swift thuds beneath my palm....

I placed the swaddled newborn in her bassinet, brushed the black down of her head and tucked on her cap. Then I pressed my knees against my chest to stifle the pain of its rending, cracking, buried my face and braced my body as it shook with silent, uncontrolled sobs.

Just for a minute, I indulged myself in overwhelming grief. I swam and pushed as if it were a pond of black molasses, soothing and sweet and suffocating. Then I toweled off.

Sometime later, my stiff, drowsy body was unfolded from the chair and settled into a warm embrace. His hands stroked my head as if he comforted a child.

"You've got *me*, firecracker," he whispered. "God knows, you've still got me."

"That man hasn't been by again, has he?" asked Dani. "The one who approached you outside The Garden Market?"

"Javier? Not a trace." I rubbed Christina's back as she snuggled into my neck. Dani flipped through a picture book with Gabe, wincing every time he jabbed his small bony knee into her tender midsection.

Samuel's lawyer had cracked down on NixieNet.net and Alan Murphy for publicizing his beloved author's daily whereabouts, and after they filed a strongly-worded cease-and-desist, he agreed to share only Sam's 'official appearance schedule.'

"After all I've done to mobilize his fan base, you'd think he'd be grateful!" Alan had snipped, when I ran into him outside the Lyons Diner. He furiously swiped blonde hair from his eyes.

"It's not like he has security detail, Alan. What if someone wanted to hurt him?"

He was too offended to see reason. "I thought he appreciated his fans, but he's just a jackass like the rest of them…"

Since that difficult confrontation, Samuel's Nixie fans were scarce, but so was Javier.

Samuel had been scarce, too. Baja California was the current destination. It was difficult to keep his trips straight as he traveled across the border states and Mexico (despite Javier's ugly warning), met with missing persons agencies, followed cold trails and poured cash into local economies for tips that ultimately led nowhere. He just needed *something* to offer beleaguered Mexican law enforcement that didn't have the time or resources to search for a "drug-addicted cartel mule."

Marieta had just…disappeared.

Sometimes Alonso and Uncle Carlos traveled with him, sometimes Santiago. He racked up so many border crossings on his passport, I was certain he'd be flagged. (No one does that many international trips for 'book research.')

I switched tiny Christina to my other shoulder as she worked up a burp. Ugh. Dani grinned, pleased it was my shirt this time that was sullied by her little minion. She waved the burp cloth I'd forgotten to place over my shoulder.

"Take this to Auntie Kaye, *chulo*."

Gabe tossed the cloth in my lap and I tried to scrub spit-up off my shirt while bobbling Dani's child. She finally had mercy and took her infant out of my arms.

"Is Sam still hunting for that girl?" Dani's voice was flat.

"He thought his sister might have sought out your great aunt Belinda in Baja, but that was a dead end."

Dani was not sold on Marieta's claims. I wondered if it had more to do with sharing the 'sister spotlight' with another woman who, if you took mutual childhood experiences out of the equation, actually had a closer blood claim than Danita. Her nose crinkled.

"I know that expression."

"I don't understand. He has family here, obligations here. If this woman wanted to have a relationship with him, she would have found him a long time ago instead of waiting until— surprise!—she needed money."

I handed Dani a diaper as she cleaned a gurgling Christina. "It's more complicated than that."

"She's a con artist and a leech." She wadded up the fouled diaper and chucked it in the pail.

"Maybe she is, but Samuel still needs to try. Remember what happened when he was a child? It has shaped so much about him."

"Because he was adopted?"

"Yes, but first he was abandoned."

I struggled to remind myself of the things I'd told Dani: Samuel needed this, he was doing something good. But with each trip he left me behind, my resentment grew. My longing for him also grew, which made our interactions awkward to the point of ridiculousness.

"How was Baja?" I asked, a touch too snarky.

He replied in Spanish so quickly, he obviously knew I couldn't keep up. Something about fishing for sea bass with Carmen Miranda and eating grapes from her fruit hat.

"Hilarious."

He gave me a biting grin. "Your Spanish has improved over the summer."

"Your attitude hasn't."

"Likewise."

"Having the last word is something teenagers do."

He simply raised an eyebrow. Dammit. I retreated to the kitchen, taken down by an Olympic heavyweight. But he was right, I always had to have the last word, which was why, an hour later, I served up a meal laden with passive aggression.

He stared at the pot of hearty, steaming, carb-heavy spaghetti I'd placed between us on the trivet. Without a word, he scooped a pile onto his plate, swiveled his fork through the mess of jarred sauce and bleached white flour noodles.

"Oh! I forgot the garlic bread." I hopped up from my chair, grabbed my oven mitts, and removed the most delicious, buttery, Parmesan-sprinkled loaf of bread imaginable. I slapped that sucker on the table like a handful of aces.

Another eyebrow raise. "I'm shocked you didn't break out a bottle of red wine."

"Eat up, darling."

Gaze locked on mine, he lifted his fork, slurped the noodles into his mouth, and chewed. He winced as starch coated his mouth for the first time in years.

"Good?" I innocently sipped my water.

"Hmm. I'm wondering what happened to the roach bait in the utility closet." I snorted and, to my mortification, water came out my nose.

Samuel's steely face cracked as he tossed me a napkin. "Am I going to die soon?"

"I promise, there's nothing more sinister than gluten and carbs. I'll microwave a pouch of quinoa."

He placed his hand on my forearm. "Nah, don't. I haven't had spaghetti in a long time, so let's just enjoy it."

Once again, we managed to patch up a spat, but tension was an underground train rumbling below our feet. Some evenings, our two-bedroom apartment was as crammed as a passenger car. I'd hear his breath, the *click-clack-click-clack* of his keyboard, and an unexplainable and deeply disturbing urge to smother him with a tasseled throw pillow would overtake me. So I'd jerk on my sneakers and suck in fresh air. First-world complaints, but I couldn't deny it: our giant new home would be awesome.

The contractor promised we'd have the outside completed before the first snow, which came early in the foothills, usually October. While Samuel traveled, I spent time on our new property exploring, hiking, watching the frame go up, then the roof, the walls, the floors. Solid. Sturdy. I even hauled our whitewater stuff out to the new storage shed and reacquainted myself with the twists and turns of Left Hand Creek.

Samuel was a man obsessed with combing the seedy streets of underground Mexico in search of a damsel in distress.

I was a woman obsessed with conquering mountains on that four-teeners list: Shavano, Kit Carson, Bierstadt, Chimney Peak.

One by one they fell as Hector, Luca and I clawed our way to their summits. My hands and knees were raw. My muscles were stiff. My face was red and chapped with wind burn. Adrenaline coursed through my body so frequently, it was as if an IV dripped espresso into my veins. But after each climb, the IV drip switched to morphine and I collapsed into bed, blissfully unaware that, once again, I was losing Samuel Cabral.

Oh, we still wore each other's rings. He still kissed me goodbye before he boarded another flight. He kissed me, but he was already two thousand miles away.

The last thing I wanted was an '*Ex* Ex-Ex,' and I knew what needed to be done:

Don't be selfish.

Let each other into the ugly parts of life.

So why didn't we? Frankly, we were nearly depleted. I didn't need Samuel Caulfield Cabral to climb a mountain. He sure didn't need me with him in Mexico.

"Explain," I begged as he crammed his carry-on with clothing, yet again.

"I don't know if it's possible. It's as if I'm being pushed from the inside-out. I don't expect you to understand—"

"If you don't *help* me understand, then how can I possibly understand?"

"Have you ever had a gut feeling that wouldn't go away, that you were meant to do something and if you didn't, no one else would?"

"Yes." *Be a mother to the child I dreamt about.* I kept silent, but he heard anyway, my heart pounded so loudly. He paused, then quickly kissed my lips. Oh yes, I understood this gut feeling all too well. And I saw—we both saw—the destruction of our marriage in those gut feelings.

How sad, that I'd fallen back into that hydraulic of thrill-seeking self-slaughter from which I'd climbed, nearly four years ago. The end of summer approached and I was thoroughly drenched from my spins in that inescapable river.

It was there, caught in the hydraulic, that the rain began.

Literally.

The lead Samuel was desperate for ultimately came from Jaime Guzman. I scrolled through the text, hardly believing what I read:

IT WOULD HAVE HELPED IF YOU'D TOLD ME SHE WAS A CABRAL!!!! M. Cabral & D. Rodriguez, detained in Brownsville w/ false docs & illegal entry into U.S. Status: Deported.

"Sam!" I scrambled to the living room where he was glued to a Red Sox game and bashed my shin on our coffee table.

Samuel winced. "Ow, done that a few times. You okay?"

I gripped my leg and forced words through my teeth. "She was deported, that's why she returned to Mexico." I shoved my phone in front of his startled face. His eyes widened as he read.

"Ah! She used 'Cabral' at the U.S. Border. I didn't think to check for our father's *apellido*, she hated him. That's why we didn't get any hits the first time. But who is 'D. Rodriguez'? And why does Jaime Guzman know about my sister?"

"Because we need a lead and Jaime can get it for us. Can you believe she's a hacktivist with ....Oh my God." I replayed Sam's question, then reread the text: she was deported with a *'D. Rodriguez.'*

I rubbed my bruised shin as I pieced together the news stories. "Marieta was with Daniel Rodriguez. He's the Unknown who did the data drop on the Zacatón Cartel, the one from La Vereda. Sam...he was kidnapped weeks ago. Do you think that's why she wanted your help? To get Daniel back?"

"And now Marieta is missing, too." He flicked off the Red Sox baseball game, which meant serious business. "That's why she was back in Mexico, living in the Tizilicho slum. Her bank account in the U.S. was seized because it was under a false name."

"Maybe she was living in the slum because it's a good place to hide..."

He pinched the bridge of his nose. "Call Jaime, find out as much as you can about Daniel Rodriguez—this is the proof we need, the *Policía Federal* have been all over the Rodriguez kidnapping case. I'll call Uncle Carlos and ask him to meet me in Brownsville."

I gasped as I put weight on my sore shin. "No! You just got back. Angel's stateside in a few days and you need to be here to welcome him home."

"Kaye, my sister needs me." He pulled his suitcase from the closet, but I was right there behind him, putting it back.

"Maybe she's gone underground and doesn't *want* to be found. For goodness' sake, just pick up a phone and *call* the Mexican Feds!" I waved my phone in the air. "Your family needs you here. I need you *here*." We stared each other down, the suitcase between us. Finally, he tossed it in the depths of the closet.

Jaime didn't have anything new, save for speculation.

"I worked under the assumption that Marieta Sanchez and Daniel Rodriguez were acquaintances," she said through my phone. "La Vereda is a hamlet, you can't empty your chamber pot onto the dirt streets without the entire village knowing about it. Marieta's a rebel, Daniel's a rebel...you do the math."

"You think they were lovers?"

"You don't get deported together unless you're romantic or work at the same meatpacking plant." She cut off my protest. "I'm just keeping it real, Kewpie.

"Here's what I think: Daniel joins Marieta in the U.S., only to be deported two years later when they're busted with false documentation. He finds work in Ciudad Victoria while Marieta lays low in Mexico City, and the Tizilicho slum is no Acapulco resort. He's sick of the Zacatón Cartel terrorizing his friends and family, sick of being separated from Marieta. He decides to fight back, and what better way than cyber warfare? Daniel dumps the dirt on the Dark Web but first wipes anything about Marieta, and that includes Samuel's data. Sadly, some ass-hat rats him out (there's a million of them in Unknown). So the cartel kidnaps him."

I hopped on her train of thought. "Marieta was going to ask Samuel to pay Daniel's ransom, but she changed her mind. Or maybe she saw this Javier guy skulking around."

"You find Daniel Rodriguez, you find Marieta."

I bit my lip, asked what I didn't want to ask. "Do you think the Zacatóns killed them?"

"I dunno. Their MO is broadcasting it to the world. That's how they keep people in fear."

"Bodies on the highways. Shallow graves. Is it any wonder Daniel Rodriguez wants them exposed?"

Death was heavy in the air between us, bleeding into our skin.

Chapter 16
HOT ACHES

*A hot ache is felt when fingers flair back to life
after going numb in frigid temperatures.*

Samuel bounced his knees with the restlessness of a little boy. Sure enough, on my other side, *el changuito's* heels kicked the bleacher in a rhythm-less fidget. In fact, the entire row of Cabral and Valdez family members were wringing hands, squirming in their seats, or twirling hair.

Today, everyone had reason to bounce with an excitement worthy of Ritalin.

Any moment now, the 460th Wing would be dismissed to the arms of their waiting families. The room was draped with stars-and-stripes swags and flags, balloons and homemade banners, patriotic music. My fingers curled the corner of a banner we had painted in the backyard of the Cabral home. It was long enough for an entire football team to run through. Samuel had pointed out the logistical complication, but Dani had insisted.

"It has to read: *'Hey, I just met you & this is crazy, but my name's Christina & I'm your baby.'* No exceptions."

So paint it we did, down to every fuchsia sparkle in Dani's perfect bubble letters, to honor the auspicious moment in which Christina met her daddy (conception aside).

Sam bumped my knee and looked skyward. Rain clouds had dissipated, unfortunate for a land deep-seated in drought.

Behind us, Alonso and Sofia discussed our "surprise" for Angel, and whether it would survive. We'd asked people all over the Mexican neighborhood if we could attach red, white, and blue balloons to their mailboxes. Unfortunately, a front moved through just before we left. High winds whipped many of them into the air, at the mercy of the sky.

"That was a waste of three hundred dollars," grumbled Alonso. Sofia poked him in the ribs.

"Not at all! Now everyone knows he's returning."

"They would have known anyway, with that gigantic banner—"

"Please *Papá*, not the banner again." The baby smacked Dani with an impatient fist. Without blinking an eye, she popped the child off one breast and settled her on the other. Having children certainly seemed to strip one of shyness, and Dani had very little to begin with. All of a sudden, Danita lunged forward, and I wondered if Christina had gummed her too hard (was that possible?). Pure joy lighted her face and I saw the direction of her gaze.

Lieutenant Angel Valdez, in the flesh, sporting the biggest grin I'd seen on the man. He saluted his wife. She bobbed in her seat. Christina mewled in protest and swung—yes, *swung*— her fist at her mother (if a baby couldn't eat in peace, was nothing sacred?). By this time, *el changuito* had also spotted his father and nearly streaked down the bleachers when Samuel caught the back of his tee shirt.

"Easy there, little boy. They'll dismiss *Papá* in a minute."

Everything seemed right in the world as a tearful Angel and Danita pressed their foreheads together, their children between them. Angel said something to Dani and she nodded and tried to take Gabriel from Angel's arms, but the toddler latched his fingers around the collar of Angel's uniform. Dani laughed and brushed Christina's baby fingers against Angel's five-o'clock shadow.

Samuel gripped my hand. "*This* is our family, Kaye."

Warmth and love eased the fractures in my chest. Still, the fractures were there: a longing to hold our own children between us, our hands protecting tiny fingers. Somehow, I had to root out this longing once and for all.

———————— ••• ————————

The first day of the Rocky Mountain Folks Festival dawned bright and beautiful. Sunshine. Not even a hint of autumn in the air, as summer clung to the first days of September with the tenacity of a blueberry stain. And that blue was freaking hard to get out.

I studied my fingertips, cuticles—a weird purple color—as I made my way (solo) to Planet Bluegrass. I'd spent the morning helping my mother can blueberry jam, and now it was time to catch the first bands on the Folks stage. I patted my purse, where I'd stashed two small jars and a pack of gluten-free crackers for Samuel. If there was one thing he couldn't cut out of his diet, it was my mother's blueberry jam. That stuff was a drug. In fact, I couldn't be certain she didn't spike it with something illegal, but whatever. We would empty that jar before the banjo finished pickin' 'Dixie.'

I spread my blanket and plopped down, waited. He was supposed to have returned from Brownsville this morning, and after a shower and nap, would meet me east of the main stage. But an hour passed, then two. I checked my watch. The second group finished their set. Checked my watch again—six p.m.

Familiar hurt and anger simmered on the backburner. *Let's give him another hour before we do anything rash, shall we?* Rocky Mountain Folks was special. It was 'our thing,' had been since we were little. When he'd been gone for seven years, I'd kept it sacred, something between the two of us. After all, when one loses her virginity to the love of her life in the midst of a music festival (well, not literally *at* the festival, we were at my mother's house), said music festival goes up on a pedestal.

I whipped out my phone for the zillionth time. Nothing. Something must have been very wrong for him to skip Folks. Had he finally confessed to carrying those kilos of cocaine? Surely it was only a matter of time before it came to light. This wouldn't be his first drug charge, either. After the last arrest, his lawyer warned him a third offense might land him in jail. But maybe if he was cooperative, they'd be lenient and downgrade... I chewed my thumb nail.

Or what if it was worse?

How easy it was to swap Samuel's name into news stories of Zacatón murder victims. Another man was on the news this morning, thirty-four, drawn and quartered, his body spread along a two-mile stretch of the main highway bisecting Tamaulipas as if he'd been chucked out a window like wadded up fast food wrappers. Was it a face dear to me, frozen in panic, staring up from a ditch hundreds of miles away? Had he known what they were going to do to him?

I hadn't noticed I'd held my breath, and I gasped for air.

Grounded...switch frequencies...Rocky Mountain Folks...

My stomach grumbled, but still I sat, held vigil, waited. Finally, just as the sun began to set behind the Rockies, my phone buzzed:

Kaye, missed my flight, staying a day longer. Be home tomorrow night. Apologies for skipping Folks.

Right. Now that simmering pot of anger bubbled. I gritted my teeth. *You will not cry, Aspen Kaye. Don't be fifteen. Don't be an emotional, needy basket case-of-a-wife. This is important.*

But Folks was important.

Fudge it. I jerked open my purse and pulled out the blueberry jam and crackers. Gluten free. What I wouldn't give for a flaky, buttery cracker. Just a single, round, golden, sun-like Ritz cracker.

"Hey Kaye, those crackers empty your bank account?"

The crackers flew out of my startled hands and scattered across the blanket. "Hector Valdez! What are you doing here?"

"Tricia has a shift tonight, I think, haven't seen her in three days." Tricia seemed to work a lot, lately, but I didn't pry. "Thought I'd see what all the fuss is about. It's okay, if you like folk music."

"Who doesn't like folk music?" I said in mock astonishment.

"Er, I could think of a few people. But not me! Put a dulcimer in my hands right now, sister!"

"Wow, you never cease to surprise me."

He leaned in, secretive. "Santiago dated the dulcimer gal a couple of months ago, remember? He studied up on that thing for a week before asking her out." He brushed crackers to the side of the blanket and sat. The hairs on his arm tickled my calf. "Where's your soul mate?"

The sour way he'd said 'soul mate' didn't sit well. "Still out-of-town with Alonso. They'll be back tomorrow night."

"Perfect!"

"Oh?"

"Yep. That means we can tackle one of the Ivy League peaks, lady's choice: Harvard, Princeton, Columbia, or Yale? Just you, me, and that big hard sun."

Just the two of us...that didn't sit well, either. "What about Luca?"

"What about him? You and I have done lots of stuff together. Seven years' worth, remember?"

Tattoos twisted and snaked up the arm next to my leg. It was so close, I saw where dark blues faded into flesh. "I don't know, Hector. It's different now."

"Why, because we're both married?" he laughed. "If Samuel is that insecure about his wife spending the day with another man, that's his problem. Maybe he should hit the gym."

I shoved his shoulder. "Don't be a jerk, Hector, you know that's not it. It just seems...disrespectful."

His face lost its joviality. "You know what else is disrespectful? A husband bailing on something that means the world to his wife, for any reason short of hospitalization. Once again, you're alone at Rocky Mountain Folks."

There was that simmering anger again, spitting and steaming, set to boil over. "You know what? You're right. It's just a climb. Anyway, what else am I supposed to do: pace around the kitchen like a little woman, waiting for him to come home?"

Hector grinned. "There's the spitfire. Pick you up at four a.m."

Mount Yale
September

Was it possible to be high on fresh air? Perhaps it was a lack of oxygen this high in the sky, atmosphere so thin, so free of humidity it made me giddy, but I couldn't stop laughing. Hector rolled on the cold ground and gasped for breath. Tears streaked from my eyes, drops of ice on my cheeks.

"*Ay*, Cabral was so pissed I asked you out before he did. Remember, right after you turned sixteen?"

I smudged away tears with fleece-covered fingers. "You took me to that terrible slasher movie right before Halloween." I remembered my friend, skin greasy and porous in the throes of puberty, his killer smile covered by metal braces. "You know, I never knew Samuel had been angry until he wrote about it a few years ago. I had no idea about a lot of things."

Hector shook his head. "Oh *mamacita*, I was crazy about you. You featured in a lot of my teenaged fantasies."

"If you cherish our friendship, don't tell me about your sixteen-year-old romance with Luciderm."

"Trust me, you don't want to know." Silence stifled our laughter as we rested on the summit of Mount Yale, thoughtful. The sky was so bright, so blue, we stared into the core of a flame. Hector continued. "I never got it…why you didn't even consider me."

Warning bells tinkled. "I did, after Samuel left. You know I did. You also know why it never happened."

"Look, I know Samuel is a good guy. But he's done some really ugly things, too."

"So have I. So has everyone."

"Quit making excuses for him, Kaye. All I know is you are not the woman you once were, ever since he came back. Frankly, you used to be fun."

I ground my fist into the rock, an outlet. He wanted the ol' 'spitfire'? He was about to get it.

"First of all, you and I both know Samuel has never stopped me from doing dangerous crap with you, despite the pain it might cause him. I stopped *myself*. I didn't want to break my head, my back, or my neck just for an adrenaline fix. I grew up. And I swear on my mother's farm, if you don't grow up too, Tricia will be a widow before she's forty."

An angry flush burned up and under his stocking-capped head. "I once thought you were something special. Though the others lost their passion—Angel, Santiago, Dani, Molly—lost themselves to the trappings of a safe, boring existence, you never would. But here you are, a mere photocopy of that bright, wild woman. Where is your soul, Aspen Kaye?"

I jumped to my feet and flipped him the bird. "Get off my mountain, asshole."

With flagrant defiance, he stomped right up the summit and towered a foot above me.

"Make me."

I shoved his shoulders, but he didn't move an inch. I growled and shoved again. His lips curled. Soft, cruel lips. My middle churned as if I'd just been thrown into a skydive. The smile dropped from his face. His eyes brightened and he inched down, and for a panicked, torturous second, I thought he was going to kiss me. In that torturous second, a single thought blinded my judgment: I should let him.

Don't you do this, Aspen Kaye Cabral.

This man sees me, I argued. He's not afraid of my passion. He doesn't see my carelessness as a flaw.

Neither does Samuel.

Just one kiss.

Just one will scar your marriage forever.

Hector's mouth, his warm breath, those soft-looking lips, waited. *Oh my God, Kaye, what are you doing?* I stumbled back and fell, so hard, I cracked my elbow on the summit rock. "What the hell, Hector?"

Hector straightened, his eyes now cold, full of accusation. He wiped his hands against his jacket, his pants. Then he turned his back on me. "Whatever. Let's head down."

I shoved myself off the ground. "Hector Valdez, you come back here. We need to talk!"

He spun around and pointed a finger at my face. "There's nothing to talk about. Nothing happened."

"How can you pretend—"

"Very easily."

And he could, too. We trekked down Mount Yale for miles, our huffing breaths and drip-drops of sweat our only conversation. The void left me ample time to consider what I'd almost done, what I *had* done, and what this would do to Samuel.

Because I would have to tell him.

There was no other option.

And I feared, dreaded, that our separation was not simply a horrible possibility. It was imminent.

Oh the irony. Here I was, pacing the kitchen like the little woman I swore to Hector I wasn't, waiting for my husband to walk through the door.

I'd nearly kissed another man. I was *that* woman—that self-centered, careless cheater about whom I'd been oh so sanctimonious. I wasn't one of *those* women, so swept off her feet by the first charming guy who came along, she forgot her marriage vows and the man she claimed to love.

I even knew what it felt like on the cheated end, to see the person you'd given yourself to in the arms of another. What would Tricia say if she found out? What would Samuel say?

I bit my fingernail. Was this some delayed, passive aggressive revenge for Samuel's dalliance with the brunette in the brownstone, all those years ago? I paused. No, definitely not.

While still painful, I'd forgiven him, long ago.

What, then? Was my head so easily turned? Again, no. I'd clung to Samuel's memory long after we'd signed those divorce papers. If I'd been seduced by Hector, we would have hooked up when Samuel lived in New York for seven years.

I clattered around in the kitchen, made hot chocolate. It cooled in my hands, untouched. Something stronger? A fruit bowl occupied the place where my wine rack once sat. I rested my forehead against the granite counter-top, the coldness easing my flushed cheeks.

You know why you did it. You are hungry for attention. An embrace. The warmth of another body. A man to appreciate you, to peer into your heart and like what he sees.

But I didn't want this from Hector. I wanted it from Samuel.

This is easy, Kaye. In the seven years Samuel was gone, to whom did you go for companionship? All those ski trips, mountain climbs, ski-dives?

Hector.

And who petted your ego and told you how gorgeous you were?

Hector.

And who conversed with you for hours about your hometown, your friends, your adventures?

Hector.

I dumped my mug of cold chocolate down the drain, rinsed out the sludge. Hector and I had all the ingredients of romance, minus the romance. It had to stop or I'd lose Samuel.

Had I already lost him?

I didn't want to return to that dark and lonely place. Not seeing Samuel's brilliant blue eyes across from me in the morning. Not having his magnetic presence fill our apartment, fill my heart. *Never again, Aspen Kaye.*

As it turned out, it was so late when Samuel rolled in from the airport, he simply grabbed my hand and pulled me into our bed, asleep in minutes. But I tossed and turned over one final question:

How can anyone look into my heart and love what they see, when I don't love it myself?

I slept fitfully in his embrace, afraid of what morning would bring, when I'd confess.

Morning did come, and I did tell him.

I forced myself to feel the hurt in Samuel's glassy eyes. His nasty green smoothie sat at his elbow and his whole body was motionless. A tear streamed down my cheek, but I wouldn't look away.

"You didn't kiss him, but you wanted him to."

"Correct."

"Why didn't you kiss him?"

"Because I won't betray you."

"Do you love him?"

I shook my head vehemently. "No. Do you hate me?"

His hand fell away from his face and his blue eyes pierced me. "I can't believe you just asked me that. Have we really sunk so far?" He pushed away his smoothie and strode from the room.

"Where are you going?"

"For a run. Just—" He warded me off. "Give me some space, okay?" I sniffled and nodded.

"I'll be back in a couple of hours."

After he left, I watched the door for a full minute, then resumed my 'worry route.' Pace.

Fix a cup of coffee. Review financial reports and invoices. Pace. Check email. Drink coffee.

Pace. Put laundry in dryer. Check email again.

Just as I put the last glass from the dish washer into the cupboard, Samuel returned. His shirt was drenched with sweat and his hair dripped. Red dust coated the backs of his legs, shoes, socks. He'd run hard. Really hard, which meant he was really upset. Without a word he crossed the kitchen and took the clean glass from my hand, filled it with water, and chugged. Then he rinsed it (who rinses away water with water?) and placed it in the empty dish washer. I was dying during this entire performance. Finally, he met my eyes.

"Here's the deal. I'll be damned if we drive this marriage into the ground after fighting so hard to get each other back. You with me?"

My heart unclenched. "How...how are you now?"

"Furious at you. I want to kill Hector. Kicking myself for not giving you what you need."

He growled and all but slammed the dish washer door. "The thing is, I've walked your shoes and I've experienced crushing guilt. Remember the woman at the brownstone?"

I dropped my gaze to my fuzzy slippers. "How could I ever forget?"

"Exactly. I'm afraid trust is always going to be an issue for us."

"Trust isn't a light switch. We've both dealt some heavy blows and it takes time to recover."

"And God knows I haven't been there for you this summer, considering this mess with Marieta."

"Sam—"

He held up a hand. "Let me finish. It's put a lot of strain on us, so this next trip is going to be my last and then I'll let the *Federales* and Uncle Carlos handle it. If they can't find her, then she's so well hidden the Zacatóns will never find her, or…or dead.

"But it's time to fix us, before we do something that's hard to come back from. So here's what's going to happen." He shoved his hands in his pockets, all business. "First, you are not to be alone with Hector. Period. No climbs, no lunches, no conversations unless I'm along. Do you think this is unreasonable?"

"Not at all." I wrapped my arms around my middle, fearful and hopeful.

"Second, we're getting a new marriage counselor. The one we have sucks."

"Agreed."

"Finally, you have got to talk to me. No more kid gloves, even if I'm as batty as an underground cave, or as dark as one. I'm not going to leave you, Kaye Cabral. Get it?"

I tugged a stray curl, thoughtful. "You've been a guarded person since the moment I met you. I suppose it's hard to drop that privacy screen."

"And you've walked eggshells with me since the moment I met you."

"True."

He took my hand and studied my fingernails, smoothed my veins. "This distance between us is killing me," he murmured.

I stepped closer. "Not gonna lie, it's been a rough summer."

"Hmmm." He eyed me up and down—pale gray tank top, flannel sleep shorts, tussled blue hair. I tucked it behind my ear, self-conscious.

"You have any plans?" His voice was suddenly husky.

"It's Sunday. We're supposed to meet your family for church."

His sensitive mouth curled, so soft, so alluring. My heart lurched. This expression was an old friend to me. "I think we need to tend to our own today." He stepped closer, traced a finger along the edge of my tank top, slipped it beneath the left strap.

"What did you have in mind?" I whispered.

"Let's go swimming."

I blinked. Surely I'd misunderstood. "Now? Where?"

"The pond on the back of your mom's property, where we used to swim when we were kids."

"That algae-infested thing?"

"It's her competition week, remember?"

I thought about it. Never failed, Mom's heirloom tomato competition in Pueblo was always the weekend of Rocky Mountain Folks, and Sam and I had a long-standing tradition of doing naughty things in an empty house while she was away. A grin broke over my face.

"Lemme brush my teeth first."

Algae was alive and well in the pond. I threw a rock and broke the lime green carpet, and wondered at the sagaciousness of putting my body in the middle of that nasty thing. How had this not bothered us when we were children?

I grimaced. "You first."

Without a beat, he pulled his tee shirt over his head, stripped away his jeans and boxers. My stomach bottomed out when he gave me a sideways glance. The man was still beautiful, more so than ever. Long limbs, sinews tightening and hardening as he aged. His neck, face, arms, were browned from hard summer labor, but beneath his clothing his torso was pale, smattered with whirls of dark brown hair—a secret for my eyes only. I watched him unabashedly as he waded into chest-high cattails and vanished, only to surface with a resounding splash. He shook pond scum from his hair and looked to me.

"Your turn."

Straightening my spine, I dragged my sundress over my body and reveled in my husband's slackened jaw. When one plans to skinny-dip, one doesn't bother with underwear. Pinching my nose, I dove through the cattails and cannonballed into the water, keeping my mouth closed so I wouldn't contract some obscure disease. I kicked to the surface and gasped for air, only to be yanked backwards by Samuel. We played in the water like kids, splashed and gasped, dove for each other's' feet, raced from one muddied bank to the other. Sunlight refracted across the water, glittering paths that widened as algae recoiled from our kicking limbs. Sam grabbed my hand and dragged me to him, up against his body, and suddenly those two children were gone. Brown water trickled down his skin. I pushed a strand of wet hair from his forehead.

Blue eyes watched me.

"You are more breathtaking than anything I could ever hope to write."

I leaned into his body slick with muck. He groaned and pulled my mouth to his. Punishing. Needy. He wrapped his arms around my hips and lifted me out of the water. Cattails brushed my breasts and legs as we pushed through reeds and up the bank. He tossed my sundress aside and laid me down on his dry clothing, and this moved me more than his pretty words.

Blood coursed through my veins, awakened my dormant body and excited my mind. I'd needed my husband's touch for so long. His mouth sought my skin, nipped, bit with a pain fringed in tenderness. Samuel had always been a good lover. Maybe it was because he knew my quirks and tells, just as I knew his. I dug my hands into his hair and yanked. He winced.

"It seems I need to remind you of a few things, *mi vida*. You gave yourself to me, nearly four years ago, at the Boulder County Courthouse. Do you recall the vows you made?" His hand snaked under my back and gooseflesh prickled my skin. I guided his shoulders until he rolled onto his back.

"You said some vows too, Samuel Cabral." My lips glided over his skin. Fingers dug into the clay on either side of his rib cage. "You better damned well keep them."

"Then we're in agreement. We belong to each other. There's no room for anyone else between us, is there?" Suddenly, I was beneath him again. He lowered his heated body to mine and drove home his point.

Our lovemaking was frantic, aggressive, a battle to reclaim, outdo, prove to each other why no one else could possibly make our bodies sing. The first time left me with an ache in my hips. The second time was slow and affectionate, as Samuel repossessed every inch of me. The summer sun baked mud and algae onto our skin until it crackled and flaked away. Sam tenderly brushed a streak of dirt from my cheek and lowered his mouth to my ear.

"You are the only one who can break me, Kaye. Not my birth parents, or fame, or those killers in Mexico. Not even this disease in my head." He cupped my shoulder blades, my bottom, traced my spine. I cried out my sorrow and he held my shuddering body tight. "Symbiosis, remember?"

"I remember. Sam, forgive me, forgive me," I sobbed again and again.

He tilted my chin and I saw his sky eyes, clouded with sadness, and it cracked me in two.

"I will always forgive you. Forgive me, too."

"For what?"

"For neglecting you."

I pressed my palms to his beloved face, kissed the corners of his lips, his chin, his cheeks. They came to rest over his heart.

"Symbiosis."

Chapter 17
BETA

*Second-hand knowledge a climber receives from another
climber who has previously tackled a specific route.*

Hydraulic Level Five [WORKING TITLE]
Draft 1.117
© Samuel Caulfield Cabral and Aspen Kaye Cabral
LEYENDAS de MONTAÑA

"So you're in Nuevo Leon."

"Monterrey, to be exact," he shouts over the roar of rain.

"Isn't that awfully close to Tamaulipas?" Aspen's voice is thin with
worry, so Caulfield treads carefully.

"It is… I'm on my way to Tamaulipas."

"You told me you wouldn't go back there!"

"You *asked* me not to go to Tamaulipas, but I never agreed."

"Dammit, Caulfield! Both Mexican coasts are about to get hit by
hurricanes, and you're driving straight into Ingrid instead of away." He
hears the tears. *This* is a hurricane, obliterating his marriage. Honesty
is especially crucial with Aspen because she's been deceived so much in
the past.

"I'm not going to lie to you, firecracker. I could have told you I was
returning to Mexico City, or simply staying in Monterrey."

"That makes me feel so much better. Dammit, Caulfield!" she says again.

"Uncle C says the only way Mexico's anti-kidnapping unit will investigate my sister's disappearance is if we have solid proof she's connected to Rodriguez. And I can't get proof at home, on our sofa. The answers are in La Vereda."

Silence stretches all the way from Boulder to this pock-marked highway, deep in the Sierra Madre Oriental. Rain hammers the car, as if a massive bag of frozen peas has been ripped open and dumped over the entire coastal state of Tamaulipas. He pictures the bags under her eyes, the way her entire body sighs in defeat as she utters her next words.

"If anything is off, if someone tries to stop your car, you and Alonso drive all the way to the border. Please just *come home*."

"I love you, Aspen. I promised this would be my last trip."

"Love you." He barely hears her whispered words above the storm before she ends the call. This *is* the last trip. It has to be the last trip, or he'll lose his wife. He's felt her departure, a dull butter knife sawing at the ties between them, so slowly, he barely notices until that rope is but a few frayed threads. Another snaps every time he closes the door to go to the airport, to cross the border, to put his life at risk for a woman whom he knows nothing about, except that they share blood.

That's not true. He knows his sister is lonely, an addict, a head case. He knows she's like him.

Is it possible to love someone you know nothing about? Aspen would say it is. She loved their nephew and niece before she held them in her arms. She loves a child she's never met, that doesn't even exist. And she chose to love Caulfield when he was nothing but a broken boy in a ghost costume.

The gas gauge dangerously flirts with 'empty.' Not an envious position, driving a lonely highway in the middle of the night through miles of Zacatón killing fields, just as Hurricane Ingrid flexes her muscles and pours out her fury in the Gulf, one hundred miles east. But bright, sunny days have never stopped the cartel from picking off cash cows from pastures.

Amazingly, his father sleeps in the passenger seat, head lolling against the glass. He hasn't noticed how gray he's gone, more salt than pepper, and Caulfield has caused most of those silver streaks above his temples. Heart disease runs rampant in his family. Caulfield never met his paternal grandfather, who was just fifty-nine when a heart attack stole his golden years. *Papá* is fifty-nine.

His father says love is a choice, an action. His father chose to love him all those years ago, when no one else was left to do so.

Caulfield has chosen to love this woman *because* she is his sister, *because* she is lonely, *because* she is an addict.

Because he knows where she's been.

Because someone was there to love him.

Aspen gets this. She'll let him do what he needs to do, that's her way.

Two days later, Caulfield downshifts the four-wheel-drive rental all the way up mud-slicked mountains west of his ancestral hacienda. She couldn't have possibly gone home, could she? Back to where people know her, back to where the Zacatóns most certainly will find her? Could she have gotten out again, in this weather? Now he walks the street of her village, looking lost and suspect in his rain slicker while his *papá* visits the town's only grocery store. Thirty years ago, his birth father had been welcomed with red festival ribbons and honeyed lips. But the cartels have fleeced their young and sacrificed them along highways, loaded them like pack mules with kilos of cocaine, sold them to 'resorts' who cater to rich perverts from all over the world.

The air is sickly-sweet with dying orange blossoms.

The blooms are long gone, but he sees why their ghosts still linger.

In an old woman's lap is a pestle and mortar and she crushes dried petals into a powder, presumably to make a fragrance. She sits in a lawn chair outside a cinder-block home, dry beneath a frayed awning. Only the first level is painted bright blue. The second is unfinished with rebar sticking up like flagless turrets. A halo of flowers sits upon her head and she is draped in once-bright colors, now faded to pastels. Does she often sit in drizzles, like one of his nixies?

She crooks her finger.

"I remember you."

"*Buenos dias, Señora*. We meet again."

She nods, neck stiff with arthritis. "You look like your father."

"Excuse me?" He glances through the store window at his *papá*.

"The man who would visit the Sanchez girl all those years ago." She points across a street that is little more than two tire tracks. The home is the same cinder-block as the rest of the village, but without flourishing gardens, the ramshackle home is drab, lifeless save for weeds that glisten with a thousand drops of rain. "She lived there with her daughter."

"Marieta?" Caulfield's heart races.

"You are the girl's brother, the son in Boston. Oh yes, you look like your father."

"I've been told I look like my mother."

The woman grins, toothless as a newborn. "Gringo eyes, gringo skin. But the rest of you…" Her eyes travel up and down Caulfield's body and she leers in a way old women can get away with. "You are an Aztec rain god, sleek as a panther. Your father was just as handsome. I will never forget as he walked up this very street and swept her away. She was ruined by him, but I think it must have been worth it."

Caulfield clears his throat. "Do you know where Marieta is now?"

"I do not." His spirit falls, but the woman isn't finished. "As I told her uncle, she was only here for a few days and then she left."

"Her *uncle*? When?"

"Not six days ago and then she vanished into the night, just as she arrived. *La Llorona*, that one." She crosses herself.

Six days. Caulfield missed her by six days. "*Señora*, are you referring to the uncle who is a mule for the cartels?"

"So they say. He threw his only sister out of his home when she was round with child. Your *abuela* came to them often, good Catholic woman."

Inspiration strikes, and he takes the photo out of his backpack: the only picture he has of his sister, given to him by the migrant farmworker.

"Yes, that is them. Marieta, her uncle, and…" she squints, then suddenly spits on the ground. "That woman is a *bruja*. We don't speak her name."

Caulfield runs a desperate hand through his hair. The man who stalked him this summer, who claimed to be her neighbor in Tizilicho…he is her uncle.

Has her uncle found his niece and saved her? Sold her to the Zacatóns? The woman touches his hand. "*Señor*, no one in our village told him she returned. We all remember how he sang beautiful songs to our children, weaved illusions and lured them away to the drug lords. We hate him."

"How do you know I won't do the same?"

Her smile is a black, gaping hole. She gestures to the dirty glass table beside her, where tattered paperbacks hide beneath a bushy, potted Mexican orange blossom. "Because I like your Nixies."

Of all things.

He holds a hand out for the well-read book. He flips to the dedication page, pulls a pen from his zip pocket, signs his name. Only a slight hesitation, knowing he may be sealing his death warrant, then jots down his burner phone number and a message:

M—Please call me.

He returns the book. "*Señora*, you'll make sure she sees this?"

She wraps thin, frail arms around her prized possession, her face grief-stricken. "I will, but she will never return. The man she loves is dead. They found my poor boy, God rest his soul." She crosses herself. "No head, hands…only his feet. A grandmother knows her grandson's feet…"

Caulfield pales as he and his *papá* descend the mountain. Mist enshrouds them, thick and heavy, as if they've fallen into the crease of his own dark folktales where creatures like *brujas*, wicked uncles, and feetless ghosts stalk the slopes. *Her uncle.* Now what should he do? Should he entrap him before he himself is entrapped, lure him back to the states and into the arms of the border patrol? Is this uncle good or bad?

"Look." His father catches his elbow and points.

He nearly misses the wild cat in the rain-speckled brush, watching him, waiting. He freezes. No, it can't be.

A *leoncillo*.

Caulfield crouches, astonished. He's never seen this creature of myth, surely it's as fantastical as the ghosts of these mountains. A harbinger? His eyes are unable to leave the clear amber of the animal's irises.

"Well, my friend," he whispers, "you haven't told us anything we don't already know."

We are drawn to the light. The sun pulls us to our doors and into the waking world after a long sleep. Our ancestors hovered over the crackling glow of fire, mesmerized by dancing flames as sweat trickled down necks and soaked wool. We are hypnotized by the fluid pictures of electronic screens, information and entertainment illuminated within the confines of a magic box. How often had I studied my husband as he wrote behind his laptop late into the night, his face reflecting its pale light like the moon against a canvas of black?

People are lights. I'd witnessed countless human moths drawn to these light carriers. Samuel hadn't set out to be a light carrier, yet people drifted to him because they ached for warmth, or illumination, or simply to be seen in the darkness. Samuel had a moment for them all.

A word of inspiration, his name in their books, or simply an ear as they told *their* stories.

He was born to be a light.

When I was nine and Samuel was on the new side of twelve, I spent a rare summer at home instead of being shipped off to Gran's in Durango. The neighborhood children played baseball at the Lyons field, next to the St. Vrain (everything in Lyons is next to the St. Vrain Creek). Most of the boys had been in Little League, with a few exceptions. One of these non-Little-Leaguers was a weird kid named Rafael. I now know he had Asperger's, but back then we didn't understand. He struggled to get the other kids to use his real name, but everyone had irritatingly called him "Fello" since preschool and continued to do so until the day he graduated and got the heck out of Lyons. Rafael wasn't a sports kind of guy, but his mom had confiscated his video games and forced him out into the sunshine. So, with great reservation (and a touch of hopefulness), Rafael joined our pick-up game.

He was chosen last.

He was also an easy out, because 'Fello' didn't know a lick about baseball. If I had been Rafael, I wouldn't have returned after the first baseman told me to step off the base and then tagged me out.

I trailed Samuel and Angel on the way home, my star-struck eyes glued to the jaunty tilt of Samuel's backwards baseball cap (I was an innocent kid, so my eyes hadn't learned to stray lower). It was difficult to understand their conversation, but I saw in the fiery set of Samuel's shoulders that he was upset.

"Firecracker, why do you think Rafael gets dumped on? Doesn't it bother you?"

I shrugged, played it cool in front of my crush. "It's not nice, I guess. Maybe if he learned the rules of baseball..."

"You're right, absolutely. I'm going to teach him."

For an entire month, Samuel pedaled over to Rafael's. I tagged along, nothing better to do. My most helpful contribution was "never run for second base when the shortstop has the ball." Samuel loaned him his old glove. Showed him how to 'swing thru,' and 'keep your eye on the ball.' By August, Rafael knew enough to remove the big bully target on his back.

When Samuel was team captain, he never chose Rafael last. If one of his Little League teammates told Rafael to steal third base, Samuel shouted "¡No seas gacho!" And they listened.

You know why? Because Samuel was a light. He set the bar so high, we were forced to stretch.

I think we are all born to be lights. But sometimes our hands are so out-of-practice, it's hard to strike the flint, catch the kindling.

Snowmass Mountain
September

"Is that a wild cat?" I grabbed Luca's sleeve and pointed to the underbrush where I swore there'd been a pair of amber eyes. He squinted.

"Don't see a thing. Sorry."

"It was like a mountain lion, only smaller."

"A bobcat, maybe, or a lynx? Keep your eyes open."

"We don't have to worry unless it's rabid. Stealthy creature."

I dragged up my tee and wiped sweat from my face. The heat of early September was nearly unbearable, hitting record levels and mercilessly cracking an already arid land. Still, no rain. Angel, Luca, and I battled up Snowmass Mountain, the trade-off a dramatic temperature shift that brought sweet relief from the castigating summer.

I collapsed on a boulder, its solid, wind-smoothed surface an ice pack on my skin. There were no trees, no shade, nothing but cool wind and sunshine. Glorious.

"That's it. I'm building a cabin right here in the tundra."

"I'm sure it'll hold up next winter," Angel laughed.

"Better yet, I'll burrow a hole next to this marmot colony. Do you think they would mind? Would you mind, little friend?" I asked a fat marmot tucked in a bed of columbine. The furry guy scurried and slid down the hill, off to warn the slope's inhabitants of my sinister plan.

"What number is this for you?" Luca dug through his pack and tossed each of us a Clif bar.

"Twelve, I think? Hector's just two from his fifteen, though." I hadn't planned to climb today, but when Hector backed out because of a 'last minute commitment,' I didn't think twice about lacing up the ol' Tevas. I'd been glued to the weather channel's radar for too long, staring at two red and yellow pinwheels: one barreling toward Mexico's Gulf Coast and the other, its Pacific Coast. I couldn't turn away, as if I could change the course of Hurricanes Manuel and Ingrid. Samuel was in Nuevo Leon, the state directly to the west of coastal Tamaulipas. At least he was inland.

"There's still time before November," I continued. "The Canucks also have three more peaks to go, but winter hits the Canadian Rockies a lot earlier than our Rockies. We've got this in the bag."

"Right on, Sister Blue Hair." Angel and I bumped fists like dweebs.

I didn't tell them Hector and I would finish out our fourteeners challenge separately. There would be no more climbs with him, alone or with a group, at least not for a few years. My heart ached at the loss of my friend, but if you're allergic to bee stings, you don't keep a hive in your backyard.

I turned a complete three-sixty, my beloved Rockies rising around me, range after range, like massive choppy waves frozen in a split-second. Far to the west, more than a hundred miles over the Uinta Basin, the sky was the steely gray of storms, thank God. The duel hurricanes in Mexico warped normal weather patterns, even this far north. By the time we left Snowmass, we'd be drenched. I said as much to my climbing partners.

"We better hit the trail," Luca agreed. "Get off the more treacherous parts of the mountain before this gully-washer." But no 'gully-washer' arrived. Something happened to the storm we saw, so far away, between the western ranges and us. It stayed in the Uinta Basin. Little did I know, those storms building and churning, stuck over the Uinta Basin, would produce a flood so ruthless, it would wash away anything in its path.

———————— •✦• ————————

When Angel asked to see the new place, I jumped. Reluctant to return to an empty apartment with Samuel in Mexico, I needed distractions.

Potholes rattled my teeth as Angel's pick-up truck bounced up the road to Samuel's and my new home. Left Hand Creek barely trickled thru its rock bed, the summer heat and lack of rain having depleted its supply. Angel slapped his knee as his country music station blared something about booze, rain, open roads, and American-made pick-up trucks.

"Been a rough summer, hasn't it?" said Angel.

Said the same thing myself, the other day. But I wasn't singing about it. "Not much rain. We're playing catch-up just to meet normal rainfall levels. Turn right."

He cranked the wheel. "I'm not talking about the weather, *hermana.*"

"I can't complain. But I want to hear about your deployment overseas."

He rubbed his military cut, the skin on his neck leathery and darkened by an oppressive desert sun. "Look, I know I've been gone a long time and it's hard to jump back in. But can I tell you what I see?"

"Sure." Guess we'd go there after all. He parked in the driveway.

"When I left in January, I saw my smiling, loony sister-in-law carry herself with a confidence that made complete strangers stop and stare. Now, nine months later, she's not smiling. She's still loony, but that confidence is gone. You're thinner."

"Not a bad thing, Angel."

"It is for you. Your whole body kinda drags when you walk."

"Like an ape?" I scratched my armpit and puffed out my cheeks.

Angel frowned. "I swear you're twelve."

I lurched into the backseat for my Tevas and eased them over blistered heels. "Things between Samuel and I...haven't been great. But we're in counseling, we're committed to each other, and we'll survive. So, while I appreciate your concern, your job right now is to spend time with your wife and your two beautiful babies."

"Danita sent me."

I should have known. Despite my downplaying the severity of my marriage crisis, she always saw. "Tell her I had wild redneck sex in a pond with her brother Sunday morning, while she was at church. That should shut her up."

A slow grin spread over Angel's face. "Believe me, it would be an honor."

We meandered over the hill, grass crackling under our feet. It was dried, dormant, desperate for water. Angel whistled. "Nice place. How many stories you building? Four?"

I hip-checked him. "Just two. Someone has to clean it. The roof goes up later this week, then the windows." I pointed out the creek, the trail ascending through the trees toward the old mine. We walked the perimeter of the property, wobbly on legs nearly shot from two days of mountain climbing.

He scratched his neck. "So...what's this insanity about a drug addict posing as Samuel's sister?"

"Despite what Danita believes, she really is his sister. If you met her, there's no way you could deny she's a Cabral."

"I get that. But you and Sam are so close to the situation, you aren't considering other possibilities. See, this is where being gone for six months comes in handy. Maybe she doesn't want to be found?"

"She wouldn't have asked for help if that were the case." I examined a downed tree we'd need to chainsaw into firewood when Samuel returned.

"Here's what bothers me. Isn't it entirely possible the whole thing is made up? Samuel's got a big bank account."

Dread crept into my bones. "You know, I'm not sure. Javier's creepy. But she seemed so…" I looked for the right word. "Genuine. Maybe she was coerced?"

We made our way back to the pick-up truck and climbed in. But Angel only sat behind the wheel, thoughtful. The air grew stale and stifling, and I cranked down the window. The air outside wasn't much better.

"Here's a scenario for you," he said after some minutes. "Marieta's scraping by in Mexico City, finding work, making friends. But then she learns something about this Javier she doesn't like. Perhaps he's sold her out to the Zacatóns, perhaps he's a human trafficker, I don't know. She flees, tells no one where she's going. Javier knows Marieta has a famous brother in Colorado, someone with money, and thinks maybe she's gone to him. Samuel's a prime target. Trouble is, Sam's off the grid after that debacle in Boston. His people are tight gatekeepers."

"But until recently, NixieNet.net posted his comings and goings." I muttered Alan Murphy's name like a curse.

"So he joins a group of migrants working the Front Range farms, stalks Samuel and reels him in with 'Marieta's address' in Mexico. But Sam is street smart: never reveal your travel plans, don't use unofficial taxis, surround yourself with an entourage, etcetera. He doesn't simply follow Javier to that Mexico City slum. Bro takes Santiago and his Uncle Carlos, who has guns and balls as big as his Mexican belt buckle."

"But I've seen Javier around town when Samuel's gone."

Angel stared me dead in the eyes. "Maybe he has a plan B." A shiver slithered down my spine and my brain raced, trying to pinpoint times I'd made myself alone and vulnerable. "No contact with this guy, *comprende*? If he comes knocking, lock yourself up tight and call the police."

"I can't call the police, because he's done nothing to threaten me. Being brown isn't illegal, *hermano*."

He rolled his eyes. "Then call *me*, Lily-white."

"Loud and clear, Lieutenant."

Just like that, Angel's job was done. He literally wiped his hands, relieved to have completed his task. "Let's head back. I need time with my baby girl, teach her how to power-five like a Wonder Twin."

Angel's truck rumbled to life and cool air poured into the cab, sweet relief. My mind zipped over unexplored angles in this deepening cavern. But one crucial question veined this scenario's walls like glowing lublinite, begging for attention:

This fragile, rumpled woman I'd twice met in Paddlers, the one who looked like Samuel... what was Marieta's angle?

The night before the Great Flood began, Samuel called me from Mexico. I told him Angel's theory about Javier. I assured him I would stay with Angel and Danita.

"Reminds me of the rabbit and the coyote."

"No clue what you mean." Samuel must have found the local *toloache* peddler.

"That old Mexican folktale. Surely you remember my father telling it to us when we were kids."

He told me to get comfortable for a bedtime story.

"Everyone knows a coyote's favorite meal is rabbit. But rabbits are tricky creatures. Once upon a time, a particularly hungry coyote chased a rabbit into the hills. He lost sight of his prey but soon found him, leaning against a rock high atop a cliff. Just as he was about to devour him, the rabbit cries 'no, you mustn't eat me. For who will keep this boulder from tumbling down the cliff and destroying the world? Quick brother, hold the boulder while I find a stick to brace it!' So coyote holds the boulder and the rabbit scurries away. Coyote waits and waits, braced against the rock until his limbs ache and he can't hold it anymore. 'Let the world be destroyed,' he cries and runs as fast as he can, only to find the boulder still perched high above on the cliff. Rabbit has tricked him."

Hazy memories wrapped around me, warm and colorful like Sofia's old peacock quilt, of being tucked into Danita's trundle bed while *Papá* Cabral wove this tale in the shadows of the bedroom lamp.

"Well, now the coyote is hopping mad. He tracks the rabbit across the plain and comes upon him lapping water from a lake, when the moon is round and bright. Just as coyote is about to devour him, the rabbit cries 'no brother, don't eat me! Eat this delicious cheese at the bottom of this lake. Do you see it?' Coyote's eyes widen and his belly gurgles. He asks rabbit how he can get the cheese from the water. 'We must drink our way to the cheese,' says rabbit. 'Drink quickly, for you are bigger than I.' So coyote drinks until his belly hurts and he is more sodden than a sponge. Water pours from his eyes and ears and he looks for the rabbit, only to find him vanished. Coyote has been tricked, once again."

"I remember this," I said as cobwebs retreated into the night. "But how does this correlate to you, Javier, and Marieta?"

"For the life of me, I can't figure this out: who is the rabbit and who is the coyote?"

We spoke for an hour about our new house, the latest news in Boulder County, the drought. He asked about my climb and I told him Hector hadn't been along. "I trust you," he said, but I wasn't sure he did. That was okay, we had lots of time.

I asked him about his trip. "You're in Nuevo Leon."

"Yes, Monterrey."

"Isn't that awfully close to Tamaulipas?"

A pause. I pictured him running his hand through his hair, the way he did when he was anxious. "It is. I'm actually on my way to La Vereda."

Frick frickin' mother frick. Anywhere but there. "You told me you wouldn't go back."

"I didn't tell you that."

"Dammit, Samuel Caulfield Cabral! Both Mexican coasts are about to get hit by hurricanes, and you're driving straight into Ingrid instead of away. You are going to get yourself kidnapped or killed."

"I won't. Ninety-nine percent of travel in Mexico is safe, at least for the next couple of days."

"Is that a promise?" I said with a voice too sarcastic to be loving.

"I'll talk to you as soon as I can, Kaye." End of call. I slammed my phone on the counter, so hard the case popped loose.

Morning dawned bright and beautiful, and I opened the curtains in Dani and Angel's townhome to another summer simmer. I turned on the news as I rifled through their pantry for cereal. A box of disgusting bulgur wheat was shoved to the back of the shelf, the same stuff Samuel ate. *Do not think about him in Tamaulipas. Do not check your phone for the thousandth time. Do not get in your car and hop an airplane. Do not, do not, do not...*

The anchorman was as cheerful as the sunshine outside the window:

"Relief from the heat is on its way, folks. The sprinkle we had yesterday was a foretaste of things to come. Clouds will build midday and that nice cold front we've been telling you about will move in, along with an unusually high level of moisture in the atmosphere. Some much needed rain is on the horizon..."

Yeah right. Rain was elevated to 'myth status' on the Front Range. But as I darted into Fischer's Deli for a turkey and Swiss, clouds billowed high into the sky. Rain pattered the pavement just as I ducked inside TrilbyJones, lunch in hand. Only a quarter of an inch total rainfall, but rock and clay doesn't absorb water. The rain raced down the foothills and settled nicely into our parched creek beds, a blessing for a land in a forty-year drought. My blue hair frizzed out like it hadn't in years, turning me into a Muppet.

How could we have possibly known that this miniscule quarter-inch of water was the first of what experts would one day call a 'thousand-year rain'?

That night, I sat beside my window and watched rain cascade down roof eaves and gush from the gutter, mesmerized. Its wetness tickled my nose. Fresh leaves and grass and earth perfumed the air, and I sucked in an exuberant breath.

My phone rang. I snatched it up. "Samuel. Are you alright?"

"I'm fine, just killing time at the airport. Listen, you and Angel were right about Javier." I sat up, sobered by his voice. "I'm almost positive he's working for the Zacatóns."

"For the love of all that's holy, get out of Mexico."

"As soon as I can. This is something I can promise."

"Please be careful."

"I need you to ask Jaime to search the Dark Web again. Instead of looking for info on me or Marieta, see what turns up about Javier Sanchez."

My mouth popped open. "'Sanchez,' as in related to Marieta Sanchez?"

"That's right—he's her uncle."

"Holy schnikes!"

"Try this address in Mexico City. Are you ready to write?"

I grabbed a pen and paper. "Shoot."

He read an apartment number in the Tizilicho slum, one number higher than Marieta's.

"I want to know everything she finds on him, his wife, his children. If she can discover who he's working for, even better. And read the chapter of our book I'm sending you..." He cleared the sorrow from his throat. "I love you. I'll be home soon."

I texted Jaime the information and settled in with Samuel's newest chapter, hammered out in a busy airport while he waited for the next flight. Four hours later, I buried my face in my pillow and slid into fitful dreams of babies crying and *La Llorona*, wailing into a starless Mexican sky.

———————◆·◆·◆———————

I downed one, two cups of strong, black coffee the next morning, still haunted by my husband's discoveries in La Vereda. So Javier was the brother of Marieta's mother, and he ran drugs for the cartel. (That explained his chilly warning about Border Patrol and how he knew Samuel and Marieta had dumped those kilos in a Texas farm pond). Javier would not be awarded a "world's greatest uncle" mug anytime soon. Why, then, had she lived next door to him in the Tizilicho slum? Was she still running drugs, too?

I gazed out the window and thought of Marieta. Did she know Daniel Rodriguez was dead? Had she watched his funeral procession leave the tiny village church and travel into the cemetery, where his family buried only his feet beneath a wooden cross? Was she concealed in some hole-in-the-wall, alone, mourning for the man she loved?

Unless she was dead, too.

So many questions. I shivered and calculated the time until I'd see my husband's Subaru pull into the driveway. It all depended on the next flight out of Mexico.

Heavy rain brawled with whipping tree limbs through the night. As morning passed, the TrilbyJones foyer became an obstacle course of open umbrellas and galoshes, a common sight in Seattle, perhaps, but not arid Boulder. The storm lashed and rattled the old Victorian and, in a moment that struck panic in my heart, caused the electricity to flicker. But soon it died to a steady sprinkle and the day became another blah Tuesday.

Jaime called, just as I debated whether to pay her a visit after work.

"If you do, I'll feed you to my Labs," she warned.

"How about I skip the social visit and you tell me what you've found on Uncle Javi?"

"Not much. No record of Javier Sanchez in the slum apartment next door to Marieta. A woman lives there, Camila Flores García. In Mexico, those two *apellidos* are as common as 'Smith' and 'Jones' in the States. So no red flags, until I traced her back to her hometown. Let's see how smart you are."

"La Vereda."

"A-plus for you. It gets more complex. Javier's 'wife' is not a wife, at least not on the books. No marriage between Javier and Camila that I can find, no record of children, either."

I absently twisted my wedding ring. This branch of Samuel's family tree was more complicated than sex in a hammock. "Maybe Javier also lied about having kids."

"Or they're simply off the books, too."

Unclaimed children…unclaimed lovers… I thought of my dad up in Cheyenne, managing his buddy's property. With his good looks and easy smile, surely he'd found another woman to love him by now. Did women cling to Javier Sanchez like my mom and I had clung to Tom Trilby? Had Marieta begged Daniel not to expose the Zacatóns, just like I'd begged Samuel not to return to Tamaulipas?

"I'm trying to dig up Daniel's passport and photo, but it's proving hard. He probably wiped all his identification off the Dark Web, so I'll have to go straight to the government sites."

"Daniel's dead, you know," I said flatly.

"*¡No mames!* Are you sure?"

"His family found a few stray body parts along the highway, feet included. They buried him last week."

Jaime hissed. "How did I not hear about this?"

"I suppose none of La Vereda's fifty residents have surfed the Dark Web lately."

"That's too bad, he was a decent guy. But Javier also seemed like a good one, in the beginning."

"If Javier sold out his own niece to the Zacatón Cartel, then he's a monster."

"People do horrible things to save their own hides. In my line of work, I've seen spouses turn their backs on their husbands and wives for far less. A lover, a salary raise, even a bowling league. It doesn't take much."

"How depressing."

"Now you see why I keep my relationships superficial."

My laugh was completely void of humor. "Now you see why I don't."

Samuel called later that evening, just as I finished a conference call with Molly.

"Are you out of Mexico?" I asked the minute I picked up my phone.

"Yes, but we're stuck in San Antonio at the airport and we can't get a flight until tomorrow. I'm too tired to mess with a car rental."

I breathed a sigh of relief. "No trouble in customs?"

"Just the usual extra ten minutes of questioning—my passport stamps are beginning to tell a shady story."

"Any sign of her?"

"We got close. But now that I know who Javier really is, it's too risky. She obviously doesn't want him to find her and I'm not doing her any favors by playing his tracking dog."

"Good thing this is the last trip. You've given the Mexican Feds more than enough to work with."

"Hmm."

Chapter 18
GRIPPED

One is gripped on a climb when
immobilized by terror.

Wednesday morning, the gully-washer arrived. Rain pounded the windows, wind thrashed the trees. I watched a mail truck careen through a puddle six inches deep, judging by the water it kicked up. No way was I going out to the mailbox in this weather. As it turned out, not only did I check my mail, I had to make a trip out to Left Hand Canyon. My contractor called, concerned about erosion around the foundation where grass had yet to grow.

"What can we do about it?" I asked.

"Me and some guys will haul sandbags out there if it's needed. Take a look yourself, let me know what you think."

I grabbed my rain coat and boots from the lobby and grumbled about paying my contractor to sit in his warm, dry office while I sloshed through a downpour to check out the condition of our home. Ash, my intern-slash-Nixie fan stopped me.

"Be careful on the way out to the canyon. Remember the exhibit we promoted for the Front Range Museum?"

I racked my brain. "The one about the Big Thompson Canyon floods in the seventies?"

"They're saying on Twitter we might get close to six inches of rain today, and that means flash floods. Don't go all Neelie Nixie on me, bestie."

I looked skyward. "Thanks for the heads up."

"Someone has to write my recommendation letter for grad school, which I need by Friday," she hinted.

"Oh crud, it's almost done. Lemme finish it up right now."

I tossed my raincoat over my desk chair and restarted my computer, opened the file. I had just printed and signed the final page when there was a rap at my door. All six feet of Hector Valdez leaned against the doorframe. His hands were jammed into his pockets, his tattooed muscles flexed with that ceaseless, restless energy that filled the space around him. His clothing was damp with rain (he hadn't bothered with an umbrella). He grinned, all joy and, I had to admit, my heart flipped. Bro was laying it on thick—he really wanted something from me.

"What is it, Hector?"

"Nice manners, *mamacita*. What happened to my polite, rosy-faced Cabbage Patch doll?" I chucked a promotional pen at his head. He ducked.

"You call me 'Cabbage Patch' again and I'll use my ninja skills."

"And what, nunchaku me with your stapler? Listen, I didn't swing by to be maimed by office supplies. You see that beautiful downpour outside?"

"Is that what it is? I thought Boulder had the power washers out today."

He shook his head. "Oh Kaye, marriage to that stick-in-the-mud has ruined your sense of humor. You used to be funny."

"Says the man-child who thinks hippie puns are hilarious."

"That reminds me. What kind of cigarettes do hippies smoke?"

"The illegal kind. Now what about the rain?"

He poked me in the shoulder. '*Yours,*' you dummy. *Ay ay ay*, there's no hope for you. But yeah, the rain. It's supposed to hit six inches by the end of today."

I lifted my red rain-booted feet. "Some are predicting nine."

Hector whistled. "Even better."

"Why on earth would nine inches of rain be a good thing? Do you know the kind of flash flooding it will cause? Tomorrow's gonna be ugly."

"Kaye, now you're really scaring me. Seriously, what has happened to my adventuress? Can you even fathom the kind of rapids this rain will kick up in the watershed? We're talking level five the *whole freaking ride*, sweet cheeks, the likes of which Colorado has never seen nor will see for a hundred years. It's our one chance. All of the river rats will be out."

"I don't think so, Hector."

"Is 'Mr. Trilby' still out of town?"

"He is."

"Then what's stopping you?" His mouth curled, sultry, seductive.

Until that moment, he nearly had me. I could feel the power of the rapids break against my face, my body, the lurch of my stomach as we rose and dipped, raced and braced and conquered the river. But then, like an unexpected kick to the back of the knees, he floored me with his disrespect.

"What is this about?" I asked, suspicious.

Hector straightened, his eyes now cold, full of accusation. He wiped his hands against his shirt, his jeans, and shrugged. "I asked you to go kill the rapids with me, you said no. Whatever. I'll give Luca a call."

"Nuh-uh. We never dealt with what happened up on the mountain. I think it's time, don't you?"

"You want to air your dirty laundry for your whole office to hear? Be my guest."

I sputtered. "No. I...I just don't like..."

"*Mamacita*, don't." He sighed, closed my office door and plopped into the chair across from my desk. "I called you out for your boring life, your safe marriage. You got all fired up and feisty, and it turned me on, nothing more. But sometimes, argh!" His hands curled into fists. "Sometimes you drive me insane, lady."

"Hector, you're married, I'm married. I love my husband."

"I know, okay? I see what you have, and that's the rub of it. I see the way you love him, the way he loves you, and I hate it. I don't even *want* you like that, Kaye."

"Then why...?"

He growled and scrubbed his bald head. "Sometimes I just want to...to kiss the hell out of you, touch you and everything else, but I don't want to keep you. You're beautiful. You have this smile, and eyes, and man, you've got guts. I'm a terrible friend just telling you this—how sometimes I want to use you up and throw you away. But I'm your friend first and I wouldn't do that to you, even though I can't stand Cabral!"

My body flushed, as if I stood over a hissing radiator and allowed steam to scald me. My hands trembled and I struggled to ignore this man who I thought I'd known, but maybe didn't know at all, and continue typing whatever the hell I'd been composing before he'd upended my uninteresting, rainy morning. How was it possible to feel so desired and cheapened at the same time? Whatever angle Hector worked, he'd twisted me into a gob of fluster and fury. Dropping the pretense, I slammed my laptop shut.

"I don't understand. Why do you dislike Samuel? Why do you hate what we have? Why would you even say these...these *things* to me?"

"Because you left me alone, Kaye! You abandoned me, what *we* had, for *him*—the guy who ditched you, who's *still* ditching you. You used me, your little Band-Aid for the Samuel-sized hole in your life. When you and Cabral fought, who's the first person you called to drag you on another adventure?"

Oh. The spitting radiator cooled, and guilt and shame sat so heavily upon me, my body sagged. *This was my fault, too.* "Hector, I'm sorry. I've always had an ugly selfish streak. But in all fairness, I've also been honest with you about Samuel."

He shrugged. "It matches your ugly jealous streak. Don't think I didn't see the ice you used to shoot Jaime. You don't do it to Tricia, though."

Because he doesn't love Tricia, not the way a husband is supposed to love his wife. I could never voice this, but I didn't have to.

"Samuel warned me I was in danger of an emotional affair. That's what we've been doing, isn't it? It all seemed innocent—climbing partners, tackling fourteeners together, you helping me get my mountain legs back." Heck, the climbs had even been Samuel's idea. He'd trusted me and I'd betrayed that trust.

"It was going well until the gringo dropped out," he spat.

Heat rose again. "Samuel did what he had to do. The fact is, I should never have gone alone with you. When I married, when you married, when anyone marries, relationships have to change. Maybe you think I'm a photocopy of my former brilliant, carefree, careless self. Whatever. That's your opinion. But at least I'm *faithful*, at least my husband knows I will always choose him over those mountains, over my friends, over my career, and certainly over a stupid adrenaline rush. Can your wife say the same?"

He sneered. "Can you say the same about your husband? Word is, he's chasing some woman in Mexico."

I rolled my desk chair back so hard, it banged into the wall and a motivational poster clattered to the ground. I skirted around him and yanked open the door. "Out of my office."

He jumped up from his chair and shoved it into my desk. "Fuck you, Kaye, and your shitty friendship."

"Ride the piss out of those rapids, Hector," I called as he stomped out of my office. "At the rate you're going, you won't be here for Christmas!" He had already rounded the hall.

Stunned eyes peered over cubicles as embarrassment flooded my face and mingled with angry purple. I pushed a hand into my curls, exhaled. Screw it.

I grabbed my raincoat, closed up my office, and called it a day.

Time for a trip up to the new house, see why the contractor was concerned. Hector Valdez would be dealt with another day.

As I wound into the Canyon, I was shocked to see the banks of Left Hand Creek filled to the brim with rushing water, a swift transformation from the docile trickle at the bottom of the rock bed. Tree branches and other woodland debris bobbed in and out of sight and piled at the culvert, damming the waters. Alarm bells rang. If the culvert was clogged, wouldn't that force the raging creek back into the canyon? That, or it would swell up and around the culvert, over the road. Disaster was stamped all over those rising waters.

When I reached our new home, I was relieved to see the surrounding earth work was holding steady against this never-ending downpour. It was a mud pit, but it was still there. My boots sucked and popped as I walked the perimeter. It was difficult to tell if our home was snug and dry against the deluge. I dug into my zip pocket for the house key then promptly dropped it in a puddle. My fingers were numb and shaking. I hadn't even noticed the rain was cold. I sloshed through water until I came up with the key and unlocked the house. Dry, fresh timber tickled my senses. I ditched my waterlogged boots, socks, and raincoat in what would be the mud room and crept across the cold but thankfully dry floors, checked the foundation.

Watertight.

Surely the rain would let up in an hour or so. I wasn't in a hurry to put on cold wet socks, so I spread out my sodden items to dry. A pity I hadn't stored any extra clothing or blankets, even a flashlight out here. *Samuel keeps one in the trunk.* I squinted through the fogged window at my Jeep. It was only late-afternoon, but heavy storm clouds blocked the sun and what little light remained would be gone soon, up here in the mountains. I'd have to hit the road. With a sigh, I trudged back to my pointless rain gear. At least the soggy socks and boots would save my feet from hidden nails and other dangers on a construction site. With one last glance around the dry, cheery home, I stepped back into the torrent and secured the door.

The drive east into the canyon was slow and perilous. Water from Left Hand Creek now flirted with the edge of the road. Not good. The farther I drove, the harder it became to navigate the tight curves of the mountain blacktop in the deep gray of twilight. Branches, rocks, other debris littered the road. Water trickling down the slopes morphed into streams. As I neared the bridge, a small, niggling voice grew louder until I was so uneasy with its shouting, I stopped the car.

Check the bridge.

Was it safe to cross? Should I try it? I wavered behind my steering wheel, not wanting to subject myself to the biting rain.

Check the bridge, it repeated, urgent.

Sighing, I flipped up my hood, opened my car door, and peered down at the bridge. What was all over the surface? It looked like a patch of black tar. Mud? I couldn't quite tell, but it was fluid, gushing...

Mother of pearl. I popped the trunk and hoped the flashlight was there. It was. "Thank you, Samuel," I whispered. The beam bounced over the bridge. Rather, what *should have* been the bridge. What once was pavement was now a roaring river...I hadn't seen tar, or mud, or even puddles, but the creek itself, rushing through a massive, gaping hole where the bridge had crumbled away.

I closed my eyes. *You're royally screwed, aren't you, Kaye?*

I scanned the left side of the road, the right, even up, hoping against hope another way might appear. The only option was the way I'd come. I squared my shoulders and returned to the Jeep.

The windshield wipers heaved aside rivers as I inched back to the house. Water from the creek now sloshed over asphalt—in less than an hour, the road would be completely swallowed into wild rapids. My phone buzzed in my purse. Clutching the steering wheel, I ignored it and navigated an obstacle course, teeth clenched, until I reached what I thought was the turn-off for our home. My tires spun and slipped, struggled to get up the hill.

"Come on!"

I hit the gas and careened up the slope, then wrenched the wheel and side-swept into gravel to keep from sliding back down. My Jeep barreled into a pile of covered timber and a black tarp fluttered loose, wrapped around the side mirror, a tree, and then sailed into the air.

Perfect. I grabbed the flashlight and my purse and shot out of the Jeep for the door.

Once I'd shed all of my wet things a second time, I curled into a corner next to the window and savored the smell of fresh wood beams and sheet rock. Nothing to do but wait the storm out. I absently traced the white ink tattoo of a trilby hat on my foot, bones beneath thin skin, callouses on my ankles, pads, heels. Counted scars on my legs, knees, elbows.

Eleven...twelve...thirteen...fourteen...fifteen...until the last bit of daylight succumbed to the storm, the mountains, the night.

My child was in my arms. His downy head was wisps of cotton against my cheek. His breath was a warm, southern breeze. His tiny body rose, sank, rose, sank against my chest. *He's mine.* The cloying scent of over-ripe oranges permeated the room. There was movement, and my heart stopped when a woman crouched next to my rocking chair, her hand around my child's tiny foot. My muscles bunched like a cat's as it readied to leap, but she held a finger to her mouth.

"Don't wake him." I swear her lips didn't move, but the room was dark…only a nightlight in the corner, so it could have been a trick of the shadows. My eyes zeroed in on her hand, playing with the baby's toes. Blue, purple, right down to the tips of her fingernails. Paint? No. I'd seen a hand like this before… It wasn't a trick of the light, the rest of her skin was brown, as brown as my husband's family. So familiar. Not Danita…slender face, sharp cheekbones, wide mouth, so much like Samuel's.

Understanding blanketed me. "I remember you."

She nodded to the baby in my embrace. "He is precious." Once again, her lips didn't move.

"Yes." I brushed the sleeping boy's face, kissed his hairline.

"He is loved."

"Very much."

She rose and turned for the door, then beckoned me to follow.

"Where are we going?"

"La montaña. Mi casa."

She slipped through the blue door, into the white.

I followed into the white…

The snowfield of Longs Peak was white, spotless, as if miles of sun-bleached linen had settled onto the mountaintop. Its light was so dazzling, my eyes watered. I turned to Molly, but she wasn't there. Neither was Cassady, the other hikers, any of our gear. All was wiped clean, as if the mountain had returned to its infancy.

Only me.

No, not only me. A single hand rose up from the field of snow, blue to the tips of her fingernails and as frosted as the sky above. Familiar trembles seized me. Airways swelled shut and I gasped, gasped again. Not the panic, please God.

Breathe.

Where was the baby?

Breathe, Kaye.

But I can't remember the mantra! Roll my foot? Feel the ground? Oh God, where was the baby?

I couldn't even find the ground, under all this snow. I sank to my knees, coughing, choking, clawing numbed fingers through piles and piles of snow, always digging but never finding.

Kaye.

I shot up. Peered around the snowfield. Empty, except for the macabre blue hand, reaching up to the heavens. With stunned silence, I watched as the fingers curled into a fist, stretched, and curled again. I blinked. Was she alive?

I scrambled from the depths of the pit I'd dug and flung myself at the snow around the hand, hurled it away, scooped, dig dig dig, but the arm went on and on. Where was the woman?

Look up.

I shook my head and searched for the woman buried beneath the snow.

Why are you searching below? Look up.

"But she's right here!" I said, flinging my arm in the direction of the hand. The hand was gone. Startled, I jumped to my feet and turned a circle. Nothing but an empty field of white.

"Look up!" the voice shouted.

I scanned the horizon.

"Higher!"

My neck stretched and I squinted into the sky, more white than blue, as white as the electrified filament of a light bulb, whiter than the sun. I couldn't look any higher. I held up a hand to block the light, and was startled to find my own hand was a sickly, frozen blue...

A buzzing woke me.

I rubbed my eyes. Where was I? I patted around for the sound... my phone, vibrating in my purse. Still half-asleep, I groped through the pockets and answered.

It was Angel, his words jumbled. "Get off the mountain!"

"What?" I blinked away sleep. The room was thick with dark purples, blues, as dark as a bruise. Where was the snowfield? The light?

"Floods coming down from the mountains into the foothills, washing out everything in their paths. The entire canyon is going to be washed away—cars, houses, people. Kaye, you'll be killed. *Get off that mountain!*"

Awareness rushed through me. I'd fallen asleep in the new house. Oh my God, the floods. The road...the bridge... A sob tore through my throat. "Angel, I can't! Left Hand Creek already washed out the bridge." He cursed.

"There's no way out, I already tried."

"Maybe there's a back road." But we both knew there was only one road in and one road out.

"Samuel. Tell him that...that I love..." *Oh Samuel, I'm sorry.*

I heard my brother-in-law's heavy breath, felt his desperation. "Okay, okay. You've got a bit of time. Get higher, as high as you can. Is there shelter in the mountain? A cave or something?"

The voice of my dreams echoed. *Look higher, Kaye.*

Light as bright as that snowfield flashed in my memory. "Angel, the old mine entrance!" I'd walked that path countless times with Samuel to the old stone structure, as sturdy as the mountain into which it was carved. "It's up the hill, beneath a natural overhang. The water'll go over the top of it. Well, *might*." Honestly, I had no idea if the water would bypass the little enclave or flood it to the hilt and drown me. But what choice did I have? I squared my shoulders and decided.

"Okay Angel, I'm going to the mine entrance." I fumbled into my cold, wet Teva boots, barely able to lace them my fingers trembled so badly. "If... if you can't find me, it's up a trail into the woods, to the left of the house. Or whatever's left of the house. If you don't remember where it's at, ask Sa-Samuel." My throat caught on the name of my beloved husband.

Angel's voice broke. "I'll see you in a few hours, okay *hermanita? Te amo mucho.*" The call ended and I was alone.

My eyes flitted over our dream home. The walls were up, the foundation was solid. Perhaps it would make it. But if I remained in the middle of its false security a moment longer, I could die here. With a last bit of affection, I patted a sturdy beam and began my treacherous climb up the hill.

Wind and rain whipped my hair loose from my ponytail and stung my eyes, cheeks. Mud slid beneath my saturated Tevas, rocks wrenched loose and tumbled down the slope. Still I climbed. How much longer until the waters came? My hands and knees were cut from falls on the slick ground, but another scar didn't matter. I counted them again: *fourteen…fifteen…sixteen…* I wouldn't die on this land Samuel had so lovingly gifted to me.

Samuel, somewhere high in the air on a plane above Texas, above Colorado. Had he returned?

Was his flight in a holding pattern as the world beneath him washed away?

I peered through the heavy curtain of rain. The forest edge. Water rose faster around my ankles…the wave was coming. Branches lashed and swayed as the storm brought trees to life in a dance of limbs and fingers. I forged through this animated army, my hands in front of my face, holding back the wind and water. Samuel and I had walked this trail numerous times, under the summer sun, the breeze warm and gentle in the trees, on my face…

Turn left.

My feet stumbled over the path, little more than a deer trail, through undergrowth invisible beneath the rising water, red with clay. An obscene giggle rumbled through me—the mountain was bleeding. Then I saw it behind a tangle of wild morning glories and weeds. Ripping aside the vines, I stumbled through the entrance and into sudden relief as the tempest howled behind me. I shook my frozen hands, wrung water from my hair. My phone was zipped into the lining of my rain coat, still working, thank goodness. Its battery charge sat at twenty percent, not good. I'd need to conserve its power, but before I shut it off, I had one call to make:

Samuel.

My signal was choppy at best and ended up dumping my call before I'd connected.

Come on!

I tried again. No contact.

One last effort. With trembling fingers, I texted a message to my husband:

Samuel Caulfield Cabral es mi mejor amigo.

A thought entered my head and wouldn't let go, as potent as my dream... *La montaña. Mi casa.* In a leap of faith, I added this:

Go to Marieta's mountain.

Because that was her true home, wasn't it?
I pressed "send." The little icon spun, spun...
Message sent.
With that, I settled against the dusty, dank rock wall and waited for the end.

Cold filtered into my bones and my skin, muscles, very veins turned to icy flint as I cowered in the mine entrance. Water streamed down the rock walls, over my head, ears, between my shoulder blades. Was I becoming a part of the mountain itself? My teeth chattered and my entire body trembled, soaked as a blanket forgotten in the rain. I pressed my palms to my ears, trying unsuccessfully to draw water away from my eardrums. Unbelievable that, only three days ago, I'd wished for an end to the unbearable heat. What I wouldn't give for that summer sun.

Beyond me, to the west, I heard it. At first, I thought it was the rumble of thunder, but it was constant, grinding, grumbling, louder and louder, like an approaching freight train. I ducked out of my hidey-hole and shone Samuel's flashlight through the canyon, into the west. Its beam bounced off movement—uprooted trees, huge objects churning in the distance. It really was an approaching freight train. With alarm, I examined the canyon's topography and judged where those objects would hit. Bits of homes, tree branches, all kinds of debris... Our own home was right in their path. Tears welled.

Nothing to do about it now. Just hold tight. I clung to one of the boards nailed over the old mine opening. Splinters burrowed into my skin, but I held fast. Water swirled around my ankles, the tops of my feet, rising slowly, then not so slow. Confused, I reached down to see where it lapped against my cold-deadened legs. It was just below my knees.

No. Deadly realization poured through me like a poison. I'd chosen wrong.

Sam had picked a good place for our home, alongside this peaceful creek, these towering mountains, so safe, like sentinels guarding our piece of land. Scenic, where the canyon bent and curved south...

The canyon curved on our property. Countless times, when Hector and I skied the backcountry, we swayed side to side through paths on our way down the mountains, skimmed around tight curves that had us leaning so far into the mountain to maintain our balance, we brushed our fingers along the ground. In the winter Olympics, I recalled sleds rounding those bends so sharply, their blades crept to the edge of the pipe, on the verge of flying up and out.

It was the same with water. If you sent it racing through a pipe and it rounded a curve, what did it do? It rose. Swept higher into the curve, up the canyon slopes.

And I was smack dab in the middle of the bend.

I squeezed my eyes shut as the very end of the earth rumbled closer and closer until it roared in my ears, shook the ground and forced me to cry out in the face of this apocalypse. Fear paralyzed me. Panic seized me, stole my breath one last time. I coughed, gasped for air, but what was the point? I was staring down death anyway.

"Oh God, what do I do?" I cried.

Go higher.

I shook my head, pressed my palms to my ears to stifle the roar.

Go to the top.

"I can't go higher, it's too late!"

Go now!

Like a shot from a cannon, I hurled my body into the maelstrom outside, through the waterfall cascading over and around the mine entrance. I was not going to die in this hole, but in the open air, under the aspen trees. Like an ant scrambling for its life up the bark of a tree, washed down only to scramble up again, I scraped my way up the side of the mountain on pure adrenaline. Seconds, minutes, hours, I pushed my way up that slope as the flood debris drew near. I had nothing left. My hands had lost their grip long ago, my mind had certainly lost its grip, but still I clawed into the mud, split my fingernails open on rocks and roots, up, up, up through the trees as rain rushed down. I grunted and cried when stinging pain streaked through my palm and something heavy crashed into my rib cage, but I pushed on, my boots digging into the ground and holding fast because my feet refused to let me tumble down into the abyss below.

I climbed until I couldn't climb any higher, and there, on the top of my mountain, my clothing and skin shredded and bloodied, I tethered my arms around the trunk of a stumpy old tree and watched the world wash away.

I was still alive.

"Thank you," I breathed. "Thank you."

At last, on the summit, I rested. The rain beat against my forehead and I laughed, partly from exhaustion and partly from a break with reality (if this could be called reality), but I laughed and laughed. How hilarious was it that I'd just summited a mountain?

"I don't suppose you're a fourteener?" I patted solid rock as the storm swallowed my voice. "I didn't think so. Damn."

My dreams were restless, if they were dreams at all. Crouched on top of the mountain, open to the elements as blood trickled and clotted...sleep was difficult. Yet my exhausted body must have slept, because I saw Samuel: young, maybe sixteen, seated in the Cabrals' family room. He hunched over his Spanish guitar, a peaceful smile on his mouth as he strummed a haunting, beautiful acoustic version of "Silent Night." The room twinkled with fairy lights, gold and shadow. Pine garlands twined around the stair banister, lined the mantle. Behind him, brilliant and shining with rubies, emeralds, jasper was their eight-foot-tall Christmas tree covered in glass ornaments. He hummed softly.

Silent night, holy night.

The mountain was as silent as the stars, void of life save for my beating heart.

All is calm, all is bright.

Long fingers danced over guitar strings. His wiry frame hugged his guitar, strength on the cusp of manhood, ready to burst and bloom.

Another memory, not so long ago. Samuel, stepping out the shower, rivulets of water running down his back, swirls of hair plastered to his arms, his legs, everything. He grabbed a towel from the rack and scrubbed his hair dry. It curled and waved all over his head, damp clumps so soft and fresh-smelling, I wanted to run my hands through it, feel the dampness, the softness. I wanted to press my cheek against his back and feel his clean, clammy skin. Why hadn't I? Every morning during this so very ordinary, so very erotic routine, *why hadn't I?*

One more vision. That's what it had to be, this couldn't possibly be a memory. I'd know that set of shoulders anywhere, even far away, high up this mountain. Sweep, sweep, raking leaves from the slope. His hair was thick and silver. Still so strong, graceful, even as he tended our yard. Our house was further down the slope. Bittersweet years had settled deep into the walls. He worked in rhythm; he must have had some song playing through his head. Was I in this vision, raking leaves or in the house, watching from the window? *Please let me share this with him.*

I would love him forever, this boy, this man, to the day his gray head bent and his eyes closed for the last time. And beyond that, I would love him.

Chapter 19
SHAKY AT THE CRUX

The crux is the most difficult portion of a climb route. Best not to be shaky.

The ground radiated a dull orange as morning dawned over the mountain. My body was as rigid as the tree to which I still clung and I groaned, tested my icy fingers and toes. Oh mother of Tom, was I sore. If I extended my joints any further, my limbs would pop out. And my neck. I gritted my teeth as I gingerly raised my head. My clothing was in tatters, shredded by sharp rocks and sticks, crusted with blood. Pain and stiffness shot through every vertebra along my back, but nothing was broken. My wrist was a different story. It hurt, badly. As the sky lightened, I saw its swollen, bruised state, all the way to the tips of my bloodied fingernails.

With my good hand, I pulled out my waterlogged phone, tried to turn it on. Dead as a doornail, of course.

The sun had been up for a full hour before I mustered enough strength to haul myself off the mountain. My stomach rumbled with hunger, even as pangs of nausea doubled me over. Unbelievable. Even surrounded by a world of water and nearly drowning in it the previous night, I was dehydrated. I tripped over a branch, but with sudden inspiration, it became my hiking stick as I carefully picked my way down the mountainside.

How does one describe an aftermath? 'Aftermath' implies great destruction, the end of a way of life. The end of naiveté, though I'd traveled that path more than once. The things of this world never ceased to hurl my previous state of oblivion in my face.

The lower two-thirds of the mountain had been stripped bare. Massive trees were uprooted and strewn across the slope like pick-up-sticks. Pieces of homes, a window frame here, a sofa there. The highway had buckled like a bedspread kicked out of the way by a three-ton foot. Boulders had tumbled into the bottom of the canyon. The massive 'creek' roared over and around them, muddy waves crashing and breaking against their rock sides. I laughed. Hector had actually wanted to navigate those waves.

And our new home...washed away, save for a few dangling timbers. But the foundation remained, unmoved, stubborn and sturdy as the ground in which it was built. Filled with red clay water, but still there. Tears trickled down my cheeks. Not sad tears. Tears of awe, of survival. The foundation was *still there*. We could rebuild, maybe stone next time, but we would not be wiped off the face of this earth. I smiled. That sturdy foundation would make a great in-ground pool.

Wind flicked debris at my raw, chapped skin as I made my way east, one cautious step at a time. Twelve flipping miles to the canyon entrance. I'd hoped the road beyond the bridge washout had been spared, but after seeing how that bulldozer-of-a-flood had flattened an entire canyon, I doubted it was drivable. No matter. The Jeep was long gone.

In retrospect, I should have stayed close to the mine entrance, or whatever was left of it, but my weary brain told me to move. As far as I knew, I was the only thing alive in this barren place, save for the occasional bird darting up and over the canyon to whatever lay beyond.

My ears throbbed, especially my bad ear. Waterlogged, maybe even ruptured. Still, I pushed on, matching my footsteps to each pulse behind my ears, my heart, until I could walk no farther. My boots were soddened, my feet blistered and wet with mud and blood. I'd passed the washed out bridge an hour ago, and still, nobody. My gut ached and so did my head. My legs buckled and I dropped onto my bottom, curled into the ground, soft and squishy as a foam mattress.

I lay on the ground and absorbed its energy. Wind swept over and around, wearing me down, smoothing rough edges. Roaring, always roaring in my eardrums, though I couldn't tell if it was the wind, the water, or injury. Soon the roaring sounded like a rhythmic *thwap-thwap-thwap*. Before long, the rhythm overtook the roar and I peered into the silvery sky.

There it was. A helicopter—military –coming from the west. I lifted a hand to wave it down. Could it see me, as muddy and bruised as the mountainside, or would I simply be unnoticed, a camouflaged body against the landscape? Closer, closer. No signs of slowing. Now it was nearly overhead.

I need to find Samuel.

With one last burst, I pushed myself off the ground and waved my arms, jumped into the air, as if I could reach that helicopter and yank it down. It slowed and hovered, its ring of wind flattening the injured slope. I blocked the sun with my hand and tried to see into the chopper. A side door popped open and a man emerged, clad from head to toe in an Air Force flight suit. A rope lowered him down, down, down, until he was face-to-face with me. He smiled, then grimaced as he took in what must be my grisly appearance. He said something to me and I shook my head, confused. Then he pushed up his visor and I saw him clearly, my own personal angel.

My brother cupped my cheek, afraid to touch me. I collapsed against his chest in a mess of sobs and then his arms came around me, hugged me to him as tightly as he dared. I sank into his warmth, his dryness.

Angel sought out my good ear and shouted. "I told you we'd come for you, *hermanita!*"

Vaguely, it registered that I hadn't been rendered completely deaf after all. He hooked a harness around me and then we were lifted into the sky, a foot, a dozen feet, farther and farther from the destruction below us.

Once I was safely inside the belly of the helicopter, I saw the other half of Angel's 'we.'

Pale and trembling, fear was etched in every deep line of his face, in the dark circles beneath his eyes, rumpled clothing, the thin press of his mouth. At once I was in the embrace of my husband, fierce, not at all careful. What little composure he'd maintained collapsed, and he buried his face into my bedraggled, stringy hair and wept.

"We couldn't find you. We couldn't find you," he cried, again and again, his arms solid and painful around my ribcage. Someone handed him a fleece blanket, which seemed to bring him back to himself and he released me, tenderly wrapped the scratchy thing around my shoulders, covering my tattered appearance that left absolutely nothing to the imagination.

Once I was decent, I burrowed into him and stayed there as the helicopter circled the canyon. A medic flashed a light in my eyes, checked my vitals, and began to catalog my injuries. I gradually became aware of my surroundings. The Air Guard medic attended two other survivors, in much the same state as I. Another peered out the windows or communicated with the pilot, directing him to washed-out homes, specks of color or movement, any life in the devastation below. The medic pressed a bottle of water into my hands.

"Slowly, okay?"

Unbelievable, how my skin was wrinkled and swollen from a night in the rain, but my innards were absolutely parched. I sipped and coughed. Samuel dragged his fingers along my spine in a soothing pattern, back-and-forth. He watched me, and I realized he'd asked a question. I tapped my bad ear and he frowned. Something was definitely wrong with my eardrums. I jammed my fingertips into them, suctioned them with my palms to no avail. Tears welled in my eyes. What if both of my ears were now bad? Of all the things to cry over, additional hearing loss seemed low on the totem pole, but it pushed me over the edge.

As I cried, Samuel took me back into his arms, and together we shook with fatigue and relief.

After a long while, he stared straight into my eyes with determination. "Can you hear me now?" he said (shouted, more likely). A little laugh burst out as I remembered those annoying cell phone commercials.

He smiled. "I think it's just Swimmers Ear, firecracker."

"What did you say a few minutes ago?" I asked (more than likely shouted, also.)

"I said, 'Do you know how we spotted you?'"

"How?"

He tugged one of my nasty locks. "Your blue hair."

"No. Really?"

"God's honest truth. Only speck of brightness on that mountain-side, saw you a mile away."

Well. Wait until I told Danita.

My body was warm, cocooned in soft, dry, blankets. No more roaring, no more wind or cold.

"Kaye."

I shook my head, which was a mistake. Ow.

"Kaye."

I cracked open an eye to see Samuel peering down at me. His sensitive mouth twitched.

"Hey," I croaked.

"Hey."

"Where am I?"

"Boulder General. You have a long rap sheet here."

"The info desk keeps butterscotch candies behind the counter, FYI."

"Good to know." He brushed hair from my eyes. "Your head hurts because you're severely dehydrated. Your left wrist is splinted, just a sprain. Cracked rib, once again. Numerous contusions and cuts on your legs and arms, like you nearly lost a fight to a mountain lion. You've got an IV in your right arm, so try not to move it. And, of course, Swimmer's Ear. Doctor emptied a gallon of water out of your head. It was enlightening."

"Duly noted." As he said this, I realized I could hear him more clearly than...how long had I been here? I reached up and took his fingers, and saw that my hand was swathed in gauze, shielding a plethora of lacerations. Dang. No one could accuse me of having banker hands. "My mom?"

"Safe in Longmont."

"Danita and the kids? Your folks?" My eyelids were twenty pound weights. They fluttered as I struggled to open them.

"Marooned in Lyons, but safe."

"The Paddlers boys?" I mumbled. "Jaime? My TrilbyJones staff?"

"Go back to sleep, sweetheart." I didn't argue.

———————— •◦• ————————

A "thousand year storm" is what they would call the disaster that hit our small corner of the world that September. Those hurricanes I'd fretted over for Samuel's sake, so far away in Mexico? Well, far-away hurricanes have huge impacts in your own backyard. That ample tropical moisture from Hurricanes Manuel and Ingrid combined with the stalled storms in the Uinta Basin, which we spotted on our mountain climb. What resulted was epic rainfall over our drought-beleaguered Front Range: twelve inches in three hours. Eight lives lost, another six missing. Fifteen-hundred homes destroyed, a billion dollars in damage. Those are the numbers.

But I'm not a numbers person.

It was as if a giant from Samuel's stories had upended a massive trough of mud and debris onto the Front Range, filling every ditch, gully and crevice with brown muck and withering branches.

Big Thompson Canyon homes were reduced to rubble, plucked from the sides of mountains and hurled onto the rocks below.

Old trees with roots twenty feet deep were effortlessly torn from the ground like saplings.

Highways broke and buckled. Two-ton SUVs glided across parking lots like matchbox cars, so great was the force of the water as it swept them away. Even my mom's truck was upside down and half-sunk into a bed of mud.

Rescue workers removed a retired teacher's body from his home after both were crushed by rocks and muck.

"We heard branches snapping in the tree line just above our backyard, thought it was a bear," Sofia shared. "I asked Alonso to check, and he asked if I was trying to off him for his life insurance," she chuckled, though there was no humor in her eyes. "It wasn't until we heard trees and boulders crashing into the St. Vrain, that we realized we had to leave our home or die in it."

She was right, too. I saw what was left of their home…even now, sickness settled into my bones as I recalled memories, sodden and scattered across a slope of putrid mud, alongside Alonso's treasured library. Sofia's Mexican folk art was destroyed. The old family room in the basement was stripped of the upper level and filled to the brim with two tons of mud. And Sofia's flower beds, tended by slightly arthritic fingers? Crushed.

Seeing the remains of the Cabrals' home on 24/7 news coverage had me bolting out of my hospital bed, wincing against the pain in my ribs and wrist as I fruitlessly tore through my suitcase for my ruined Tevas. But I was still hooked up to my monitors (and some pretty strong pain meds), and my skyrocketing stress levels brought a nurse running. The nurse told my doctor, my doctor told Samuel, and now I was banned from watching 24/7 news.

Three days in the hospital.

Did I mention my roommate was Ash, my TrilbyJones intern?

"Do you think Samuel will be back this morning?" (Not 'your husband.' She called him '*Samuel*.') She peered at me from her hospital bed, where her leg was in traction. Apparently, she'd walked across a flooded road, but Boulder Creek had different ideas and slammed her into a streetlight.

"I'm sure he will."

"I saw the interview he did about the flooding on the national news, encouraging donations to the Front Range Flood Relief Fund."

"Yes, we watched it together, remember?" We watched everything together. Everything that *she* chose to watch, because my loving husband placed the television remote in her hands and instructed her not to let me watch the news. So now I was her new BFF. (Or rather, the wife of her new BFF.)

"Can you imagine the devastation he must have seen when he took that helicopter ride with the governor?"

I rolled my eyes. "I have an idea."

Samuel had become some sort of celebrity spokesperson for relief efforts. He had my full blessing, of course, because I'd much rather have him out there, helping, than stuck in this hospital room while Ash monopolized our conversations. The Boulder Hospital was overcrowded, so the roommate situation was unavoidable. I got it, I really did, and tried to make the best of it because Boulder had much bigger concerns than whether I had an annoying roommate. But even a drawn curtain couldn't shut out her enthusiastic six a.m. calls to some chick in Baltimore who went by the handle 'MNN.' (At first, I thought Ash called her 'M&M', but then I realized the Baltimore chick's full handle was "Missus Nicodemus Nixie', as in, "Are you awake? Missus Nicodemus Nixie, brace yourself. You will never believe who was just in my hospital room! Eeee!")

Somehow, I'd escaped hell-on-earth in the canyon, only to have landed in another kind of hell. I needed a friggin' jailbreak.

"You in here, flower?"

My dad poked his head around the door and I sat up, elated to have a visitor. My mother followed him into the room and my joy grew.

"Mom!" I reached for her like a toddler and she bent over, gave me a quick pat and pulled up a chair. "Samuel told me you got out okay, but it's good to see you with my own eyes."

Dad took the other chair. "I thought your room would be crawling with friends and family, but it's quiet, huh?"

"I told you Tom, Lyons is an island right now. The Cabrals can't leave unless they hitch a ride on a Guard helicopter."

"Which is supposed to happen later today, according to the local news," I pointed out.

Mom frowned. "Samuel said you weren't supposed to watch the news until you were released from the hospital. Doctor's orders."

I tossed up my hands. "What else am I supposed to do? My phone is gone, my laptop was in my Jeep, which is also gone, and one can only read FIT magazine for so long before one wants to rip out one's IV and do glute lunges through hospital corridors. Is it a crime to want to know how my hometown is doing?"

My traitor roommate gave my mother the television remote. "I bet you could find a *Law & Order* marathon."

I groaned and leaned back in my bed.

"I can tell you what's happening out there better than the television. You heard the farm flooded?"

I leaned forward, itching for news. "Sam mentioned something about canoeing off the land?"

"St. Vrain Creek, Highland Ditch, Rough and Ready Ditch—all look like they're ready for barge traffic. The ground's completely saturated, so there's no place for the water to go except up. Well, the water kept rising, so I got the sheep out of the pen while I could still see the ground, the chickens, loaded them into the trailer and took 'em up to Mark Watson's place on the hill. All except Loppy. I kept her with me until the water in the basement spilled onto the first floor. Then we untethered the canoe and paddled across the farm until the bottom hit mud."

"Your mom shouldered that sheep and waded through the muck until she reached the highway, then hitched a ride into Longmont where she called me from a gas station. Sheep still on her shoulders, mind you."

"And here we are."

"Ahhh, where's the sheep?"

Mom grinned. "In your father's Prius. Don't worry, she's diapered."

Good lord, Gran would turn in her grave. I eyed my parents. "So, are you two...?"

They immediately shook their heads. "Definitely not," said my dad.

"I wouldn't touch that hairy hippie with a ten-foot hookah pipe. Saw Audrey at the school gym and she said the same. Apparently, we're friends now, after a night playing Rummy under the bleachers."

"That's good, I guess."

Suddenly, Ash squealed with genuflects and thank yous. Samuel had returned, armed with a gigantic balloon bouquet and an even larger bouquet of flowers. He placed the balloons on my roommate's nightstand.

"These are for the best reader in the world." I swear his white teeth twinkled. As Ash lost herself in a fit of hysterical euphoria, Sam knelt next to my bed and placed the paper-wrapped flowers in my lap. "And these are for my strong, amazing wife." He leaned over and kissed my head, then my lips, tender and cautious of my abrasions. His smile held firm, but his eyes were dark blue, sober and serious. I wondered at the things he'd seen.

"Don't sugarcoat it."

He rubbed his neck. "Well, I'll say this: Our neighbors have a sense of humor. There are more garage sale signs today than all of this summer."

"A woman at the school gym told me the water hurled her refrigerator up to the second floor," Mom said.

"Probably along with every other appliance in her house." The destruction of his parents' home reflected in his eyes. I didn't ask if he'd been to our own home, scattered across the ruin of our mountain before we'd even slept under its new roof. "I just got off the phone with Danita. The National Guard is going to airlift them out of Lyons within the hour."

"Do they need a place to stay?"

"*Mamá* and *Papá* have friends at their church who will put them up. Dani and the kids are taking our guest bedroom until Angel is off duty. After that, I don't know."

That was the story for more than a thousand of my Front Range neighbors. Leaving town wasn't as simple as hopping in a car and driving away. Traversing from Longmont to Boulder was like escaping from a hundred-mile maze.

But the sun did return and the waters did recede. And soon, my family trickled through my hospital room with their own harrowing tales. Sofia and Alonso, Dani and my sweet nephew and niece, and then Angel after Guard duty. Even Luca and his family. All somber-faced, full of half-stories and careful words.

They were hiding something.

Tears spilled down my cheeks when Molly's beautiful red head peeked around my hospital room door, her frame nearly obscured by a gigantic care package.

"For you and Ash." She hauled the thing onto the table between our beds and unloaded an endless stream of magazines, pre-packed snacks, and music. Ash loosed a shriek so piercing, birds dropped miles away.

"O. M. G.! This is a galley proof for Samuel Cabral's mountaineering book! NO ONE has this yet!"

Molly winked at me. "Courtesy of your husband. That should buy you an evening of quiet," she whispered as she gingerly hugged me around my tubes.

"What are you doing here?"

"Someone has to man the home office while you're laid up. Seriously, do you really think I'd hide away in Alaska? I'm where I need to be."

"And Hippie?"

Molly's smile dropped. "He's where he needs to be. Far away in Alaska."

"Oh Molly, I'm sorry."

"Don't worry about it. He's driving Betty the Campervan down when the roads improve, and then he's off to Minnesota or something. Alaska's 'not doing it for him anymore.' Don't even." She swatted my outstretched hand. "Funny, it's so anticlimactic. No big fight, no dramatic exit." Her voice cracked. "Oh, I think my heart is going to be broken for a while, but I'm not what Cassady needs and he's not what I need. Where are those Kleenexes?" As she dug through her purse, a tear skimmed the bridge of her nose and dripped. I offered her the box on my nightstand. When she was in control once again, she slapped her thighs.

"Long story short, don't you worry about our baby. TrilbyJones is in good hands."

I assured her of my undying gratitude and she tutted, gathered her things to 'scope out the food situation in the cafeteria.'

"Oh! Before you go, can you find out how the Valdez family is doing? I haven't heard from a one of them, save Angel. Hector's not surprising, he's probably still miffed. Santiago, though…"

Molly and Ash exchanged a covert look, but I caught it.

"What? I've gotten this all day, from Samuel, Sofia, even my mom, and I'm about ready to take a hostage if I don't get answers."

Molly faltered, bit her lip. "I need to talk to Sam first." She ducked through the door, leaving me flabbergasted. I turned to Ash, but she'd already popped in her ear buds and buried her nose in Samuel's galley proof.

Fear settled into my bones…there was a reason Samuel was scarce today, and it wasn't just because of his flood recovery efforts. But my body was tired and demanded sleep, and my brain obeyed. The aftermath would hit, soon enough.

Days' worth of scruff coated my husband's face and scraped my cheeks as he bent to embrace me the following morning. His eyes were rimmed in dark circles. His limbs moved with the exhaustion of a ninety-year-old man, and I wondered at the things he'd seen in the 'outside world.'

I sighed into his warm, stubbly neck. "Good news. Doctor said I can leave in a couple of hours. Why don't you pull around the Subaru and we'll bust out of this joint like Bonnie and Clyde."

"Ah, problem with that. No Subaru."

"What happened? Where is it?"

"Somewhere in Left Hand Canyon. I tried to go after you when I returned from Mexico, despite Angel telling me there was no way to get through. I ended up ditching it after nearly being impaled by a road sign and hiked back to Olde Stage."

I gasped. "Are you okay?"

He shrugged. "I am now."

"So, no Jeep and no Subaru."

"I've got Angel's truck on loan, but Dani also needs it. Everyone else's vehicles are stuck in Lyons."

"Okay, okay. Let's make some calls, see if we can borrow a car."

But twenty minutes later, after countless voicemails and dead ends, we had nothing.

"We could buy one," I suggested.

"Not a single dealership is open within a fifty-mile radius. Even if there was, gas lines are two hours long at the few stations still operating."

"Good lord, it's like a post-apocalyptic movie."

"I've got a car," Ash chimed in.

Sunlight poured from my intern's face as she realized it was her turn to play the heroine in a Samuel Caulfield Cabral story.

'Car' was a loose term for Ash's land-boat. It was a box of lime sherbet on wheels. Bright green, sharp angles, her ancient Chevy Impala was the height of luxury…in the seventies. It was longer than Longs Peak and more solid, too. She passed Samuel the keys over her painfully-tractioned leg, brimming with excitement and flushed with embarrassment, a curious meld. "I'm so, so sorry it's an ugly rust-bucket. I know you're used to cars that are, well, awesome and…and beautiful. Just like you."

Samuel held out his arms for a hug, the smooth-operator. "The car is a classic! You are one generous young lady, and I am completely indebted to you."

She loosed a nervous giggle. "Oh, no way! I am, just, *totally* happy I could help you out. Not like I'll be driving it anytime soon. Can I just…Do you mind?" She pulled out her camera phone.

"Not at all."

As Samuel posed for selfies, I took in the sad state of Boulder one last time, from my hospital window. God help the souls who'd landed in the river's merciless flow.

Samuel grabbed my overnight bag. "Ready to go?"

I wrapped my arms around my middle and nodded.

My birthday was a quiet affair; no one was in the mood to celebrate, though Samuel tried to make Sofia's Mexican Chocolate Cake, the sweet man. I watched from the couch as he and Danita shuffled around each other in the kitchen and threw together a red pork *posole* with the dried chilis we'd stashed in the cupboard. Soon the comforting smells of the Cabral home filled our apartment and my heart calmed, until I remembered that the Cabral home was scattered across the base of Steamboat Mountain.

Baby Christina slept against my shoulder and *el changuito* was tucked into my side, wide-eyed and jumpy from the chaos of the past few days. Still he made a big show of being brave and tough, the Valdez machismo in his genes shining through… Angel, the soldier.

Santiago, the playboy.

Hector, the adventurer.

A century ago, they would have been the stuff of old west legends, those untamable cowboys. My thoughts turned to Hector. *Pendejo*, out there kayaking those treacherous rivers as the whole world crumbled, whitewater turned brown with trees and mud, the mountains it had toppled in its wake…

"Can you believe Hector wanted to go kayaking, once the rain broke? I bet Tricia's hopping mad, what with all the E.coli and chemicals swimming in that water."

No answer. Dani and Samuel exchanged a look. *Not on her birthday*, he mouthed, but I saw the words—fearful, devastating words—and *then I knew*.

No. No, I didn't know anything. Breath escaped my body. I couldn't move, couldn't blink.

I tried to force that metal door back into place, but it wouldn't budge.

Samuel stepped forward, slow, hesitant. My body began to quake. Danita slipped the baby from my arms, pulled *el changuito* into her lap. I shook my head, slapped Samuel's hands away as he tried to hold me. I leaped up.

"You know how Hector is! How he goes off on these trips and sometimes doesn't call because of crappy service. We used to do that all the time! Dani, remember, before Samuel came back, how you always used to get on my case about not calling?"

"Kaye. He's missing."

I pushed past Samuel as he again tried to embrace me and fled to our bedroom. I slammed the door but Samuel caught it, gently closed it. I backed into a corner.

"Of course he isn't missing! I just told you, he'll surface in a day or two when he's done playing. I mean, look at those rivers! He'll never have a chance to tackle rapids like that in Colorado ever again!"

"They found his gear, his kayak. They just haven't found his—"

"Shut up!" I pressed my hands to my ears, begging for the roaring to return, to drown out Samuel's words. I struggled in his arms, but he was persistent, firm, brought me to my knees and then to the ground.

"Listen, firecracker, I'm not going to hide the truth from you. They're searching for his *body*. Not him."

"Hector wouldn't drown. He can't drown!"

"He can! He's human, just like you're human, so fragile and breakable. Don't you see?"

"Of course I do, I nearly got flattened by that avalanche on Longs Peak, but Hector didn't!" I pushed him away and crawled over to the closet, dug out my hiking gear. "They might be searching for a body, but I'm going to find my friend. Where are my waders?"

"The back of our Jeep, long gone in Left Hand Canyon."

"My Tevas?"

"Ruined beyond saving. I threw them out."

"Good thing I have backups." I hauled out a pair of worn boots with frayed laces and jerked them on as best as I could with a sprained wrist.

Samuel started digging out his boots, clothes. I shook my head. "Don't try and stop me, Samuel."

"I'm not. I'm coming with you."

All night we sloshed through the swamps of the St. Vrain greenspace, flashlights darting against felled tree trunks, house siding, interior debris of lives swallowed by the river. My mending ribs creaked and ached. The painkillers I'd downed had worn off hours ago and my barely-healed body was giving out under me, each time I pulled a water-logged boot out of the muck. One of my frayed laces broke, and Samuel wordlessly knotted it as best as he could. He plodded behind me, silent, until the moment I burned through my reserved energy and collapsed in a squishy heap.

"It's time to go home. Your body can't take any more."

I shook my head, even as a slick film of exhaustion coated my brain.

"This area has already been searched. Angel, Santiago, my parents, Molly...we've all been out here. We did what we could."

"If he disappeared at Left Hand Creek, it could take days for him to reach this part of the watershed. We have to search again."

He hauled me into his arms and tromped on. Vaguely, it registered that for the past hour, he'd guided us back to Ash's boat-of-a-car. Sweaty and filthy, I sank into the seat. But first, one more time…

I opened the wood-trimmed glove box and took out Sam's phone. He sighed as I called Tricia for the third time. No answer. Frustrated, I shoved it back into the compartment.

"I told you, she's gone to her parents' home in Greeley."

"Why isn't she looking for her husband?"

Samuel shot me a warning. "She did, for forty-eight hours straight, until they found his gear."

"And she's just going to give up?"

"Don't you dare judge her, Aspen Kaye. Not until you've walked in her shoes, and I pray you'll never have to do so. You don't know what's in her heart. But I bet she feels he's gone, deep inside." He turned back to the windshield, his face grim as he took in the devastation. "People know."

My stomach churned, weak thing that it was. I crammed a fist into my mouth, and Sam pulled over to the side of the road. Nearby, the St. Vrain still swirled over its bank, monstrous, angry. I opened the door and hit my knees. For long minutes I heaved, choked, until nothing more came up. And still, my body jerked. Samuel smoothed gnarled hair behind my ears. When I was finished, he handed me a bottle of water. I rinsed my mouth and leaned against a car tire.

"You're right. People know." *Angel. Santiago. His parents and little sister. His wife.*

"That's why I kept looking for you hours after I saw the footprint of our new home, the flooded mine entrance. Angel thought you were gone. I hoped you weren't." Tears mixed with the sweat on my cheeks, dripped from my chin. "You know Hector. He may be reckless, but he's not heartless."

I sniffed. "He'd never chase rapids for days on end, while his friends and family dug through the ruins of their homes. He'd be right there beside them, helping. Stupid…cocky…" I slapped the dashboard once, twice, three times with my injured hand, anger burning bright, until Samuel caught the grimy thing.

"You're going to do real damage."

"The damage is already done. The idiot would have gotten both of us killed! He wanted to drag me along with him. He goaded me, told me I was losing my sense of adventure. I said terrible things. But I should have gone just to keep him out of that poisoned water." Guilt chased the blood through my veins. Why hadn't I tried to stop him?

"Shhh, sweetheart, no. This is not your fault."

"He never would have let me go alone! You always have a partner, just in case."

"Luca was with him. He couldn't save him."

"Luca's a newbie!"

"Kaye, you couldn't have saved him."

"You don't know that, Samuel."

"*Kaye*. You couldn't have saved him."

"I bet he didn't even have on his life vest, and Luca's too sweet to speak up. Once the hydraulic catches you, you spin and spin, and something needs to guide you up to the surface. Angel, Santiago, we're always reminding him he has to wear the thing, but he never listens!"

Samuel's eyes were flinty in the dim console light. "Listen to me, Aspen Kaye Cabral. I am damned glad you weren't on that river. If you'd gone with him like you would have a few years ago, I'd be planning your funeral right now. You couldn't have stopped him. No one could. Hector Valdez was a man so lost in his addictions, only he could claw his way out. *But he didn't want to.* He went down exactly the way he lived—all *cajones* and no consideration, and that's the naked, unadorned, ugly truth."

Truth grabbed me by the throat.

Here's the thing about cold, hard truth: it's as comforting as strong arms when it connects what you know in your head to what you feel in your heart.

I couldn't have saved Hector. I'd tried, he hadn't listened. If I'd been there on that river with him, I would be dead. I studied our joined hands, the soft, dark hair of Sam's forearms, let it tickle my fingertips.

"Do you ever wonder if God brought you back here to save my life?" I whispered.

"If he did, I'm grateful. I know you've saved mine."

I buried my face in Samuel's sweat-stained shirt, breathed in years and years of summers, mornings wrapped in sheets. If I'd saved his life, it certainly hadn't been at my expense.

"Take me home, please."

"Oh Kaye, you are home."

Chapter 20
GROUND UP

*Climbers begin a route at rock bottom and work
their way up. They may lose a hold and fall, begin
again, fall, begin again.*

"Have they found his body yet?"

Three days later, I sat on the floor of Luca's home beside Jaime's legs. Luca was beside her on the couch, his face littered by small cuts from river debris. Somewhere behind us, the same bluegrass song looped on a speaker, twanging banjos unsuitable for the somber mood. I asked Jaime about her phone, but she absently gestured to the couch cushions so I let it play on.

"We were over in Spruce Gulch yesterday, or what's left of it," I said. "Nothing. We couldn't get close to Left Hand Creek because the roads are out. Maybe if we hiked in…" She focused upon some invisible speck on the wall.

"I knew he was dead." She turned to his brother. "I knew it before you told me how his kayak was swamped by that hydraulic, how the water sucked him under and never kicked him out. The moment my phone rang and I heard your voice, I already knew."

Tears streamed down my cheeks. I saw Hector, his strong tattooed arms gripping his paddle as he pushed his yellow kayak like a warrior and battled rapids too powerful for even him. I heard his cries of excitement grow panicked the moment he knew he wouldn't make it out of the river alive. "Oh Jaime, I don't know what to say. I promise we'll find him…"

Her face hardened. "That's the trouble with you, Kewpie. You never know when to shut up. There's nothing to say. You can't tell me he loved me because that would be cruel to his wife. You can't tell me he missed me, he was thinking of having an affair with me, because people don't say that about someone who's deceased. What good does it do now? What good did it ever do? The truth is, Hector Valdez loved too much, and he didn't love anyone. Loving him was like a kick in the ribs to a stray dog after a warm bed and a full food dish." She buried her face in her brother's shoulder. Luca tightened his grip.

Long minutes passed. Her shudders slowed, and then she pierced me with reddened eyes.

"Let's shoot some stuff in Luca's backyard."

"We can't. This is a residential neighborhood."

"Well, let's visit the Labs. I have them in Luca's sports shed."

He frowned. "You should see what they did to my snow shoes."

I followed her out the door and grabbed a rubber ball from the toy crate. Her dogs swarmed our legs, tongues lolling and tails waggling, their fur crusted with dried mud from a backyard that now resembled the Florida Everglades.

I chucked the ball and three of the Labradors scurried across the grass, kicking up waterlogged clumps. Jaime let slip a tender smile as she watched her babies play. "Bastard reminded me of a Labrador, you know? Big and boisterous, smart until you wave a stick in its face. They want that thing so bad, they'd chase it into hot lava." The smile hardened.

"Do you want to talk about something else?" I hedged.

"God yes." Air burst from her lungs and she was all lawyer. "Before the flood and…everything…I did some digging into Marieta Sanchez's home village, La Vereda? The young men aren't the only ones vanishing. They have an abnormally high number of missing women and children. The whole mountain region does."

That's right, Samuel's sister is still lost. I struggled to board a train of thought from what seemed a lifetime ago.

I tugged the drool-glazed ball from a dog's jaws and threw it again. "You think it's related to the cartel's drug operations?" A dream hovered at the periphery, a woman in the nursery. *La montaña. Mi casa...*

"The Zacatóns' criminal activities aren't limited to drugs and weapons, you know."

I'd read the reports of women, men, children who had vanished into the rush hour congestion that was human trafficking. I couldn't help but put the faces I loved on those of the victims, and I closed my eyes at the horror of it.

"Here's what you need to find out. What's the uncle's role in all of this? Good guy or bad guy?"

"Well, Marieta rented the apartment next to him and this Camila woman in the Mexico City slum. But then she ran. Years ago, he threw Marieta's mom out of the house when he found out she was pregnant."

"Nice dude. Not much respect for women."

"An old woman in La Vereda said they hate him in the village because he was recruiting young people to run drugs for the Zacatón Cartel."

"What if he was doing more than recruiting young people? What if he was harvesting them?"

Evil hung between us, the idea that one human being could do such a thing to another...

"Here's a scenario," Jaime continued. "Six years ago, Samuel helps Marieta get away from the Zacatón Cartel, but she's deported back to Mexico. A repentant Uncle Javier tells her he wants to get out too, and because he's family she has compassion for him. So, they hide together in Mexico City and start a new life."

I jumped aboard. "Javier hooks up with Camila Flores, also from La Vereda. Every now and then, Daniel travels from Ciudad Victoria to see Marieta. What happens to ruin it all? Daniel could have uncovered something about Javier when he hacked the cartel's files."

"Possibly. Marieta was once a drug runner herself, but I bet she drew the line at selling kids to pedophiles. There's a family brawl."

"Do you think Javier sold out Daniel and Marieta?"

"I don't know, Kewpie. For all I know, he's a decent guy who just wants to help. But you've got to admit, there's stinky shit piled all over this."

"Exactly. Why lie to Samuel about his identity?"

"Maybe because he was here on a false ID and didn't want to get deported. Or maybe because he wants Samuel's money. Either is plausible."

"What do we do?"

"You stay out of this and live nice long lives in Colorado. Or you try to find Marieta before the Zacatón Cartel does, if they haven't already. You smuggle her out of Mexico, maybe get her a job at that nice Tex-Mex restaurant down the street."

I looked skyward. "You have no filter, do you?"

"I'm Chicana. I can use the racist stereotypes, unlike you, Snow White. That reminds me. I've got something for you from a friend who owes me for winning full custody of her cat during her divorce." Jaime held up her phone. It was a scan of a Mexican identification card for one Daniel Rodriguez. I zoomed in on the grainy photo and examined it... thick black hair, full lips, dark eyes, stocky build. Perhaps in his early thirties?

I touched the brooding face, sad. He was a handsome man... Tragically, now a handsome dead man.

We packed up the rubber balls as the dogs whined, stripped off our mud-coated boots (which was really hard with one good hand). To my surprise, Jaime helped me zip my fleece.

"I'm gonna do something really nice for you, Trilby, so good, years from now you'll thank me."

I lifted a dubious eyebrow.

"You have Hector's permission to stop searching for him."

"I don't understand."

"He's gone, Kaye. If he were able, he'd tell you to quit wasting your time looking for his body and go save someone you still have a chance to save. Dwell on the living, not the dead."

My lips twitched. "That's what Hector says." *Said.*

"No one lived more than him, that's for sure. He wasn't afraid of death."

"I think it was a case of not acknowledging mortality. Lemme tell you about the night after my Gran died…"

The winter of my senior year of high school was the first time Hector Valdez deliberately shared an awful hippie joke.

I'd sat in the corner booth of the Lyons Diner, tucked away from the early dinner crowds, a cup of hot chocolate and a slice of pie on the table. Both were untouched. My Gran had succumbed to cancer the previous day, alone in Durango, save for a hospice nurse. My mother had planned to travel down, but once Gran entered hospice, she'd passed six hours later.

Mom wasn't one to grieve with anyone but her gardens, but there wasn't much to grow in January, so I'd fled to give her the solitude she'd craved. The Cabrals were spending the last of winter break in Southern California visiting Uncle Carlos and Aunt Lucia, so the diner was my best option.

It had snowed, so the tile floor was slippery as patrons tracked slush through the door. The bell tinkled and in walked Hector Valdez. His skin was still free of tattoos, and a head-full of black hair curled over his forehead, around his ears (how I wished he'd never razed that dishy mane). He spotted me in the corner and flashed a killer smile, but as he strode toward my booth a puddle jumped up and attacked him. I saw it in his face, the moment he realized he was going down and there was nothing he could do. He groaned, hauled himself off the floor. Then that smile was back, now a touch rueful as he rubbed his tailbone and waved away a waitress' profuse apologies.

The booth wobbled as Hector crashed across from me. "You gonna eat that?"

I shook my head and he grabbed the slice of lemon merengue pie, bypassing the fork.

"Stopped by your house and your mom told me you'd be here. Wanna go skiing while pretty boy is out of town?"

"Not really. My Gran died."

He scooped up half the pie and crammed it in his mouth. "Yeah, I heard," he said through cheeks-full of lemon filling. "So why are you here, all by yourself?"

"Mom needs space. The Cabrals won't be home until Thursday night, Dad's being dad and high off his butt, such a hippie. This is the best I've got."

"You've got me. I'll be your distraction."

I lifted a shoulder. "It's not like I can forget. It's here, in my chest, a fifty-pound weight pulling me down."

"Sure you can, you just have to think about living instead of dying. I bet I can help you."

I lifted an eyebrow and he gave a flamboyant gasp. "Not like that! Mind of a sex perv, I swear." He polished off the last of the pie and sucked his fingers clean. "Speaking of hippies, what do you call a hippie who breaks up with his girlfriend? Homeless!"

I snorted. "You have no idea how true that is."

"Tom and Audrey on the rocks again?"

"The opposite, actually. Thus, the ready supply of pot. Tell me another."

"Why did Hippie Tom cross the road?"

"I assume that's where the ditch weed grew."

"Nah, but good guess. Who else would follow a chicken around?"

My mouth cracked a smile, despite the sadness that clung to me like a wetsuit. Hector pointed. "See, *mamacita*? Dwell on life, not death."

I shifted against the broken spring. "Got any more of those?"

"Give me time. Hey." He reached across the table, slid the lukewarm mug from my grip and replaced it with his hand. "Why don't you tell me a story about your Gran?"...

Jaime shook her head after I finished my story. "'*Héctor es comediante*,' said no Juan ever. Swing by later. I've got some really dirty stories about that jackass."

"Thanks Jaime." I stepped onto her front porch. "Just...thank you."

"Just...go away," she snarked as she closed the door in my face, "and do something about that ugly blue hair!"

I felt more like my old self as I tousled my freshly cut blonde curls, now stripped of blue.

I could almost pretend the floods hadn't happened. I took the stairs two-at-at-time, up to our apartment. "You'll never believe this. Jaime found a picture of Daniel Rodgri…"

My voice died in the doorway. Samuel sat on the sofa, elbows on his knees, hands clasped, though they'd left fretful, messy trails through his coffee-colored hair.

Though his mouth was grim and silent, his ice eyes poured pity.

He didn't even need to say it.

They found Hector.

The Valdez boys discovered their brother's body that very day, tangled in a debris pile where St. Vrain converges with the South Platte River. Like war veterans who'd seen unspeakable things, they kept the details between the two of them. Years ago, when the Colorado River was unusually heavy with spring snow melt, I'd seen the distorted, swollen carcass of a dog. Actually, I'd smelled it first and my eyes unthinkingly sought out the source of the horrendous decay. But I couldn't un-see it and un-smell it, and I kept my kayak pointed forward and my oar in the water until a mile down, then put the boat out and immediately vomited into the weeds.

There was a reason Hector Valdez's casket was closed at his wake, instead of the traditional white sheet draped over his body.

Tricia wanted a traditional Mexican (read Catholic) funeral, though everything about it was wrong because nothing about Hector Valdez was traditional. But everything was wrong about the way he'd died, and everyone shook their heads as they ate food and drank *velorio*, as if a vibrant sunflower had been deadheaded at the cusp of its bloom. And wasn't Tricia allowed to have something traditional in the death of her marriage, if not in life? No husband to come home to, no babies, no long years and gray heads. That's what they all said.

I couldn't remember what Santiago and Angel said in their eulogies. Tricia asked Samuel to play his Spanish guitar while I sang because she wanted tradition, and neither of us dared tell her it wasn't traditional.

And oh lord, the *novena*. Nine days of recitation and prayers, masses and mourning. I wondered how long it would take for Tricia's veneer of stoicism to crack, and two days seemed to do it. As the prayer ended, we stood, shoulder to shoulder: Molly, Sam, me, Danita, Angel, Tricia, Santiago. Together we stared at the sprawling tableau of framed photos that chronicled Hector's life: lived to the fullest and never lived at all. Tricia's body trembled as she desperately fought to hold back a flood that had already ravaged her world.

"What can I do?"

Tricia turned to me, brittle, clinical eyes sweeping my healing injuries. "How are the ribs?"

"I've got good painkillers."

"Hmmm, I bet. About three weeks of healing…no chest infections?"

"None."

She nodded, all doctor. "Good, good. I've been so busy at the hospital and…and…" she cleared her throat and refocused on my offer of help. "The family clinic is still a mess, especially the basement. Smells like a sewer. We could use a clean-up crew, if you're up for it. Keep the bandages loose, lift nothing more than twenty pounds. And bring a mask and gloves."

That was our duct tape over cracked foundations: physical labor. Samuel had asked Uncle Carlos to continue the hunt for Marieta Sanchez in his place, and he had obliged. Frankly, she and Daniel Rodriguez were far from my mind as we went house-to-house, following insurance inspectors through neighborhoods with shovels, mops and buckets of bleach. We demoed rotten walls and put up new sheet rock. We cleaned inventory at Paddlers but pitched most of it. Helped my TrilbyJones clients put their businesses back together in whatever way we could, because when I threw myself into the needs of others, I didn't have time to rage over the set of tattooed arms who no longer worked alongside us and never would again.

Hey mamacita, sky's as clear your criminal record. We jumping today?

But at night…

When all was dark, when the hard labor of the day stilled and red clay coated the tiles of our bathroom shower…

There's fresh snow in the backcountry. First tracks are ours if we get up there before dawn.

When our dishwasher quietly rattled in the kitchen…

When the security light flickered, cold and pale. When dry, mountain air fluttered our curtains and coiled around our skin like satin ribbons…

Two Fourteeners left, don't you bail on me now.

"Come here, firecracker." His voice was soothing, warm.

I curled onto my husband's chest and released my pain.

There, safe in his arms, I slept. I slept and dreamed of a blue door… a sad mother and her baby, lost on *la montaña.*

Two weeks later, it still took me twice as long to navigate the beleaguered streets of Boulder. The creek had cut a strong path right through the heart of the city, severing roads and toppling traffic lights. While I'd been trapped on the mountain, my quick-thinking office manager had organized a rapid removal of any files and boxes stored in the TrilbyJones basement. Dude was getting a big fat bonus this year. Sump pumps had run 'round the clock until we'd lost power, piping water out and away from the foundation, sparing our home.

Even though the car dealerships had reopened, we'd neglected to replace Sam's Subaru. He rode with Angel or Danita up to Lyons to help with clean-up, and I'd finally just paid Ash for her boat-of-a-car until I did some legitimate car-shopping. I parked the rust bucket and hauled myself up the stairs. Another morning at the office, another afternoon of demo, this time the Snowy Marmot Discovery Center, whose outdoor patio was beyond saving. I wasn't expecting Samuel home for another hour, when the sun set and work on his parents' property ceased. So, I was surprised to find the living room lights on.

"Sam?"

"Back here," he shouted from the bedroom closet.

A suitcase was open on the bed, a familiar, disheartening sight. He emerged from the closet with an armful of clothing and shoes.

"Where are you going?"

Worried eyes sought mine. "Marieta finally called. She needs help getting out of Tamaulipas, and I can't do nothing. I'm sorry, I know I promised—"

"Give me five minutes to grab my bag and my passport, and I'll go with you." I pulled my hiking bag out from under the bed.

Samuel shoved it back under the bed. "Absolutely not, Kaye. You're still recovering from a sprained wrist and cracked ribs."

"Which have given me little trouble during the flood clean-up."

"You are *not* going with me to Mexico. I'll call Santiago—"

"He just lost his brother, Sam. His family needs him."

"My Dad—"

"And he just lost his house! This time there's no one except me. You've reached the bottom of the barrel," I said acerbically.

He rounded on me, his face near wild. "This has nothing to do with a lack of faith in your capability! Is it so difficult to believe I want to keep the woman I love beyond anything safe from harm? This isn't a sightseeing jaunt. These people have guns and no value for human life, and they won't hesitate to pull the trigger if you get in their way. Do you get it?"

"Do *you* get it? I would rather risk my life beside you than risk living without you, alone in Colorado." I took out my bag again and stuffed it with clothing and hygiene items.

We fired harsh words over our shoulders in our race to pack, until he grabbed his suitcase and pounded down the stairs. I shouldered my hiking pack and followed him, determined not to watch him drive away from me yet again. We got to the parking lot and he froze. The only car we owned was a lime green 1977 Chevy Impala behemoth that once belonged to my intern.

And I had the keys.

A slow smile spread across my face. Samuel cursed and slapped a hand against the roof of the car.

I squealed. "Yes! I win at life. I'm buying this baby a custom low-rider conversion when we get to Mexico."

Troubled blue eyes swept over my fading injuries, newly healed ribs, paused upon the fresh pink scar along my hairline. "I will never forgive myself if something happens to you."

"You'll just have to remind yourself that I wouldn't take 'no' for an answer. That, and I own the car."

"I'm deadly serious, Aspen Kaye."

"So am I!"

"What kind of husband would I be if I took you into the most dangerous place in Mexico?"

I tossed the keys into the air. "I get that every fiber of your being wants to keep me safe. But I'm ready to hunt for someone I can save. Hector's dead. But maybe, *maybe,* we can save your sister and if you climb into that car without me, I'll follow. I'll borrow Jaime Guzman's car—she'd loan it to me—plug in the Garmin and drive south across the border until I reach that tiny village in the mountain. You know I'll do it, Samuel. But I'd rather be in this ugly green Impala with you."

Silence followed my outburst. His iron-rod posture relented. "Why do you always have to fight me, firecracker?"

"History and experience have taught me, if I don't fight, I get left behind."

He closed his eyes and mumbled something under his breath. His face was carefully blank, but I knew his brain raced, formulating a plan. Finally, he gave a slow, decisive nod that concerned me more than it thrilled me, because, knowing the lengths Samuel had taken in the past to protect me, *it couldn't be this easy.*

"Fine. Get in. But if I tell you to get back in the vehicle, you better race for the border, do you understand?"

I saluted. "Yes sir, Sergeant Pepper."

"This is going to be a disaster," Samuel grumbled as he took my bag and tossed it next to his suitcase.

We flew south down the highway, past Denver, past Pueblo and into Oklahoma. Red rocks and mountain slopes gave way to tornado-prone flatland, field and shrub and a sky so big and wide, I felt small.

"Playing devil's advocate: are you sure the woman you spoke with was your sister?"

"Yes."

"How?"

"She called a burner phone I set up specifically for her. I left a message with Daniel Rodriguez's *abuela* in La Vereda." Love, loyalty, and plain blind hope were driving this Chevy Impala into Mexico, and it didn't stop for doubt.

"What are we going to do when we get there?"

Samuel nervously drummed the steering wheel. "I'm still working that out in my head."

Night fell somewhere in Texas, and we lost ourselves in a blur of yellow lines and dark hulking shadows. I drove while Samuel slept, and then we switched. The adrenaline of our race from Colorado had long receded and what followed was a painful stillness.

Until recently, I hadn't much experience with death. When Gran died, we'd known it was coming. The last summer I spent with her, before my senior year of high school, was a litany of chemo appointments, weakness and nausea, and scouring Durango boutiques for elaborate scarves to cover her hair loss. Gran's glitzy streak was so prominent a print on her genetic fabric, I'd often wondered if my salt-of-the-earth mother was adopted. Her coffin was lined in a red satin so deep and shiny, it could have been re-purposed drapes from an Old West brothel. But that was Gran. She'd wanted to be framed in brilliant crimson as people snapped one last mental picture.

Hector's face flashed, bright and intense. Only his brothers had that final glimpse. I wondered if my imagination was worse than reality.

My heart clenched and I gasped. Sam glanced at me. I curled into the passenger seat, squeezed my eyes shut. If I could just sleep for another hour, I could shut down the thoughts. But I'd already slept through Colorado, Oklahoma, and half of Texas. My body simply didn't need another minute of rest.

My husband reached over and rubbed my neck. I leaned into his touch, a contented cat.

"We'll be at the border soon. I thought we'd stop for a stretch and a bite in Brownsville."

The blue glow of the dashboard clock read five a.m. "Mmmhmm."

"The text you sent me the night of the flood... of all things, why did you want me to go to my sister's mountain?"

I stretched my arms, yawned. "You'll think it's crazy."

"Remember who you're talking to."

I smiled. "I had a dream. A beautiful, sad dream. I was back in the nursery with a baby, except your sister was there with me. Marieta." I tried to conjure the feel of it. "She told me to follow her to the mountains, to her home. We walked through a bright blue door. It seemed really important."

"Important enough to make it your last words to me?"

"I suppose that's what I did."

"When my sister called ..."

I watched Samuel's troubled face. "Yes?"

"She was sobbing, hard to understand. She asked me to go to her family on the mountain. She didn't elaborate, but she said I'd understand." He fell silent, lost in the echoes of my dream.

"Do you...do you think she's dead, Kaye?"

"I don't know." I remembered the light, the snow, her blue hands... but was she real, or the product of an exhausted, traumatized brain?

"The floods, the devastation, the deaths. The Front Range is your home and it's hurting. Yet you chose to leave it behind for me. Why?"

This I could answer. "Simple. I love you. There was no choice but to go with you. You're okay with this?"

He gave a mirthless laugh. Something dark and sad possessed him. "Nothing is okay about this. But I swear, I will do anything to keep you safe."

"I'd rather you promised I'll never have to chase your back."

The intense expression lifted, and once again his face was careful, blank. He threaded his fingers through mine. "I love you, so much, and I'm afraid you won't see my love for what it is. Are you with me?"

I searched his profile, his jaw working overly hard to maintain control, and I did indeed struggle to understand. Still, I answered, "I'm with you."

We claimed a booth at a Tex-Mex joint that had me grabbing the hand sanitizer, and spread out plates of loaded eggs and peppers, tortillas, bacon—all things Samuel wasn't supposed to eat, but that was shelved for the time being. I swirled my fork through a mess of eggs and cheese, watched the prongs until my eyes blurred.

"Hey." Samuel's voice was kind. "You still with me?"

"Yes." I straightened my slouching back and made an effort to eat.

"I need you to hear this. When we go through customs, keep your answers short and unadorned. We're visiting family on the outskirts of Ciudad Victoria. We plan to return in one week. We aren't carrying any merchandise."

"Do you think you'll have a difficult time?"

"I've crossed the border seven times in the past three months. I'd be disappointed if they didn't search every crevice of my person."

That earned a smile. "Disappointed, huh?"

"They have gentle hands at the Port of Entry."

I choked on my water. "Jacques H. Cousteau, don't let Hector hear you say that or—"

Samuel's eyes softened as he watched my face crumple. He slid into the booth next to me and tucked me under his arm.

Long minutes passed. Soon my mind caught up with my fragile emotional state, and I felt the curiosity of a dozen eyes. I peered at the booth across from us. A girl whispered in her mother's ear and the woman instructed the girl not to stare. Wiping my eyes with a napkin, I pulled myself together.

"Let's get on the road. We have somewhere we need to be."

Chapter 21
LAYBACK

*A strenuous climbing technique in which the hands
and feet oppose each other as one pulls and the
other pushes, creating leverage to maneuver
up a difficult rock face.*

"You didn't pack distilled water? You're going to get sick!"

"Relax, Molly. We'll buy it when we get there."

"That includes brushing your teeth. And don't open your mouth in the shower."

"I tell you we're going to find Samuel's missing sister with cartel connections, and you're worried about drinking water?"

Her huff was so loud, she nearly cracked my phone speaker. "Well, I already advised you to call the Mexican FBI—whatever they're called—and you shot me down with the whole 'they've done all they're going to' B.S. What else am I supposed to tell you?"

"I just wanted you to know, and to apologize. I'm a horrible business partner."

"No more horrible than a business partner who moves to Salmon's Butt, Alaska for a boy. Oh wait, that was *me*." We chuckled half-heartedly. "Besides, the floods seriously set back most of our clients. Who has money to spend on marketing when they're gutting storefronts and tearing out moldy insulation? The next couple of years are going to be really rough—like, layoffs rough. It might be time to tell a few of the underlings to start job hunting."

Guilt and shame filled my gut. I was responsible for these people, and here I was, bailing on them. "Molly, sorry isn't enough."

She sighed. "This would be happening whether you were here or not, okay? I've. Got. This! Me, and Ash the Intern. Just... please come home alive. We can't take another hit, and if we lost you and Samuel..." Her words became teary. "Don't be stupid for a woman you don't know."

The distance between me and Molly was more than miles, but if anyone could understand the foolishness of abandoning your home, your family, and your business to follow a man into the unknown, it was Molly. To the world, her risk hadn't paid off. But I knew in her heart, it had.

That's why I hadn't called Danita first... I left that chore to Samuel.

"How was it?" I asked as he slid behind the wheel.

"Bad. I don't think I should repeat the things Dani called me. Or *you*, for that matter."

I took one of the water bottles he offered and cracked it open.

"She's worried out of her mind."

"I get it. But we had to tell them. If something were to happen..."

"They need to know."

"Tamaulipas is not Cancun," he said. I raised an eyebrow. "But it would be patronizing to explain this to you."

I wouldn't have known Tamaulipas from Cancun anyway, save for a distinct lack of beachfront resorts and spring-breakers. I'd never before seen a lick of Mexico. I'd imagined what it would be like to cross this foreign country, to have this missing puzzle piece, to complete this landscape of brightly colored contrasts that was Samuel Caulfield Cabral: familiar and mysterious, sensible and neurotic, compassionate and bitter. This land was fraught with strangeness. Like home, old brick and iron mixed with sleek modern buildings, but everything was blindingly bright, colorful...even the grayest of stone. Parts of Tamaulipas could have been a corner in the Hispanic neighborhood of Lyons. Spanish words plastered on billboards and above ramshackle grocery stores were a language of love to my ears. Even the mountains were southern sisters to my beloved Rockies.

There was a disproportionate number of VW Beetles on Tamaulipas roadways. The memory of a childhood car game, Slug Bug, made me smile. Whenever one of us spotted a Bug on the road, we'd shout, "Slug Bug!" and pound each other in the arm. Danita had a particularly bruising punch, with her boney fingers and pent up aggression.

In a moment of inspiration, I thumped Samuel.

"Hey!"

"Slug Bug."

He rubbed his shoulder. "Seriously? You can't play Slug Bug in Mexico. Half the population drives a VW."

"Best time to play."

"Oh, little girl, you're going to rue this day. Slug Bug." He walloped me in the arm, just as a white Beetle cruised up the opposite lane.

Admittedly, resurrecting Slug Bug was not the best idea.

Farms slid past in the early morning light, miles of rippling sorghum and maize. Samuel tuned into a Latin pop station, then classical, then finally turned off the radio. As we drew closer to Ciudad Victoria, nervous ticks resurfaced. Bouncing knees, drumming fingers. When we stopped for gas and I returned from the station with two coffees, I witnessed his hand tremble as he replaced the gas cap.

We eased into the Sierra Madre Oriental foothills just shy of noon. These mountains were more like mounds than the jagged peaks of home, smoothed over by green foliage. Cinder block homes and rusted roofs jutted out of the hillsides. Old cars lined street curbs or sat in border gardens of fruit trees and giant red blooms. The torrential rains of Hurricanes Manuel and Ingrid had seeped into underground streams, and now the land was as lush as a sailor on shore leave. Soon we were on the outskirts of Ciudad Victoria. Samuel turned onto a gravel side street and parked the behemoth.

"Just a quick stop. Stay in the car please."

"Where are we?"

"*Tía* Mariángel's place in town. I need to borrow something from my uncle, and then we'll book it to La Vereda." He rubbed his jaw, sensing my confusion and, I admit, hurt. "It's not that I don't want to bring you in to the *familia*, Kaye. But..."

"This isn't a social visit," I finished, forgiving. "I also know relationships are strained, so do what you need to do. I'll wait."

He closed the door. I watched him jog up to the concrete house and enter the garden. A curtain covering one of the front windows fluttered and I thought Mariángel peered around it. I waved and it dropped back into place.

Club music blared over a radio from the home across the street. A wooden fence was overgrown with vines and flowers, but through the gaps I saw two girls practicing cartwheels. Next to the fence, a mongrel dog lay in the shade, tongue hanging out of his mouth when he wasn't scratching his hide, his haunches. A normal neighborhood on a quiet, sunny day.

A familiar face exited a gas station a block up and strode across the street. I bolted upright. He was an older man, garish purple Aloha shirt flapping over his gut, sunglasses pushed high on the bridge of his nose. Uncle Javier. He scratched his whiskers and glanced my way, then froze. I ducked below the dash, hoping he hadn't spotted me in this sore-thumb-of-a lime monstrosity with Colorado license plates. When I peeked over the dash a minute later, he was gone. But, parked as we were outside the Cabrals' bungalow, our cover was busted.

I jumped as the car door opened and Samuel slid in.

"Good to go?" I asked.

His hand hovered over the ignition, and I wondered if he'd just prefer to remain in the quiet of the car, on the safe side of the street.

"Guess who just moonwalked out of that gas station?" I told him about my sighting, camouflaged as Javier was in a motif of palms and hibiscus.

Tiny lines formed between his brows. "It sounds as if he wasn't expecting to see you, which means he has a different reason for being in the neighborhood."

"Cartel business?"

"Possibly. Or a residence. Either way, someone is watching my aunt and uncle's house."

"And if he has connections in La Vereda..."

"They know we're here."

Frickety-frick. "You still think the woman you spoke to was your sister, that this isn't a set-up?"

No response, just his old fallback: a judiciously blank face.

"Why'd we stop, anyway?" We pulled into traffic and cruised past shopping centers, restaurants, hotels.

Finally, he answered. "I borrowed *Tío* Tomás' gun."

Blood drained. A search of his torso produced a gun tucked in his waistband, beneath his shirt. "Aren't guns illegal in Mexico?"

"When I told you this was going to be dangerous, I didn't mean 'driving over the speed limit' dangerous. And believe me, if it comes down to us or them, I won't hesitate to pull that trigger."

My breaths became shorter. How the heck had I—naïve, back-country Aspen Kaye— ended up playing peek-a-boo with a drug cartel? Stuff like this only happened to people on *Forensic Crimes* episodes.

This wasn't one of Samuel's Nixie adventures, a thrilling showdown between water sprites and demons. Rivers didn't roar at my command. Snow didn't crash down mountainsides at the clap of my hands, and winds didn't swirl and gust with my every exhale. I'd felt my frailty on the snowfield of Longs Peak, as torrents of white swept away all signs of life.

Hector had been a scholar at reading rivers. Every dip and eddy spoke to him in his native language, and in the end, it hadn't been his to conquer.

Samuel was not infallible, either. He may have a genius brain and a working knowledge of Mexico's underbelly, but in real life, it only took one bullet.

None of us held the keys to Hades. In the end, we would all die. Some earlier, some later, and if I went earlier fighting for those I loved...I could live with it. *Well, not live with it.*

My gasping breaths slowed and peace settled into my body, my mind, my heart. All was in agreement.

As we traveled southwest, city limits gave way to country slopes covered in green and sand, giant cacti, and spiky plants that might have been agave. The mountains loomed blue and hazy before us. Not too far.

Samuel pointed out a drive that veered off the main road. "The Cabral family's hacienda. It's more of a weekend home for family gatherings. Utility and maintenance expenses are too high to justify permanent residence, once my *abuelo* died and the farming operation ceased. I imagine it will be uninhabitable in a decade or two." His tone held disapproval. "Last I heard, it was falling into disrepair, but the family would rather see it topple to the ground than accept my money. *Se creen mucho.*"

I craned my neck to see where Alonso had spent his childhood summers, but the house was obscured by unruly mango trees and overgrown, flowering bushes, so I only glimpsed its white walls and arches before we sped by, one final, resigned glance in the rearview mirror.

"Can we stop on the way back from La Vereda?"

That pinched, uneasy look returned. "Maybe."

Minutes later, Samuel steered into an old gas station, its pavement crumbled by thousands of tires like the dredges of a potato chip sack. "Pit stop," he mumbled and headed toward the faded "*baño*" sign. I leaned back in my seat, closed my eyes.

My mother tromped into my head with her sturdy rubber boots and colorful handkerchiefs, many of them once having belonged to Gran. Was that how Mom kept her near? Gran's cancer scarves? If I died, what would my mother choose to hold onto? And my father.

Dad wasn't one to hold onto anything or anyone, but I hoped he might make an exception. I took out my phone and started to dial, but paused.

Samuel startled me as he opened the door. "You should call them, Kaye. Don't worry about international."

"It's not that. I just don't know what to say. Anything I would tell them, I already did when I was in the hospital. That's okay, isn't it?"

"Sure. You don't horde your 'I love yous' until it's too late."

If that proverbial red flag had only fluttered before, now it whipped around like crazy.

"Do you think we're driving into a trap?" The sun was sinking over the southwestern sky as we left the main highway and bumped along a deeply rutted road.

"I don't know. I'm flying blind here, firecracker, and a part of me hates that I wasn't strong enough to make you stay home. The other part is elated you're here. Frankly, it's terrifying."

Soon we turned off of that road onto an even sketchier path up a steep hill that flirted with mountain status. At the base was a shuttered building, its wood slats long stripped of paint, now little more than a termite buffet.

"The old market. Farmers, rural folk would buy and sell at the road crossing decades ago. *Papá* and my father—Antonio—would stop on their way up to La Vereda. But it was too isolated, unincorporated as it was, to be safe. I believe the owners had enough and moved into the village."

Humidity clung to my skin, leaving me feeling clammy and dirty, so unlike the thin, dry air of Colorado. Overgrown foliage swiped the sides of the car with every hairpin turn. As we traveled higher, thick undergrowth gave way to sparse shrubs and blonde, crackled rock. A boxlike house jutted out of the hill, followed by another, and around the bend was a cluster of homes, some blue, some peach, others not painted at all. A cinder block building with a cross painted on the wall sat on the corner of two intersecting streets. A handful of businesses followed it up the hill—a grocery store that was little more than a shack, a municipal building, perhaps a *cantina*.

"Now what?"

Samuel rubbed tired eyes beneath his sunglasses. "Come on, I'll introduce you to the locals."

We passed the few storefronts, homes, people walking on the streets, sweeping driveways or hammering rebar for home construction. All met us with closed faces and few words. I wondered if Alonso would have been a better companion for Samuel.

"They don't trust me much," I whispered.

"They don't trust outsiders much, but can you blame them? Outsiders have lured away their young people. This way."

He took my hand and led me into the neighborhood, where an ancient man and woman sat at a table. The couple's skin was as brown and weathered as the bark of the pine-oak forest that sheltered the village. Between them was a gorgeous potted plant, straining at its ceramic confines. The last of its fragile white blossoms spilled over the edge of the table and fluttered to the paving stones. I plucked one from the ground and inhaled. Citrus?

"Orange blossom. It will go there in the spring." The woman pointed to a small dirt patch by the door. She spoke in a Spanish so regional, I struggled to translate. Her eyes were red and clouded with cataracts, but when she met my gaze, I saw sharp intelligence.

While her fingers deftly threaded a needle, the paperback in the man's hand shook as he turned a page. Not just any book—one of Samuel's nixie stories.

"Kaye, may I introduce *Señor y Señora* Rodriguez. They are the grandparents of Daniel."

Startled, I wiped a clammy hand and held it out in greeting, stumbling through an expression of sympathy. They turned to Samuel.

"*Señor* Cabral, I am honored to see you again," said the old man. "All is ready?"

Señor Rodriguez gestured to the house. "It is secure here. He is up the street, at the *mercado*. Guard your back, young man."

Wait, '*he*'? Not '*she*'?

Samuel grasped the man's hand and pressed his cheek to the woman's face with deference. "*Gracias Señor, Señora.*"

Her eyes met mine again. Her hard gaze was that of a hawk's, hovering over a ditch as it waited for mice to surface from the tallgrass. The hairs on the back of my neck prickled.

Something wasn't right. Dread filled me as I watched Samuel push open the door of a dark, windowless home.

It's windowless...the other houses have windows. I grabbed my husband's sleeve and held firm.

"Samuel, don't go in there. Something doesn't feel right."

"I'm not going in. You are." *What?*

He pried my fingers from his sleeve. "I'm sorry, Kaye." His voice was suddenly tortured. "But I have to go on without you."

"There aren't any windows," I hissed.

He leaned over and kissed the top of my head, then gave me a gentle push, as if he were a parent ushering a toddler into a babysitter's living room. "Stay here, please don't follow me and you'll be safe. I love you." There it was, the darkness and sadness he'd struggled to hide since we left Colorado, now laid bare to the bone. *He planned this from the beginning.* The minute I'd forced my way into his Mexico-bound car, he'd determined to ditch me. He cupped my cheek and slipped through the door before it registered that I'd let him go. The door slammed shut and clicked.

No.

He'd left me behind.

And where on earth was I? Fear shook me—that paralyzing dread on the edge of a nightmare, where darkness is heavy and wicked. Pushing at the door was fruitless. I squinted into the ink black room, the sun's ghost still bright in my eyes. *Not entirely black... a dim light.* Must and dust hit my nose and I sneezed.

Silence.

"Samuel?"

No answer. I took a tentative step into the room. Hardwood floor? No, packed dirt. I groped with blind fingers and feet in this stuffy, sunless room. My feet hit something and I fell to my knees, put my hands out to break my fall. Fire shot up my newly healed wrist and I cried out.

"Sam?" My voice was a pathetic whimper. My good hand patted the floor but instead of cold hard dirt, it found fabric. A body?

Breathe, Kaye. I willed my eyes to adjust to the low light of the room. Not a body, but a basket of fabric scraps and a half-woven rug. I scanned my surroundings—wooden table, two rocking chairs, tiny wood-burning stove. A sofa, its once-bright flowers faded to threadbare pastel.

I hauled myself off the floor and settled onto the sofa, tucked my knees under my chin and replayed Samuel's blank expressions, shaking hands, careful words. When had he arranged to dump me on these poor, grieving strangers? *The pit stop at the gas station...he must have called ahead.* My face landed in my hands. I couldn't believe I hadn't anticipated this...this *deception*, and just when we'd begun to again trust each other. But that was Samuel Caulfield Cabral to a tee, wasn't it? High-handed, arrogant, always three steps ahead...

And afraid. He'd told me as much, hadn't he? Afraid I wouldn't understand why he chose what he chose, that I wouldn't understand his love for me. Oh, I understood. He loved me too much to leave me brokenhearted and fragile in Colorado, yet loved me too much to allow me to risk my life for his sister.

But did he understand how much *I* loved *him*?

Pure, pristine fear—not for myself, but Sam—clawed at my brain and drove me from the sofa to pound on the thick door panels and shout for liberation.

"He only wants to keep you safe."

I halted at the sound of the voice, deep and temperate. The ancient man entered through the only other door in the room, hands raised as if to calm a skittish colt. Though frail, a straight back and buoyant stride belied strength beneath papery skin and sinew. But it wasn't the man who ultimately held my attention. It was the door he latched behind him. A door that was washed in *bright blue.*

Blue, like the door in my dream.

I watched *Señor* Rodriguez.

The man looked heavenward. "My wife is a Nixie fan. She would do anything for 'SCC.' Settle in, young lady." He explained how his wife knew all the comings and goings of La Vereda, how she sat outside their home on the street with her sewing in her lap and her Nixie books, how she watched my husband and knew him instantly, and knew for whom he searched.

Comprehension filled me as I recalled Sam's writing. "He left the burner phone number for Marieta, in the Nixie book."

"And that book has not left the table."

So Marieta hadn't returned. Who, then, had found the number in the book? Fresh eyes landed on a cluster of framed photographs, proudly displayed on a shelf opposite the stove. I nodded to them in silent question.

"Please do. You are a guest in our home."

Most of the photos were black and white, grainy with age, of unfamiliar relatives posed in gardens, front steps, long-dead cars.

Many were adorned in what must have been cheery flowers and cross-stitches, but two color photos outshone the others. The first held a boy and a girl, perhaps eight years old. Behind them was the tiny commercial street of La Vereda. The boy was vaguely familiar, but the girl stole my breath as memories of my own childhood sweetheart shone through her smile, the tilt of her chin, high cheekbones, feathery eyelashes. This could only be Marieta Sanchez. I studied the boy's face again. Heavy eyebrows and full lips, a scowl that said he was too cool to smile.

The second picture confirmed my suspicions: Daniel and Marieta, now grown, beaming and brightly embroidered in Mexican tradition. I'd only seen dresses like this at…

"They're married!"

The man brushed a gnarled finger along the top of the frame. "Three years ago."

"I wondered, but I didn't know. How beautiful they are."

The old woman—Daniel's grandmother—slipped through the door and leaned against it, keeping a wary distance. "And few knew of their marriage. Because of her past with the cartel, we thought it better. Those butchers bend people into obedience by attacking their families. It is why your husband asked that you remain in our care until…" She swallowed. "Until he returns from the *mercado*."

Concern again had me turning for the blue door, but the man grasped my arm. Definitely stronger than he looked. "Let him deal with Javier Sanchez on his own, *Señora*. Money is why they lured him here, and money is what will speak to them. But if you were to storm into their sanctuary, you'd become a bargaining chip. No one could prevent them from shipping you far away."

My throat went dry. "Human trafficking?"

The man nodded and eased into the chair, rested his aged legs.

The woman sat in the rocker beside him, pulled a slippery fringe shawl from the back and wrapped it around her thin shoulders. "It was this evil that my Daniel and Marieta fought."

"What about Javier Sanchez and Camila Flores? They lived in the apartment next to Marieta in Mexico City."

"Their life there is a mystery to us. I do know that Marieta was finished with the cartels, but Javier is a selfish man, too weak, too cowardly to get out. And Camila!" She crossed herself.

"She knows the old plants and poisons, and she's wicked enough to use them. Some say she even drugged women and children for the cartel, in the way of the Aztecs. I would think Marieta would run far away from them. Especially with—" She clamped her mouth when her husband gave her a sharp look.

"Especially with..." I prompted, but this was a dead end. I rubbed my temples. "But Javier has a photograph of the three of them, together. It looked recent. If Marieta wanted nothing to do with them, then why was she in front of a fountain, smiling, with her arms around them?"

"I'm afraid only Marieta could answer that."

I sank onto the sofa, struggling to take in all that they said. "Do you think she's...gone?"

The man was grim. "We have not heard from her since Daniel's funeral, but that is not unusual. For all we know, she has left Mexico altogether."

"Then who called Samuel at the number in the book, if it wasn't Marieta?"

"Probably *la bruja*," *Señora* Rodriguez grumbled.

"We don't know," her husband answered. "Regardless, your husband needs to finish this business, not only for him, but for his family."

My blood turned to ice as I remembered the borrowed gun. Samuel hadn't locked me away to go find his sister, or get answers, or even to pay a ransom. Samuel locked me away because, in his own words, *he wouldn't hesitate to pull the trigger.*

When would the man ever learn that *familia* meant you never had to fight bad guys alone?

I bit my lip, took stock of the frail couple before me: stooped back, deep fissures from decades of hard labor. For what? To have their family torn to pieces by bloodsucking cartels?

They didn't seem to be the type of people who sat on their hands.

"I bet you're beyond angry."

The woman's black eyes glinted. "Anger doesn't begin to describe what we feel. They have stolen our grandson."

"And Samuel's retribution is your retribution?"

The man shrugged. "When I was young, I could have fought them with my fists. Now?" He held up his hands for my inspection, knobbed and curled by arthritis. Now I can't even pull a trigger to save my family."

"But Samuel can." I nodded to the shotgun that hung above the shelf. "I can too, if you'll show me where to go."

Señora Rodriguez tutted. "Don't be ridiculous."

But *Señor* Rodriguez took in my petite frame, short blonde curls— I was probably Shirley Temple in his eyes. His cracked lips thinned. "The scar along your hairline. How did you get it?"

"Would you believe a fist-fight with Mexican street gangs?" He didn't laugh, and I sighed. "I had a run-in with the ground in a skydiving accident."

Bushy eyebrows rose. "And the scars on your knees?"

Embarrassed, I tugged at my frayed cut-offs. "Oh, who knows? Mountain climbing, roughed them up in caves, maybe even bottomed out on a ski slope."

"Ah, you're an *aventurera*."

"Something like that. Or I was…"

"There are many types of adventures, *Señora,* and not all involve carabiners." He squinted at the old clock perched upon the mantle, quietly ticking, and I caught a hint of worry in the deep crags of his face. Samuel had been gone too long.

"Tell me, do you believe in God?"

His question was sudden, and I opened my mouth to offer a pat answer. But I paused, reflected. "I think I've always known he's there, though I never gave him much thought. I blamed him for a lot of the bad, but I don't know if I gave him credit for the good, until he—" I hesitated, knowing how crazy it sounded. "I think he told me to climb a mountain in the middle of a flood, and it saved my life. Does a voice in my head make any sense, or is this a disconnection with reality?"

The man gave me a patient smile, as one would patronize a young lady off her rocker. But then he surprised me. "I think you're just the person for the job. Marieta believed so, too. Let's check on your husband, shall we?"

His wife scoffed. "Foolishness! You old goat, you will get her killed."

"Hush now, she'll go there anyway. I'd rather she not knock us to the ground to do it." He padded over to his wife's rocker, held out his hands.

With a shake of her head, she drew the filmy black shawl from her shoulders and tossed it to me. "Tie this over that bright head. You're a walking target."

Were they letting me go? Hope flitted in my chest and I obediently tied the scarf over my head like a bandana, feeling ninja-ish. *Señor* Rodriguez went through the blue door and returned with an old cigar box. Inside was a smaller box—ammunition. He placed them in my hand, then plopped a black Stetson on his head, as if to leave the house. But first, he took the shotgun from the wall and held it out with reverence, like a samurai passing on a sword (if samurais wore cowboy hats). Making sure the safety was on, I slid the business ends of shells up into the loading flap, just as Jamie had taught me. He nodded his approval.

"She'll dislocate her shoulder with that old thing."

"It does have a terrible kick, so your shoulders will be bruised," he said apologetically. "But do what you must and listen to that voice. *La cabeza y corazón* are in agreement."

Chapter 22
FREE SOLO

When a single climber scales a mountain without the aid of a belay rope, harness, or climbing partner, and depends on skill alone. It's a long, long way to the ground.

Señor Rodriguez had a quicker stride than I'd expected as I scrambled up the dirt path behind him, weaving the forest line on the outskirts of the village like a ninja. Determination had knocked twenty years off of his shoulders. Clouds of mosquitoes from dewy grass swarmed my ankles and feasted on my exposed skin. I gritted my teeth, unable to swat them away because of the monstrous rifle.

We stopped behind a cluster of homes, little more than one-room shacks. He put two fingers to his mouth and loosed a sharp whistle. Only night sounds replied, the chatter of bugs and pines and breeze. But then a man emerged from one of the homes, similarly black-hatted and armed, then another, and another. One brushed crumbs from his shirt and I wondered if he'd been in the middle of his supper.

"It's time," said Rodriguez.

Their faces were stone-cold, but their jitters belied an eagerness to be done with the venomous snakes nesting in the backyard woodpile. They wordlessly fell in line behind Mr. Rodriguez like well-trained soldiers. We crept up the mountain slope, prowling behind sheds and animal pens; far enough in shadow not to startle the village dogs, but now and then, someone threw treats into yards. How many times had they done this?

After a half mile, the village gave way to darkness. "I thought we were going to the *mercado,*" I whispered to the man in front of me. He put a sausage-like finger to his lips and pointed at the well-lit house on the edge of town. This did not look like a grocery store; perhaps '*mercado*' also translated to 'creepy backwoods drug den.'

Light pooled like a moat to ward off enemies. A watchman stood outside the door, little more than a teenager, huffy and bored, the metal on his fingers glinting under security lights. Metal also gleamed at his jean-clad hip. Nuts. He leaned against the wall and lazily puffed a cigarette, eyes half-closed. Then they flew open and I saw that one of our party had slipped around the house and pressed a muzzle to his back.

A slow tremor melted from my head to my toes, because I was ambushing a Mexican drug cartel with a local vigilante group armed to the hilt, and *this doesn't happen to small-town advertisers from Colorado.* My heart flapped against my ribs like goose wings. One of the village men gave me a shove, repeating what I'd missed.

"Go around back and hold that gun on anyone who makes for the tree line," he said in a vernacular I could barely understand. "That's the safest place for *you.*"

Not liking the emphasis, I grabbed the man's sleeve. "Don't shoot my husband, okay? Or hurt him, even."

The man rolled his eyes as if to say, "I'm not an amateur, crazy gringo," and shooed me toward the building.

I didn't know what to do, so I staked out a place on fairly even ground and took off the shotgun's safety, my senses attuned to the sounds coming from the other side of the building.

Two minutes...three... Enough time for me to marinade in the absurdity of this pickle...

Once, when I was eleven, in a fit of terror I ran headlong into a thorn bush.

My mother was in the thick of fall harvest, so Sofia invited me to stay the week. Angel was having a sleepover with Samuel, and the two had claimed the basement for video games, which forced me and Dani into the lingering afternoon light. We had a beautiful array of gold, red, orange leaves drying on the deck when the boys tromped through, Sofia calling from the depths of the house to 'get some fresh air and work out your teenaged aggression, for heaven's sake.'

Angel chomped his teeth. "One minute's head-start to hide, on the count of three.

One...Two...THREE!"

Dani and I shrieked across the yard, splitting up when we reached the trees. I knew exactly where to go. I'd staked out this hiding spot a year ago—a newly fallen tree, it's rotting, hollow trunk filled with pale fungi. But Samuel had lost all interest in playing Search & Destroy with 'children.' (He'd had his eye on Cherry Chapstick Girl, and jealousy licked through my veins because *she'd* had a whole summer of his attention, while I'd languished in Durango with my grandmother.) Now Samuel would seek out *me*. With glee, I shimmied my boyish body into the log and waited.

Sweet pungent wood rot tickled my nostrils. Not a breath.... maybe a bit of air...I evened my breathing, melded into the sponge beneath me.

Minutes passed. Dapples of sunlight gave way to mute oranges, which faded into cool October shadows. The boys' sneakers tromped by, but they never waded into the brush that camouflaged my tree. Temperatures dropped. Faintly, I heard Angel: "Oh Aspen Kaye, come out and meet your doooom!" Heck no, I wasn't falling for that old tactic. Then Dani's voice: "We give up. Come on, *Mamá* won't let us eat until we find you!" Wow, thanks bestie.

Silence blanketed my corner of the wood. Now the only thing keeping me in the log was belligerence and sheer determination. Once, he would have known where to find me, because we would have discovered the log in the woods *together*. Heck, we would have hidden in the *Same. Flipping. Log.* But he was thirteen and I was eleven, which meant I'd become so invisible I might as well have been a toddler, for all the seriousness he gave to my opinions, or heartaches, or interests. He couldn't even bother to find me here, only steps off the beaten path.

A rustle in the brush broke through my prepubescent angst and I froze.

Human footsteps? No.

A quiet growl, then a hiss.

I hurled my body out of the log, not caring that my jeans snagged and the knee ripped wide open. No way would I be a sitting duck for…whatever kind of rabid animal lurked in hollow logs. A badger? Mountain lion?

In retrospect, the likely culprit was a raccoon, but when one is wrapped in the eeriness of an autumn wood, logic and raccoons fly out the window.

That, ladies and gentlemen, is how I ran headlong into a thorn bush, where Samuel found me covered with a thousand burrs and tree rot… …and laughed.

…and tagged me out.

What would Samuel say if he saw me crouched in the shadows, ready to fend off cartel henchmen with a weapon so heavy, I barely balanced it? If I tried to fire, would I catapult backwards, through the shack? Fear slammed me, the same terror of an eleven year girl who ran straight into thorn bushes. This was, *by far*, the stupidest thing I'd ever done, and I'd done *a lot* of stupid things.

Voices cut through my panic. I held my breath. A quiet conversation—*Señor* Rodriguez and a woman inside the house. The voices grew louder as the conversation turned into an argument, then all hell broke loose as the door banged and feet clambered down wooden steps. Ah crud. I lifted the gun, but no one came around the house. Flannels streamed into the woods, pursued by bounding black Stetsons whooping Latin war cries, firing their guns into trees, bullets whizzing and cracking branches.

Like our old game of Search & Destroy, it seemed the drug thugs frequently ran from the townies into the woods, only to creep back to their club house. *Unlike* our old game of Search & Destroy, these people had grown-up with realities on their shoulders, realities where their young men and women vanished.

Where was Samuel?

I searched for my husband's tall, slender frame in the villagers who remerged from the woods and stomped down the hill toward town, but he wasn't among them.

The night fell quiet. The air was thick with heady earth and shadow, crisp breeze ruffling the canopy of trees. The moon was huge and low and orange, the same harvest moon that had hovered over Lyons just days ago. If I closed my eyes, I could be home, crouching in a log, braced for an animal's growl.

Now what was I supposed to do? Go back to town? Wait here? As I waffled, a twig snapped to my right. I swung the shotgun toward the noise and, as I did, something sharp stung my neck. A mosquito this was not. Just before I dropped like a sandbag, gun and all, I swear I heard someone say "tag!"—a punchline so ridiculous and poetic, I would have laughed if I hadn't been out cold.

The first thing that cut through the fog was pain. Fire licked up my freshly reinjured wrist. My head throbbed, so I put my good hand to my cheek and it came away warm, sticky. Had I hit it when I fell? I gingerly probed the gash. If I made it to seventy, I'd have more scar tissue than skin. I buried my face into...what was I lying upon? Tree rot? I shifted and it rustled. Straw mattress. Was I in the building with the moat of light, or had they moved me?

Samuel.

I sat up and groaned when my brain tried to beat its way out of my skull. Concussion, perhaps? No, I'd had concussions, and this nerve-numbing blanket wrapping my body felt more like the haze of strong meds.

"Sam?" I whispered into the dark. A light flared in the corner, and pain shot through my head. Was I hung over?

"What did you do to me?" I slurred.

"*Toloache.* You should still be asleep; my dosing was off. I don't understand..." A woman, distinct Spanish dialect like the other villagers. She clapped her hands and I flinched. "Of course, the altitude.

Your blood runs thin because you come from Colorado. Mountain people have higher tolerances."

Toloache. I'd heard of it before…Alonso's story…

'We would travel through the villages…once, they gave my brother toloache for a sprained ankle and he hallucinated he was trapped inside its thorny fruit…It is what the Aztecs used to subdue their human sacrifices…'

"You gave me that crazy Aztec plant?"

She straightened her back. "Consider it a small mercy. The Zacatón wants me to bash your head so he can transport you to Nuevo Laredo, but I won't let him do that."

"How generous."

I struggled to make sense of her words, but it was like listening to a weak static signal on a radio station. The woman sat in front of an oil lamp, darkly silhouetted like a Madonna profile edged with gold in a medieval icon. She rose from the table and I saw her more clearly. Smooth, sumptuous skin and eyes of glittering flint, oval face, piled hair. She looked much younger than the heavy cares that streaked her hair with gray. An herbal scent filled my nostrils.

"I've seen your photo. You're Javier Sanchez's wife, Camila Flores."

She smiled thinly. "Something like that."

"Where's my husband?"

"Same place as mine." I watched balefully as she poured something into a cup. "Drink. It will ease the pain."

I gave a harsh laugh. "There's no way I'm going to drink that."

"*Toloache* won't kill you, only give you strange dreams."

"Oh lady, I don't need another flipping strange dream. I've had my quota, thanks."

Camila frowned. "It's difficult for you to believe, but I'm not a bad person. You weren't supposed to be with the writer. If that *cholo* takes you to the Nuevo Laredo Treiños, you'll never see home again. But they don't have to know we have you. Once your husband makes the bank account transfer, Javier and I will return you to him. I'm trying to save your life."

"Or you could let me go now. That seems easier."

"Drink." Exasperated, she held out the mug. *Not a chance, sister.* I stubbornly clamped my mouth shut, terrified if I drank, I'd be dead like those long ago Aztec prisoners.

Two bottles were on the table. One was a brown liquid—the *toloache*. The other was clear liquor. Camila rolled the clear bottle between her palms—homemade *raicilla?*—and the liquor sloshed against the sides. "It won't kill you," she repeated. "I'm a medicine woman. I've gathered plants, dried them, and worked the markets since I was a *niñita*."

Boots clomped up the stairs. The door she'd been eyeing swung open and in stomped the watchman. So he'd given the villagers the slip. For one so young, his face was red and splotchy with exertion.

"Car is gone, the others have it," he wheezed, and grabbed the bottle the woman held.

"Please, help yourself." Camila glared at the arrogant youth.

Forgoing a glass, he splashed a generous amount down his throat and gave a satisfied smack. "Still the best in Tamaulipas, better than your grandmother's, even. She wasn't good for much else." He spotted me. "*Ay Dios mío,* this one isn't dead after all. You are a hell of a lot of trouble."

What had I done except get myself drugged?

"Your husband just couldn't leave well enough alone. Had to drag the *Federales*, border agents, the damned P.I. into our business. Thinks he's so smart, that he can pay his way out." The man faced me now, wavering oddly, as if I viewed him through the sloshing liquid of the woman's *raicilla* bottle. Drops of his spittle landed on my cheeks and I wiped it in disgust.

"I don't suppose if I apologized, you'd let me go." I shifted against the straw mattress as another wave of nausea hit me. The man's eyes grew dark and hungry, a predator, and I belatedly realized that small movement caused what little cleavage I had to jut out. I hurriedly zipped up my hoodie to my neck.

The man chuckled and grabbed his crotch. "*¿Hoy cena Pancho, eh?*"

I tucked my knees further into my body. Even I knew the implications of that crude phrase.

The woman huffed. "If your mother could see you now, she'd whip your backside. Besides, if we kill the writer's wife, we have no chance of accessing Samuel Cabral's bank accounts."

"I've not killed a woman yet with *this*." Good lord, the man was obsessed with his crotch. "Anyway, she's of no use to us. Send her to the Treiños."

"Such big words for such a small, stupid boy! It doesn't matter which one of the Cabrals we're holding, as long as the other is free to pay their ransom."

The man ran a hand over his holstered gun. "Be careful, old woman. The Zacatóns are calling in retribution on you and Sanchez for 'losing' their goods. If we don't get the account information, you are as good as dead…"

My eyes darted back and forth as I tried to follow their volley. "Lemme get this straight," I slurred. Why wouldn't my mouth stop flapping? "You and Javier lost the cartel's goods—how do you lose something that belongs to a drug cartel? Did it fall out of your pocket?—and you want to use our money to pay this debt. So you lured Sam down here to hold him for ransom, but that plan now blows because I'm not in Colorado to authorize…the…bank…" My vision blurred.

How did four bottles appear on the table? I tried to meet Camila's icy stare with one that was equally threatening.

The thug snorted. "Bitch is *loco*. No one's going to pay money for her." He waved his gun in my direction. "Just hit her with your bottle and be done with it."

Yep, I needed to get out of there, stat. I grabbed for the nearest diversion. "Okay no need for blunt force trauma. Just give me the cup." The wife tentatively held out the mug and I snatched it, sniffed. It was some herbal, nasty smelling thing and I crinkled my nose.

"Do it." The lackey impatiently waved his gun above his head.

"Really, *wey*? You want me to drink this? Maybe you *should* just knock me out."

"*Pinche perra*, just drink the damned thing!" His fingers were loose on the handle, lax at the trigger. He swayed on his feet, stumbled into the table. The homemade *raicilla* bottle clattered to the floor—it must have been powerful stuff, because the guy was as drunk as a skunk. This was my chance.

I hurled the foul mug at his face and it chased the *raicilla* bottle across the floor. Just as I gripped the door handle, a shot ripped through the room and lodged in the wall, followed by a second that whizzed by and hit the door behind me. My arms flew up.

"Mother of Tom!" *Wey* may have been as wobbly as a landed trout, but he meant business. "I give up! I'll drink."

Camila's scowl was full-on ugly. She marched across the room, refill in hand. "Do you have any idea how difficult it is to find these plants? Don't spill. In fact, here." She yanked the man-boy by his white tee and instructed him to force my mouth open as she put the mug to my lips. The foul liquid sloshed down my throat, and before I could spit, she forced my jaw shut.

Helpless, I gagged and swallowed.

"Did she drink enough?"

"Enough for flying unicorns." Camila hunched over me as if to check my vitals and whispered. "For God's sake, be quiet and don't fight."

"Unicorns don't fly," I grumbled.

Minutes passed as I sat on the straw mattress and plotted. The *cholo* bit his fingernails and spit them on the dirt floor. The woman opened one of Samuel's Nixie books and flipped to an oft-read passage, judging by the crease in the binding—probably that sex scene I'd been chaffed about when it was first published. A Nixie was a Nixie, regardless of nationality, age, and criminal intent.

Everyone jumped as the door banged open and Javier strode through. His Aloha shirt was so bright, my poor drugged eyes watered. My heart pounded out of my chest.

"What have you done with Samuel?" I garbled. Ugh, my tongue was a thick clump of oatmeal clogging my mouth.

Javier assessed my extremely stoned state. "Is the writer here, too?"

"No. I thought you were going to get him," said Camila.

"They took him before I could intercept them. If he's not here, he's at the old market."

The old market…that was what Samuel had called the boarded up building at the base of the hill.

"What are they going to do to him?"

Javier turned to me. "He's on his way to a 'financial meeting' with Treiño's 'chauffeur,' down from Nuevo Laredo." He even used air-quotes, the idiot, as if I didn't know what he was talking about. "They'll want to sell the girl," he said to the Zacatón.

"It shouldn't be a problem."

My head roared at Camila's false promises. They had no intention of releasing me, and I wished I'd spent more time learning about the horror of human trafficking rather than stressing over new homes and babies and marital problems.

"And Samuel Cabral?" Javier asked.

"The usual. He pays, we ask for more. He will keep paying, as long as there is hope of her return."

Sickness roiled in my stomach. I truly was going to end up on an episode of *Forensic Crimes*, a twenty-minute blip of morbid curiosity for other people safe on their couches, people who had enough sense not to mix with evil cartels. *Not going to happen.* Grim determination blossomed; I'd get out or die trying.

The room grew fuzzy. I gripped my head.

At that moment, the thug mirrored my actions. He shook his head and slumped against the wall. His eyes flew to Camila.

"Wha...what did you give me, witch?"

"Only *raicilla*, child, better than my *abuela's*."

Mother cliffhucker. *They'd played him.*

The Zacatón henchman slid to the floor. Javier towered over the man and leered, then reared back and delivered a blow. He cried out, but Javier was merciless.

"It wasn't enough for the cartel to have me, Marieta and Daniel. Now you devils want the children*, and I will not allow it.*"

"Please," said the Zacatón but determination was in Javier's beefy fists. I pressed my body as tightly against the wall as I could, unable to watch as he brought his judgement.

"Javier! He's only a stupid little boy from La Vereda. If the cartel doesn't kill him, the police will."

Javier ignored her. "Greed. Revenge. Power. You bathe in blood, yet you are never cleansed. And now I'm just like you. I have my niece's blood on my hands. Oh, Marieta."

"Enough," Camila said quietly.

I winced at the lifeless heap on the floor…I didn't want to look but I had to know. Sure enough, his chest still rose and fell. My head swam again, and as I watched Javier dig through a bag and tuck an envelope in his shirt pocket, his arms blurred and split in two, like zippers. My eyes bugged out as he fragmented further, and soon he had bones for arms, waving and rattling like those *Dios de los Muertos* skeletons propped in windows and hung from doorways. I would have preferred unicorns.

Keep your focus, Kaye, get yourself out of here. I looked again. Brightly colored bones and animals danced upon the walls, jaguar fur billowed down from the ceiling. Wow, it was pretty. So soft, like the mountain *leoncillo*. I touched the delicate bristles.

"It's beautiful…" I murmured.

"*Now* I have the correct dose," the medicine woman sighed. At least, it sounded like her. A second skeleton sat in the chair, her head wreathed in bright red roses, and I was fairly sure I had toppled into Alonso's folktales.

Perhaps it was the *toloache* coursing through my bloodstream and causing a trip worthy of The Beatles post Strawberry Fields. More likely it was an absolute lack of inhibition combined with the knowledge that Samuel was nabbed by inhuman butchers. Either way, it was time to leave. Legs as wobbly as a fawn's, I pushed myself up from the straw bed and stumbled for the door, or where I thought the door had been, because the walls swirled and wafted like a brightly painted ship sail. If I had to somersault my way back to the village, I would find him.

"We can't just turn her loose, you don't have the money yet. Besides, she'll never make it back to the village." The skeleton woman's voice was hollow as black crept into the corners of my vision.

"You must take her. Return her to Rodriguez, they'll keep her safe until the *toloache* leaves her body."

"And Samuel Cabral?"

"Samuel," I lamented. I had to find him.

A pause, then a calm voice. "I will help your husband, Mrs. Cabral."

Somewhere behind me, the woman skeleton cried, pleaded with the man. As they clung to each other, I lurched and swam through a swirl of colors, deep in this Aztec ocean. Then bone fingers clutched my arms and the man was inches before me, scintillating eyes holding mine. "*Señora*, I don't know if you can understand me, but I pray you remember when you are again yourself."

I started to scream for Samuel, but the man covered my mouth.

"Go to the cave, up the mountain. You'll find the children there."

"What children?"

"The children Marieta took from the cartel. That is what we do. We help them to escape."

"They are the 'lost goods' the cartel boy spoke of," Camila explained.

"You must return them to their families. Please *Señora*."

My head lolled and I tried to hold his gaze. His words were a jigsaw puzzle, thousands of scattered pieces. "I don't understand. Why are you letting me go?"

"Because *mi sobrinita* is dead, my sister's beautiful girl. *Ay*, Marieta. She was good to me. You cannot let her boy fall into the hands of those monsters, or she will have died for nothing. Go. I will help your writer escape."

Pieces fit together in a moment of clarity. *Poor Marieta. Samuel would be devastated.*

"They'll hurt you," I said, my voice strange and childlike.

"Do not worry what they will or won't do. I carved my coffin long ago." With that, he shoved me out the door and into a foreign night.

I tripped through the muck of the forest, vaguely aware of boney fingers clutching my sleeves, pushing me, guiding me as I ran. Cool air filled my nostrils and the moon swam into view above a body of glowing water.

"I cannot go any further or they will find me," the woman with the skeleton hands said in a low voice. "The village is up the hill on the other side of the lake. Stick to the road and for God's sake, don't fall in. Tell *Señor* Rodriguez to take you to Marieta's cave. He will know."

She gave my back a small shove. "Go! Run!"

I began to scramble up the hill but froze. What about Samuel? He wasn't *up* the hill, he was *down* the hill, at the old market. I dropped to my hands and knees, dug my fingers into dirt and gravel to ground my panic. If I went for the children, could I trust Javier to save Samuel?

But the children... the Zacatóns had scattered into the forests. How long before some cartel goon found them in this cave? Or, what if I tried to save Samuel and they killed me? Who would tell the village how to find them?

I cried in agony, because there was never a choice. Up the hill, in a cave, there were scared children who'd been wrenched from homes, parents, lives, trafficked like chattel and saved by my fearless sister-in-law, a woman I would never know. Up the hill, in a cave, was her boy.

I bowed my head. I knew what Samuel would want me to do. Heartsick, I forced my eyes up the hill into the darkness...up the road...up...around the lake...up...up.

The *toloache*'s grip on my mind weakened as I stumbled up the road, the woman in the quiet nursery guiding me.

Look higher.

I ran through dark streets, pounded on doors, heedless of distressed voices on the other sides. Why couldn't I remember which home belonged to the old man and woman? *Go to the Rodriguez home*, her voice echoed in my head, the voice of my dreams. *Look up.*

I looked up, slipping over seaweed, pushing through river rapids. A bright blue door, the door Marieta had opened in my dream.

"Please! *Señor* Rodriguez, *Señora*. Open the door."

The butt of a rifle met my face, and then dropped. The door flew open and the old man pulled me inside.

"Thank goodness! I just returned from the house, but there was only the Lopez boy, passed out on the floor."

Words tumbled from my mouth, about Marieta and the children she rescued from the cartel, about a cave, and Javier and Camila and Samuel.

Señora Rodriguez clutched her brightly woven shawl to her chest. "The cave! Of course, she would take them to the cave on the south slope, where she and Daniel played. We didn't look there..."

"They're going to kill Samuel. He's at the old market."

The old couple shared a look. Then he shouldered his rifle and slipped out the door.

"Some of our men will go to the old market, and some to the cave," said the *señora*. She studied my pupils with concern. "What have you taken?"

"*Toloache*. It's going to paint me, like the *leoncillo*."

"Oh my. How much did you swallow?"

"I don't know, just a bit. I threw the rest at the skeletons."

She looked heavenward. "Good girl. Unfortunately, it gives you *loco* dreams, for an hour at least. Come, lie down."

Even as she said it, I followed *Señor* Rodriguez and his rifle out the door because I couldn't let the demon Aztec plant win.

"Where on earth are you going?" The *Señora* tugged me back into the house, but I was no match for her.

"To the cave. I have to find them."

She gave up and grabbed her shawl. "Very well, come with me. *Gringa estúpida*, I can't let you kill yourself on this mountain."

Contrary to the woman's intentions, her words filled me with a sense of comfort, probably because I'd heard them a thousand times. "*Señora*, you aren't the first person to tell me that I'll die on a mountain."

Chapter 23
SCREAMER

*When a climber takes a whipper, or a long fall,
and it's accompanied by screaming.*

Hydraulic Level Five [WORKING TITLE]
Draft 1.123
© Samuel Caulfield Cabral and Aspen Kaye Cabral
SUMMITING THE SIERRA MADRES IN A CAR TRUNK

He was supposed to write mountains for her.

Caulfield twists his tied wrists. His kidnappers are really nothing more than boys, but they know what they are doing. He can't help the wryness in the smile on his painfully split lips. Aspen was right... he's going to end up on an episode of *Forensic Crimes*.

Caulfield has never seen a murder. Suicide? Yes. OD? More than once. Not surprising, considering the sketchy places he's holed up. So the first murder he'll witness will be his own. (Would he actually see himself die, or does one's brain simply shut off moments before impact? Another tally mark, another corpse heaved onto the heap of fodder his brain mucks through at night.)

It's dark inside the trunk. It's literally pitch-black, though there's metaphor to unearth as he bounces along, bent into himself, bound by a plastic zip-tie that cuts his wrists. Sightless. Motionless. Helpless.

Wealthy, naïve Chicano American is lured into cartel country, only to become a victim of kidnapping and ransom. How cliché.

And that's the rub of it. Not that his fingers and toes will be strewn along the 101. Man, he hates the hopelessness that sucks him under, the bipolar that pulls down an already drowning man, a concrete block tethered to his ankles that bars him from kicking to the surface. He conjures Aspen's face, the girlish curve of her jawline, the softness of her body when he draws her close. Kick for the surface, the light.

God, don't let it end like this. Surely you have more for me to do than write fairytales.

His wrists are slick with what he thought was sweat, but now they sting so it must be blood. The car hits a pothole and jars his spine against the underside of the trunk.

They slow to a stop.

Muffled voices, laughs, silence. A shout now: "*¿Que pedo?*" Two loud pops.

Caulfield braces, ready to kick and fight and hurl his body against these punk kids because he's not going to die in such a helpless manner. The trunk squeaks open, then a silhouette. Not the teenagers, but a man, older, slower. Caulfield squints against the blinding beam of a flashlight.

"Turn around, I'll cut you loose."

He knows the voice. It's his sister's uncle. The man lowers the flashlight beam, and under the nearly full moon, he can see him clearly. Cragged forehead, eyes drooping like a hound, at odds with the colorful splashes of flowers on his shirt, this man looks as resigned as Caulfield felt moments ago. Behind him are the two kids slumped on the ground. One moans incoherently, the other is obviously dead.

The minute his hands are free, he rips the duct tape from his mouth. "Where's my wife?"

"Your wife is safe in the village, exactly where you left her." The uncle's mouth twitches at some unknown thing. He tosses Caulfield's backpack at his feet and pulls the borrowed gun from his waistband, handle out. "These belong to you."

Just like that, it's over.

In retrospect, Caulfield should have said *thank you*, because, as surely as he still breathes, he's face to face with a dead man. But all he says is "Why?"

His sister's uncle lifts a shoulder as if the fact that the cartel will slaughter him for his betrayal is no big deal. "Why? Because you loved Marieta when no one else did." He studies Caulfield as if he's never before seen him. "You look like her. Do you think she would have forgiven me?"

Caulfield swallows. He could condemn this man for the evil he'd brought into Marieta's life. He could tell him 'of course she would forgive you,' but truthfully, he doesn't know, so that's what he goes with. "I do not know my sister well enough to answer that."

The uncle laughs. "Yet you and your wife ran into the mouth of a lion to save her. Why?"

"Because she's my sister."

"No. Because she's *you*. Ah, I see I've caught you. No worries, you'll have long years to ponder this." He loops his fingers over his belt. "Just wait until you're a father. Because that is what you are now."

He narrows his eyes. Is this a trick?

"Do you not know we have a nephew? A little boy, just turned three. He's yours now, you'll find out why when he tells you his name."

Caulfield shakes his head. "I didn't...I don't..."

"We saved as many as we could," the uncle continues, as if he hasn't just devastatingly knocked the wind from Caulfield's body. "Now you must save *him*. That's what she wanted from you, when she knew Rodriguez was dead and she would be, too."

"But my sister..."

"Is gone."

No. *No. Oh, Marieta.*

He can't do this here. *Hold it together. Find Aspen.* Caulfield rests his forehead against the cold metal of the car...

The toy car. A bit of metal painted yellow in the Mexico City slum, a bright thing forgotten in a dark room, and he hadn't seen it. Not a neighbor's child as the grocer had assumed, and he'd assumed, and they'd all assumed. Of course. *Of course* his sister has a child.

A father...an orphaned nephew.... he feels the chill of a long ago Boston morning, a child's despair built on the balcony of a five-star hotel. For his nephew, it would be humid October nights in the mountains of Tamaulipas.

Not for his nephew. For his son.

Because that's what he has to be, now: a father.

Denial and panic and duty battle in his broken brain like dogs pissing for the same backyard. He struggles to chase off the strays. Finally, only one dog stands.

Caulfield's laugh is mirthless, bitter. Oh, the irony. Months of fighting with Aspen over a baby, to the near detriment of their marriage. Every sound argument he'd put forth about his mental health, his lack of dependability, his inability to parent. In the end it doesn't matter a whit, because only a single path lay before him.

The uncle gives him his flashlight, pushes an envelope in his hand, and points him north, up the mountain. "Go find your wife and Marieta's boy and live a long life together. Tell him about his *mamá*. Tell him how his uncle loved them, but not until it was too late. Say "*Hijo, don't wait until it's too late*"...

Sierra Madres Oriental
November

One month later, the southern sun baked my face. I stretched like a lazy tabby who'd found a sunny spot and half-listened to *Tía* Mariángel and Sofia. Swathed in bright florals, the matrons lounged on the patio of the Cabral hacienda like two potted dahlias heavy with blooms.

"...they found her purse and identification cards in a plastic bag by a hotel dumpster. Her jacket and shoes were in a ditch south of Nuevo Laredo."

"But no body? Are you sure she's...you know?" *Tía* Mariángel had a habit of dancing around uncomfortable words.

"Yes, quite sure. She wouldn't abandon her child in a cave. At least, Samuel says she wouldn't."

The wind carried the pungent fragrance of neglected mangos that had ripened and rotted on their branches, and smoke. In the hacienda's garden, Alonso and *Tío* Tomás dragged overgrowth into a burn pile. Though the Mexican Feds' presence was felt all over this part of the country as they rounded up cartel remnants, the two men still kept watch like sentries defending their castle, each with a gun tucked beneath layers of sweaty, dusty work clothes. I'd only met Tomás a handful of times, and his shy demeanor had led me to the erroneous conclusion that he was apathetic. But then I learned he stockpiled firearms in his pantry, concealed in empty cereal boxes (I suppose that's what one did when cartel thugs attended your street festivals). Some people were all bark and no bite, but not Tomás. The man was point-blank tenacious.

As the women chatted, I paged through the browning sheaves of paper which Samuel had dug from the bottom of his grandfather's desk and manically scribbled upon. He then paced between shelves of dusty old books, where Cabrals before him had fretted over hacienda expenditures and college lectures. He tried to process all that had changed in the past few days, months, even years, but a saturated sponge can only absorb so much before water dribbles back into the bucket. As the first rays crested the hills, he jerked on his tennis shoes and tore out of his family's hacienda to force his body and mind into submission.

I hope he took the gun. Nostalgia panged for the days of my old friends Tweedle Dee and Tweedle Dum, the meddlesome (but non-violent) paparazzi. I longed for our home in Colorado, but all that I'd drawn comfort from had been stripped and splintered and twisted into something unrecognizable. And now, here in Mexico, we'd landed in the vortex of a massive criminal investigation whose fronds reached deep into the Zacatón Cartel.

Long story short, we wouldn't see the Rockies anytime soon.

"But we really know nothing about her, do we?" continued Mariángel.

"We know Samuel tried to help her. We know he loved her."

I curled into the chair and caught a moment's rest, having nothing to add. Marieta was gone...

Señor Rodriguez and I found the children in the cave, just as Camila Flores had instructed. Four of them, ages eight to three, filthy and freezing, huddled together in little more than a giant hole beneath a rocky overhang, concealed by curtains of butterfly vines and brush.

I'd squirmed through the entrance on my stomach (still reeling from the *toloache*, but the hallucinations had receded). When my flashlight beam bounced over their frightened faces and gleaming black eyes, I cried out in horror and relief.

"It's okay, you are all right," I assured them, though I couldn't possibly know if it was okay, and if they'd be all right. "I am Marieta's sister."

Watchful, they inched toward me and *Señor* Rodriguez, who had wiggled his arthritic joints into the cave behind me. Marieta had smuggled them from the back of a semi at a station not far from here, the oldest child explained, brought them food and water and blankets, and anything else they needed, until she could safely move them out of the Sierra Madre Orientals and into the care of 'the good people.' But she hadn't returned for nearly a week.

They asked many questions: Were their loved ones looking for them? Could I help them go home? Even why my temple bled, but they did *not* ask what happened to Marieta.

They didn't need to. If she were still alive, *she* would be here rather than me.

One of the children—a boy, perhaps three or four—cautiously scooted closer as the children told me their names. His fingertips brushed my shoe, the lightest of touches, as if testing whether my sneaker would burn his skin. He moved into the beam of my flashlight. *Señor* Rodriguez gasped. Then he lurched toward the boy and embraced him. To my surprise, the boy did not fight but went limp, a possum playing dead.

"You are Daniel's," the old man lamented as he rocked the startled boy. "As sure as I know my own face, you could be no other's. My grandson! I have not seen you since you were a baby."

I squatted low to meet the boy's eyes. "What is your name, *hijito?*"

Deep brown peered at me beneath thick, matted hair. A grimy finger slipped into his mouth. "Samuel," he mumbled around his finger.

"Of course you are." My voice cracked. "I would know your face anywhere, Samuel, and I am very, very happy to meet you…"

"And Samuel believes it was she who called him in Colorado? It could have been anybody!" Mariángel's high-pitched voice pierced my thoughts, pulled me away from the soft glow of an oil lamp and back to the hacienda patio.

"We'll never know, I suppose. But Samuel and Kaye are safe. The children were found and returned to their families, and that's the important thing."

Samuel still held fast to his belief that his sister called him just before she was killed. I thought it was someone involved in the ransom plot, Camila Flores, perhaps, but I wouldn't try to convince him. He needed the comfort of those last words, distressing as they were.

I arched my back into the dusty wicker chair to ease the knots. Though we'd never tell Mariángel, the guest room mattresses were so thin, it was as if we slept on bedsprings. Samuel called it quits after three nights and dragged a blanket to the floor.

"Join me."

I wavered, not wanting to insult *Tía* Mariángel's hospitality.

"Join me, please." His words were as soft as a caress. I crawled off the mattress and tucked into his warmth. His lips found the curve of my shoulder. "I'm sorry I misled you, that night in La Vereda. I wanted you out of the way, and I chose convenience over candidness."

"It was pretty high-handed. But I do have an ugly stubborn streak, so I understand."

He rested his head against my sternum, listened to my heartbeat. Every warm breath tickled my skin. He sighed. "In the end, I only accomplished a betrayal of your trust."

"It's forgiven." I swept his thick hair from his forehead, kissed his bruised temple. "And I am truly sorry about Marieta. You just wanted to help her."

In his grief, Samuel's only reply was to lace his fingers with mine and lose himself in my body. As sweat and tears mingled, I held him and whispered words of love, and life, and forgiveness.

It had taken time to forgive his deception, though I knew why he'd done it. When Samuel had stumbled into the Rodriguez home that night in La Vereda, after Javier freed him, puffy-eyed and bloodied, shirt shredded as if he'd been mauled by one of Alonso's *leoncillos*, I'd let him have it.

"Mother!" (I slapped his arm). "Cliffhucker!" (Another slap.) "Friggin' hamster balls, Samuel!" The effects of the *toloache* still lingered, so my words were fuzzy and not-at-all stinging (though I'd earned enough street cred that night to drop an F-bomb or two).

He gently secured my flailing arms and held me. He offered no apologies, but I didn't expect him to. He searched my limbs, assessed my injuries. He brushed the new gash on my forehead, as if he could erase it with the pad of his thumb. My vision wavered, and I worried he was a ghost of that awful concoction.

"Are you dead?" My voice was laced with wonder (and strong hallucinogens).

A pause. "Are you drunk?"

"No!" I shoved him away. "I'm poisoned."

After a closer study of my muddled state, he looked to *Señora* Rodriguez.

"The *curandero* gave her *toloache*."

"Good God!" And that was all he said, though he embraced me a little tighter.

It wasn't until later, when the *toloache* ran its course and both Mexican and U.S. Feds combed every inch of La Vereda, did we share our stories. Samuel reread the letter Javier had shoved into his hand. He passed it to me.

"Look at this. I'm still trying to process it."

I devoured the hastily-written words...

Señor Cabral,

I may not have the opportunity to deliver this letter. Assuming you are still alive, here is what you need to know:

Your sister slipped under the border and sought you out in Colorado because she hoped your money would buy Daniel's freedom. But after she met your wife and friends, saw your happy life in Colorado, she chose not to place you on the cartel's radar. She loved you; how proud she was of her talented, successful brother. She left Colorado and returned to her work with Anti-Trafficking International, and to her son, who was in Camila's care. I agreed to keep an eye on you, in the event someone had followed her. (Our safety has been precarious since Daniel dropped the Zacatón data bomb. Rodriguez was a radical, and I admit there was no love lost between us.)

My niece and I had mended fences, after I proved to her that I was done with cartel life. She was so hungry for family, she believed me. The truth is, I fell out of favor with the cartel. I was old, lacked the understanding and technological proficiency to stay in the game—the curse of middle-management nearing retirement age.

And here is my confession...

I arranged for those cartel low-levels to take you. If I could lure you to Mexico, I would regain the Treiños' favor and reimburse them for the 'cargo' we stole...they cannot even call them 'children.' But one does not make deals with the devil and win. Just as I encouraged the cartel to increase their presence in La Vereda, my niece, foolish in her grief, returned to see the grave of Daniel Rodriguez and fell right into the palm of those who hunted her. They took her not five days ago.

I bought back my life, only to find my dear Marieta forfeited hers. Who is left to care for her boy? Not a selfish old drug mule whose clock is winding down.

I cannot save Marieta Cabral Sanchez de Rodriguez. But I can save her son...

The cartel now believes it was me who helped Marieta dispose of their ten kilos of cocaine. It's already done.

Contact the U.S. federal agents at the Naco Port of Entry in Arizona—I have tipped them off about the ransom deal, and they'll take me seriously. With the Federales swarming your family home in Mexico and U.S. feds watching your interests in the States, you become a high risk target to the cartel, and not worth the effort.

Also contact Anti-Trafficking International. You will know what to do when you speak to them.

I leave this as my gift to my nephew...my life for your freedom. Javier Sanchez

It turned out, the feds at Naco *did* know Javier, and they also suspected they would not hear from him again. Whatever role Camila Flores played—hero or villain (or somewhere in between)—would remain a mystery. She had also vanished after she'd pointed my *toloache*-drugged butt toward the village, and we had not seen or heard from her.

I had a feeling she knew Javier was dead...

The wind shifted, and now clouds of smoke from the burning brush piles drifted onto the hacienda's patio, irritating our eyes and throats. But Mariángel pushed forward with valiance as she expressed shock over her brother's long-concealed progeny.

"I still cannot believe it," she said, peering over her sunglasses in disbelief. "All this time, I had a niece growing up ten miles from here and *Mamá* never said a word to anybody. How *could* she?" Mariángel crossed herself.

Sofia raised an eyebrow behind her coffee cup. Nobody who bore the name Cabral could possibly judge another for sweeping secrets under the rug.

"Not only a niece, but now a grand-nephew! Next, I suppose I'll find out I have a long-lost twin."

"Not even Samuel knew about the boy," I reasoned. "Anti-trafficking is dangerous work, and I'm sure his parents wanted to shield him from the cartels as long as possible."

Again she crossed herself at the mention of the cartels. "Evil business, and right here in our beautiful Tamaulipas."

Sofia could no longer hold her tongue. "Perhaps if we had given Antonio's girl the family she so desperately needed, that evil business would not have touched us, or her. Perhaps she would be alive."

I remembered the shy, fragile woman I'd met at Paddlers, so briefly. How had I missed her longing? Her underlying strength? Like a spoiled child who only saw what I didn't have, I'd taken much for granted. Chiefly, my family. But I'd never walked a trial alone, had I? They were always beside me, imperfect, but shoulder to shoulder.

Molly and her unwavering optimism.

Danita with her tough love.

Angel, my protective big brother.

Santiago and his loyalty.

Jaime and Luca, yin and yang.

Hector. Gone though he was, his passion for life wasn't.

My parents. Not the best decision makers, but they loved me.

Sofia and Alonso and their steady, unswerving faith.

And my brave, compassionate Samuel, who saw the best in people, but never the best in himself.

Life changed. People moved and married, lived and died, but love was constant. Whether we walked in Colorado or New York, or Alaska or Afghanistan or Mexico, we walked together.

This was what Samuel had wanted for his sister, if only she'd allowed him to give it to her.

But we could give it to her son...

That night in La Vereda, as the last of the police had trickled away until morning, my husband and I studied the sleeping boy's features and compared him to the photos on the mantel of the Rodriguez home. From his broad forehead to his snub nose, he looked like Daniel Rodriguez, save for the high cheekbones. That beautiful feature was pure Cabral.

Señora Rodriguez sat beside the child and I watched as she cradled his small hand, slack with blissful sleep. The old woman kissed the crown of the boy's head, inhaled deeply. Young Samuel sank deeper into the pillow and my heart wrenched.

"He should stay with you," I whispered. "We're strangers, and he's been through so much. How can we possibly take him away from everything he's ever known?"

"You are young. So is he."

"But he's your grandson."

The old woman shook her head. "We've decided. My health is poor. How long could we give him? Five, ten years? And the violence here…we could not bear it. But…" The joints of her chair squeaked as she leaned forward. "That old hacienda which stands empty, the one in the foothills? It belongs to your family, does it not? Perhaps you need not go so far away, just yet…"

A legal nightmare awaited us. Immigration petitions, visits to the U.S. embassy, court hearings, criminal investigations, identification and documentation… We didn't even have proof that his mother was deceased. And this was just the procedural hurdles.

"Surely they will allow you to return to Colorado with him," said *Tía* Mariángel.

"He's traumatized," I explained. "Everything and everyone he has ever known and loved is gone. How can we simply pack up and go back to Colorado? He's already so lost…"

Sofia squeezed my hand. "*Mi corazón*, we will stay with you as long as we can."

"And you may continue to use the hacienda for as long as you like." Mariángel's eyes sparked at my surprise. "What? My nephew has been after me for years to let him pay for the upkeep, like we are some poor, third-world relations. If he wants this old place restored so badly, let him do it himself. Then he'll learn what a headache it is. Perfect for children, though." She gave her wicker chair a fond pat, as if to soften the blow. "Though you may want to install the best security system money can buy. He can certainly afford it."

"Samuel—*we*—would like that."

Tía Mariángel nodded at the pages of scribblings Samuel had dropped in my lap. "Is he writing a new book?"

"Not really. It's how he lets me into his head." I didn't elaborate, because some things were too personal.

"Should we be worried about him? I don't know much about his…" she waved her hands around her head.

Sofia shifted in her chair. We were all concerned.

I rubbed tired eyes as I struggled over Samuel's cramped handwriting, frustratingly lacking in punctuation and grammar. I wanted to tell her not to worry, that he was still on his meds, but his health history and his relatives' icy treatment of him were still an open wound.

Sofia could handle that battle.

A whimper sounded from the monitor app Samuel and I had jimmied up between our phones. I watched the grainy camera footage of our nephew in the guest room. He was still asleep but crying.

"All is well?" Sofia gently asked.

My body sagged. He often cried large beads of tears as he dreamed of his mother. Then he would wake up in a strange place with no mother at all and cry some more. I was frantic to hug and coddle and shield, but I would only overwhelm him, so every move was calculated. Samuel fared better, using ball games as an opportunity to pat his back, ruffle his hair, feed his little nephew the affection he craved but could not trust us with.

Another moan on the monitor, then a sigh as young Samuel Rodriguez shifted. It wouldn't be long before he woke. I set my husband's notebook aside, ready to greet my inconsolable nephew who cried for a woman I wasn't, a woman he would never again see on this earth, whose place I could never take. I would have slept on the floor next to his bed, stayed by his side every waking and sleeping hour if it helped. But when I was near, he watched me with caution, his little body rigid. How could I comfort him? How could I be enough?

Sofia must have seen my desperation. She rose.

"Walk with me, *hija*?"

We meandered along the crumbling outer wall of the hacienda, stepped around prickly plants and suspicious-looking mud heaps. Sofia crossed her arms over the rusting gate, closed her eyes and absorbed the sun. Her brows pinched; she looked very much the way I felt inside.

Then her face cleared. She seemed…peaceful.

"I was recalling when Samuel, *big* Samuel," she clarified with a smile, "first came to us. Oh Kaye, how good God is."

"How…how can you possibly say that?" I stammered. "Look what he took from Samuel. And now the *same thing* has happened to his nephew."

Her gaze was steady. "And because of what Samuel has lived through, he knows how to help his nephew."

I shook my head. "I just…how could he possibly allow such a horrible thing to happen all over again?"

"You are asking why God would allow evil things to happen. That is a question millions have asked for thousands of years. This world is filled with so much evil, is it not?" Sofia tucked a stray hair behind my ear. "But there is also so much love. My hope is that one day the evil will be gone, and all that will be left is the love."

Feeling churned inside of me for my little nephew. Righteous anger and grief on his behalf threatened to choke me. I swallowed it back, but it was a losing battle.

"I wonder," she murmured, "would we know compassion if we did not know suffering?"

I grabbed the metal gate, wanting to bend it in two but I wasn't strong enough, would *never* be strong enough.

"I am at a loss. I have known this little boy for so long, in my heart. I have...I have longed for him. Wanted him to be mine, but not like this! *Never* like this. It's unfair, and...and *cruel*. And I can't *make it better*." I dug through my pocket for a tissue but came up empty. Sofia placed one in my hand, and I wiped my nose with the inelegance of a preschooler. Then she firmly took my arms.

"I know, *hija*. Oh, how I know. When you raise a broken child, you are truly in the trenches."

We continued our walk. "At first he'll fight you. He will not want your love, but he'll need it. Anger, tears, pushing you away one day and clinging to your legs the next. He will make himself as unpalatable as possible so you'll leave him, just as he expects. And when you are still there every day, unwavering in your love, he'll begin to trust. It's the way of children who have seen wickedness."

I thought of the haunted boy I'd known, years ago. He had been too young to see the bigger picture...he only knew his mother was gone and this stranger was trying to be his mom. Sofia was good at being a mom, but he didn't want a *good* mom...he wanted *his* mom. On the outside, Sofia seemed patient, joyful. But she must have felt frustrated and inept for *years*. 'In the trenches' indeed.

My phone crackled again, and a child's voice echoed through a hacienda guest room, hastily converted for a toddler. "*Mamá? Mamá...*" He didn't cry for me, but still, I would answer. His soft pleas quickly devolved into a wail and I hastened toward the house. Before I could escape, Sofia caught my hand.

"Together, you are enough."

Just then, a voice came through the monitor. "*Hola, hijito.*"

Together, we watched the screen as my husband, having returned from his run, crouched next to his nephew's bed and laid a hand on the mattress near the boy's forehead, leaving enough space to set the boy at ease. Controlled, soothing, though he'd spent the night in manic restlessness.

"*I miss your mama, too. But I am very glad you are safe, here with me.*"

Sofia patted my hand. "Raise Daniel and Marieta's boy in Tamaulipas or America, or both—whatever is best for him. If you choose to stay, bring him to Colorado in the summer so he knows his family. His American *abuelos.*"

I squeezed my eyes shut but tears escaped anyway.

On the monitor, Samuel played with the boy's small toes—the only part of him he dared hug at all, lest he frighten this boy, his son. Samuel disappeared from the screen, but soon we heard the unmistakable twangs of a Spanish guitar. It was the lullaby, the one about lemon balm and jasmine. The one Sofia sang to him as a child.

My heart swelled and cracked. *Not like this, never like this.* Such a bittersweet thing, to know your child is only yours because he has suffered tremendous loss.

"Whatever you do," my mother-in-law said, "please. Remember my son. Where he has been. How far he has come. Always growing, always learning. It *is* possible, *hija.*"

Finally, I understood Sofia's and Alonso's hearts. Though imperfect, they'd navigated the waters as best as they could. Samuel only became their son after trauma and mental illness and death left their ugly scars beneath his tiny ribcage. With their very last heartbeats, they would make sure Samuel was safe and loved. After all, this was parenthood. To cling tightly and then, slowly, gingerly, peel back your grip and release your child, whether three or thirty-three, into the unknown.

I vowed to do the same for our boy.

"I love you. You're safe." I touched the small figure on the screen of my phone.

Chapter 24
RIDGE WALK

Scenic terrain beyond the timberline, where climbers emerge from the forest to a breathtaking view.

Three years later, some things never change...

"Arrrrgh! Angel!"

The yellow duckie jerks and bobs as we back it toward the frothing, roaring hydraulic.

This is the year. We're going to surf that wretched thing once and for all.

"Paddle Kaye, paddle! No...yes...lean!"

Frigid whitewater crashes against the sides of our kayak, spills into our laps, pools around our ankles. We sputter and throw our backs into propelling the kayak onto the wave. It stalls and rumbles in perfect harmony with the motion of the river. We rise as the river spins below us, surfing the wave...for two freaking seconds.

Before I can scream out in triumph, the duckie dips and my world is upended as my feet fly over my head. We're pearling. Again.

Tuck...roll with the current like a beach ball, the water...oh crap, so frickin' cold! ...sky...gray...sky...gray...same old, same old... And nothing but glorious, blue sky.

A hand plunges into the ice water and grasps the back of my life vest, hauling me to the surface. Samuel, who waits for me on the other side of the rapid in the catamaran, drags me away and simultaneously grabs my abandoned paddle. My hero.

"We al-m-most g-got it that t-time." I'm hoisted into the cat, next to him. Behind me, Jaime helps Angel right the duckie.

His well-shaped lips curl. "Almost had it, firecracker. Last try?"

"Last try." Angel and I both agree—we have too much to lose for one stupid hydraulic. It isn't worth the brutal, tragic months we weathered after Hector drowned.

My little guy needs me alive.

Some things never change. Then again, everything changes…

Bit by bit, our sad boy unfurled his tightly rolled leaves and basked in the sunlight. Not long after his fourth birthday, he told us he wanted a new name: Sam-Rod.

"Are you sure about that nickname?" Samuel, dubious, asked.

"We have the same ah-peh.. ah…"

"*Apellido.*"

He nodded. "See?" He pointed to his huge, navy-colored jersey with 'Rodriguez' emblazoned on the back, a gift from Dani.

"But he's a *Yankee*. And we're Red Sox fans."

"I like the Yankees," 'Sam-Rod' whispered.

I actually heard Samuel's heart break.

"Well, it would make it easier to tell the two of you apart," I teased. Sam-Rod giggled, one of those rare, golden moments, and hugged my knees.

"Thanks, *Tía* Kaye," he mouthed, and trailed his Valdez cousins up the hill, to the swing set we'd just installed in our backyard. I pressed a hand to my chest. For the price of a hug, I'd call the boy 'Jedi Master Sam-Rod of the Cabralsan System' if he wanted…

Glacial water swirls around my fingers as I dangle them over the side of the catamaran. Samuel steers the raft toward the bank and we take out. "You okay?" he shouts over the rapids, searching my body for injuries. Next to him, Jaime cackles.

372

"Hey, nice maneuver. They teach you girls how to fall out of kayaks down in Mexico, do they? So big strong alpha-males can rescue you?" Samuel has the indecency to laugh.

I flip both of them the bird, my finger quivering with cold. Jaime passes me a flask of whiskey in apology.

Before we journeyed to Glenwood Canyon, our small family—Samuel, Sam-Rod and me—made a pilgrimage to La Vereda, as we did every year.

It was a rainy spring in Tamaulipas, and the slopes were a mess of mud and delicate green grass. My hand rested between Sam-Rod's solemn little shoulder blades as he scattered orange blossoms across the mountainside, and I felt his noiseless shudders. The cave, where he had last seen his mother, rested up the hill. He still hadn't spoken about the autumn he spent on the run from the cartel. One day he would. When we returned to Colorado, our little man crawled into bed between us, and together we listened to the snowmelt trickle down the mountainside and into the creek below, as if the world were nothing but dripping icicles. Finally, he drifted to sleep.

So much love had been poured into our new home. The original foundation survived the Left Hand Canyon flood, and now the walls are solid, sturdier than ever.

The house has a small media studio for Samuel to do interviews. It's great for book tours, but even better for our work on behalf of Anti-Trafficking International. One day, when Sam-Rod's grown-up, we'd like to establish a shelter for victims of human trafficking. I still remember listening to an audio clip of Marieta that the ATI shared with us…

"They come up from southern countries like Guatemala and Honduras, down from the States, our very own Mexico and are snatched up, sold like cattle. They need people to help, strong and well-financed, connected, unafraid to take risks."

What would it be like to permanently live in a land drenched with sun, the air so thick with moisture, I felt twenty pounds heavier? To renovate the hacienda, reinvent our future…our very lives? Could we build another charity from the ground-up? And to have one eye over my shoulder until the day the cartels came knocking (and they surely would). To carry a weapon, to dig into the gutters for lost souls, seek them out in the dark of night, on the fringe of street lamps and alleys…

It's a dozen years down the road, but we'd need time to convince *Tía* Mariángel to let us use the hacienda.

Whether in Colorado or summering in Tamaulipas, Samuel works from home when he can. It helps to preserve his mind, which often teeters in a delicate balance despite proper meds and diagnosis. There are times when, despite measures we've taken, bouts of mania and depression are as inevitable as ripples on a lake.

The most recent slide came on the heels of the publication of his first nonfiction book, which took a real, harrowing look at drug and human trafficking, framed by the life and death of Marieta Rodriguez. Reviewers were stunned by the beloved Nixie author's abrupt genre pivot. A heated debate sparked, as some critics told him to 'stick to what he knew,' and others roared for a follow-up.

But that's Samuel Caulfield Cabral…he keeps people on their toes. Two weeks into his book tour, I held him when his mind was buried under layers of dank sediment and mire, and he couldn't leave our bed for days. I held him and loved him.

When he teeters toward mania—*those* are the times I curse being tied to Colorado. His jittery limbs and spastic moods could try the patience of Gandhi. Throw in the relentless, emotionally-draining energy of Sam-Rod, and it's no wonder I sometimes locked myself in the bathroom with a paperback. If I find I'm contemplating the drive time from Boulder to a Caribbean island, I'll call Sofia.

"I'm this close to purchasing a one-way ticket to St. Lucia."

"I'll be right over."

I guess Sofia told Samuel about one such conversation after he'd leveled out, because he actually took me to St. Lucia for some R&R, while Sam-Rod went to 'grandma camp.' Next time he swings toward mania, I'll tell Sofia I'm retreating to an exclusive spa in the French Riviera.

Some things change… marriages and splits.

Santiago and his dulcimer girl got hitched. Honestly, we all thought their relationship was brushing feathers with the dodo, so it was a happy surprise. (They split a month later, which was not a happy surprise.)

My parents never rekindled their romance (thank goodness). Molly and Cassady never did, either.

"At least I put my whole heart into it. We just didn't love each other like we thought we did," she told me over a plate of Havarti and diet coke. She didn't trust herself not to drunk-dial Hippie if we uncorked a bottle. "Now I can go anywhere I want." She chose Glenwood Springs as her new home, which proved to be a killer move in expanding our TrilbyJones client base.

Fall changes to winter, which changes to spring...and another...and another...

Tonight, we've taken over Molly's mountainside home, high on a bluff overlooking the Colorado River. Surrounded by tiki torches on her outdoor patio, we toast Hector. Jaime's here.

Molly's new guy mans the grill. I was shocked when she told me she met someone special in Glenwood Springs. Not just anyone—the very man we pulled from the Longs Peak snowfield avalanche.

"He kept staring at me in line for coffee one day, and I thought he was a creeper. He told me he thought I was an angel. Literally. When he saw my face after we dug him out of the snow, he truly thought angels had rescued him. I told him it was hypothermia, but, well, if the glove fits! He'll probably think you're an angel too, when you meet him."

New guy is quite a bit older than Molly, with graying temples and eyes that crinkle around the corners. But he has a youthful exuberance and love for life (and for Molly) which make me believe he's in it for the long haul. I wonder what he was like before the avalanche, and if he also had an epiphany after barely scraping by with his brain intact. He has two teen boys who absolutely adore Molly. Their mother isn't in the picture and I know it will crush them if Molly and this guy don't work out. But Molly knows it, too—how painful it is to be a child discarded by someone you love, which makes me think she's also in it for the long haul.

Santiago hears from Hippie occasionally, and he's happy wherever he's at—somewhere in southern California. It's still strange without him, but we're all making an effort to get to know the new guy.

We've changed, gotten a little older, hopefully a little better. We're camping in Molly's home instead of under the stars and, quite frankly, I'm more than okay with it. The cousins have claimed the basement. I creep around scattered cushions and toys, spilled popcorn, wince when a Lego finds my arch. The soft glow of the nightlight shows me they've finally fallen asleep beneath a pile of sleeping bags. I find my own sweet boy and tuck his bare foot beneath his camouflaged bag. He moans and flops over, and the foot pops out again. Oh well. Another baby tooth is going to pop out any day now and I'm trying to figure out the logistics of a tooth fairy visit beneath that heap of stinky, snoozing children.

I return upstairs, quiet so as not to disturb Dani as she nurses baby number three back to sleep. Once, I would have felt pangs of jealousy. But now I know that's not part of the plan for me. When Sam-Rod came into my life, the strange dreams about the nursery and the baby flitted away, lost in the realities of daylight. Was it possible that, for a time, I was allowed to cradle him, rock him, my precious boy?

I know in my heart it was *him* I longed for.

And some portion of my son's heart will always long for Marieta. He forever asks to hear about the time I met her in Paddlers, and how beautiful, and brave, and special she was, and how much she loved him. Our son will always know he is loved.

I slip under the covers of the guest room, shiver at the chill. Samuel is beside me, bare-chested and glasses perched on his nose, typing away on his laptop. Sometimes I worry—just for a second—when he's in his writing groove, that he's slipping into mania. He must have a finely-tuned worried-wife radar, because he'll set the laptop aside and gently rock my world.

He's going to do that now, I hope.

"Hello, Aspen Kaye."

"Having trouble sleeping?"

"Mmm. Just sorting out my thoughts on paper."

"Electronic paper."

"Symbolic paper."

"Can I read it?"

He rests his computer on my lap like a sacred offering, and I scan his words. Just a couple of paragraphs, but it's an epic in my eyes. An epic that isn't found in soaring peaks, cloudless skies, or wild hydraulic rapids. Breathtaking as they are, mountains and skies and rivers could never satisfy my soul. I could climb a thousand fourteeners and not be fulfilled until I came home to the people I love. That's our epic, Samuel's and mine. To give. To serve. To love. Because we're not meant to simply exist...we're meant to *live*.

"What do you think?" Samuel's cheek hovers over my shoulder. I can't speak through the tears.

So I type this note at the bottom of the page:

S—It's perfect. Are you going to publish it? –K

Hydraulic Level Five [WORKING TITLE]
Draft 1.whoevenknows
© Samuel & Kaye Cabral EPILOGUE

Aspen,

This is my goodbye letter to you.

I have a grown-up love and her name is Kaye. She's a gorgeous, brave, stubborn woman. Sometimes I see your youthful vibrancy when she laughs, or plays her guitar, or scribbles on my head with Sharpie markers while I'm asleep, and it makes me feel seventeen. But I don't want to be seventeen again.

I want Kaye for the rest of my life. Her faith in me makes me a better man. She's my wife.

Somewhere, across this immeasurable earth, we have children waiting for us to bring them home. Children who look nothing like either of us but will break my guitar strings and dance horribly like their mother. Our children will have grandparents, aunts and uncles, and cousins who dote on them when I'm not feeling well.

No illness, distance, red tape, or dollar amount will keep us from them. Kaye and I will scour the icy water of St. Vrain Creek, just like we used to, and we'll show our children rainbow rocks and tadpoles and cattails. We'll scale mountains and raft rivers…

Please trust that you will be safe and cherished, tucked away in the corners of my mind.

And you won't be alone, because I'm leaving Caulfield with you. You prefer him to me, anyway.

Love,
Samuel Caulfield Cabral

S—It's perfect. Are you going to publish it?—K
No, Kaye. Our story won't be finished for a long, long time.—S

END

Acknowledgments

To my husband Nathan: thank you for your patience and encouragement when daily tasks fall by the wayside as the writing bug bites. You are my friend and partner in every way, and I'm grateful to have you as the "work horse" of our family.

To my children: how creative and free you are! Your stories inspire me.

To Mom and Dad: this book would not have happened had you not left your home behind to make a new home down the street. I am grateful my kids know what it's like to have grandma and grandpa a mile away.

To Emily and William: I adore your farm stories! Thank you for allowing me to mine your experiences and give them the "fiction treatment."

To my family: you didn't blink an eye when we became foster parents and welcomed every child without hesitation or question. Thank you.

To my Women of the Word ladies: Thank you for allowing me a safe place to express my insecurities and concerns, never judging, always praying. You have helped me to grow and thrive in my own skin.

To my editor, publisher, and long-time champion and encourager, Elizabeth Riley with Omnific Publishing. You have stood by this project for years and welcomed me back with open arms after my writing hiatus. Your belief in my work and personal interest in the story helped me to dig deep and find emotions previously unexplored.

To Stacey Spangler, my spirit sister: I'm glad I can walk this writing journey with you. Both of us are a bit different (in good ways!) and we've chosen to embrace this God-given creativity through storytelling. I miss seeing you every week but we're where we need to be.

To the Leonard sisters, who allowed me a glimpse into the lives of military families and have cheered me on since I was an extremely awkward eight-year-old.

To the teachers and librarians who motivate a new generation to love books—my kids included!

To the readers who have waited patiently for this book, understanding and encouraging us as our family helped broken kids and parents.

I thank my God for always lighting my path when I walk in unknown places.

About the Author

Sarah Latchaw was raised in eastern Iowa. After college, she left behind everything she knew to venture into the great wild of Des Moines. She has travelled across Europe, explored the Middle East, climbed mountains, and braved Legoland with her husband, son, and daughter. Sarah was awarded her MA in Creative Writing from Iowa State University. In recent years, she and her husband were licensed as foster parents and now call many children "their kids." She lives for the special moments when she tells her kids not to jump on "the couch," "the car," "the cat," or "your brother's head."